DARK SURF

Surfing's in their blood...

a novel by

T.C. Zmak

ISBN: 0692258175
ISBN-13: 978-0-692-25817-0
Library of Congress Control Number: 2014913252
Zmak Creative, Marina, CA

For information: www.tczmak.com

CreateSpace, Charleston SC
Printed in the United States of America

First paperback edition, August 2014

For Steve Zmak, my eternal inspiration

DARK SURF

Prologue – Blood in the Water

Five minutes after the sun dipped below the Pacific horizon, the screaming began.

"Shark!"

The slate-gray fin, which thrust through the ocean's surface to reflect the last red streaks of the sunset, dropped out of sight again.

The teenage surfer on the far left felt one tooth, then another and another pierce the flesh of his calf. "Aaaaah!" he screamed. "I'm bit!"

The boy felt the shark unclench its jaw. He hoisted his leg onto his surfboard, leaving a murky red trail in the water. Terrified, he whipped his head around, looking for the predator.

The boy's girlfriend, who was surfing next to him, paddled over, grabbed the back of his head and shoved his face into his board. "Paddle!" she commanded.

The three boys and two girls, who moments earlier had been sitting on their boards enjoying the remnants of the sunset, felt the adrenaline surge through their muscles as they wildly swung their arms over their heads and down into the ocean, desperately trying to reach shore before the great white shark surfaced again.

The boy, whose blood spilled onto his board and into the sea as he swam, felt movement beneath him. Slam! The shark's nose rocketed into his surfboard, catapulting him into the air. His body arched, limbs flailing, lungs burning as he screamed. He splashed down. Bubbles encircled him as he plunged into the water. Halting his downward momentum, he pushed his arms and hands through the water and kicked to reach the surface. He broke through, only to be dragged down again by teeth tearing into his thigh.

"No!" his girlfriend wailed, turning back to see him pulled under again.

"You can't help him! Just go! Go!" yelled one of the other surfers.

The four teens furiously swam toward the beach. "Shark!" one shouted, warning others in the water to get to shore.

The boy managed to free himself again and struggled toward the surface. He pushed through, hearing the fading shrieks of "Shark!" in the distance. Before he could fill his lungs with oxygen, he was pulled down into the darkness. Multiple spikes of pain tore across his chest and abdomen. He twisted his body, left and right, trying to get free. But struggling only plunged the serrated teeth deeper into his flesh.

He stopped twisting and gazed into the shark's eye. *Is that satisfaction,* he wondered, *or recognition? How can that be?* As he looked deeper into the eye, the shark's upper and lower teeth clamped down, crushing the life out of the soul trapped between its jaws.

The killing had begun. Again.

1 – Jake

While Jake Ryder had never met the teenage boy who was killed by the shark, he heard about it on the local news. And two months later, he knew exactly how the boy's friends felt.

Jake's experience confirmed his belief that surfing, like death, is solitary.

It's true you can surf with other people or even die with other people, Jake thought. *But when it comes down to it, you do the deed alone. And how you choose to surf, or choose to live or die, is ultimately a mirror of who you are, a reflection of your soul.*

Surf the right way and you'll have the most amazing day of your life. Skimming the water's surface, you are no longer bound to the earth. You fly, suspended by a layer of hydrogen and oxygen particles swirling beneath your board. You feel the ocean's power beneath you, lifting, carrying, propelling you forward, defying the laws of gravity. You feel invincible.

Surf the wrong way and you could get yourself killed or kill someone else.

The day my best friend, Cody, died I had been with him all day, surfing. But in the end, he died alone.

2 – The Wrong Trunks

In Jake's opinion, the Del Norte Reefers were notorious for surfing the wrong way. They were arrogant and dangerous. They didn't respect the ocean or the people or animals in it. They descended on the beach like they owned the place. To them, no one else existed. If they wanted a wave, they took it. It didn't matter who else was there—other surfers, bodyboarders, swimmers, kids.

Jake and Cody usually surfed the stretch of coastline between 15th Street in Del Mar and Fletcher Cove in Solana Beach but heard the waves were going off at Seaside Reef, where the Del Norte Reefers congregated.

Situated just north of the Solana Beach border in Cardiff-by-the-Sea, Seaside is one of the few North County beaches with a decent-sized parking lot, which means it can get crowded. One aggro surfer can wreak a lot of havoc, especially since it's a popular spot with bodyboarders, too.

Jake and Cody started surfing Seaside a couple weeks after the Labor Day weekend crowds cleared out. Their second afternoon there, the Del Norte Reefers showed up. There was one guy in particular who Jake hated.

Jake didn't know his name but, over the course of a week, he snaked five of Jake's waves and purposely collided with three other surfers including Cody. Jake knew it was the guy's way of staking his territory and trying to intimidate others into leaving. But, in Jake's mind, there was no way some territorial surf rat was going to intimidate him and Cody into leaving a public beach.

For fun, Jake sometimes razzed Cody because he and the surf rat kind of looked alike. They were both tall, lean and tan. They both had shoulder-length blond hair, streaked platinum by the sun. And they both had neon pink swim trunks that could be seen a mile away.

Cody liked to say the pink trunks were a "chick magnet." The first day he wore them, as soon as he saw the look on Jake's face, he held up his palm and said, "Don't dis the trunks, man. Women know a man who's got the guts to wear these must have a lot going on underneath!"

In spite of, or maybe because of, the trunks, Cody had no shortage of girlfriends. Everybody loved Cody.

Unfortunately, Jake thought, *those were the trunks that got Cody killed.*

3 — Cody's Last Wave

That sunny September day—the day Jake let his best friend surf, and die, alone—turned his life upside down.

It was Jake and Cody's second week at Seaside Reef. They were having an awesome time, as they usually did when they surfed.

Jake remembered the day well. *It was the kind of day where everything feels right with the world—where you don't know darkness is waiting, ready to swoop in and destroy everything you've ever known.*

Jake and Cody had been surfing all afternoon. They saw the worst Reefer early in the day but then he moved down the coast and kept out of their way. *Good for us*, Jake thought, *but bad for whoever is down the beach.*

As the sun drifted low on the horizon, Jake felt a sense of euphoria from being out in the sun and salt water all day. He felt physically exhausted and exhilarated at the same time, as endorphins pulsed through every cell of his body, leaving a blissful trail behind.

"Dude! I'm ready to go in," Jake said, as he and Cody sat on their boards, staring at the blue and orange horizon, waiting for the next set.

Cody slumped his shoulders and sighed. "C'mon! It's not even dark yet."

"Yeah, give it 20 minutes," Jake said. "The sun's just about to disappear."

Ten seconds later the fiery orb melted into the ocean, leaving blood-red splotches spattering the surface.

"Seriously, I'm done. Well done." With his index finger, Jake pressed a white spot into his lightly sunburned skin. "Let's catch the next wave in. You with me or against me?"

"With. But you take this one and I'll get the one after that. I want my last wave all to myself. You know, to give the ladies on the beach a show," Cody joked, pointing to his pink trunks.

Those were the last words Jake ever heard Cody speak.

Jake caught the next wave and wiped out. When he emerged, he saw another surfer. *He must have passed right by me while I was getting worked underwater.*

Jake noticed that the surfer's gaze seemed fixed on Cody. He didn't get a look at the guy's face but saw his board was emblazoned with a giant shark with bloody teeth. *Gnarly.*

Jake hoisted his body onto his board. Lying there, he watched the guy approach Cody and start talking. Wanting to get a better look, Jake sat up and plunged his legs into the water, straddling his board. At that moment, he thought he felt the water move beneath him. Instinctively, he jerked up his feet. He whipped his head around, looking down to the left and right, but couldn't see anything.

Jake glanced at Cody again. Cody saw him and pointed toward shore. He raised his hand, five fingers extended—five more minutes he wanted. Cody waved him on again, so Jake paddled toward the twinkling gold lights dotting the landscape.

Once back on the shore, Jake slung his board under his arm and ambled across the tan- and black-streaked sand toward the parking lot. The smooth stones beneath his feet felt warm from the afternoon sun.

As he approached the black pavement, he noticed a woman in cut-off jean shorts and a black bikini top, walking with a friend. She pointed at his foot and said, "You're bleeding."

Jake looked down and noticed bits of broken green bottles around him. *Probably from the Del Norte Reefers.*

He lifted his head to strike up a conversation with the women but they continued strolling toward the water. He bent down and examined his foot. Blood seeped from his toe, but he didn't see any glass in the cut and it didn't seem too deep.

It was then Jake heard the scream. He turned in the direction of the noise, toward the beach. He saw the same woman and her friend. Their hands flew up to their mouths. There were more screams.

Jake felt a sinking feeling in the pit of his stomach. *Cody. Something's wrong.* As he scanned the water, he saw Cody's board wash up. Then he saw Cody's face and body; Cody was still connected to his board by his leash.

Jake dropped his board and sprinted to the water. He splashed in, frantically grabbing beneath the surface. He thrust his arms under Cody's arms, dragged him out of the water and laid him out on the sand. *Blood. There's a lot of blood.*

"Cody!" Jake yelled. Cody's eyes remained closed.

Jake tilted Cody's head back and placed his ear above Cody's mouth to see if he was breathing. He then pressed two fingers below Cody's jawbone to check for a pulse. *Nothing.*

Jake glanced up at the lifeguard tower. It was after Labor Day so it was empty. "Somebody call 911!" he shouted.

He started CPR. There was more blood. *It's escaping his body fast—too fast.*

Jake didn't know how much time passed before the paramedics arrived. They pulled him aside and took over. As they worked to revive Cody, he studied the gashes on Cody's body. There were marks on the left side of his abdomen, his left thigh, and the left side of his neck. *Are those ... bite marks? What could cause that?* Jake scrunched his eyes, trying to make sense of what he was seeing. *Shark?*

He heard voices next to him. "He's gone." "Okay, let's get him into the ambulance."

Jake rushed toward the paramedics. "He's not gone! Why are you stopping?!"

A detective who had arrived on scene pulled Jake back.

"Stop!" He gripped Jake's shoulders, shaking him to get his attention. "Son, stop! Listen to me!"

Jake looked away from Cody, who was still lying in a pool of blood. His eyes connected with the detective's.

"Son, I'm Detective Garrison. This deputy needs to ask you a few questions. Now calm down. What's your name?"

"Jake. Jake Ryder."

"Jake, was anyone else in the water? Anyone out there with your friend?" the deputy asked.

Jake knew the deputy was talking to him but he had trouble comprehending what the deputy was saying. "What?" He shook his head, trying to get a grip on everything going on around him. He felt like the beach was spinning but he was standing still. He couldn't quite connect.

"Listen, whatever did this to your friend is still out there." Speaking slowly, as if to a young child, the deputy asked again, "Is anyone else in the water? Do you understand me? Did you see anyone else out there?"

"No, I was surfing with my friend and I came in and … Wait! Yes, I saw someone else paddling out when I was coming in. I don't know who it was. Some blond guy, a surfer. He was talking with Cody …" Jake looked out at the horizon again. It was nearly dark. He could barely see anything.

The deputy lifted his flashlight and swept it across the water, back and forth. "Do you think this other guy could've come in and you didn't notice?"

"Maybe," Jake answered. "My back was turned. I was walking toward the parking lot. There were these women. I cut my foot. I looked down … I dunno."

The deputy sprang into action. "We may have another surfer out there! Let's go!"

Turning away from the commotion, Jake glanced toward the parking lot. He saw the detective talking to a blond woman.

She held something out, like an ID card.

Over the detective's shoulder, Jake saw the paramedics loading Cody onto a gurney. "Wait!" he yelled, running toward them. "Where are you taking him? I'm going with him!"

4 – Gone

The paramedics wouldn't let Jake in the ambulance so he followed them to the hospital in his truck. He paced in the waiting room for what seemed like an eternity. He didn't have a clear grasp on time since leaving Cody in the ocean. *Has it been minutes or hours?* he wondered.

Finally, a doctor appeared. Jake rushed to him. "Cody Hansen, the surfer who was brought in? Tell me," he pleaded.

"Are you family?" the doctor asked.

"He has no family. I'm all he's got."

The doctor motioned to a chair. Jake collapsed, realizing he hadn't sat down since he arrived at the hospital. *How long has it been?*

The doctor began, "Son …"

Why does everyone keep calling me "son"? When people who are totally unrelated talk to a woman, they don't say, "Daughter …"

Seeing Jake was distracted, the doctor touched his arm. "Son? Your friend suffered very severe wounds. He died quickly, so he probably felt no pain." The doctor thought this would bring Jake some relief but his mind flashed back to the blood, all that blood.

"I can't say for certain yet, but it appears your friend was bitten by a great white shark," the doctor continued.

"A great white?" Even though Jake had seen the bite marks himself, he had a hard time believing it.

"Great whites are pretty rare in this area. Even more rare are instances of a shark attacking a human. For years, beaches here on the West Coast have been among the safest in North America. But attacks do happen. And when they do, 90 percent of the time it's a great white. Do you remember the story about the teenage surfer killed by a shark off Imperial Beach about two months ago—happened at sunset, he didn't make it but his four friends saw the attack and survived? They found two tooth fragments in the body, indicating it was a great white." The doctor considered going on but saw the strained look on Jake's face. "Is there someone I can call for you? To take you home?"

"No." Jake turned and walked away. He had nothing left to say. Cody was gone.

5 – Cody's Encounter

Shortly after Jake decided to go in and started toward the shore, Cody saw a blue-eyed surfer with shaggy blond hair approach. There was a big shark with bloody teeth on his board. *Cool,* Cody thought.

"What's up?" Cody lifted his head with a slight nod.

The surfer turned to him and smirked. "You broke the Rules."

"Rules?" Cody asked, grinning. "What rules?"

"*The* Rules."

"What are you talking about? Did Jake put you up to this?" Still smiling, Cody wondered if Jake was pulling some prank. He spotted Jake across the water and pointed to shore, telling him not to wait. Wanting to catch one last wave, he signaled "five" with his hand and waved him in again.

Seeing Jake turn toward the beach, Cody directed his attention back to the blond surfer. "Seriously, dude, what are you talking about?" he asked, still friendly and grinning.

"I saw you here last night after sunset. You dropped in on *my* wave, nearly took out me and my board. You trashed the parking lot and beach with broken beer bottles. I heard from a friend you were terrorizing kids in the water down the beach earlier today and that you've been messing with people all week." With each accusation the surfer hurled, he grew more and more agitated. "And that's just the tip of the iceberg."

"What?" Cody's grin disappeared from his face. "I wasn't even here last night. And I've been here in this spot all day, not down the beach."

"Stop lying." The surfer pointed his finger in Cody's face, "YOU are ocean trash and YOU need to be taken out."

"Dude, I'm not lying." Cody glanced toward shore hoping Jake was looking in his direction but Jake's back was turned.

Cody looked past Jake to the beach but realized he was so far out, no one on shore would be able to see him well enough to realize he was in trouble, especially in the rapidly dimming light. "Hey, wait, I think you mean that Reefer who's got pink…"

Cody didn't get to finish his sentence. In a flash, the surfer hurled his body at Cody, pushing him off his board, backward into the ocean. Encircled in bubbles, Cody saw a white streak and felt something pierce his neck. He grabbed his neck with one hand and kicked toward the ocean's surface. A second after he glimpsed the great white shark, he felt another white-hot flash of pain. It felt like a metal bear trap clamped down on his left side, knocking the air out of him. Then he felt another steel trap slam shut on his thigh. The crush of pain made him black out.

When Cody opened his eyes again, he realized he was still underwater. He glanced up and saw a man with dark brown hair shove the shaggy blond surfer. No longer able to move, Cody sank deeper into the dark water, then jerked to a stop, his foot still encircled by his leash. He had a vague sensation of warmth as blood poured from his body and diffused in the water around him. He looked up through the murky water and saw the blond surfer's face, terrified, eyes wide, staring down at him. Then blackness washed in and Cody lost consciousness.

On the ocean's surface, the brown-haired surfer, Tristan, held the shaggy blond surfer's face underwater. After a minute, he violently pulled the surfer's hair, yanking his head out of the water. "What did you do, Rick?!"

"What do you mean? I took out the trash," the blond surfer gasped, his voice an octave higher than usual.

Tristan stiffened, trying to maintain control but still grasping Rick's hair in his hand. He pointed underwater to Cody. "That is not trash. You've got the wrong guy."

"No! That's the guy. The pink trunks. He nearly knocked

me over last night and I heard he almost killed a couple kids on bodyboards today right down there," Rick pointed south. "And he …"

"You idiot," Tristan cut him off. "*That* is a different guy. Couldn't you tell the difference? Couldn't you smell it? Didn't you taste it after your first bite?"

Rick lowered his head and shook it left and right. "Tristan, I'm sorry. I thought he was the guy. I'll do better next time. I'll check. I'll double-check."

"Rick," Tristan emphasized the "k" so it hung thick in the air, "there's not gonna be a next time."

After a couple minutes, Tristan emerged from the sea, alone. He found Rick's board, surfed to shore and walked up onto the sand, about a quarter-mile north of all the commotion. He glanced at the parking lot and saw the ambulance. He looked at Jake for a split second, trying to determine what, if anything, he knew about what went down. But then Jake got in his truck and sped away after the ambulance.

"Another time," Tristan said and headed home.

6 – Lani

Special Agent Lani Marley arrived on scene the night of Cody's attack, shortly before the ambulance took him away. The ambulance and sheriff's vehicles' lights flashed in the parking lot. People darted back and forth—some trying to treat the injured surfer, others trying to find the missing surfer. A crowd of bystanders gathered to watch.

Lani saw an older man, who looked like a detective, talking to a young deputy. She walked over to them. "What happened here?"

"And who are you, little lady?" Detective Garrison peered down at Lani, who without heels stood at 5'1".

Great, she thought, *another one of these guys*. "Special Agent Marley, FBI."

A look of disbelief spread across the detective's face. *How can this little pixie be an FBI agent?* he wondered.

Lani, who was 29 but looked at least five years younger, had seen the look before, often, and did her best to ignore it.

Lani was petite and slim, with blue eyes and straight blond hair that reached a few inches past her shoulders. Her looks were often an asset when trying to get information out of people, men in particular. But they were a hindrance when trying to get some people, men in particular, to take her seriously.

"FBI?" Garrison asked. "Aren't you a little, uh, young? And isn't this a little out of your jurisdiction?"

"Depends. Shark attack, right?" Lani asked, knowing it was before he answered. She'd heard the call over the sheriff's radio. It was like the others.

"We don't know that yet, little lady," Garrison said.

"Special Agent Marley," she corrected, wanting to shove the detective's condescending face into the hood of his car. She briefly considered it but went on. "And you are …?"

"Detective Garrison."

"Well then, Detective Garrison, what can you tell me about what happened here?"

As Lani listened to what little the detective knew, her mind filled in the missing pieces—some of them at least. It *was* like the others. A surfer washes up on the beach. The medical examiner says the death was caused by one or more bites from a great white shark. The problem was that shark attacks, while not unheard of, used to be pretty rare off the California coast. But they were increasing fast. And they seemed to occur in the company of a nomadic tribe of surfers, led by a man named Tristan Pierce.

Lani didn't share any of this with the detective. In truth, she wasn't really on a case. She had tried but failed to convince her boss there even was a case. Technically, she was on vacation, the first one she'd taken since she joined the Bureau.

But Lani knew the beaches and she knew the ocean. There was something going on. A shark attack was a natural occurrence but very rare. This was something … unnatural. She knew it in her gut. And she decided she would not rest until she found out what. Even if it meant she had to become Leilani Waters again.

How ironic. After all these years running from my past, now it might be exactly what I need to break this case. My parents would be so proud, she thought wryly. *No, not proud. They'd be … probably too stoned to care.*

7 – Hunger

When Jake awoke, he didn't remember how he got home from the hospital. He rose from the couch and lifted the curtains with one hand. He saw his truck parked in its usual spot. It was dark outside. *What time is it?* he wondered. *Was I at the hospital tonight or did I sleep through to the next night?*

Jake's stomach roared. He walked to the fridge and opened the door. *Two beers and a bottle of hot sauce. That's not going to work.*

He quickly showered and drove down Highway 101 to Rubio's. He stepped up to the counter, "Three fish tacos, for here." He paid the cashier and ambled over to the salsa bar. He filled one container with tomatillo salsa and another with chipotle salsa, and then watched some tropical fish swim around a saltwater tank a few steps back from the counter. His head tingled from hunger.

"Jake!" the cashier yelled.

Jake picked up his tray of food and sat at an open table in the corner. He unwrapped the first taco, opened the corn tortilla, squeezed a lime wedge across the beer battered fish, and drizzled salsa across the fresh cabbage. He devoured the taco in two bites. He tore through the second and third tacos, not even bothering with the lime or salsa. He ordered six tacos to go, filled a few more salsa containers, and took everything home.

A few minutes later, Jake set the bag on the kitchen counter and opened it, digging out a pile of tacos. He ripped open a wrapper and ate one taco and then another and another. He reached in the bag again. It was empty.

Jake wandered over to the window, lifted the curtains, and peered into the darkness. *Maybe it's the nine fish tacos I just ate. Or maybe it's the 24 hours of uninterrupted sleep. Whatever it is, I need to surf. Now.*

8 – Surfing Through the Darkness

Jake ignored the shark warning signs posted on the beach and sprinted to the water. The wet sand felt like mounds of velvet beneath his feet. As he entered the ocean, he heard the roar of the waves crashing around him. It sounded like applause, encircling him, coming at him from all directions. Emboldened, he paddled out into the blackness.

He sat on his board in the lull, waiting for the next set of waves. The water gently chipped away at the despair and loneliness he felt. *Cody.*

Jake wondered about the shark that bit Cody. He saw the bites himself but couldn't shake the feeling the other surfer was involved somehow.

He looked over his shoulder. Surprisingly, he felt unafraid. *Shark, no shark—either way, I'm surfing tonight.*

Jake almost hoped he did find the shark that killed Cody so he could return the favor. He also wanted to find the surfer who was the last person to see Cody alive and maybe the first person to see him dead. *Is that surfer dead, too? Did he get eaten by the shark? Or is he alive? It seemed like he was targeting Cody when he swam out to him, like he needed to talk to him or confront him about something.*

Jake remembered the surfer's fixed gaze. Thinking back on it, he felt the same bad vibe he felt when he first saw him. The memory sent a shiver down his spine.

He reached down to his ankle, where he'd strapped his titanium dive knife. *If I do run into that shark, or that surfer, I can protect myself. And avenge my friend. Would I really kill him, if he murdered Cody? Could I?*

Jake glanced over his shoulder and saw a tasty wave rolling toward him. He paddled, looked over his shoulder once again, and leapt to his feet. Taking the drop, he could immediately tell this was no ordinary wave. The wave crested over his head and he was in the green room. He dragged his index finger across the wall of water. *This is epic. Perfect.*

With each wave Jake rode, he felt better, stronger. *It feels like Cody is with me,* he thought, *which is good since I never surf alone at night.*

Jake recalled how, from a young age, every surfer learns about the buddy system. *Anything can happen in the ocean during the day. You can get slammed into a rock, get knocked unconscious, break your bones, slice open your flesh. You can get trapped under a wall of water, pinned to the ocean floor by wave after wave. Or you can sit for hours waiting for a wave that never comes. Whatever the case, having a friend out there is vital to your survival. At night, the risks are magnified a thousandfold.*

A couple hours before dawn, after a night of awesome waves, Jake made his way back to shore. He emerged from the black water and was struck by a single overwhelming thought: *I can't surf during the day anymore. There's no way. It'll be too painful without Cody. In the darkness, I can imagine he's here. In the daylight, I'll know he isn't.*

Jake turned back to the ocean and made a solemn promise. *I won't let you die for no reason, Cody. I'm going to find that surfer and find out exactly what happened to you if it's the last thing I do. Tomorrow the hunt begins.*

9 – The Nomads

After leaving the beach, Tristan returned home. Home, for the last eight weeks, was a rented Spanish-style house on the bluffs above the ocean in Encinitas.

He threw Rick's board in a bedroom and marched down the street to Skylar's house. He pounded on the front door. "Skylar!"

She unlocked the door. "What? What's going on?"

Skylar was a 28-year-old surfer from Huntington Beach. She was, by almost universal standards, gorgeous. She had long, wavy chestnut brown hair with sunkissed streaks that made her bronze skin glow. She had large, almond-shaped brown eyes and a smile that lit up a room, that is, when she did smile.

Skylar, who stood at 5'6" but seemed taller because of her "kill-or-be-killed" attitude, was Tristan's second-in-command. She knew when he used her full name instead of her nickname, Sky, someone was in trouble.

"When everyone returns, I want a meeting at my place. Immediately." Tristan turned and headed back to his house.

Ten hours later, shortly before 6 a.m., the last Nomad returned home. Skylar rounded them up. "Tristan wants a meeting. Now."

Logan, Cruz and Torrey followed Skylar to Tristan's house. Skylar let herself in and led them into the living room. They all lined up to face Tristan, who had his back turned and was staring at a large black-and-white photo of the Big Sur coast on the wall.

This is definitely not good, Skylar thought. "Rick isn't home," she reported to Tristan.

"Yeah, I haven't seen Rick all night. Where is he?" asked Logan, who at 19 was the youngest and newest member of the Nomads.

Tristan slowly turned around. His brown eyes darkened as he glowered at Logan. Logan averted his eyes to the floor.

Tristan clenched his jaw. "I'll ask the questions tonight. Do you all remember the incident off Imperial Beach two months ago—and the Rules we discussed, again, after that fiasco? You know, the fiasco that was splashed across the news, where an innocent *young* surfer was killed by a shark and his four friends saw it happen? You remember that, don't you? The faces of crying teenagers on TV for days?" Tristan asked.

The surfers nodded in unison, "Yes."

"And do you remember how we had to find the Rogue who did that," Tristan spit the word "Rogue" like it left a bitter taste in his mouth, "and make him pay for what he did?"

"Yes," they quietly answered.

"Well then what is it about my Rules—*our* Rules—that's so hard to understand? Skylar, what's Rule number 1?" he demanded.

"Rule number 1: Do not kill a child," she answered.

"And what's the penalty for breaking the Rule and killing someone who hasn't yet reached the ripe old age of 18?" Tristan asked, even though everyone in the room knew the answer.

"Death. You will be killed to make up for the human life you took and prevent the taking of another," Skylar replied.

Tristan gave her a slight nod. "And Rule number 2?"

"Rule 2: Do not kill, unless you're certain it's a righteous kill."

"And what's the penalty for breaking Rule 2 and killing someone who doesn't deserve it?" Tristan asked.

"Death," Skylar answered.

"*That*, Logan, is what happened to Rick. He broke Rule 2," Tristan explained.

Skylar gasped.

Tristan glared at her. "Skylar, please continue with the Rules since it appears some of us are having trouble with them."

"Rule 3: Do not trash the ocean or the beach. Rule 4 ..."

Tristan was the oldest of the Nomads, both in human years and actual years. But that's not what earned him the Nomads' respect.

Tristan was the first vampire shark—and their creator.

10 – Tristan's (Re)Birth

Tristan, who was born in San Francisco in 1905, became a vampire when he was 31 years old. He and a buddy had been at the 365 Club on Market Street, drinking gin out of coffee cups all night. After leaving the club, Tristan, who was quite drunk, made a wrong turn into an alley. In the darkness, he heard a deep voice say, "A meal *and* a martini. Nice."

Tristan peered down the alley to see if he could tell where the voice came from. Seeing nothing, he turned back toward the street. Half-a-second later, he felt someone grab him from behind. As Tristan tried to break free of the arms wrapped around his chest, he felt two sharp pangs on the right side of his neck.

The man pressed his lips against Tristan's neck and began to suck his blood. Tristan struggled but realized it was just making the bite deeper and more ragged. There was no way he could free himself from the grip of the monster slowly draining him of his life. Tristan stood there, immobile, trying to make sense of what was happening through his alcohol-induced haze.

After a few minutes, the man pulled away from Tristan's neck. "Mister, how much did you drink tonight? I'm already soused." He pushed Tristan aside, into the wall of a building, and stumbled down the alley to the street.

Tristan slumped against the building, clutching his neck to try to stop the flow of blood. A couple minutes later, he passed out. He lay in the shadows, in a small pool of his own blood, the entire next day.

When Tristan awoke that evening, he lifted his head, which felt about twice its normal size and weight. He glanced down at his shirt and saw it was bloody. *Did I get in a fight?* he wondered. He smacked his lips; his mouth was parched and his tongue felt swollen. His body hurt. *I am so hung over. How much did I drink last night?*

But that was only part of the reason Tristan felt so strange. With each passing moment, he was becoming less human.

Twelve hours later, after drinking 64 ounces of water and lying awake all night in his bed, Tristan still felt odd. He felt uncomfortable in his skin. His head and body ached. The city smells wafting through his open window grew increasingly intense, making him feel queasy.

Tristan mustered his strength and rose from bed to close the window. As his foot crossed into the morning sunlight burning a bright swath across his floor, he jumped back, as if scalded.

He collapsed on the bed and threw his arm across his forehead. *What happened? I went to the bar. I drank gin. Okay, admittedly, a lot of gin. I left the bar ... and then what?* Slowly, he remembered the stranger in the alley. *Did that even happen? It seemed so surreal.*

Tristan walked to the bathroom and stared in the mirror. He was taken aback by how pale he looked. He craned his neck. There they were: two round burgundy dots with jagged lines, about half an inch long, radiating from each.

One by one the puzzle pieces drifted into place. Tristan could no longer ignore the truth. The inability to stand in sunlight, the keen sense of smell, the desire for blood—he felt it all.

Tristan had heard stories about vampires in the city for years but thought that's all they were—stories. Something parents told their children to keep them from wandering the streets at night. Something men told women to get them to cling to their arms a little tighter on the foggy stroll home.

This is unbelievable. Literally unbelievable.

Tristan waited for darkness to fall and ventured out into

the mist. As he rounded the corner, he didn't know how but he smelled another vampire across the street. The vampire's scent was slightly metallic. Tristan wondered if the vampire had recently dined on human blood. He ran over and offered to buy him a drink.

Over a round of martinis, Tristan learned he had indeed been turned into a vampire and that life as he knew it would never be the same.

11 – Newborn

"So you're telling me I can't go outside during the day anymore?" Tristan asked anxiously.

"No, no, not at all," said the other vampire, a wrinkly gray-haired man named William. "You just can't go out for a while. When you are …" He paused and looked around to see if anyone was in earshot. "When you are one of our kind, everything is intensified. Everything. Mostly that's a good thing, if you catch my meaning." William winked and nodded.

Tristan smiled politely, trying to avoid envisioning the wrinkled vampire doing anything the wink could possibly imply.

William continued excitedly, "Now that you are one of us, you will find all your senses—sight, sound, smell, taste, touch—are magnified. That gives you superpowers in a way. You will be aware of things before regular people are. You can react to something before anyone else perceives it. If someone approaches you from behind, you know what they're up to almost before they do. You can read people, with or without seeing their faces. You can hear their heart beat. You can tell by their smell if they feel scared or excited. You can tell by the way their pupils expand or contract if they're aroused or ambivalent. You can hear tones in their voices they're not even aware they're communicating."

"That all sounds nice. Really. But what about going outside in the sunlight?" Although there were more foggy days than not in San Francisco, when it was clear, Tristan loved to stroll through the city feeling the sun on his face and the wind in his hair.

"Think of it this way," William said. "You are like a newborn baby, only your skin is even more sensitive. You need to gradually—very gradually—build up a tolerance to the sun. If you go out in the sunlight tomorrow, you'll disappear into a pile of ash."

Tristan gasped.

"Don't worry, Tristan. You just need to be careful. You can start by exposing your skin to the light reflecting off the moon. Be careful during a full moon though. You'll get burned if you stay out all night with your skin exposed."

"Moonburned? I don't believe you. Are you trying to have a laugh at my expense?"

"No, I'm being completely serious," William assured him. "That is sunlight reflecting off the moon, is it not? During a full moon, it's so bright that regular people, without supersenses like ours, can walk around at midnight and see perfectly well, right? That means those rays are powerful. Look at my face. How old do you think I am?"

"I don't know. In human years, I'd say 70," Tristan guessed.

"No. In human years, I'd be 55 but I look 70. Do you know why? Because I did not take care of my skin. I was careless in my youth, as so many are. If I can give you one piece of advice, it's this: Protect your skin. You're going to have it a very long time. You might as well look your best, right?"

"What do you mean by a 'long' time? How long do we live exactly?" Tristan asked.

"Technically, I'm 552 years old."

Tristan lifted his brows in disbelief.

"It's true." William stood up to leave. "Life is long, Tristan. Make the most of it. Do what you love. Accept nothing less than that. And now I must go."

"Wait!" Tristan pleaded. "I have so many other questions."

"You're a smart man. You'll figure it out. It's really not all that complicated." William shook Tristan's hand and headed toward the door. Halfway there, he turned around and pointed his index finger at Tristan. "Protect your skin, young man. You'll thank me later."

In the days and decades that followed, Tristan heeded William's advice and was careful to protect his skin as he built up a tolerance to the sun's powerful rays.

He also quickly learned to blend into human society as a vampire. He continued to eat as a human but preferred his meat cooked rare, if at all. He sometimes fed on animal blood. *Pets go missing in the city all the time. No big deal,* he thought.

On rare and special occasions, he dined on human blood. His favorite meal was "surf and turf," as he called it.

A few times a year, Tristan would venture down to the pier in the dead of night and stow away on a sightseeing boat that did twilight cruises of San Francisco Bay. Once the boat was at sea, Tristan would emerge after sunset and look for a person standing alone on deck, gazing out at the darkening water. Upon finding his prey, he'd sneak up from behind and snap the person's neck. Tristan thought it was the humane and practical thing to do. He didn't want his meal to feel pain, nor did he want his meal to scream or thrash and cause a ruckus. After feeding, he'd simply toss the body overboard. No muss, no fuss.

Sometimes for fun, after throwing the body into the sea, Tristan would anonymously yell, "Man overboard!" He liked to see the panic and flurry of frantic activity that followed. *Dinner and a show*, he'd muse.

Most times, however, he let the sea carry away the body, which would eventually be eaten by scavengers. *Circle of life*, Tristan thought.

12 – Vampire Adrift

In November 1972, 36 years after becoming a vampire, Tristan bided his time on a research vessel travelling from Pier 43 in San Francisco to the Farallons, a group of islands and rocks in the Gulf of the Farallones 30 miles outside the Golden Gate Bridge.

A few minutes after sunset, the boat turned and made its way back toward the city. Tristan emerged from the engine room and spotted a lonely figure leaning over the railing. After Tristan finished his dinner, he lifted the body over his head and prepared to toss it overboard.

At that moment, a rogue wave hit the boat, knocking Tristan and the body into the frigid Pacific Ocean. Here, near the edge of the North American continental shelf, the ocean floor plunged to more than two miles deep.

Tristan, however, wasn't concerned for his safety. He was stronger than the average human so he knew he could swim the 30 miles back to the city, if necessary. With his vampire body's superior thermoregulation, he knew hypothermia wasn't a threat and that he could survive in the 55-degree water for hours.

What Tristan didn't know was that from 1946 to 1970, under the authority of the Atomic Energy Commission, the sea around the Farallons was a nuclear dumping site. As Tristan swam east toward San Francisco, he was blissfully unaware of the 47,800 barrels of low-level radioactive waste littering the ocean floor beneath him.

Another thing Tristan didn't know was that one of these barrels was leaking—and transforming the ecosystem around him.

13 – Predator and Prey

Splashing along the ocean's surface, Tristan caught the attention of a great white shark, one of many who live around the Farallons. While this particular shark normally dined on elephant seals and an occasional sea lion, she was intrigued by the unusual creature with long limbs swimming above her.

The 15-foot shark approached Tristan from below and took an exploratory bite of the meaty part of his calf, just to get a taste. She released Tristan and swam away, pondering the unfamiliar flavor. Deciding she liked it, she circled back and zoomed in for the kill, excited about the idea of eating something foreign and exotic, even if it was a bit bony.

For Tristan, the instant he felt the bite on his leg, every cell in his vampire body went on high alert. *I am the one who bites*, he thought. *Not the other way around.* Although that first exploratory bite wasn't serious—it was more like a bite from a puppy with sharp teeth—Tristan was not about to let another happen.

Seeing the steel-gray shark circle and swim toward him, Tristan leapt into attack mode. As the shark thrust her head toward him and opened her jaw, her milky white skin pulled back to reveal rows of jagged teeth. Before her mouth was fully extended, Tristan swung his arm back and punched her in the nose as hard as he could. Dazed and confused, the shark flew backward through the air, exposing her white underbelly.

As the shark hit the water, Tristan jumped on top of her. He grabbed the shark by the steel-gray gills lined up behind her head. He tore into her, his fangs covering her face with bite marks. As she thrashed in his iron grip, Tristan drained her blood. He then tossed the mangled body aside and continued swimming toward the city.

A few minutes later, another female shark hit Tristan from

below and threw him into the air. He whipped his body around, mid-air, and plunged into the ocean, fangs first. He ripped into the 12-foot shark's mottled gray and white snout, and tore ribbons of flesh from her gills. Once again, he drank the shark's blood and set the body adrift.

Just before he reached an island, a third shark appeared. Tristan and the 11-foot male wrestled, splashing on the ocean's surface and tumbling a few feet below. Teeth gnashed, puncturing flesh and spilling blood.

Tristan climbed onto the rocky shore, victorious, wet, and ready to burst from ingesting so much blood. As he lay on the rocks, patting his distended belly, he gazed at the razor-thin crescent moon and pondered how exactly he was going to swim all the way back to San Francisco in shark-infested waters. *How many sharks can I fight?* he wondered.

14 – Vampire Stories

While Tristan digested his shark dinner, he reflected on the mythology surrounding vampires and laughed to himself about how easily humans jump to conclusions.

During his evening with poor, wrinkled William and in conversations with other vampires since, he learned vampires are not immortal. They simply have longer life spans than humans. A healthy vampire can live to be up to 800 or 900 or even 1,000 years old. *A very long life? Yes. Immortal? No,* Tristan chuckled.

Another fallacy is that vampires are dead. In actuality, vampires' hearts beat so slowly, the beats are almost imperceptible to humans.

In fact, the whole reason humans think vampires sleep in coffins is because so many vampires have ended up in a coffin after falling asleep.

Vampires are notoriously deep sleepers. In the days before technology transformed modern medicine and autopsies became commonplace, a sleeping vampire was often thought to be a dead human since no heartbeat could be detected. The sleeping body was then placed in a coffin and prepared for burial, or even buried on occasion. Upon waking, the groggy vampire would freak out to find himself or herself trapped in a coffin. He or she would throw open the casket lid, sometimes surprising the mortician or funeral attendees or gravedigger or any other humans who happened to be around. Hence, vampires became known as the "undead" and "walking dead."

Like more than a few vampires, Tristan was slightly claustrophobic. The fear of being trapped in small places was sometimes passed from the DNA of one vampire to the next—like a fear of spiders or snakes has been passed from one generation of humans to the next for millennia.

Another myth is that vampires eat only blood and must ingest blood to survive. While vampires, like humans, need to eat to live, they usually eat once every three days or so. Because vampires have a heightened sense of smell, like dogs, raw flesh and blood smell quite appetizing and taste delicious. Humans, of course, are disgusted by this, conveniently forgetting that animals in the wild eat raw flesh and blood all the time.

Since most humans prefer their animal flesh dead and cooked, with the occasional exception like sushi or steak tartare, they think a raw diet is vicious and uncivilized. *Hypocrites*, Tristan scoffed. *Humans love to bend and twist the rules, ignoring contradictions and creating double standards whenever it suits them.*

To blend in, most vampires eat regular human-grade food, albeit rare. But they do have blood on occasion as a special treat. Blood to a vampire is very much like chocolate to most humans. Some days you can resist it, some days you need only a little piece, and occasionally you gorge.

Since vampires are neither immortal nor dead, they can be killed. It just takes a lot more effort. A wooden stake through the heart is usually the most efficient way to kill a vampire, since humans rarely get more than one try. And guns are far too noisy. Many humans have been surprised to find their guns snatched from their hands before they finished cocking the weapon or placing an index finger on the trigger.

Because vampires are stronger and faster than humans, and their five senses are so finely honed, they have both an offensive and defensive advantage—which suited Tristan just fine.

15 – Metamorphosis

After a couple hours lying on the rocks thinking about the differences between humans and vampires, and why vampires are vastly superior, Tristan still felt uncomfortably full. He had never eaten so much blood at once—a human and three sharks. But it wasn't just his stomach. His entire body felt strange, like it was shimmering on the inside.

Tristan held up his arm in the faint, silvery moonlight. He turned it from side to side. His pale skin glowed and pulsated. *That's weird,* he thought.

The waves of light emanating from his skin coincided with the waves of nausea that began to hit. Tristan clutched his stomach and doubled over, unaccustomed to feeling sick since becoming a vampire.

He began to vomit. Pieces of shark flesh hurled from his body. Just when he thought the worst was over, more shark bits and blood poured from his mouth.

After a half-hour, his stomach was finally empty. He collapsed on the rocks. His head throbbed. His skin felt cold and slimy. *What's happening to me?*

Tristan slipped in and out of consciousness. He dreamed of swimming through the ocean. He swished his tail fin from side to side. Pectoral fins outstretched, he felt like he was flying. Gathering momentum, he turned upward. Faster and faster, his caudal fin swished until he propelled himself out of the water and into the air. He opened his mouth, sucking in a cold blast of oxygen from above the ocean's surface. Droplets of water wisped behind his body as he sailed, dorsal fin grazing the sky. Closing his mouth, he splashed down into the ocean. The water whizzing past his gills felt amazing. As he plunged, he stretched his pectoral fins again, flying.

When Tristan awoke, he lifted his head. There was no nausea and his headache was gone. He slowly climbed to his feet. *I feel fine now. Better than fine actually. The last time I felt this good was after dining on human blood for the first time. But this is even better!*

Tristan ran to the ocean. Wading into the black water, he wondered if sharks lurked nearby but felt no fear.

Remembering his dream and the profound freedom he felt, Tristan began to swim. Before long, he felt exactly as he had in the dream. Sleek, smooth, powerful, invincible. It was at this moment Tristan realized he was no longer in his own body but in the body of a great white shark.

Tristan clamped his jaws together. He flicked his caudal fin back and forth. From head to tail, his body tingled. *Alive. I feel so alive!*

Though he didn't know what it was called at that moment, Tristan was feeling his lateral line, a series of fluid-filled canals just below the skin of a shark's head and along the sides of its body. The canals, which open to the water through tiny pores, contain sensory cells. As the water movement around Tristan displaced the hairlike projections, the stimulation triggered nerve impulses to his brain. He enjoyed the sensation as it rippled through his body.

When he approached a seal, the tingling in his head intensified. It felt like a heartbeat, growing stronger and stronger. As the seal swam away, it faded.

Tristan would later learn the feeling in his head was caused by his ampullae of Lorenzini. Unique to sea creatures like sharks and rays, these electroreceptors create an extensive sensory system around the head. The ampullae pores lead to jelly-filled canals, sensory cells and nerve fibers that can detect the electromagnetic fields produced by all living things. As a shark, Tristan now had thousands and thousands of these sensing organs to help him find prey.

Excited by this sixth sense, Tristan set out to find another animal. Before he could see it or hear it, he detected the faint electrical pulse of a fur seal's heartbeat. *Amazing!*

Reveling in his newfound hydro-senses and speed, Tristan propelled himself toward San Francisco. When he crossed under the Golden Gate Bridge, he wondered if he could change back into his human body as easily as he had transformed into a shark. But since it was still broad daylight and he didn't want to expose his skin to the sun, he explored the bay, hunted and feasted on a harbor seal.

When darkness fell, Tristan found a remote spot and swam to shore. As soon as he had the thought to start walking, he found himself in human form again. He emerged from the sea, naked and dripping.

Laughing to himself, Tristan set out to find some clothing. It was that night he met Julianna.

16 – The Hunt

The evening after Jake's first midnight surf session, he headed to a bar near Seaside Reef where local surfers go to drink, rehash their exploits on the water, and talk tides and swells. *If anyone knows anything about this mystery surfer or what happened to Cody, this is the best place to start,* he decided.

Jake took a seat at the bar and ordered a pint of Wipeout IPA from Port Brewing. He took a sip. *Mmm, hoppy.* He took another drink and looked around the dimly lit room. He held up his hand and motioned to the bartender.

"Yeah, a friend of mine told me to meet up with a guy who surfs at Seaside. He's blond and has a cool board with a big shark with bloody teeth on it. You know him?" Jake hoped he sounded casual and not like a guy on a mission to avenge his best friend.

"Why do you wanna know?" the bartender asked.

"I just wanna ask him about the surfing around here."

"Really? Now why don't I buy that?" the bartender grumbled as he wiped down beer glasses.

"Okay, man," Jake lowered his voice, "the truth is, I need to talk to him. I think he might know something about that shark attack that happened a couple days ago."

The bartender was unimpressed with Jake's confession. "What's it to you?"

"It was my friend that got killed. By the shark."

The bartender loudly inhaled and exhaled. "Yeah, I might know the guy you mean. Haven't seen him in a couple days." He paused again, then continued in a hushed tone. "There's a group he hangs out with. A guy, Tristan, a girl, Skylar, and a couple others. They come in here sometimes. I've seen the guy with 'em once or twice. But you didn't hear it from me."

"Thanks, man. But how will I know them?"

"Don't worry. You'll know," the bartender snickered and turned away.

I guess this conversation's over. Jake decided to wait it out and sipped his beer.

Ten minutes later, the door swung open and a cool, salty breeze whooshed into the bar.

"Speak of the devil," the bartender muttered under his breath.

Jake turned and saw a dark-haired man glide through the door. He was 6 feet tall with broad shoulders and a muscular build. He wore a tight black T-shirt, black jeans, and sunglasses.

That's a little weird, Jake thought. *It's dark outside.*

Following behind the man was a stunning woman with glowing bronze skin and wavy chestnut brown hair. She, too, wore sunglasses, and a black tank dress. Jake's mouth fell open at the sight of her. *Oh god, I hope she didn't see that.* He turned back to the bar and took a swig of beer. *Focus, man.*

Jake used the mirror on the wall behind the bar to spy on Tristan and Skylar as they scanned the room for a table. He saw Tristan pause behind a blond who had taken a seat to his left. He watched Tristan inhale deeply and start to turn to her, as if to say something, but then he thought better of it and continued walking. As Skylar passed behind Jake, he caught the scent of the ocean mixed with something sweet, like a tropical-scented shower gel or shampoo. *Focus.*

From the corner of his eye, he saw them take a seat at a table past the bar and remove their sunglasses. Jake took another swig of beer and sighed. *For Cody, talking to a woman like that would be no problem. For me? Let's just say I've been known to forget my own name when asked a direct question by a woman only half as hot as her.*

He stole a glance at Skylar again. *This is going to be tougher than I thought.*

17 — A Different Hunt

At the same instant, Lani had the exact same thought. She, too, had come to the bar on a mission. She had scoped it out the night of the shark attack and knew the Nomads sometimes visited since it was a popular hangout for surfers. She hoped to infiltrate their group and do some digging.

Earlier that evening, sitting near the window, Lani was surprised when she saw Jake walk in and take a seat at the bar. She recognized him from the beach, the night of Cody's death. She sized him up. He looked to be about 23 years old, 5'7", medium build. He had a roundish face, dark brown hair, and greenish-brown eyes. *He's nice-looking,* she thought.

As Lani studied Jake, she felt bad for him and was stunned to see him out so soon after the loss of his friend. *But I guess it makes sense you'd want to have a drink, or many, after your best friend was savagely killed*, she ruminated. Though, having never lost anyone close to her, she didn't know for sure.

When Lani heard Jake ask the bartender about the blond surfer he'd seen at the beach the night Cody died, her ears perked up. Wanting to eavesdrop, she slammed her beer, strolled up to the bar and sat two seats to the left of Jake. She waved her empty glass to signal to the bartender she'd like another.

The bartender set a full beer on the bar. As she reached for it, he let his fingers linger on the glass, so she'd accidentally touch him. "You let me know if you need anything else, beautiful." He brushed his fingertips against hers. "A-ny-thing."

Lani cringed, disgusted by the bartender's unwelcome touch. She wanted to snatch her hand away so she could use it to smash his face against the sticky wooden bar. *Knock some manners into him*, she thought.

Instead, she smiled sweetly and said, "Thanks," thinking

she might need to get some information from him later about Tristan and his crew.

Lani turned away from the bartender and took a big gulp of cold beer. She nearly choked, however, upon seeing Tristan enter the bar. She knew from his description and a couple grainy photos that he would be good-looking and nicely built, but she had no idea he would be this beautiful. Gazing at his hypnotic dark brown eyes, smooth dark brown hair, and perfectly tanned skin, she struggled to swallow her beer without coughing and drawing attention to herself. *This is going to be harder than I thought.*

Lani knew it had to be more than just a coincidence that the Nomads seemed to turn up in a city right around the time a surfer went missing or was found dead at the beach. *Are the Nomads the cause of the disappearances and deaths? Or are they seeking the cause, like I am? Or do they just have really bad timing?*

Her inner cynic, which usually ruled her brain, told her option A was most likely the correct answer. But, upon seeing Tristan, something inside her wanted it to be option B or C.

She tore her eyes away from Tristan's chiseled jaw and Adonis-like body, and took another drink of beer. She tried to stop the blushing in her cheeks and focus on getting into character—Leilani, lifelong surfer. Her character was actually a former version of herself, but one she voluntarily left behind. Until she realized it could help her investigation.

Come on, Leilani. You used to love to surf. Tristan loves to surf. You can do this. Just ignore the fact that he is, without a doubt, the most gorgeous man you've ever seen in your entire life. He also might be a murderer. And it's up to you to find out.

With that chilling thought, Lani was back on the case. She turned to her right to strike up a conversation with Jake. But he was on his way over to Tristan's table. She hoped she'd be able to hear their conversation.

18 – Lolo

Both Lani's parents, Jeff and Linda Waters, were die-hard surfers. That's why they named their only daughter Leilani; it sounded like a surfer girl's name. Her middle name, Marley, was for Bob Marley, their favorite musician. And having Waters as a last name for a family of surfers was destiny or a stroke of dumb luck, depending on how one looked at it.

Leilani grew up in Hawaii, never living more than a few blocks from the ocean, usually in the most dilapidated place in the neighborhood. Her parents, both high school dropouts, eked out a living doing odd jobs and, mostly, selling marijuana—that is, what they didn't smoke themselves.

When she was a toddler, Leilani's parents nicknamed her "Lolo." Leilani liked the nickname until, at the age of 8, she found out it was short for pakalolo, a Hawaiian word for marijuana. She immediately asked them to stop calling her "Lolo." She told them it sounded too babyish for a girl her age, but really she didn't want to be named after a weed, especially one that made her parents so forgetful and annoying.

From the time she could walk, Leilani spent as much time as she could at the beach. She loved the roar of the ocean. It drowned out her parents' voices and the voice in her head telling her she was different, at least in the Waters' household.

Even as a child Leilani was driven, impatient, and quick to anger when she knew she wasn't being taken seriously. She also had an intense curiosity and delighted in asking question after question about the world around her.

Her parents were the opposite. "Chill, Lolo. Stop asking so many questions. Just be," they'd tell her, over and over. But the more laid back her parents were, the more angry and resentful Leilani got.

Seeing Leilani as their golden ticket, Jeff and Linda pressured her to join the pro surfing circuit. Leilani, who was naturally athletic, had always been a hard worker. With her innate drive to succeed, she performed well in competitions and showed no fear, even on the most massive waves.

Leilani's anger and defiance made her feel invincible. She wanted to show her parents someone could be a surfer and a law-abiding, contributing member of society. Each time a wave challenged her, she thought of her parents and the ride was a cakewalk, so to speak.

But the more Leilani won, the less her parents worked and the more they relied on her. Instead of teaching them a lesson, she realized she was the one learning a lesson. Her parents were taking advantage of her. They supplemented their meager income with her prize winnings and sold most of the merchandise her sponsors gave her.

As a teenager, Leilani grew weary of her parents' lazy lifestyle. She quit surfing at the beginning of her junior year in high school, after getting thrown head-first into coral at Sunset Beach in Oahu. The blow was so hard it knocked her out for about 10 seconds. When she opened her eyes, still underwater, she found herself face to face with a great white shark. To her surprise, the shark stared at her for a while, sized her up, and then swam away, apparently not interested in a meal at that particular time.

Although the experience was harrowing, Leilani knew she could overcome it and surf again if she wanted to. But she used the concussion and close encounter with the shark as her excuse to quit surfing altogether. She was tired of her parents exploiting her. She also wanted to focus all her energy on school. Leilani set a goal to get a scholarship to a college far away, study criminology, and pursue a career in law enforcement—much to her parents' dismay.

Leilani's parents had always talked derisively about "the Man," meaning the law or any part of the establishment. They relished the fact that their lifestyle was a daily rebellion against mainstream society. The word "Rebel" was often tossed around as a term of endearment between them, like the way other couples say, "Honey" or "Dear."

"Hey Rebel, you wanna hit the beach?" or "Hey Rebel, did you remember to feed Lolo today?" or more commonly, "Hey Rebel, where's the lighter?"

Of course, they failed to see the irony that their daughter joining mainstream society was, in fact, an act of rebellion against them. But instead of calling her "Rebel," they started calling her "the Man."

"Oh no, it's the Man!" they'd say, pretending to hide the bong when she arrived home from school. "Don't bother the Man. She's studying," they'd scoff, when she'd ask them to turn down the TV. They thought it was funny. It wasn't to Leilani.

The day Leilani turned 18, she left home and legally changed her name to "Lani Marley" in an effort to distance herself from her parents, their checkered past, and her life in the Waters family.

She'd always liked the name Marley and the music of her namesake. She loved Bob Marley's vision of "one world, one love," and aspired to have the patience and peace of mind to actually live by that vision someday. And she had nothing against the surf subculture that enjoyed partying with pakalolo. Most of the surfers she met through her parents were really cool, peaceful people who'd give you the shirt off their back if you asked. She felt bad when they came to make a purchase because she knew her parents had rigged their scale to be off by a tiny percentage, in their favor of course. They often joked about their "administrative fee," never feeling remorse for the customers they ever-so-slightly short-changed.

What Leilani didn't like was being a member of the Waters family, which in her mind was a family of leeches.

But now, 11 years later, Lani realized that her history as Leilani Waters might come in handy. With her background, she knew there was no one better for this case. It was hers to solve. And, it was rumored, Tristan had a thing for blonds. *How fortunate*, she thought.

19 — A Chance Meeting

When Tristan walked into the bar that night, he was surprised to see Jake there. Even more surprising was the blond woman sitting at the bar, two seats away from Jake. He didn't get a good look at her face but as he walked behind her, her scent seemed familiar. Like an olfactory déjà vu.

As Tristan sat down at an empty table, he leaned over and whispered in Skylar's ear, "The guy from the beach is here."

Skylar threw him a worried look. "What do we do?"

"There's nothing to be concerned about yet. Let's see what happens," Tristan murmured.

Skylar relaxed, enjoying the warmth of his breath on her neck.

Tristan pulled away and leaned back in his chair as Jake shuffled up. *What, if anything, does this guy know about that whole screw-up with Rick?* he wondered, as he looked up with a smile.

20 – Frenemies

"Hey man, can I talk to you for a second?" Jake broached.

"Sure. What can I do for you?" Tristan asked, wanting to seem pleasant and approachable.

Seeing Tristan be so welcoming, Skylar shot Jake a friendly smile and gestured to the empty chair, "Here, have a seat. Join us." Warm honey dripped from her voice.

Jake decided he couldn't make up some ruse about the blond surfer. It was hard enough to concentrate knowing Skylar's warm mocha-brown eyes were now staring at him. *I'll just tell the truth and see if they know anything.* He sat down. "Thanks. I'm Jake."

Tristan grasped Jake's hand, "Tristan. Nice to meet you."

Skylar then offered her soft, tan hand, "Skylar."

Tristan motioned to the bartender, "Sam, a pitcher of Pizza Port's Sharkbite Red."

The name of the beer made Jake's stomach flip. *Get a hold of yourself, man.*

"So what can we do for you?" Tristan asked, still smiling.

"Um, you know the shark attack the other night at Seaside?" Jake asked.

"Yeah, man, tragic. Someone died, right?" Tristan looked at Skylar and then Jake, as if asking for confirmation.

"Uh, yeah. His name was Cody. He was my best friend, actually. I was out surfing with him the day it happened."

The bartender delivered the pitcher of beer and three glasses.

Tristan poured and continued, "No way. Sorry, man. What happened? Was it really a shark, like they said on the news? Sky and I surf there but have never seen a shark. That's crazy."

"Yeah. The doctor said he died of bites from a great white," Jake replied.

Tristan could see the pain radiating from Jake's eyes as he thought of Cody. Tristan, knowing that pain all too well, shifted in his seat.

"I didn't actually see a shark though. After I left Cody, I saw him talking to another surfer. The guy had shaggy blond hair and a black board with a big shark on it with bloody teeth." Jake paused, looking at Tristan and then Skylar to see if they showed any recognition. Their faces were blank.

"He was the last one to see Cody alive so I wanted to ask him if he saw anything, but no one's been able to find him. Search and rescue crews spent all night looking for him but found no sign of him or his board. They think the shark might have gotten him, too," Jake explained.

"Wow. Like I said, man, I'm sorry about your friend. So, what does this have to do with us?" Tristan scrunched his eyebrows together and tilted his head, as if trying to understand.

Jake didn't want to rat out the bartender so he decided to tell a small lie. "I was at the beach earlier asking around if anyone knew this guy, and … You know the Del Norte Reefers?"

"Yeah, those guys are losers," Tristan said.

"Well one of those guys said he thought he saw the blond guy with you and your friends a couple times out on the water."

Skylar took a drink of red ale, waiting to see how Tristan handled this.

"The Del Norte Reefers?" Tristan wrinkled his nose, like he smelled something foul. He folded his arms. "Are you friends with those guys?"

"No, I can't stand those guys. But I was asking around and that's what they told me," Jake said.

"Sky and I and some other friends have been surfing there on and off for a few weeks. You say it was a black board with a big shark on it?"

"Yeah, with bloody teeth."

"Bloody teeth …" Tristan unfolded one arm and raised his fist to his mouth. He lightly tapped his closed hand against his lips a couple times. "Yeah … I know that guy. Blond hair? About your height? Yeah, he was solo so asked if he could hang out with us a couple times after sunset." He stopped and peered at Jake. "Surfing alone at night is dangerous, you know?"

Why's he looking at me like that? Jake wondered. *If I didn't know better, I'd say he knows I went out surfing by myself last night. But how could he? And why would he even care?*

Tristan continued, "I can't say I knew the guy real well. I think his name was Rick."

"Yeah, Rick," Skylar chimed in.

"What did you think about him, Skylar?" Jake asked.

"He seemed fine. I mean, I wouldn't go out with him or anything, but he seemed fine to surf with." Seeing Tristan smirk, Skylar kicked him under the table.

"Yeah, he seemed okay. Not like the Reefers. Why?" Tristan asked.

"I dunno. I just got a weird vibe off him. He was the last one to talk to Cody and he's been missing since Cody died. Maybe the shark got him too, but you think his board would've washed up or something." Jake tried to fit the puzzle together but kept coming up several pieces short.

"Huh, that's weird. I wish I could help. Hey, how about some more beer?" Tristan offered.

Jake didn't really want to stay but thought maybe Tristan knew more than he was saying. "Yeah, sure."

Tristan lifted the pitcher and topped off Jake's glass.

Skylar raised an eyebrow and shot Tristan a look that said, "You really want to talk to this guy some more?"

As Tristan leaned over to fill Skylar's glass, he whispered in her ear, "Friends close, enemies closer."

Skylar smiled.

21 – An Invitation

When Tristan pulled away from Skylar's ear, Lani happened to look over and catch his eye. He held her gaze just long enough to make her blush again.

I know her, but from where? Tristan wondered, slightly raising the corners of his mouth into a smile.

Lani smiled and turned away. She looked down into her glass, widening her eyes in amazement at his beauty. She then crinkled her eyes in disgust at her ability to forget she was working on an investigation when she gazed into Tristan's dark, magnetic eyes.

Skylar also noticed Tristan's gaze and the slight smile. *Great*, she thought, *another blond*.

As Tristan took a drink, he wondered if he should be concerned about Jake. *I don't think he could identify Rick in a line-up, but he definitely knows Rick's board. That could be dangerous. I never should've taken Rick's board home. I thought it would be better to hide any evidence of him but I should've let it wash up on shore. Lesson learned for next time.*

Tristan steered the conversation to surfing. "The surf's firing north of here. We're heading out tomorrow about 7 p.m. You wanna join us?"

Jake hesitated. "I can't tomorrow. It's Cody's memorial."

"I'm sorry," Tristan said. "How about the next night? It might do you some good."

"C'mon, it'll help take your mind off things," Skylar said. "I'd really like you to come."

Staring into Skylar's soft brown eyes, Jake felt his resistance melt away. "Yeah, okay."

"Great. We should go but we'll see you the night after tomorrow." Tristan rose from his chair. "Gimme your number. I'll tell you where to meet us. We know some secret spots."

Jake programmed his number into Tristan's phone. "Okay. See ya."

Skylar brushed her hand across Jake's shoulders, sending an electric pulse down his spine. "Bye, Jake."

As Tristan strode toward the door, his eyes wandered back to the blond at the bar. *I know her. And it's not just because she kind of looks like Julianna.*

22 – Julianna

That dark, moonless night in 1972 when Tristan emerged from the Pacific Ocean was one of the best nights of his life.

Still exhilarated from his undersea adventures as a shark, Tristan climbed from the ocean and set out in the darkness to reach his home or find some clothing, whichever came first. He clung to the shadows to avoid arrest for indecent exposure. He hid in doorways, ducked around corners and crouched behind dumpsters as he crept through the city toward his apartment.

Four blocks away from his apartment, Tristan ran into a woman exiting her front door.

"I'm so sorry!" He jumped to the side and pressed his body up against the building, covering his backside with his hand. "I mean you no harm. I lost my clothes and …"

"I gathered that," she laughed. "I could see you down the block from my apartment. It was pretty amusing watching you scurry down the street."

"I'm glad you find me so entertaining," Tristan chuckled. He glanced at the woman, who clearly was not afraid of a strange naked man at her doorway. She had long blond hair, straight and parted in the middle. She had a petite frame but appeared to be physically strong, like an athlete. *She's pretty,* he thought.

She extended her arm to him, "Here, put these on."

He took the clothing from her hand. "You're very kind. Thank you. Um, would you mind?" He drew a circle in the air with his index finger.

"Oh, you want me to turn around?" She turned her back to him while he hurriedly put on the sweatpants and t-shirt. "Modesty is a nice quality in a man. These days, most guys like to let it all hang out," she giggled.

"All done. You can turn around. I'm Tristan."

She turned and reached toward his outstretched hand. "Julianna. So tell me, Tristan, how does a man end up naked, wandering the streets of San Francisco?"

"It's a loooong story."

23 – The Conversation

Jake sat for a moment, dazed by Skylar's touch. He grabbed his pint glass and returned to the bar. Someone had taken the seat he was in before, so he sat one barstool to the left of it.

After a minute, Lani turned to him, "Are you okay?"

"What? Yeah, I'm okay," Jake answered, doing his best to sound cool. "Are you okay?"

"Yeah, I'm okay," Lani replied. "Sorry, I thought you looked a little dazed or something."

"Nah, I'm fine. I'm Jake, by the way."

"I'm Leilani. Nice to meet you. That couple you were talking with … They look familiar. Do you know them?"

"Not really. I just met them tonight."

Lani wondered how much she could pry without arousing suspicion or hitting a raw nerve and causing him to completely shut down. She decided to dive in. "You look familiar, too, actually. Were you at the beach a couple days ago? The night that surfer got killed?"

"Yeah, I was there." A dark cloud swept over Jake's face. "It was my best friend that died."

"I'm so sorry." Lani instantly regretted bringing it up. It was too soon. His pain was too raw. She placed her hand on top of his hand on the bar. "I can't imagine how devastating that must be."

"Yeah, it was pretty bad." Jake tried to will away the tears that threatened to slip from his eyes. *Don't cry. Not now.*

"Listen, if you don't want to talk about it …"

"No. It's fine. That's actually why I'm here tonight. I wanted to ask Tristan, that guy I was talking with, if he knew anything about that night and what happened."

"Oh." Lani was eager to learn more but didn't want to press too hard, seeing how difficult it was for Jake to hold himself together. "Was he there that night, too?"

"No, but he knew the guy who was the last one to see Cody alive."

Jake explained what he recalled about his last day with Cody—and about the blond surfer who paddled out to talk to him. He then shared his conversation with Tristan and how he learned the guy's name was Rick.

Lani listened patiently, feeling bad for Jake and a little guilty about making him relive that day. She realized Jake knew even less than she did about the Nomads.

But then Jake added, "I'm going surfing with Tristan and Skylar the night after tomorrow."

Lani flashed a bright smile. "You are? Do you mind if I join you?"

Jake hesitated. It wasn't that he didn't want Leilani to come along. It was just highly unusual that not one but two beautiful women asked to surf with him on the same day.

"You surf?" he asked.

"I do. But I don't want to impose. I shouldn't have invited myself."

"No, it's not that. It's just that I don't know these guys very well so I wouldn't feel right bringing someone along. At least not yet. But how about the day after that? We could grab some dinner or something and then get a session in?" Jake offered.

Lani paused. *What am I getting myself into? But I could ask him about his night with the Nomads. He may be my way in.* "Yeah, that sounds great."

Jake gulped. *Did I just ask this woman on a date? Or are we just hanging out?* He gazed at Leilani's perfect white smile. *Whatever it is, she seems cool. But that Skylar ...*

24 – Dinner for Five

After Tristan and Skylar left the bar, they headed home.

Logan greeted them with their boards. "The Reefers are out causing trouble again at the beach. They sent four kids to the hospital—a board collision and a fistfight. Territorial trash. We should do something, right?"

Tristan reached for his board. "Yeah. This has gone on long enough. Let's finish what Rick started and screwed up. Where are Torrey and Cruz?"

"At the beach. Watching. They didn't want to make a move without you," Logan said.

"Good," Tristan said. "Let's go."

Tristan, Skylar and Logan jogged to the beach. They joined Torrey and Cruz who were monitoring the Del Norte Reefers.

Cruz raised his hand to greet Tristan. "Dude, I'm glad you're here. Can we move on these guys? I'm hungry."

Tristan looked around. Except for the Nomads and the five Reefers, the beach was deserted.

"Sky, you're with me. Let's head down the beach. I don't want them to see us. Torrey, Cruz, Logan, give us a few minutes to paddle into position just past the impact zone. Then attract their attention. Lure them out. Hope you've got empty stomachs because we're feasting tonight. Sky, let's go."

Tristan threw his arm around Skylar as they headed to the ocean. "Just like old times, eh?"

"Yeah, old times," Skylar smiled, unable to hide the wistfulness in her voice.

Before Cruz, Torrey and Logan joined the Nomads, it was just Tristan and Skylar. Skylar remembered the night Tristan turned her.

25 – The Proposal

"Do you want to surf forever?" Tristan had asked her. Although it was 10 years ago, to Skylar, it felt like last night.

The two of them had been sleeping together and surfing together for six months. For Skylar, it was love at first sight. For Tristan, it was lust at first sight. Skylar, overwhelmed by her feelings for him, believed he felt the same way she did. From their first kiss, she believed they were perfect together and it was simply a matter of time before he proposed.

So when Tristan invited her out for a picnic dinner and surf session one balmy July evening, Skylar could feel it in her bones. *Tonight's the night.*

Tristan spread a blanket on the sand. He opened a cooler. He reached inside and took out three plates. He placed one in front of Skylar, one in front of himself and one in between. He removed a candle from the cooler and set it on the center plate. He cupped his hands over the candle and lit it. A moment later the ocean breeze extinguished the flame.

"I tried, right?" he laughed. Skylar giggled.

Tristan served Skylar her favorite meal, bay shrimp salad. She liked to call it baby shrimp salad; she thought it sounded cuter. He spooned a pile of chopped romaine lettuce onto both plates. He sprinkled green onions and bay shrimp on the lettuce. He dropped some alfalfa sprouts on top and then drizzled everything with a lemon vinaigrette. For the finishing touch, he scattered toasted almond slivers on top.

"Voila!" Tristan opened his cloth napkin with a flourish. "Dinner is served. Oh, I almost forgot. Champagne?"

"Yes, please." Skylar clasped her hands together. *This is it. I wonder where he has the ring. In the cooler? In his pocket? Maybe he'll put it in the champagne flute!*

Tristan poured the champagne and raised his glass. "To Sky, my favorite surfing partner."

"Thank you, Tristan. This is perfect. Cheers!" She clinked her glass to Tristan's. *No ring inside. He must be waiting for the perfect moment.*

They drank and ate and talked. After dinner, Tristan cleared the plates and glasses and put everything back in the cooler, which he moved into the sand. He settled down on the blanket and motioned for Skylar to come sit in front of him. She sat between his legs and leaned back, resting her spine against his muscular chest. He wrapped his arms around her. They sat like that for a while, hypnotized by the tide's ebb and flow.

"Shall we surf?" Tristan asked.

"Sure." Skylar wondered why he hadn't asked yet. The moment was perfect—the two of them alone, watching the ocean, under billions of stars.

Tristan jumped up and ripped off his t-shirt. Skylar stood and lifted her white sundress over her head to reveal a new white bikini. She thought white would be appropriate for the occasion.

"Wow! Is that new? You look amazing, Sky."

"Thanks." *C'mon, Tristan. White, wedding gown, me.* She tried to will him to get on with it. *Propose, propose, propose!*

"Let's go." He clasped her hand and they ran to the water. They paddled out and climbed on top of their boards.

"Hmmm, it's kind of calm now." Tristan looked west. "We may need to wait for some decent waves."

"That's okay. This is nice."

"It is. Say, Sky, there's something I want to ask you."

"Yes?"

"Do you want to surf forever?"

26 – Taking Out the Trash

"Sky, you ready?" Tristan asked.

She snapped back to the present. "Yeah, let's do this."

From the ocean, they watched Logan, Torrey and Cruz on shore.

Gripping their boards under their arms, the three Nomads ran past the five Reefers, hooting and hollering, "Losers!" "Kooks!" "Zonies!"

"What the …? Let's get 'em!" the Reefer in the hot pink trunks commanded. The five Reefers leapt to their feet, grabbed their boards, and chased after the three surfers.

"Let's smoke these Reefers," Logan snarled, nearly bursting with excitement as he, Cruz and Torrey splashed into the ocean.

The Reefers followed, not far behind. When all five Reefers were in the ocean, duck diving under the breaking waves, the Nomads each leaned to the side and plunged into the water, leaving their boards to float on the ocean's surface. They wiggled out of their swimsuits and tied them to their leashes.

After the Reefers passed under the last line of breaking waves, they popped out of the water and looked around. "Where'd they go?" one asked. As they glanced around, shark fins appeared. "Are you guys seeing what I'm seeing?" another asked.

The Reefers couldn't believe their eyes. Five great white sharks surrounded them. Then, one by one, the Reefers started to scream. "Aaaaah!" "Something's got me!" "It's biting me!"

Each Nomad plunged his or her teeth into the calf of a Reefer and dragged him underwater. Five sharks circled, each with a Reefer in its mouth.

Logan tossed his Reefer into the air, caught the flailing body in his jaws and swung his head back and forth. His serrated teeth sawed through the Reefer's flesh, all the way to the bone.

He opened his jaw and clamped down again before diving underwater with his prey.

After a minute or two, the Reefers' thrashing and screaming stopped. The feeding continued a while longer. One after the other, the Nomads' heads emerged from the water.

"That was easy!" Tristan exclaimed, clearly pleased with the way the evening had gone. "How was dinner, guys?"

"Best ever!" Logan grinned from ear to ear.

"Fine, but mine was kinda salty," Torrey joked.

"Yeah, mine too," laughed Cruz as he leaned over to give his wife, Torrey, a kiss.

Skylar didn't answer.

"Sky? Earth to Sky … How was dinner?" Tristan waved his hand in front of her. He noticed she showed none of the excitement the others enjoyed from a righteous kill.

"Mine was pretty drunk," she mumbled. "I'm going in."

"That's a good idea," Tristan said. "Let's all head in and get rid of the Reefers' mess. I don't want to leave any evidence of them behind."

The Nomads surfed to shore. They cleaned up the trash, beer bottles and cigarette butts the Reefers had strewn around their bonfire.

"Can we keep their boards?" Logan asked.

"Not this time," Tristan replied. "There's still too much attention on the death of that Cody guy and Rick's disappearance. Let's take them to the landfill and bury them."

Skylar picked up her board. "Count me out. I'm going home."

"Why? Are you okay?" Tristan asked.

She ignored him and kept walking.

Tristan puzzled over why Skylar seemed so distant but came up empty. For someone as old and wise as he was, he sometimes had no clue, particularly when it came to Skylar.

27 – A Misunderstanding

Skylar plodded home and flopped onto her bed. *Why doesn't Tristan love me? Did he ever love me? Will he ever love me?*

Her mind wandered back to that night at the beach 10 years ago. "Do you want to surf forever?" he had asked.

Skylar, of course, thought that was Tristan's way of proposing. She was wrong. Dead wrong.

Tristan was actually asking the question in a very literal sense, although the word "forever" was an exaggeration. What he really meant was, "Do you want to surf for centuries?"

The thought of marrying Skylar had never crossed Tristan's mind. He liked Skylar and enjoyed being with her, both in and out of bed. He loved surfing with her because she was fun and fearless on the water. But he never loved her. He hadn't loved anyone since Julianna and doubted he'd ever love anyone again. Which was fine with him because it was much easier that way.

Skylar, however, thought he did love her, which is why what happened next was so shocking.

"Yes, Tristan! I will surf with you forever," she answered in reply to his question, as they floated side by side on their boards.

"You're sure this is what you want?" he asked. "You are 100 percent certain?"

"100 percent." Skylar saw Tristan open his arms and thought he was leaning in to kiss her. But instead, his lips brushed down to her neck. The pain was immediate and nearly unbearable as he plunged his fangs into the soft flesh on the side of her neck, a couple inches below her earlobe.

"Tristan, stop." She tried to push him away. "Tristan!"

He continued to drink her blood. The third time she yelled his name, he finally heard.

"Tristan! What the hell are you doing?!"

Tristan pulled his head back. His lips were crimson with her blood. "What do you mean? I asked you and you said yes."

"What?!"

"I asked if you wanted to surf forever and you said yes."

"I said yes, I'll marry you. I didn't say yes to … to … to whatever this is!"

"Marry me? I never asked you to …" Tristan slowly realized his mistake. He thought he and Skylar were on the same page, having fun together but nothing serious. He'd never said he loved her. "Skylar, I'm sorry. I never … I didn't … I never …"

"Shut up, Tristan! Just shut up! What did you do to me?" She clutched her neck to stop the pain and steady flow of blood.

"What do you mean? I'm a sea vampire—a vampire shark. I asked if you wanted to be one, too. I thought you said yes, so I bit you to turn you." Tristan thought it was all very obvious.

"A what? What do you mean you're a sea vampire? A vampire? Really? That's ridiculous!"

"C'mon, Sky," he tilted his head and peered into her eyes. "You knew."

"Knew what? That you're a vampire? You've got to be kidding. A vampire? That's not even real," she said, desperately clinging to the notion that vampires were only a myth.

"Oh my god." Tristan ran his hands up his face and over the top of his head. "I have made a huge mistake. I'm sorry. I thought you knew. I mean, c'mon. I rarely go out in the sun. I sleep all day. I surf only at night. I don't eat every day. When I do, I like it raw and bloody. I told you I was born in 1905 and that I could live to be 1,000 years old …"

"I thought you were joking!" Skylar interrupted. "Like you were saying you were an old soul or something. I didn't think you were literally born in 1905!" In her head, she ran through all the time she'd known Tristan. *It's true,* she realized. *We never go out during the day. We only surf after sunset and before sunrise. He likes his food raw. But a vampire? How could I possibly have known that?*

"A vampire?" she asked, sarcasm filling every syllable. "Really?"

"Yes, really. I've mentioned to you at least 10 times that I'm a vampire."

"Tristan, I thought it was a metaphor. You know, like you're a night owl. Or you feed off of other people's energy. Or you like your food bloody. I didn't think you were an actual vampire."

Skylar continued to shake her head in disbelief as Tristan told her how he became a vampire on the streets of San Francisco and then became something more—a vampire with the ability to morph into a great white shark in the ocean. A vampire shark.

"And now you're one, too. A vampire shark."

"No." Skylar shook her head. "Tristan, no."

But Skylar couldn't deny what she was feeling. With each second that passed, she felt herself becoming more connected to the ocean. Where her legs dangled in the water she couldn't tell where her skin ended and the ocean began. Her cells felt like they were dancing and swirling in the water. Her tear-filled eyes looked up into Tristan's eyes. "What did you do to me?"

"Skylar, I'm so sorry."

From that moment on, Skylar had a power over Tristan no other Nomad had. It was the same power that humans—mothers and religious leaders, in particular—had used to control other humans for millennia: Guilt.

While Tristan could never completely give Skylar the one thing she wanted most—himself—he could not deny her anything else. Even if that sometimes meant trouble for the Nomads.

28 – The Paddle Out

The evening after Jake's excursion to the bar, a memorial service for Cody was held at Seaside Reef. Earlier that afternoon, Jake had considered going surfing to calm his nerves. He pulled on his trunks and lathered up with sunscreen, but then decided he couldn't do it. He could not surf during the day without Cody.

Shortly before sunset, Jake threw his board in his pickup and headed to Seaside. When he pulled into the parking lot, he was shocked to see at least 100 surfboards sticking out of the sand like tombstones. He knew everyone liked Cody but this was more than he expected. He was also surprised so many people were willing to venture into the ocean so soon after a shark attack.

Jake found an empty parking spot and wiped his hand across his eyes to stave off the tears beginning to form. He grabbed his board and headed toward the crowd on the beach. He walked across the river of stones that separated the parking lot from the sand. The setting sun glinted off more stones that were scattered across the black-streaked sand all the way to the water.

Jake saw a space had been left for him next to Carlos, the minister who would lead the ceremony. Carlos was a surf buddy he and Cody knew from Del Mar. They sometimes ran into him when they surfed around 15th Street.

Jake looked at the long line of surfers standing in front of their boards like an honor guard for one of their fallen soldiers. He felt the tears well up again. He shoved his board in the sand behind him and nodded to Carlos.

Carlos nodded back and began, "Thank you for coming today to honor the life of Cody Hansen. Cody's favorite place was in the ocean and that's where we'll celebrate his life today."

Two teenage volunteers from Carlos's church handed flowers and leis to the surfers as they paraded into the gently rolling waves. They paddled out past the breaking waves and formed a large circle as the sun set behind them. One by one, they tossed their flowers into the center of the circle.

It's so peaceful here now, Jake noticed. *Nothing like three days ago. Man, Cody and I had so many good times out here on this stretch of coastline. North, south, we surfed it all.*

Carlos touched Jake's arm. The two of them started splashing water toward the sky and everyone joined in. "Cody! Cody!" they chanted.

In the middle of the flowers and the splashing, a dolphin appeared. It lifted its head above the water and looked around. "Hey, Cody's here!" one person shouted, laughing. Jake smiled, wishing it were true.

The dolphin dropped out of sight for a moment and then leapt out of the water, arcing its body before it disappeared underwater again with a swish of its tail. The circle burst into applause.

Carlos clasped Jake's hand and raised it toward the heavens. "To Cody!"

Everyone joined hands and raised them, "To Cody!"

As the pink hues in the evening sky darkened, the circle broke and people surfed to shore.

Back on the beach, several surfers came up to shake Jake's hand or give him a comforting pat on the back. "Sorry about Cody, man. He was a great guy." "Everyone loved him." "There'll never be another like him." "We were so lucky to have known him." "Call me if you need anything."

Jake felt himself dangerously close to completely losing it. *I have to get out of here.*

Carlos saw the pained look on Jake's face and offered to walk him to his truck. As they walked, he threw his arm over

Jake's shoulder. "Jake, I know how much Cody meant to you. I know that today, and probably for a long time, there will be grief and sorrow and tears. But it won't always be like that."

Jake narrowed his eyes in disbelief.

Seeing his doubt and anguish, Carlos continued. "You know, the reason the loss is so great is because Cody was so great. The magnitude of what you're feeling is directly proportional to how important Cody was to you, to how big a part of your life he was. When Cody died, he took a part of your soul with him. That leaves a hole behind. You can't see it but you can feel it, right?"

Jake nodded as tears began to stream down his face.

"To have a friend like that, one who is so important that he becomes a part of you, is a rare and precious gift," Carlos said. "I know it sounds messed up but you're really lucky you found that. Even though Cody wasn't here with us very long, he made such an impact. Look at everyone who was here today. They didn't care there was a shark here a few days ago. They were here for Cody. And for you. You know, the crazy thing about life is that it's often in our darkest, most painful moments that we see how rich and beautiful life really is. It's the bitter parts that make us appreciate the sweet parts. It's the full spectrum— pleasure, pain, lightness, darkness. It's all right here." Carlos lightly tapped his chest, over his heart. "Listen, I'm rambling way too much. Sorry. Sometimes the minister in me takes over. You want me to drive you home?"

"Nah, I'll be fine." Jake wiped his eyes.

"You sure, man?"

Jake nodded.

"Well then drive safe, okay? Let me know if you need anything," Carlos said.

"Thanks, Carlos. And thanks for doing all this today—the ceremony, the flowers …"

"De nada. Stay strong, Jake."

Jake placed his board in his pickup and drove home, up the coast highway. He had to keep wiping the tears that blurred his vision and turned the headlights of oncoming cars into bright white starbursts.

He thought about the paddle out and how everyone had come to pay their respects to Cody. *All these people connected by sharing a love of the ocean. This was Cody's tribe.*

Jake smiled as he remembered how Cody used to extol the virtues of the surf community any time someone would say something disparaging about surfers. *"Pick up any newspaper in any coastal town,"* Cody would argue. *"You'll find heroic stories every day. Every day, man. A teen who's swept off the rocks into the ocean—saved by a surfer. A swimmer bitten by a shark—rescued by surfers. A mom and kid dragged out to sea in a riptide—pulled to shore by surfers. Every time surfers try to save someone, they put their own lives in jeopardy. And you know what? They don't think twice about it. They do it. That's who they are."*

That was Cody. Champion of champions, Jake reflected. *And although there are occasional bad seeds, like the Del Norte Reefers, those guys are definitely the exception, not the rule. The rule is what I saw here today. A community, a family.*

Jake pulled into his parking spot. He walked into his apartment and closed the front door. He pressed his back against the door, slid to the floor and broke down into uncontrollable sobs. He passed out there, from sheer exhaustion, a few hours before dawn.

29 – Night Surfing

The following evening, Jake awoke. He ignored the messages on his voicemail and set off to meet the Nomads. He felt drained. He literally could not cry anymore. There was nothing left. He was an empty vessel, waiting to be filled again. With something. Anything.

Once again, he passed the shark warning signs.

"Jake!" Tristan opened his arms wide to welcome Jake to the group. He placed his hand on Jake's shoulder and began the introductions. "This is Logan, Cruz and Torrey."

Apparently, they don't care about the shark signs either, Jake thought as he appraised the three surfers.

At 19, Logan still carried the lanky 5-foot-11-inch frame of a teenager as well as the desire to be the class clown. His tan, boyish face was usually adorned with an infectious smile that could brighten even the darkest room. His sandy blond hair alternated between being closely cropped or longish. When he grew tired of sweeping his straw-colored bangs from his green eyes, he'd head back to the barber and have it all shaved off again.

Cruz was 24. He had narrow, dark brown eyes that were usually focused on his wife, Torrey, and smooth olive skin that tanned quickly and deeply. He stood at 5-foot-10 but his spiky black hair added another inch or two to his height. His strong, muscular build revealed his devotion to surfing and to weight training.

Torrey was 25 and 5 feet 6 inches tall. She had an athletic build and moved with an effortless grace both on and off the water. Her most striking features were her bright blue-green eyes and broad smile that made everyone around her feel instantly at ease. Her straight reddish-brown hair, which draped several inches past her shoulders, contrasted strikingly with her radiant skin and rosy cheeks.

Tristan continued, "And, of course, you know Skylar."

"Yeah, hi again." Jake looked into Skylar's mocha-brown eyes and then sheepishly down at his feet.

"These waves are freakin' amazing! Let's go!" Tristan said.

The Nomads and Jake ran to the water, which felt warm and inviting compared to the cool evening air.

Tristan caught the first wave. One after one, perfect waves kept rolling in. *Another epic night*, Jake noted.

After a few hours, everyone swam in and sprawled on the beach. Tristan opened the cooler and passed out drinks.

"That was awesome!" Logan exclaimed.

"Totally awesome," echoed Torrey as she wrapped her arms around Cruz and kissed his cheek. "Just like you, babe."

Skylar rolled her eyes.

"Did you have fun, Jake?" Tristan handed him a beer.

"Yeah, man. It was a barrel fest out there. I felt pretty crappy earlier but I feel better now. You guys can really shred. How long have you been surfing?"

Tristan flashed an enigmatic smile. "Forever."

"Hey, I hear you call yourselves the Nomads," Jake said. "That's pretty cool. Does that mean you, like, travel around the world surfing?"

"The Nomads. Where'd you hear that?" Tristan asked.

"I dunno. Around," Jake said.

"We're not like a club, you know. But we do move where the surf moves." Tristan was curious about what else Jake had heard.

"That's cool. How do you manage jobs and stuff, moving around like that?" Jake asked.

"How do you?" Tristan swiveled his head back to Jake. "I mean, I'm assuming you don't have a job you need to get to first thing in the morning."

"Yeah, you're right. I'm a freelance web designer. I handle all my clients with email and phone calls, so I can set my own hours. As long as I meet their deadlines and give them frequent updates, they don't care where I am or when I work," Jake explained.

"It's the same with us," Tristan said. "Technology makes work so much easier, right? No office, no commute, no neckties, no boss breathing down your neck."

"Totally. So … what exactly do you do?" Jake asked.

"Day trader," Tristan responded.

"You're able to make a living at that? That's impressive," Jake said. "How do you know what to pick and when to buy and sell? Seems like a lot of people lose money at that."

"Yeah, Wall Street is full of vampires looking to suck people dry," Tristan said with a sardonic smile. "But it's actually pretty easy when you think about it. I analyze the past to determine the trends of the future, and invest accordingly. I've made lots of money off of lots of companies over the years. I could tell you who I'm looking at now, but then I'd have to kill you."

"Ha, yeah." Jake was pretty sure Tristan was joking, but felt a chill when he saw Tristan's dark eyes boring into him.

Aware of the change in Jake's energy and quickening of his pulse, Tristan changed the subject. "Hey, that blond in the bar the night before last? You know her?"

"Not really. I just met her that night. But I'll be seeing her tomorrow night." Jake looked to see if Skylar reacted. She didn't. She seemed to be off in her own world.

"You mean tonight," Tristan corrected.

Jake glanced at his watch. *1 a.m.* "Yeah, tonight. We're having dinner, as friends," he added in case Skylar was listening.

"What's her name?" Tristan asked.

"Leilani. I didn't get her last name."

"Hmmm. I know her from somewhere." Tristan struggled to remember. "We're surfing here again tonight. Why don't you and Leilani join us?"

"I dunno." Jake stole a glance at Skylar.

"Dude, the surf is gonna be rockin'! Even better than it just was. You gotta come," Tristan said.

"Okay. But only if things go well," Jake replied, unsure of himself.

"Of course they'll go well," Tristan assured him. "You're Jake. You're one of us."

30 – Dinner and a Set

Eighteen hours later Jake arrived at Leilani's house. He thought he should wear something different than his usual attire, shorts and a t-shirt, but didn't want to look like he was trying too hard. So, he decided on a blue button-down short-sleeved shirt, open at the collar, and tan Dockers. *I should've worn jeans. I feel overdressed,* he lamented. *Oh well, too late now.*

He knocked at Leilani's door. She answered wearing a lavender dress with a navy blue floral print. "Hi. You look nice!" she said.

"Thanks. You do, too. I came here straight from work, a client meeting," he lied. "You ready?"

"Yeah. Let's go."

Their conversation flowed easily in the car. It felt like Jake had known Leilani for years. They pulled into the parking lot of The Poseidon. Jake parked and ran around to Leilani's side to open the door for her.

"Thanks," she said. "Not many guys do that anymore."

"I'm not 'many guys.' I'm Jake," he said, thinking back to his conversation with Tristan. "*You're one of us,*" Tristan had said. For some reason, that had given Jake confidence, which he now felt again.

The hostess led them through the bustling restaurant to a table outdoors, facing the ocean. They took their seats and perused the menu. "What looks good?" Jake asked.

Lani scanned the menu. *Fish, mollusks, crustaceans, fowl, beef. There has to be something vegetarian. Ah, there it is.* "I think I'll get the Thai stir fry with tofu. You?"

"Tofu? Are you a vegetarian?"

"Guilty," she smiled.

"Leilani, you should have told me. I wouldn't have taken

you to a seafood restaurant."

"Really, it's not a problem. This is California. No matter what restaurant I'm in, I can usually find something on the menu without a face," she laughed. "So what are you getting?"

Jake flashed a devilish grin, "Definitely something with a face. The pistachio-crusted salmon sounds good. I think I'll get that." He set down his menu, gazed into Leilani's blue eyes, and found himself at a loss for words. "So, uh … what do you do … for work?"

"I'm an interior designer."

"Oh, what are you working on now?"

Before meeting Jake three nights ago, Lani had prepared her cover story. She picked up all the design, architecture and home magazines she could find. She remembered an interview with a designer in a *San Diego Magazine* article. She relayed the story to him like it was her own, changing a few details here and there.

"So is it weird going into all these strangers' homes and trying to figure out, like, what will be perfect for them to live in day after day?" he asked.

"No, it's fun actually. You can tell a lot about people from what they have inside their homes. It's pretty fascinating," she replied.

"I'm afraid to let you see mine."

"Why? What does it say?" she asked.

He shook his head and laughed.

Lani clasped her hands together below her chin. "Okay, let me guess. It says bachelor, who knows this place is only temporary so … you haven't put a lot of thought into matching any of the furniture you've bought off of Craigslist. There's a single bathroom that rarely gets cleaned, unless a woman is coming over, of course. There are no dirty dishes in the sink because you rarely cook anything at home, but maybe a dirty glass or two. And you're probably one of those guys with a six-pack of beer and a bottle of hot sauce in the fridge, right?"

"Now there's where you're wrong," Jake interrupted, pointing his index finger at her. "It's only two bottles of beer."

They continued to chat easily through dinner. They each talked more about their work and hobbies.

Lani noticed Jake occasionally staring off in the distance. His eyes seemed to darken when he did so. *He's probably thinking about Cody. The paddle out was only two days ago,* she reminded herself.

The topic of conversation then turned to surfing. Jake felt better when he thought about the ocean. He wondered if he should invite Leilani to surf with the Nomads. He still wasn't sure about them. He glanced at the waves breaking outside the restaurant. He couldn't resist going out again. The waves were just too tasty.

"Hey, I'm having a really great time tonight. Some friends invited me, well us actually, to go surfing with them. What do you think?" Jake looked at her expectantly.

This guy is so nice he probably doesn't even realize how cute he is right now, Lani mused. "Friends? Who?"

"Tristan and those guys. I went out with them last night. We had a really good time and the surf was going off! It's even better tonight. But if you don't want to go …"

"Tonight? That would be fun. We should totally go." Lani motioned to her right. "I mean, *look* at those waves. They're perfect. So you wanna swing by my house? I can get my suit and board. What about you? You have everything you need?"

"Yep, suit's in my truck and I rarely go anywhere without my board, so I'm all set."

Jake waved his hand at the waitress to ask for the check. Five minutes later they headed out the door.

On the drive back to her house, Lani said, "So Jake, the

other night you mentioned your friend, Cody, and that you thought Tristan might know something. Were you able to find out anything about what happened?"

"No. I didn't really get into it. We were having a good time and I didn't want to launch into this whole interrogation. I thought maybe I'd get to know them a little better before I ask any more questions about that Rick guy. I probably sound crazy but I feel like I owe it to Cody to at least find out what happened to him after I left. I need to know what happened in the last moments of his life, you know?"

"I totally understand. And I think you're right. If they do know anything more about Rick, you'll probably learn more if they know you better," Lani agreed.

"Yeah. Hey, don't say anything to them, okay? I don't want it to seem like the only reason I'm hanging out with them is to get information. They do seem pretty cool," Jake said.

"Your secret is safe with me. And let me know if I can do anything to help. I know if something like that happened to someone I cared about, I wouldn't be able to rest until I knew what happened. So let me know, okay?"

"Okay. Thanks."

Fifteen minutes later they were at the beach. Jake noticed the shark signs were gone.

The Nomads arrived a few minutes after that.

Jake introduced Leilani. "Leilani, this is Tristan."

When Tristan shook Leilani's hand, Jake thought his hand lingered a little too long. Skylar thought the same thing.

"And this is Skylar, Logan, Cruz and Torrey," Jake continued.

"Wow, you all have such great names. Sounds like a soap opera or something," Lani said.

"Says the woman named *Leilani*," Tristan joked, melodically drawling her name.

"Very funny, *Tristan*," Lani teased.

"Logan and I actually go by our last names," Cruz explained. "We're both named Josh. It gets confusing. You know, you go through school, there's always at least one other Josh in your class. By the time you get to college there are so many, it's just easier to go by your last name."

Changing your name in college. How original, Lani laughed to herself. "Got it."

"And my beautiful wife, Torrey, could only have a name equally as beautiful." Cruz kissed Torrey's cheek.

"Oh please!" Skylar hated displays of affection that did not involve her personally.

The crash of a huge wave directed their attention to the ocean.

"Shall we?" Tristan looked at Leilani and then the rest of the group.

Lani hesitated. "So that shark's gone, right?"

"Absolutely," Tristan assured her. "You know sharks have to keep moving to live, right? There's no way he's going to hang around in one place, especially when he knows he's not wanted."

"You seem awfully sure," Lani said.

"We were here last night. It's fine. The city even took down the shark warning signs." Tristan pointed, "See? No signs."

Lani turned to Jake for reassurance.

"It's fine," Jake said.

"All right. Let's hit it!" Tristan said.

"You guys go ahead. I want to wax my board." Skylar sat in the sand and tore the wrapper off a bar of surf wax. She threw the wrapper into her beach bag and began massaging the wax onto the surface of her board.

"Are you coming out later?" Jake asked.

"Yeah, I'll be out soon," Skylar replied.

Logan, Torrey and Cruz paddled in one direction. Tristan, Jake and Leilani paddled in another.

Jake sat on one side of Leilani, Tristan on the other. Seeing a massive wave rolling toward them, Tristan said, "Ladies first," and motioned to Leilani.

Lani began paddling. *You can do this,* she told herself. *You used to do this every day and in much bigger waves. So what if it's been more than 10 years. It's like riding a bike, right?*

On her belly, Lani felt the wave gather momentum beneath her board. Her muscle memory kicked in and she sprang to her feet. Poised perfectly, she slid down the wave's face, feeling the rush of the drop. As the wave curled over her, she hunched down and glided into the tube. After what seemed like an eternity, she bulleted out of the barrel and gracefully ended the ride.

Jake and Tristan watched, mesmerized.

"Did you know she was this good?" Tristan asked.

"No!" Jake said, awestruck.

They took turns riding alone and together. No one noticed Skylar hadn't come out.

Skylar watched from shore, disturbed by the blond absorbing Tristan's attention. She dropped her bikini in the sand and swam toward them. She dove underwater so Jake and Leilani wouldn't see her dorsal fin and panic. She swam back and forth a few feet below the water's surface, waiting. As soon as she saw Leilani's board, she rocketed upward, launching it into the air.

Skylar quickly turned and sped to shore as Leilani splashed down into the water and grazed the sand on the ocean floor.

While Jake and Tristan rushed to Leilani, Skylar slipped on her bikini top and bottoms.

Tristan reached Leilani first. He lifted her onto his surfboard and swam her to shore. Jake trailed behind, pulling her board.

Before she knew it, Lani found herself lying in the wet sand, looking up into Tristan's espresso-brown eyes.

He cradled the back of her head in his hands. "Leilani? Are you okay?"

"Yeah. How did we get here so fast?" Lani asked.

"I brought you in on my board."

"What happened?"

"I don't know. I was just about to ask you the same thing," Tristan smiled gently.

"One second I was up and the next I was on the ocean floor getting a sand facial. And now I'm here," she said.

Jake emerged on shore, dropped the boards and rushed to Leilani. He got there the same time as Skylar, who had run down from the blankets they set up when they arrived.

"What happened out there?" Jake asked.

"I dunno." Lani slowly sat up. "I was on my board and it was weird. It felt almost like I hit a speed bump."

Tristan shot a fierce look at Skylar. She was the only Nomad unaccounted for when Leilani fell. Skylar widened her eyes and shrugged her shoulders, feigning innocence.

"Weird," Tristan said. "Are you sure you're okay?"

"Yeah, I'm fine. I think I just got the wind knocked out of me," Lani answered. "I'm a little embarrassed actually."

"You have nothing to be embarrassed about. It happens to all of us, pro surfer or not," Tristan smiled.

Lani wondered if he knew about her past on the pro circuit.

"Hey, maybe you should rest awhile," Jake suggested. "I'll stay with you." Even though he was into Skylar, he wasn't sure if he liked the way Tristan and Leilani were looking at each other.

"No, let's go back out." Lani jumped up. "I'm fine. Really."

"Fearless. I like that in a woman," Tristan said, smiling, as they all ran back to the sea.

31 – Boards

The next day, Jake and Lani arrived after dark for a barbecue at Tristan's. Feeling magnanimous after another epic night of surfing, Tristan had invited everyone over. More important, he wanted to see Leilani again to ignite the spark he knew she was feeling, too.

Tristan greeted them at the front door before they knocked. "Welcome! Everyone's out back. Follow me."

He guided Leilani and Jake past the living room and kitchen to the backyard. "You know Torrey and Cruz. Skylar's out for the night. Logan might stop by later. Appetizers are on the table. The ice chest is here on the patio. Help yourselves."

Jake pulled an assortment of local beers from a soft-sided, insulated cooler bag. "Can I get anyone a beer before I put 'em on ice?"

Tristan eyed the collection. "I think that Arrogant Bastard from Stone has my name on it. Leilani, what's your pleasure?"

"I'll take a Mermaid's Red from Coronado Brewing," she replied.

"Cruz? Torrey? What about you?" Jake asked.

"I feel like something dark," Cruz said. "How about the Ballast Point Black Marlin Porter, por favor?"

Torrey peeked over Cruz's shoulder. "The Karl Strauss Tower 10 IPA. Thanks, Jake."

Jake popped off the caps and passed them their beers. He then opened a bottle of West Coast IPA from Green Flash for himself.

After a few minutes, Lani excused herself to use the bathroom. She walked through the house, surveying each room. She saw an empty bathroom downstairs, but softly closed the door and headed upstairs. She poked her head into each bedroom. She spotted nothing unusual until she came upon a locked door. She pulled a pin from her purse and jimmied the lock.

Lani stepped inside and saw rows and rows of surfboards from different eras—longboards, shortboards, funboards—and they'd all been used. *This guy really loves surfboards,* she thought. *Wow, these are so cool! If I had all these, I'd have them displayed in every room of the house. Wait, now I really do sound like an interior designer. But these are so cool. Why would he have them all locked away in here, out of sight?*

As she flipped through the boards, she got her answer. Black board, shark, bloody teeth, the name "Rick" emblazoned on it. *This is the board Jake saw the night Cody was killed. Why would it be here, in a locked room, unless Tristan had something to do with Rick's disappearance?*

Lani heard the screen door slam downstairs. She carefully tilted the boards back against the wall, the way she'd found them. She closed the bedroom door, tiptoed across the hall to the bathroom, and shut the door. She quickly flushed the toilet and splashed water over her hands.

She opened the door and ran into Tristan. "Hey," she said calmly.

"Hey, yourself. What are you doing up here?" he asked, curious but not quite sure if he should feel concerned.

"Just using the bathroom."

"There's one downstairs, you know." He led her down the hall and downstairs.

"I'm sorry. I didn't see one."

"Right there," he pointed. "Oh, but the door's closed. Sorry, that's usually open." He twisted the knob and opened it.

"No problem. I'll remember for next time," Lani said.

32 – Sustainable Seafood

As Leilani set out to find a bathroom, Jake chatted with Torrey. "So where's Skylar tonight?" he asked.

"I dunno," Torrey replied. "She said she had something to do."

"Or someone!" Cruz yelled from the barbecue. Torrey shot him a withering look.

Jake's stomach dropped. "Does Skylar have a boyfriend?"

"No," Cruz said. "It's better that way. Believe me."

"Cruz, shut up! Sorry about him," Torrey apologized to Jake.

"What about Tristan? Was he ever her boyfriend?" Jake asked.

"Tristan isn't the boyfriend type, you know?" Torrey explained.

"Did I hear my name?" Tristan asked as he returned from the kitchen.

"Hey, Tristan. We were just talking about you," Torrey said. "I'm gonna go get the guacamole from the fridge."

"Jake, my man. What's up?" Tristan asked.

"Nothing. I was just asking about Skylar."

"Oh. She's not here. Would you like her to be here?" Tristan teased.

Jake wasn't sure how to answer. He had come to the barbecue with Leilani but, as beautiful and cool as she was, he was still thinking of Leilani as more of a friend. But Skylar ... He definitely felt something more when he was with her.

"Jake?" Tristan asked.

"Huh?"

"Never mind," Tristan laughed. *Jake isn't the first guy to fall under Sky's spell and certainly won't be the last. Although Sky might argue, she's more like me than she cares to admit,*

Tristan thought. "Where's Leilani?"

"She went to find a bathroom," Jake said.

"Maybe she got lost. I'll go find her. Be right back," Tristan said.

Jake walked over to talk to Cruz at the barbecue. After a minute, Cruz pulled some rare burgers and portobello mushrooms off the grill and offered the open space to Jake.

"If you brought something to 'cue, toss it right on." Cruz stepped away from the grill. "I'm gonna get the burger fixings from the ice chest."

"Thanks, man." Jake reached into his bag and pulled out a pound of seafood. He unwrapped the white butcher paper and grabbed two shark fillets.

As soon as Cruz got a whiff of the shark, he whipped his head away from the cooler, jumped up and charged at Jake. The force of Cruz's body tackling Jake dislodged the shark fillets from his hand. Jake hit the patio, spine first. Cruz landed on top of him, catching the fillets in one hand before they hit the ground next to Jake's head.

At that instant, Tristan and Leilani opened the screen door. "Oh my god!" Lani yelled, seeing Cruz topple Jake.

Tristan rushed over, grabbed Cruz by the collar and peeled him off Jake. "Cruz, chill! What the hell's going on?"

Tristan released Cruz and reached down to offer his hand to Jake, who was still sprawled out on the patio. "Jake, sorry man." Tristan pulled him up with one hand and then threw his other arm around Jake's shoulders to make sure he could stand on his own. "Are you okay?"

"Yeah, man. Fine," Jake muttered.

"Cruz, what happened?"

"Sorry, Tristan. But he brought shark! Shark! He was just about to throw it on the grill and ..."

Tristan put his hand up, palm toward Cruz, to stop him from

saying any more. He turned to Jake and Leilani. "Sorry. Cruz is super-vigilant about sustainable seafood. Shark is a definite no-no. Cruz, why don't you get Jake a Seafood Watch card so he can be better prepared next time, okay?"

Cruz stomped inside, still breathing hard from the altercation. He retrieved a card from the kitchen, walked back out and flung it toward Jake. "See? Shark is on the 'Avoid' list."

Feeling Tristan's glare, Cruz changed his tone toward Jake. "Hey man, sorry I knocked you down. I just hate the way people abuse the ocean, you know? Overfishing and polluting and stuff. It's wrong."

"Dude, you're right. Sorry. I didn't know," Jake said.

Torrey, who had been watching from the kitchen, decided to lighten the mood. "Guacamole!" she yelled as she walked from the kitchen to the back patio. She sat next to Cruz. Under the table, she stroked his thigh to calm him. She felt his breathing slow and his muscles relax. When the tray of rare burgers came around, Torrey offered one to Cruz.

Cruz whispered in her ear, "What I want isn't on the menu."

Torrey smiled, then stopped. *Is he talking about me?* She glanced down the table at Jake. *Or one of our dinner guests?*

33 – The Reemergence of Leilani

"Here, Jake, Leilani, have a burger. Sorry about your dinner," Cruz said.

"No problem." Jake reached for a hamburger patty.

"Actually, I'll take one of those portobello mushrooms," Lani said.

"She's a vegetarian," Jake explained.

Cruz tensed again. "It's not going to bother you that we're eating meat though, right?"

"Not at all. Just a personal decision. No judgment. I swear," Lani assured him.

Tristan glared at Cruz. "Relax," he mouthed. Cruz gave a slight nod.

"So we have a celebrity here tonight," Tristan announced with a smile. "We have the U.S. Rip/Shred Girls' Junior Pro Champion at this very table."

Lani's stomach plummeted three stories. *So he does know.* She never liked the recognition that went along with being a top surfer. She preferred anonymity, both on and off the waves. The loss of solitude in the ocean was part of the reason she gave up her surfing career. That and she had no desire to support her lazy parents at the tender age of 16.

"Leilani Waters!" Tristan exclaimed.

Jake turned to Leilani. "What? You didn't tell me that."

Lani shook her head, "It's not a big deal." Her cheeks flushed bright pink.

"Of course it's a big deal!" Tristan said.

"That is a big deal," Jake added. "That's awesome. Why didn't you say anything?"

"It was a long time ago," Lani replied. "I really haven't surfed much since then."

"Why'd you give it up?" Jake asked. "You're insane out there."

"Oh you know, fell, hit my head, got a concussion, was almost eaten by a shark, the usual surfer stuff." Lani saw the Nomads shift in their seats and glance at each other at the mention of the word, "shark." She also noticed a change in Tristan's expression.

Seeing Leilani looking at him, Tristan put on a big smile. "Well we're glad you're here with us tonight. And Jake's right. You really were amazing. It was an honor to share the surf with you and it's an honor to have you in my home. To Leilani!" Tristan raised his glass in a toast and the others followed.

"Leilani!" they shouted.

Jake nudged her and whispered, "That's pretty cool. You should be proud."

"Thanks," she said quietly.

Tristan changed the subject and the conversation veered away from Leilani, for which she was grateful.

Later, when she brought her dinner plate and glass into the kitchen, Tristan followed. "Leilani, listen, I'm sorry I brought up that whole thing about you and your surfing career. I thought it was really cool. But I didn't want to make you uncomfortable. I never would've brought it up if …"

"No, it's okay. It was a long time ago, a different part of my life. One that wasn't so great actually," Lani confessed.

"Sorry. I didn't know." He paused. "Hey, let me make it up to you. How about dinner next week? It's the least I can do for having ruined your evening twice tonight—first with that whole thing with Cruz and then with my big mouth."

Lani hesitated. She thought of Jake. *We're definitely not dating and I don't think he has feelings for me, but is it wrong to accept a date with one guy when you're here with another? Even when both dates are actually work? Eww or does that make it worse?*

"Please," Tristan asked, head down, eyes up.

Why does he have to be so sexy? "Okay, yeah," she said. "Call me next week." *If you're still a free man.*

Later that night, after Jake dropped Leilani off at home, she walked to a nearby convenience store. From the dilapidated pay phone, she disguised her voice and phoned in an anonymous tip to Detective Garrison. "Yeah, dude, you know that surfer who went missing last week where that guy got killed by the shark? I know where his board is. It's at Tristan Pierce's house in a locked bedroom. Is that weird or what?"

She felt a twinge of guilt as she gave him Tristan's address, but knew she had to, if for no other reason than to find out for herself whether Tristan was involved or not. *I really hope he's not.*

34 – Tristan's Detainment

Tristan had never worried about going three days without surfing, even when two deputies and a detective arrived at his door with a search warrant the day after the barbecue.

For vampire sharks, surfing is a biological imperative. They don't just live to surf; they surf to live.

Vampire sharks must immerse themselves in salt water at least once every 72 hours. If they don't, they age at an accelerated pace. After 72 hours, each hour spent out of the water ages a vampire shark five years. Even with a lifespan of approximately 800 years, most are dead in under a week if they can't find salt water.

"Tristan Pierce? We have a warrant to search your house. Step aside," Detective Garrison ordered.

"May I see that?" Tristan scanned the warrant. It looked legit. "Well then, please come in."

The deputies entered and went room to room, searching for the black surfboard with the shark and bloody teeth and anything else that might connect Tristan to the missing surfer, Rick Jennings.

"What's this about?" Tristan asked.

"Missing surfer."

"What missing surfer?" Tristan's question was met with silence.

When the deputies came upon a locked bedroom, they called for Tristan.

"Open the door," Garrison demanded.

"What if I refuse?" Tristan asked.

"Then we'll break it down," Garrison answered with a smug smile.

"I think I'd rather open it. What exactly are you searching for?"

When Tristan opened the door, Detective Garrison whistled, "Phewww! That's quite a collection. How'd you get so many boards?"

"I surf. I collect. Is that a crime?"

Garrison peered at Tristan. "You tell me."

"Detective Garrison?" A young deputy held out Rick's board. "Is this the surfboard?"

"Mr. Pierce, will you come down to the station with us?" Garrison asked. "We'd like to ask you some questions in connection with the disappearance of Rick Jennings."

"I'd prefer not to. I barely knew the guy," Tristan said coolly.

"Great. Then it'll be a quick interview. Shall we?"

"Why not? So long as it's quick," Tristan smiled.

Detective Garrison led Tristan to his car and put him in the back, uncuffed. Fortunately for Tristan, it was after sunset. Unfortunately, it was also after hours on a Friday. He hadn't been in the ocean since 2 a.m. Thursday morning since he didn't go surfing the night of the barbecue.

At the sheriff's station, Garrison guided Tristan to a small room with a two-way mirror and pushed him into a chair.

"May I make a call before we begin?" Tristan asked.

"What? You wanna check the surf report?" Garrison asked.

"Yeah, actually I do. Since we'll be done soon, I'd like to see how I'll be spending the rest of my evening." Tristan looked around. "A phone, gentlemen?"

"Yeah, sure." Garrison led Tristan to a phone.

Tristan called Skylar's cell. *Pick up, Sky, pick up.* Skylar's phone went to voicemail. "Sky, Tristan here. I'm at the sheriff's station. Through some exceptionally fine detective work," Tristan smirked at Garrison, "they've brought me in for some inexplicable reason to question me in the disappearance of that surfer, Rick. Clearly, they have some more detecting to do. Anywho, please come down to the station and get me as soon as you get this message. And if the surf's tasty, bring my board. Thanks, Sky. See you soon."

"Okay, surfer boy. Back to the box," Garrison said.

Detective Garrison and the deputy led Tristan back to the interrogation room. Garrison sat down at the small, shabby table, across from Tristan. "So, tell me about Rick Jennings. His family said they haven't seen him since he hooked up with you and your little surf gang."

"His family? Really? I didn't know Rick had a family. And I don't have a surf gang. They're called friends. Though I can see why that word might be foreign to you, Detective," Tristan said with a slight smile.

"So when's the last time you saw Rick?" Garrison asked. "I have witnesses who say they saw you surfing with him the day before he disappeared."

"The *day* before he disappeared? No. That wasn't me."

"Witnesses say it was. When's the last time you saw Rick?"

"Wait. I've changed my mind. If I'm going to answer any more questions, I'd like to have an attorney present." Tristan didn't really care if an attorney was there. He just wanted to make things difficult for Garrison.

"Sure, we'll get right on that." Detective Garrison opened the door and yelled down the hall to no one in particular, "He wants a lawyer!"

He shut the door and turned back to Tristan. "Though I don't see why. We're just talkin', right? While we're waiting, how about you answer a few questions for me? For starters, why is Rick's surfboard in a locked bedroom in your house?" He pointed to the surfboard in the corner of the room.

"I believe I said if I'm going to answer any questions I'd like to have an attorney present." Tristan debated the merit of continuing, but he did like to toy with annoying people—like Garrison. *This could be fun.* "But, hey, maybe I can help you out while we're waiting for an attorney. One's on her way, right? I hope she's cute," he grinned at the deputy.

"Yeah, she'll be here any minute," Garrison fibbed.

"Great. Then let's clear this up and we can both be on our way. For starters," Tristan pointed, "that is not Rick's board. It's my board. You do know that not every surfboard is unique, right? You can walk into a surf shop and just buy one off the wall. Now, of course, you don't want to be surfing next to a guy with the exact same board as you. It's kind of like showing up to the prom in the same dress as another girl. It's embarrassing but it does happen."

Tristan leaned across the table to whisper so the young deputy standing at the door wouldn't hear. "Kind of like wearing your finest pair of pink lace panties to work and seeing another detective wearing the exact same pair, right, Detective Garrison?"

Garrison gasped. *How does he know?* "Yeah right, surfer boy," he bristled. "And why does it say 'Rick' on the board?"

"I don't know. Rick is probably the name of the guy who designed the board. Or maybe it's the name of the shark. I don't know. I didn't make the board."

"And why was the door to the room locked?" Garrison asked.

"Do you know how much all those boards are worth? A lot more than *both* your annual salaries combined." Tristan leaned across the table again and whispered, "You know, if you took all the money you spent on frilly underthings for yourself and put it into a Roth IRA, you'd probably do okay when you retired. But that lace just feels *so good*, right?"

"You little punk!" Garrison reached across with one hand and slammed Tristan's face into the table.

"Garrison!" the deputy yelled.

Garrison lifted Tristan's head and smashed it into the table two more times before the deputy pried his hands from the top of Tristan's head.

Though he could have stopped Garrison at any time and killed him in an instant, Tristan chose not to. He thought getting roughed up would make the sheriff's department more eager to end the questioning and send him home. So, to attract attention to the room, he yelled, "Police brutality!"

"He tried to head-butt me!" Garrison lied. He turned to the deputy. "You saw it, right? He leaned over and tried to head-butt me. Game over, surfer boy. You're going down."

"I never touched you, Detective," Tristan said calmly. "What about my lawyer? I requested a lawyer—twice—before you began questioning me. You're really not supposed to question me after I request a lawyer. Did you miss that day as a young cadet? And beating an innocent man, completely unprovoked by the way, is just plain wrong. My civil rights have been violated. I'd like to lodge a formal complaint. Where's the sheriff?"

"Quiet, you! Lock him up!" Garrison ordered.

35 — Dry Spell

The young deputy led Tristan to a holding cell. Tristan wondered why Skylar wasn't there yet.

"You wanna make another call first?" the deputy offered, feeling conflicted about what he saw Garrison do. He didn't see Tristan try to head-butt him and he knew Garrison had a rep for overreacting to verbal jabs. But the deputy was applying to be a detective and didn't want to openly contradict someone who had been with the department for decades.

"Yeah, another call would be great. Thank you." Tristan dialed Skylar again. "Skylar, I'm at the sheriff's station. There's been a mix-up and they're holding me here. I need you to come down here now. I haven't been surfing in almost two days. Understand? I need you here. Now."

Skylar, who had met someone, a sandy-blond surf stud named Frances, didn't check her cell phone messages until 6 p.m. Saturday. She heard Tristan's voice. "Skylar. Tristan here. I'm at …"

She clicked off her phone. *I don't care where you are, Tristan. I've met someone and he's kind and he likes me for me. And I'm going to see him again tonight. So who cares where you are and who you're with.*

When Skylar returned home early Sunday evening, she realized she did care.

"Where have you been?" Cruz demanded, as soon as he saw her pull up in front of her house.

"Out with a friend. Why?"

"Tristan's missing," he answered.

"We haven't seen him in days. No one has," Torrey added.

"What do you mean? You guys haven't been surfing?" Skylar asked.

"Not with Tristan. He's M.I.A. His cell is at home. We could hear it ringing when we went to the front door. But he's not there. What do we do?" Logan asked.

"Hang on." Skylar dialed her voicemail. "Skylar. Tristan here. I'm at the sheriff's station …" She gulped. *Uh oh. I may have really screwed up this time.*

When the message ended, Skylar leapt into command mode. "He's at the sheriff's station. He's been arrested or something. They think he has something to do with Rick's death. They're calling it a 'disappearance.' I'm going to get him out. When's the last time everyone saw him?"

"The barbecue," they answered in unison.

"That was three days ago! He's in serious trouble. Torrey, you're with me. Cruz and Logan, you follow us. I'll give you instructions when we get there. Move! Now!"

They raced east, across town, to the sheriff's station. Skylar pulled into a parking spot. She and Torrey jumped out.

Cruz pulled next to her and started to get out.

"No. Cruz, drive Torrey to that motel we passed, two turns back," Skylar instructed. "Torrey you check in and start running a cool bath. Then call me and Cruz with your room number. Cruz, you and Logan go to the supermarket we passed. Buy all the sea salt you can. Meet us back at Torrey's room. Go now!"

She rushed inside the sheriff's station. "Hi, my name is Skylar Sirena. I received a call from someone in your custody, Tristan Pierce. Where is he?"

The clerk entered a few keystrokes on his computer. "They're releasing him now. He'll be out shortly."

36 – Parched

The sheriff's department decided to set Tristan free after 48 hours due to a lack of evidence, despite Garrison's claims that Tristan tried to attack him. As it turned out, Garrison found out Rick's board was not unique. At least, that's what the owner of a local surf shop told him.

After Rick's disappearance, when Jake started asking questions, Tristan had a friend make a few replicas of Rick's board. He then placed the boards in a North County surf shop, where he personally knew the owner, Mark—and knew Mark hated Garrison.

In the surf community, Garrison was persona non grata. He liked to bust teens and adults, particularly surfers, for minor infractions like drinking on the beach or smoking weed—or for nothing at all. More than a few boards had gotten dinged up or disappeared while in Garrison's custody. And, when it came to serious crimes, Garrison usually botched the investigation.

As Tristan delivered the boards, he gave Mark a bag full of hundred-dollar bills and told him he could sell the boards and keep that money, too, if he told any law enforcement officials that it was not a custom board. Mark was happy to help Tristan and grateful for the money to help his sister who, Tristan knew, had a huge pile of medical bills.

The plan worked but Tristan still paid a hefty price. There, at the sheriff's station, as he rounded the corner, Skylar saw his face and winced. His skin was flaming red and dry. It began to flake and crack. He was aging, right there before her eyes. She rushed to him. He put his arm around her for support.

"Looks like he's got the flu or something," said the clerk who processed the paperwork to release Tristan. "And don't forget the surfboard. They said he can have it back."

Skylar tucked the board under one arm and guided Tristan outside. "How long has it been since you've been in the ocean?" she whispered in his ear.

"Since Thursday morning, early—90 hours, give or take. Salt water. Now," he gasped through parched lips. He was so dehydrated he could barely walk.

As Skylar helped him into the car and strapped the board to her roof racks, she did the calculations in her head. *Ninety hours minus 72 hours equals 18 hours of damage. Eighteen hours times five years of aging per hour.* "Ninety years, Tristan! You've lost 90 years. I'm so sorry!"

"I feel like I'm dying. I guess that's because I am dying. Where are we going?"

"To a motel. The drive home or to the beach is too far. We need to get you in salt water now to stop the aging. Torrey, Cruz and Logan are on it."

Skylar got the call from Torrey with the room number and pulled into a parking space in front of the room. Torrey ran out and helped her carry Tristan to the bathroom. His cells were rapidly deteriorating.

"I've got it from here, Torrey. Call Cruz and tell them to get here with the salt now!" Skylar closed the door so it was open just a crack. She undressed Tristan and lowered him into the bath water.

37 – Shopping for Trouble

Down the street, Logan and Cruz grabbed all the sea salt they could and tossed it into a shopping cart. They ran to the only open checkstand. Cruz looked at the signs hanging from the ceiling: "3's a crowd. When there's more than 3 in line, we'll open the next available register."

He nudged Logan and pointed to the signs. "Clearly, that's a lie."

"Totally. Three's a crowd, man!" Logan shouted. "Open another register!"

Of course, no new registers opened. The line inched up by one person. Logan and Cruz loaded their salt onto the belt.

The two 12-year-old boys in front of them turned around. "What are you gonna do with all that salt?" one asked.

"Nothing," Cruz answered curtly.

On the belt in front of their salt, Cruz and Logan spied six giant packages of toilet paper and two cans of shaving cream.

"What are you gonna do with all the TP and shaving cream?" Logan asked.

"Nothing," the boys replied.

The checker, who seemed to purposely move in slow motion, finally finished with the two boys and began ringing up the salt. Logan threw it into paper bags to speed the process while Cruz paid cash. They ran past the boys and sped to the motel.

When they turned into the parking lot, Cruz's phone rang. "Where are you?!" Torrey asked.

"We're here," he said.

Torrey opened the door and waved to them. They ran to the bath and began dumping in the sea salt. When five boxes were emptied, Skylar yelled, "Out!"

She swirled the salt in the water, around Tristan's body, to help it dissolve more quickly. She took a plastic cup from the sink, filled it with salty bath water, and poured it over his head and shoulders. "Tristan, relax, okay? You should start feeling better any minute now. Just breathe."

Tristan's face twisted in pain. For the past 18-plus hours it felt like he was frying on a skillet. His tongue felt like sandpaper. The pain was so intense he would have cried, if he had any moisture left in his body to form tears.

Eventually, he felt his core temperature start to drop. Relief slowly seeped into his skin. After 90 minutes, he was feeling almost normal. That is, as normal as you could feel if you lost about 10 percent of your lifespan in a matter of hours.

Seeing Tristan recovering, Skylar sent the others home. Several blocks away from the motel, Logan elbowed Cruz as they passed a house enshrined in toilet paper and two cars coated with shaving cream.

Around 1 a.m., Skylar took Tristan home. She helped him into bed and then left. The following night, she took him to the ocean. They floated quietly for several minutes.

Finally, Tristan broke the silence. "Where were you when I called?"

"I'm so sorry. My phone died and I didn't have my charger," she lied. "I didn't get your messages until Sunday night. As soon as I heard your first message we all rushed over …"

"I know. I don't blame you. You did great. But where were you all weekend?"

"I met someone."

Tristan thought of Leilani. *This will certainly make things easier if Skylar is preoccupied with someone else.* "Do I know him?"

"No. But you will. I turned him," Skylar said. "Now, I'd like you to finish the job so he can be one of us."

38 – Reconsidering

Lani thought about Tristan throughout the weekend. *I wonder if they found anything at his place, other than the board?*

While jogging at the beach, she heard that a gang of surf punks, the Del Norte Reefers, had disappeared and wondered where that investigation would lead. *Hopefully not to a locked bedroom in Tristan's house.*

By Sunday night, Lani learned the sheriff had let Tristan go for lack of evidence in Rick Jennings' disappearance. She also heard Tristan was brutalized in some way during the questioning, which made her feel sick.

Despite the fact that the surfboard didn't prove anything, her intuition told her Tristan had something to do with Rick's disappearance. *But what?*

She thought back on her night surfing with Tristan and Jake. *I haven't felt like that in years. I felt so ... free. So, why did I ever quit surfing? To focus on school? No. I could do both. I did do both. I gave up surfing to punish my parents. But the joke's on me. I ended up punishing myself. It was my stupid parents who got in the way of my enjoyment. It was them pushing me to make more of it than it was. It was a hobby, not a job. And I chose to leave the job, which was a good move. But I also left the hobby, which I guess I actually loved.*

Lani picked up her phone. *Maybe I should call Jake and see if he wants to go surfing. I can also make it clear we're just friends. He's a nice guy. I don't want him to get hurt in all this.* She began to dial but hung up. *Or maybe I should call Tristan first and see if he's okay. No! I'm not supposed to know he was brought in for questioning. Ugh. Maybe I shouldn't talk to anyone today.*

39 – Xan

By Wednesday, Tristan was back to feeling like himself, only older. He gave Skylar the okay to bring her new boyfriend over.

"Frances, I'd like you to meet Tristan Pierce. Tristan, this is Frances Francis." She looked expectantly at Tristan, imploring him to be nice.

"Frances, nice to meet you." Tristan firmly grasped his hand. "I'm sorry," he laughed. "Frances Francis? Skylar, come on! We cannot have someone in our group named Frances Francis."

"Tristan!" Skylar gasped.

"Frances, what's your middle name?" Tristan asked.

"Alexander."

"That's better," Tristan said. "What about Xan? Is that cool?"

"Yeah, that is cool. Xan. I like that," Frances said. Growing up as Frances Francis was not an easy feat—especially for a nice-looking boy with long, wavy hair. He painfully recalled more than one occasion, before puberty, when he'd been mistaken for a girl.

"So, Xan, what are your intentions with Skylar?"

"Tristan, shut up," Skylar demanded.

"Intentions? Skylar and I intend to have a rockin' good time. She's an amazing woman. I'm lucky to have found her." Xan threw his arm around Skylar, who beamed.

"Yes, she's pretty amazing," Tristan agreed with a knowing smile.

Skylar shot him a warning look. *Don't go any further.*

"So I understand you're now a vampire, thanks to Skylar here. How do you feel about that, Xan?" Tristan asked.

"It's awesome. I thought I'd only have a couple more decades to surf. Now I've got centuries! And Skylar says you can make it even more awesome."

"Did she? What exactly did she say?" Tristan probed.

"Nothing," Xan replied. "She said I had to come to you personally and, if you approved, you would tell me more and that it would be awesome."

"Well it takes more than one meeting," Tristan clarified. "It's kind of like a screening process."

"That's cool. I can see how with your lifestyle," Xan lowered his voice, "you know, as a vampire, you have to be careful, right?"

"Right. Skylar, can I talk to you for a minute?" Tristan ushered her outside, so Xan wouldn't be able to hear them.

"I'm glad you're happy with this guy," Tristan whispered, "but don't you think you're rushing things? You just met him, you turned him, and now you want to invite him to share in all our secrets?"

"But he's really sweet and I like him," Skylar explained. "I really, really like him."

"That's great. I mean it. But we need to make sure he fits in with our family, you know? Why don't you let the guys and I take him out surfing tonight?"

"I dunno. It seems kind of early in the relationship to leave him alone with you. And Logan and Cruz," she quickly added.

Tristan knew what she meant. He had chased more than one guy away from Skylar. *They weren't good enough for her.* But he did see how his protectiveness could put a crimp in her love life.

"It's too early in the relationship for him to go out alone with us but not to turn him? C'mon, Sky. You can't have it both ways."

"Okay, okay, you're right. But don't say anything about our past. I want to start fresh with this guy. I don't want him feeling jealous and looking over his shoulder. Don't be too hard on him. And make sure he's home before dawn. Promise?"

"I promise," Tristan said.

40 – Ashes to Ashes

Tristan, Cruz and Logan met Xan at the beach later that night. Xan sat in the middle of a pile of fast food wrappers, napkins and a paper soda cup.

"Xan!" They greeted him warmly; their promise to Skylar.

"Hey, it's almost a full moon!" Logan exclaimed. "Awesome!"

Xan jumped up and grabbed his board. "Let's go!"

"Aren't you going to clean that up?" Tristan asked.

Xan got the feeling it wasn't a question but a command. "Oh. Yeah."

Littering the beach, strike two, Tristan thought. *Your first strike was distracting Skylar, who left me in jail to wither and age 90 years.*

Logan gazed up at the moon, feeling the silvery light on his face. "Ah!" He pulled a tube of sunscreen from the cooler and lathered up. Cruz and Tristan did the same.

Xan watched them, perplexed. "What are you guys doing? It's nighttime. We don't need sunscreen."

"Xan, you're not human anymore. Haven't you been out surfing with Skylar since she turned you?" Tristan asked.

"A little. We spend most of our time indoors," Xan grinned.

"I see," Tristan sighed. "Well, spending hours under a full or nearly full moon is just like being out in the sun. You see that light reflecting off the moon? That's sunlight."

"Dude, I know that," Xan said. "I'm not an idiot."

"Well, sunlight burns vampire skin, particularly when you're a newborn vampire. You have absolutely no tolerance to sun. You need to build that up. It's like tanning for humans. You have to start slow. If you rush it, you get burned and you blister and peel. Now, as a newbie or 'Non' as we like to call you," Tristan smiled condescendingly, "if you're walking around in clothes and not outside for an extended length of time under a full moon, it's no big deal. But if you're nearly naked outdoors for hours, on sand and salt water, which reflect the sunlight, you'd better lather up."

"Ooh! What if I don't? Will I get moonburned?" Xan teased.

"Yeah. Badly. But do what you want." Tristan poured sunscreen on his fingers.

"You guys are messing with me," Xan said.

"Like I said, do what you want." Tristan patted Xan's left and right shoulder blades with his sunscreen-soaked fingers, and then swished his hand across Xan's back as he said, "Go on, get outta here."

Logan and Cruz laughed and shook their heads.

Logan squirted a tiny drop of sunscreen on his fingertip. "Hey, Xan, I think you've got something on your head. Lemme see." He reached up and drew an "L" on Xan's forehead. "There. It's gone."

"Are you guys all set?" Tristan asked with a smirk. *Skylar's gonna be pissed. But she'll see this guy's nowhere near ready to be a vampire shark.*

"Yep," Logan replied. "Let's go!"

They splashed into the ocean. The sea foam glowed lavender, as if illuminated by a blacklight.

After several hours surfing under the waxing gibbous moon, Tristan, Cruz and Logan watched in amusement as Xan turned deepening shades of watermelon red. That is, except for the white "L" Logan had flicked on Xan's forehead and the sad face Tristan had drawn by slapping eyes on Xan's shoulder blades and swiping a downturned mouth across his back.

Tristan surfed up behind Xan. "Hey, why so sad?"

Logan and Cruz busted out laughing.

"Dude, what are you talking about?" Xan asked, oblivious. "Are you guys high?"

That made them all laugh even harder.

Cruz surveyed Xan's dayglow skin, vandalized with sunscreen graffiti. "Oh man, Skylar's gonna kill us."

As dawn approached, Tristan, Logan and Cruz prepared to catch their last wave to shore.

"Hey, where are you guys going? We've got some more time before sun up," Xan said, disappointed the evening was ending.

"Not really. By the time we walk home it'll be nearly sunrise. You need to come with us now," Tristan said firmly.

"You guys are too careful. Five more minutes," Xan pleaded.

"Come in now or die, newborn. The choice is yours." Tristan turned to catch his final wave in with Logan and Cruz.

Once on shore, they waved their arms to call Xan in but he blew them off. "We tried," Tristan shrugged.

When Tristan got home, he sprinted up to his bedroom and reached for his binoculars. He pointed toward the shore and adjusted the focus. Xan was still out there surfing. *Idiot.*

Tristan saw Xan jump up on his board. It was a killer wave. But a few seconds into the ride, the sun burst into the eastern sky.

Xan caught sight of it at the same time he noticed how burned his skin felt. *Maybe those guys were right about the sunscreen*, he realized.

As Xan continued to ride the perfect wave, he pressed his fingertips into his arm. Bright white spots appeared in the midst of his sizzling red flesh. *Oh no.* He looked at the sun, which was rising way too fast. *Oh no.*

Tristan watched through his binoculars. Poof! In a flash of black smoke, Xan was gone. A pile of ash collapsed onto the surfboard, which then tumbled in the wave.

"Goodbye, Xan." Tristan set down his binoculars and thought about retrieving Xan's board to add to his collection. He did not look forward to telling Skylar about Xan.

41 – Both Ways

Skylar burst into Tristan's house and found him standing in front of his bedroom window. "Where's Xan?!" she demanded.

"Let's just say it was a killer sunrise."

"Tristan!"

"I'm sorry to say it but he was a Non," Tristan said.

"He was not. You just don't want me to be happy. I can't believe you let him die."

"Sky, we tried. We told him about the sunscreen and he ignored us. We told him repeatedly to come in with us before the sun rose and he refused. Oh, and I didn't even tell you about the litter. Clearly, he didn't respect the beach and he couldn't follow instructions. If he couldn't follow instructions, how was he supposed to follow the Rules? We don't need another Rick on our hands. I'm starting to seriously question your taste in men. First Rick, then Xan. You really need to stop bringing home strays. Xan was a Non."

"He was not a Non. He was still learning. You didn't even try to help him!" Skylar shrieked.

"He was the very definition of a Non. Non-human. Non-vampire shark. Non-existent. A mere bloodsucker with no respect for anything. It's better this way. We got lucky actually. Nature took care of him for us. C'mon, Sky, you deserve better."

"You always say that. But no one is ever good enough, according to you. You don't want me, Tristan. I get that. But you don't want anyone else to have me either. As you said yourself, you can't have it both ways." Skylar enjoyed throwing Tristan's words back at him. *This is not over,* she thought. *You are going to pay for this, Tristan.*

42 – Truth Telling

Later that morning, Tristan called Leilani. "Hey, I meant to call you earlier in the week but wasn't feeling well. How's tomorrow night for dinner?"

"Tomorrow? Okay."

"How about if I pick you up at 8? Give me your address." Tristan jotted Leilani's address on a pad of paper as he smiled into the phone. "Until then."

"Until then," she said.

The next night Tristan arrived at Leilani's doorstep promptly at 8 p.m. He rang the bell.

Lani opened the door and gazed at him. *Something's different*, she noticed. *His face looks different ... older. What happened to him while he was in custody at the sheriff's station?* She immediately felt guilty again.

Tristan presented a bouquet of bright violet-blue irises from behind his back. "Flowers for you."

"They're beautiful! Thanks. How did you know I like irises?"

"Lucky guess. You didn't seem like a roses kind of woman."

Lani walked back inside to get a vase. Tristan stood at the doorway, awaiting an invitation to enter.

In the kitchen, Lani realized she'd left Tristan at the door without inviting him in. *Most guys would have just come in regardless,* she thought. *Very polite.*

"Come on in!" she shouted over her shoulder. "I'll put these in water and then we can go."

Tristan entered and looked around. "Physician heal thyself," he muttered under his breath.

"What?" Lani yelled from the kitchen.

"Sorry! I didn't mean for you to hear that."

Lani walked into the family room with the vase full of

flowers. "What were you saying?"

"I was being rude actually. I said, 'Physician heal thyself.' When I walked in, I expected to see this amazingly decorated home but it looks ... uh ..." Tristan struggled to find a word that wouldn't dig a deeper hole for himself.

"No, you're right," Lani laughed. "The interior designer with the ugly house. It's like that saying, you know, the cobbler whose kids have holes in their shoes. Or the web designer without a website. You spend all your creative energy on your clients and find there's nothing left for yourself. And then you're left with this," she waved her arm across the room.

"Right," he chuckled. "Sorry, I didn't mean to insult you."

"You didn't."

They walked outside to Tristan's black hybrid SUV. After he pulled away from the curb, he turned to her. "While I'm being rude, mind if I ask a personal question?"

"Why not?" Lani wondered where this was going.

"So why did you give up surfing? You have a gift. You really do."

She blushed. "It's a long story."

"I've got time," he said.

Lani decided to be honest. Her past was part of her cover, after all. *It's not who I am now anyway, so I won't be giving anything up.*

"Okay, but let's talk about it over dinner," she suggested. "Do you mind if I ask you a question that could also be considered rude?"

"Shoot."

"Why does your car smell like French fries?"

Tristan grinned. "I had a friend convert it to run on waste vegetable oil. I get it from restaurants and fast food places. They like it because they don't have to dispose of the oil. That means less oil down the sink, in the sewers and in the ocean. I like it because I'm not polluting the environment. But my car does smell like a diner with a deep fryer."

"No worries. I like French fries," Lani smiled.

Over dinner, Lani told Tristan about her parents and her upbringing, including the years of neglect and ridicule. She divulged her parents' sudden interest when her surfing started to generate income. She even revealed she gave up surfing to spite her parents but that she only ended up hurting herself.

"Are your parents still married?" Tristan asked.

"Yes. I mean, I think so. I haven't actually talked to them since I left home more than 10 years ago." *Wow, that seems so long when I say it out loud. Do I really hate them that much?*

"What about you? Have you ever been married?" Lani asked, changing the focus to Tristan. She'd already disclosed more than she intended. *It's time for me to ask the questions now.* She wasn't sure if she'd broach the topic of Cody and Rick or keep it on a more personal level—establish trust and intimacy before diving deeper. Like Jake was doing.

"Yes, I was married once. It seems like a lifetime ago." Tristan paused. The light disappeared from his warm espresso-brown eyes. "Her name was Julianna. She died."

"I'm so sorry. What happened?"

Tristan's face turned dark, which made him look even older. *He definitely looks older than the other night*, Lani thought. *I'm going to call Garrison and find out exactly what happened.*

Tristan started to talk and then stopped.

"I shouldn't have asked. We can talk about something else, okay?" Lani placed her hand on his hand, which rested on the table. *Intimacy. Trust.*

Tristan wondered if he should continue, but decided to be honest. "It was my fault," he confessed, pulling his hand away.

"What do you mean?"

Tristan didn't answer.

"Like a car accident or something?" Lani pressed.

"Something like that." Tristan unconsciously wrung his hands. "I was careless and as a result she died and I'll never forgive myself." He gazed down at his restless hands. He clasped one over the other to stop them from fidgeting.

"How long has it been?" Lani gently asked.

"It happened a long time ago. But it seems like yesterday sometimes." Tristan peered into Leilani's blue eyes. He saw compassion, which made him want to continue.

"I'm really sorry, Tristan. What happened?"

"She was killed by a sea vamp…" Tristan stopped abruptly. *What the hell am I doing?* he asked himself. "She was killed, in the sea, by a shark."

"Oh my god! Like Jake's friend? Where? Here?"

"No. North of San Francisco. Stinson Beach. We used to live in San Francisco and go up there on weekends."

"How old was she?"

"She was 24. We'd only been married a few weeks when it happened." Tristan stopped and tried to shake the memory. "It was a long time ago."

Lani did the math in her head. *Let's say Tristan was around Julianna's age when they married. So that was what—10 or 15 years ago?*

"Does Jake know about Julianna?" she asked. "It might be a comfort to him to know he's not the only one who's lost someone in that way."

"No. No one does actually. It's strange since we just met, but you're the only one I've told about Julianna since it happened, other than my best friend at the time. Not even Skylar knows and we've been friends for years. But I do know how Jake feels. That's why I asked him to come surfing with us. When something like that happens, some people shut down and try to escape from it all—the ocean, the beach, the coast. They develop a fear and never return. I think it's better to never let that fear develop in the first place. Just get back out there and keep doing it."

"You're right," Lani agreed. "It's hard though, when you're right in the middle of it. I gave up surfing, not out of a fear of hitting my head again or seeing a shark, but out of anger and spite. But still … in the end I only hurt myself. I couldn't see that back then though. It's nice Jake has you as a friend to help him through it, to tell him to keep at it. You shouldn't give up either."

"What do you mean?" Tristan asked. "I surf almost every day."

"No, I mean you shouldn't give up on finding someone. It's obvious you haven't let go of the pain of losing your wife. I can see it all over your face. But you can't blame yourself, any more than Jake can blame himself for Cody's death. And I think he does. He feels like he left Cody out there all alone to die. But how could he have known? How could you?"

Tristan shifted in his seat. *Julianna's death, my fault. Cody's death, my fault again. Rick's death, my fault. Xan, well, that was his own fault for not listening. But what the hell am I doing? I've got to get this under control. Why did I create so many monsters who …*

"How long were you and Julianna together?" Lani asked.

"More than three years."

"Have you been close with anyone since you lost her? Or fallen in love again—even for a short time?"

"No." Tristan pushed aside his regrets and shifted his attention back to Leilani. "No, I haven't met the right person." He stared into her eyes. "Yet."

43 – The Rogues and the Rules

In truth, it was partly Tristan's fault his wife, Julianna, died. It was also the reason he created the Rules.

After his transformation into the first vampire shark, Tristan delighted in turning young surfers into vampire sharks. "Men in gray suits," he liked to call them. Or "graysuits," for short.

"Do you want to surf forever?" he'd ask as they floated on their boards, in the lull, waiting for the next set. "Hell yeah!" they'd say or something to that effect. And Tristan would turn them, with a single bite.

The problem was, he made so many vampire sharks after his fateful trip to the Farallons, he lost track of most of them. Fortunately, vampire sharks could not create new vampire sharks. Only Tristan could. He didn't know why his venom was unique, but he did enjoy the fact that he alone had this godlike power.

Vampire sharks could, however, turn humans into regular vampires, like any vampire could. And both graysuits and vampires could wreak a lot of havoc if they wanted to.

Some of these vampire sharks, like some vampires and some humans, lacked impulse control. Others hunted and killed humans for sport, not just food. And they weren't discreet about it either.

A few weeks after he and Julianna married, Tristan sat on the beach, preparing breakfast over a bonfire after a night of surfing with his young bride. Julianna, who was still human and unaware of Tristan's true nature, waded into the ocean to rinse off cups and plates for breakfast. But, after a few minutes, Tristan realized she hadn't returned. He called her name but there was no reply.

With a sinking feeling, he darted into the ocean and raced

to where she had been. *No!* He dove in and out of the water, frantically searching. *No!* Then he found her. *No! No! No! This is not happening.* A large bite was taken out of the right side of her neck and shoulder. Her carcass was simply cast aside after the thrill of the kill subsided.

Tristan gently scooped her up in his arms. He carried her body across the sand and laid her on the blanket near the bonfire, where their scrambled eggs were now charred.

Gazing down at Julianna, from the left side, it looked like she was simply sleeping. But the right side showed the ugly, bloody truth.

Tristan, distraught over the death of his wife and furious she had been discarded so callously, sprinted back to the ocean. Within 10 minutes, he sniffed out the vampire shark who killed Julianna. It was the first time since the night of his transformation that Tristan killed a shark. In his shark form, he used his serrated teeth to shake and shred the graysuit until there was nothing left but small piles of mealy flesh.

On the swim back to shore, Tristan began to formulate the Rules. He made it his life's mission to seek out rogue vampire sharks—those who indiscriminately killed innocent humans— and eliminate them. One by one.

Tristan knew this wouldn't bring back Julianna. But vengeance, particularly in the guise of a noble cause, can be profoundly satisfying. Each righteous kill helped to fill a little bit of the gaping hole in his heart. And each made him feel more powerful, which for Tristan, was an addictive feeling.

44 – Lighter

Tristan offered his hand to help Leilani out of the SUV and continued to hold her hand as he walked her to her front door.

"Thank you, Leilani. I haven't talked about Julianna in a while. It's good to get it out there sometimes, you know?" He stared into her eyes again. *This woman's eyes are so incredibly blue.*

"Yeah," Lani held Tristan's gaze. *This guy has the most hypnotic eyes. They're magnetic. I can feel them pulling me toward him.*

"I'd like to see you again. Would you like to come over for dinner tomorrow night?"

"You mean with everyone?"

"No. Just the two of us," Tristan said.

"Yeah. I'd like that."

"Come over around 6?"

"Okay." Lani turned to go inside.

Tristan continued to hold her hand, gently pulling her back. Lani turned to him. He reached up and grazed her neck with his fingertips, just below her jawline, and leaned down. He felt Lani's pulse quicken. He softly kissed her lips and pulled away.

"See you tomorrow," he whispered.

Tristan strolled back to his car, feeling lighter than he'd felt in 40 years.

45 – Scrambled

Lani unlocked her door, walked in and collapsed on the couch. She felt scrambled inside, like she just drank a Red Bull and vodka, or a coffee stout. Her mind and body zoomed in opposite directions. Half of her felt up, excited, soaring. The other half was weighted, heavy, confused.

Lani had never done deep undercover work as an FBI agent. Never wanted to. Some people could bifurcate their brains—live one life on the outside and another on the inside. She was not one of those people.

The deeper she got into her investigation, her friendship with Jake, and her relationship with Tristan, the more she began to doubt herself and wish she'd never become involved.

Why am I doing this? It's not my job. The FBI doesn't think there's a case here. A series of shark attacks, a few deaths, a few missing surfers. No evidence of any crime anywhere. That whole thing with the surfboard at Tristan's house went nowhere. And something terrible happened at the sheriff's station. I can see it in Tristan's face. That's partly my fault for phoning in that stupid tip.

But what about Jake? He thinks there might be something, too. There's a shark attack. The Nomads know the guy who was the last one with Cody. But what's missing?

Lani again reviewed her files. She drew a timeline, listing each attack or disappearance. She then plotted the Nomads' travel, obtained through a variety of documents, including hotel bills, lease agreements, credit card and ATM receipts, and utility and phone bills, among other things.

In all but two attacks—one of those being Cody's and one in Santa Cruz earlier this year—it looks like the Nomads turn up within the first 48 hours after the shark attack occurs, she deduced. *So that means, in most of these cases, there's no way they could be involved, right? But why would they be there afterward? Maybe they're shark chasers, like those crazy people who chase tornadoes. Is there such a thing as shark chasers? Is it an adrenaline junkie thing to surf where sharks have been known to attack?*

Lani flicked on her computer, opened a search engine and entered "shark attacks + North America." Scrolling through the search results, she confirmed that shark attacks had been increasing all over the West Coast, with most in California and Hawaii.

Why are shark attacks rising? Why do the Nomads always turn up in these areas, sometimes before but usually after the attacks? What does Tristan have to do with this? Why do I find it so hard to stay focused when I'm around him? Why does he have to be so good-looking? When he said, "I haven't met the right person. Yet," what did he mean?

No. No way. I cannot be falling for this guy. Come on, a surf bum? Seriously? I've spent my entire adult life trying to get away from that. Granted, he's smart. He's charming. He's charismatic. He's gorgeous beyond words. He has a nice car, despite the diner smell, and he lives in a nice house by the beach. That means he's probably had some kind of professional success, so he's definitely not like my parents. But his life is surfing, chasing waves. What kind of life is that for an adult?

46 – Half the Truth

Tristan got home from his date with Leilani just after midnight. He decided to go for a swim to clear his head.

He strolled toward the beach and ran into Jake, who walked up with his board. "Jake, what's up, man? You surfing alone?"

"Hey, Tristan. Yeah, I felt like I needed to get wet, clear my head."

"Yeah, me too. You should've called me. It can be dangerous surfing alone at night."

"I know. I couldn't sit at home though. I feel better in the water. I just needed to catch a couple waves, mellow out."

"I know exactly what you mean. Hey, can I talk to you about something?" Tristan asked.

"Yeah. Let me get changed and I'll meet you back here."

Jake ambled over to his truck and placed his board in the back. He wrapped a towel around his waist, tucking one end to keep it in place. He pulled off his wet trunks and flung them into the truck bed. He stepped into a dry pair of shorts, pulled them up, and tossed the soggy towel on top of his trunks. He put on a t-shirt and flip flops, and walked back down to Tristan.

Jake squinted, "Man, that moon is bright tonight."

"That's why I have these." Tristan pulled out a pair of sunglasses.

"Sunglasses at night? Isn't that like an '80s song?" Jake smirked.

"Yeah. But give 'em a try. On a night like this they're kind of nice."

Jake slid on the sunglasses, looked up and down the beach, and then out at the water. The light gray tint made the sand and sea foam appear a radiant bluish-white in the moonlight. "Whoa, that's pretty cool. Everything looks normal, like I don't even have sunglasses on, but better." He took off the sunglasses and inspected them. "Is it like a polarizing filter or something?"

"Something like that," Tristan answered.

"Cool. Where can I get a pair of these?"

"I know the guy who invented these and bought stock in the company a while ago. I've got a bunch at home. Investing in my investment, so to speak. You can keep these."

"No, that's okay." Jake handed the sunglasses back to Tristan.

"No. Keep 'em. Seriously. I've got five pairs at home." Tristan wanted Jake to see his eyes when he said what he was about to say. He hoped Jake would see he was being sincere and then let the matter drop.

"Jake, I need to tell you something. The other night when you asked about your friend and that guy, Rick, who was out there with him, I wasn't entirely honest with you."

"What do you mean?"

"I knew Rick better than I let on," Tristan admitted.

Jake's face dropped.

"He wasn't like my best friend or anything like that," Tristan quickly added. "I hadn't known him very long. I surfed with him and thought he was cool at first. But he turned out to be a beach leech. You know the type. 'Can I borrow a board? I didn't bring mine. Can I use some wax? I forgot mine. Can I steal one of your beers? I didn't pack any.' So annoying."

"I don't get it," Jake said. "Why did you pretend not to know him at first?"

"I dunno. I felt bad for you. It was obvious you were in a lot of pain and it felt weird to say I knew the guy who you said was the last one to see your friend alive."

"Do you know what happened? Do you know where he is?" Jake asked. "No one's seen him since Cody died. They say he probably got killed by the same shark that took out Cody but I don't know."

"I wish I could tell you more." It was the truth. Tristan wished he could tell Jake everything. But he couldn't. The Nomads had a pact to never share their secret with a human unless that human was going to join their tribe.

"When I passed Rick in the water, he seemed like he was headed to Cody on purpose, like he wanted to confront him about something. I can't explain it but I got a bad vibe off him," Jake explained. "Do you know why he would've wanted to talk to Cody?"

"Do you think he knew Cody?" Tristan asked.

"No, I don't think so."

"Maybe it was a case of mistaken identity," Tristan suggested. "Maybe he thought he knew Cody, but actually had him mixed up with someone else."

"Hmmm, I never thought about that." The wheels turned in Jake's mind as he tried to piece together what happened using Tristan's theory. "Now that you mention it, Cody did look a lot like one of the Reefers—the worst one, in my opinion. They even had the same hideous pink trunks. I wonder if Rick thought that's who he was approaching."

"Could be. Rick was one of those guys who was always going off half-cocked and getting himself into trouble. Who needs to be around that?"

"Yeah. Like those Reefer dudes. Speaking of them, I haven't seen them in a while. You?"

"Nope. They seem to have disappeared." Tristan was unable to hide the satisfaction in his voice.

"Good riddance. I'm glad those guys are gone."

"Me too, Jake. Me too."

47 – Admissions and Omissions

Saturday afternoon Jake awoke to his phone ringing.

"Hi Jake. It's Skylar."

Jake pulled the phone away from his ear and looked at it in astonishment. *Skylar is calling me? Play it cool, man.*

"Skylar. What's up, dude?" He grimaced. *Too cool. Skylar is most definitely not a dude.*

"Uh, not much, dude. What are you doing tonight? I'm making lasagna and I'm not going to be able to eat it all by myself. I thought you might like to come over. Maybe get in some surfing later?"

Hell yeah! "Yeah, that sounds good. What time?"

"6 o'clock. My place. I live a few houses down from Tristan. I'll send you the address."

"Okay. See you soon."

Four hours later Jake was at Skylar's door.

"Jake, great to see you! Come in." Skylar wore white shorts and a peach tank top with a nearly transparent long sleeve peach blouse over it. Her bronze skin glowed beneath the sheer fabric.

This woman is so hot. Jake tried to think of something to say. *Compliment her.* "You look great."

"Thanks. You do, too."

Jake smiled and then realized he was wearing the same outfit he wore to dinner with Leilani. *Real original. At least it's clean.*

Searching for something else to say, he noticed Skylar's white shorts and said, "I was watching TV earlier. Some entertainment show came on and this fashion guy said to never wear white after Labor Day. Why is that?"

"Who cares? You should know, Jake, I don't play by other people's rules," Skylar said with a glint in her eye.

"That's cool. Rules are for people who don't know how to

do things on their own. Happens all the time. Someone goes too far and then someone else has to make a rule to prevent other people from crossing that line. They ruin it for everyone."

"Who? The people who go too far or the people who make the rules?"

"Both. Like the people who bring their dogs to the beach without a leash. It's fine if the dogs are well-behaved and listen to their owners. But you've always got someone who brings his dog there and then it attacks another dog or a kid or something. Then they create a leash law and say everyone has to leash their dogs. Then someone else brings their dog on a leash but they let it go chase some endangered birds or something. Then there are no dogs allowed on the beach anymore. Sucks for everyone."

"You're right. Hey, is that for me?" Skylar pointed to the bottle of Zinfandel in his hand.

"Yep." He handed it to her.

"Paso Robles. Nice! You're obviously a man of taste. Paso Zins are the best."

"Yeah. That and the guy at the store said it would go great with lasagna."

"Thanks, that's sweet."

"Here, let me open that for you." Jake opened the bottle while Skylar pulled two glasses from the cupboard.

"Well, I got most of the cork out," he laughed, as he poured the wine. "So what do you do, Skylar? For work?"

"Nothing."

"Nothing? That must be nice."

"I guess," she said. "I got a big inheritance from my parents. I pretty much live off the interest, travel, surf."

"Did your parents …"

"Die? Yeah. They got killed in a car crash by a drunk driver. I got a big settlement from the driver and a big payout from my parents' life insurance."

"Wow, that sucks. I mean about the drunk driver and stuff. How old were you?" Jake asked.

"Seventeen. It was ages ago. So tell me about you. What about your family?"

"My parents are gone, too. When I was in college, my mom died of cancer. My dad died less than a year later. They say you can't die of a broken heart but it's not true. I think that's what killed my dad. He never recovered after losing my mom. So, my friend, Cody, was kind of like the only family I had."

Skylar gave Jake a hug. "I'm sorry." As she pulled away, she asked, "So Tristan said he talked to you about Rick?" She then peeked inside the oven at the bubbling lasagna to avoid making eye contact with him.

"Yeah."

"I'm sorry we didn't tell you we knew him when you first asked. He turned out to be kind of a jerk."

"Yeah, that's what Tristan said." Jake decided to see if Skylar could help him with his latest theory. "Hey, when Tristan and I were talking, I started thinking maybe Rick got Cody mixed up with someone else? Because when I saw him, he seemed like he wanted to confront Cody about something. So I was thinking, one of the Reefers looked a lot like Cody. They both had blond hair and wore these bright pink trunks. Do you know if Rick had something against one of the Reefers?"

"I wish I could say." Skylar slipped on fluffy orange terrycloth gloves and removed the lasagna from the oven. She smiled seductively at Jake. "Forget about Rick. I'd rather talk about you. You're the one I'm interested in."

Over dinner, Skylar asked Jake about his favorites—movie, band, TV show, book, video game. They talked and ate lasagna and talked some more.

48 – Reality vs. Reality

Down the street, Tristan and Lani shared a similar evening of good food and conversation. They settled on the sofa after dinner and continued talking.

"Favorite movie?" Lani asked.

"That's tough. There are so many over the years. I guess I like the ones that keep you guessing—where you're looking through the eyes of the main character but you're not sure what's real and what's not. The guy is there, living his life and interacting with people, but he's in a separate reality."

"I don't know what you mean. Give me some examples."

"Well, let's look at movies from your lifetime," Tristan smiled. "Donnie Darko. Vanilla Sky. Inception. You have these fascinating characters who, in a moment, make what turns out to be a life-or-death decision—and they can't take it back, no matter how much they regret it. They try to shape their reality into a different experience but it all comes back to paying the consequences for that decision."

"Wow. That's pretty heavy."

"Yeah. Huh. I guess I've never really thought about it in those terms until now." He paused. *Gee, Tristan, could you be any more obvious?* he asked himself. *See any parallels to your own life there, buddy?* "Anyway, they're really cool movies. You should check 'em out. What's your favorite?"

"Let's just say I like it lighter."

"Like what?"

"I'm embarrassed to say now."

"Don't be embarrassed." He playfully brushed her shoulder with his hand. "What?"

"I like those John Hughes movies from the '80s," she said.

"What? Sixteen Candles? Breakfast Club?"

"Exactly!"

"Oh man," Tristan laughed.

"Hey, there were some pretty heavy themes in Breakfast Club. Bullying, suicide, child abuse, sex, drugs, and let's not forget months and months of detention."

"You're absolutely right," Tristan said. "My apologies for dissing such an important contribution to American cinema." He leaned in and softly kissed Leilani on the lips.

Lani's mind raced. *Which reality am I living in? Am I Leilani Waters or Lani Marley? Surfer/interior designer or undercover FBI agent? Am I going to have to pay the consequences for my deception? And what about Tristan? What's his reality? Surfer/day trader? Shark chaser/adrenaline junkie? Innocent bystander with really bad timing? Something else?*

Tristan leaned back slightly. "You okay?" He could sense Leilani's heart beating a mile a minute, like she was anxious about something ... or maybe excited. He hoped it was the latter.

"Yeah, I'm fine," Lani replied. *Who cares? We all have secrets,* she reassured herself, *and they always come out. It's just a matter of when. I've spent years punishing myself, depriving myself of fun, for no reason. Maybe it's time to live a little.*

"Better than fine, actually," she murmured. "Now where were we?"

After a half-hour, Tristan pulled away again. "Let's surf," he whispered.

"What?" Lani asked.

"Let's surf. It's a beautiful night." He rose from the couch. "I'm going upstairs to get changed. You can find a suit and towel in the bathroom cupboard. Meet you back down here in a minute."

"Uh, okay," Lani sputtered, perplexed as to why Tristan would end their make-out session for a surf session.

Tristan walked upstairs, smiling to himself. *Sometimes it's good to leave them wanting more. Julianna taught me that. Then, of course, once you finally do get them into bed, leave them wanting for nothing.* He stopped in his tracks. *Julianna.* For the first time, it didn't cause him pain to say her name. Tristan felt relief.

He smiled as he folded his clothes and neatly placed them on a chair. He quickly applied unscented sunscreen to shield his skin from the light of the nearly full moon and pulled on his black boardshorts.

Downstairs Leilani opened the bathroom cupboard and spotted a new wetsuit in her size. *Did Tristan have this lying around? Or did he get this for me?*

When she emerged from the bathroom, Tristan was waiting. "Does it fit okay?" he asked.

"Perfect," she said.

"Great! Let's go. I've got two boards outside for us." He draped his arm over her shoulder and guided her toward the back door.

Lani sniffed. *Sunscreen. I don't remember smelling that earlier. Maybe it's soaked into his trunks?* She had plenty of shorts and t-shirts that reeked of sunscreen, no matter how long she soaked them or how many times she ran them through the washer. *Wow. That's really strong though. He wouldn't put on sunscreen to surf at night. Would he? That'd be weird.*

49 – An Unexpected Encounter

Tristan and Lani slipped through the back gate and climbed down a hidden path carved into the bluff. They strolled to the ocean hand in hand. Silver flecks of sand sparkled beneath their feet. They planted their boards in the sand and watched the waves.

Tristan pulled Leilani to him and kissed her. "You ready?"

"Yep."

They dropped their towels and marched to the water. Tristan heard something in the distance and stopped in his tracks.

"What?" Lani asked.

He raised his nose in the ocean breeze. *Skylar and Jake.*

"I heard someone. I think it's Skylar," he said. "Let's go see."

They paddled toward two dark figures silhouetted against the moonlit sky.

Lani expected to see Skylar but was surprised to see Jake with her. "Jake, what are you doing here?" she asked before she could stop herself.

"Skylar invited me surfing," he quickly answered. "You?"

"Tristan … surfing," she stammered.

"Great!" Jake was relieved Leilani was with Tristan and not upset with him for being out with Skylar.

Lani was relieved, too, though she wasn't sure she liked Jake with Skylar. *I can't say I really know her but I don't trust her. And Jake seems too nice for her somehow.*

While they all exchanged pleasantries, Skylar glared at Leilani. She then glanced at Tristan but his gaze was focused on Leilani. Skylar sighed and turned to Jake. "Let's ride," she said, leaning over to stroke the back of his neck.

Jake, embarrassed, looked up at Tristan and Leilani. Tristan looked amused; Leilani, confused.

Jake and Skylar paddled into position, ready for the next set.

"You okay, Leilani? You look a little out of it," Tristan said.

"Yeah, fine. I'm surprised to see Jake here. I didn't know he and Skylar were … dating," Lani said.

"You're not jealous, are you?" he teased.

"No! Don't be silly. He just didn't say anything to me."

"Did you say anything to him about us?"

"No," she admitted.

"Now we all know everything, right? So we're cool?"

"We're cool," Lani echoed, still unsure.

Tristan waved his arm toward a growing wave. "That one has your name on it."

After admiring Leilani's skills once again and catching several waves of his own, Tristan jumped off his board. He loved the feel of the cool salt water on his body. Since his detainment at the sheriff's station, he felt the need to go in the ocean every day. It nourished and soothed his skin, which still felt hot and itchy like a sunburn, but at a cellular level, beneath the surface.

Tristan dove underwater, feeling grateful Skylar seemed happy with Jake and feeling upbeat about how things were going with Leilani. When he surfaced, a familiar smell punctured his bliss. Knowing smells travel faster through air than water, he wondered how much time he had to get everyone out of the ocean.

He climbed on his board and glanced around to see where Skylar was. He tilted his head down toward his chest and said, "Sky. Graysuits." He knew Skylar would be able to hear him but Jake and Leilani wouldn't.

Skylar looked over at Tristan in alarm. She knew she and Tristan could take on rogue vampire sharks by themselves if necessary, but with two humans, things could get messy.

Tristan ran his hands over the top of his head and closed

his eyes, thinking of a reason to quickly get everyone out of the water, just in case the vampire sharks were indeed hungry Rogues.

Lani paddled over to him. "What's wrong?"

Tristan decided to play it casual. "Nothing. But I think I'm done for the night. Let's head in."

"But it's only been like an hour. I thought you wanted to surf," Lani said, confused again.

"Yeah, I did but I'm good now. I think it's blowing out anyway." Tristan forced a smile. "If we go in, maybe we can pick up where we left off?"

Lani had heard the expression "smoldering eyes" but never fully grasped the meaning before Tristan. *His eyes really do smolder. Maybe we should go back to his place*, she thought.

"Okay, we can go. But we're not coming out here again later if you get the sudden urge," she teased.

"Understood. Looks like Jake and Skylar are going in, too." Tristan tried to appear upbeat, but something about his expression worried Lani.

A couple seconds after they all started to paddle toward shore a shrill voice called out from the west. "Tristan?!"

Tristan turned around. He recognized the voice. *This is bad on so many levels*, he anguished.

"Tristan! It is you!" the high-pitched female voice exclaimed.

Lani looked toward where the voice was coming from but couldn't see much.

"Leilani, go to shore now, okay?" Tristan whispered hurriedly. "Pick up Jake on your way in and go."

"Why? Who is that?" Lani hated being told what to do, especially without knowing why.

"Someone I knew once. Let's just say she's not a nice person. Go now. I'll explain everything later. Please, do this for me," he begged.

Seeing his concern, Lani relented. "Fine. But you *will* explain later."

Before Lani could begin moving toward shore, a woman on a surfboard swooped in front of her. "Hey, blondie, where ya goin'?"

Skylar heard this and turned back toward Tristan and Leilani. She had a feeling the situation was about to take a dangerous turn. Admittedly, she didn't care much for Leilani, but she did care for Tristan. And Jake.

Seeing Skylar turn around, Jake followed. "Hey, who's that woman?" he asked.

"I don't know," Skylar replied.

Lani stared at the woman with sandy-blond hair blocking her path. "I was just heading in," Lani said curtly. "Now if you'll excuse me …"

"You're not going anywhere," the woman said.

"Lisa, relax. I'll stay and talk with you but my friends are going in." Tristan gave Skylar a quick nod to make sure she understood he wanted everyone to get to shore as fast as possible.

"You don't get to make the rules anymore, Tristan," Lisa argued.

Another woman on a surfboard emerged from the west and paddled next to Tristan. "Yeah, Tristan. Rules are so 20th century," said the bleached blond beauty as she reached up to stroke the side of Tristan's face. "How are you, T? It's been a while."

Tristan jerked his head away. "Erica," he said with displeasure, "hands to yourself, please."

50 – Old Flames

Perched on their boards, Tristan and Skylar exchanged a concerned glance as they appraised the two women.

Lisa was 22 years old, with long, wavy sandy-blond hair, blue eyes and a dusting of freckles across her nose and cheeks. Erica was 25, skinny, with large brown eyes and straight platinum blond hair that extended past her disproportionately large bosom.

Tristan met Lisa in 1973, after becoming a vampire shark. He met Erica a few months after that. He'd turned both women, separately, after surfing with them a bit, back in the days when he was careless about such things.

Tristan ran into Lisa again in 1997 in Santa Barbara. They spent a month together before Tristan decided to move on. Lisa wasn't happy he left.

In 1999, he bumped into Erica on the coast of Oregon. They had a torrid rainy weekend together before Tristan tired of her and headed north.

Tristan hoped he'd never see either woman again. Now, here they were, together. *This is so not good,* he thought.

"Listen, Erica, Lisa, I'd love to catch up but we're heading in. How about if I call you? We can arrange to get together another time," Tristan offered.

"As I recall, you're not great about calling a woman when you say you will," Erica chided.

"Yeah, Tristan, that's not one of your strong suits," added Lisa.

"Fine. We can talk now. But my friends are going in and then you can tell me what brings you to town," Tristan said calmly, trying to gain control of the situation.

"Not just yet." Lisa continued to position her board directly in front of Leilani's. "You know, Tristan, it's been a long time but you still look goooood." Lisa's eyes descended from Tristan's eyes, to his broad chest, and finally to where his black boardshorts disappeared into the ocean. She brought her eyes back up to his face. "A little older maybe, but still as foxy as ever."

"Lisa, stop," Tristan said.

"What? I'm trying to give you a compliment." Lisa's faux-friendly tone failed to mask the venom in her voice.

"We'll give you two minutes. Then we've gotta go. Why don't I start with introductions? Everyone, this is Lisa and Erica. I knew them a long, long time ago." Tristan could feel Leilani's and Skylar's eyes boring into him. "So, I take it you two are friends now?" he asked, looking from Lisa to Erica.

"Erica and I go way back. We met in nineteen-sev… well, years ago. There weren't many of us—girl surfers, I mean—back then. We sort of found each other. We went our separate ways but then ran into each other again in 2002. So we decided to meet up once a year in a tropical destination for a girls' weekend. You know, to do the man-eater thing," Lisa winked at Tristan. "Imagine our surprise when on one of our trips, over appletinis one night, we learned we had even more in common than a love of surfing. We both had a soft spot for a tall, dark, handsome surfer named Tristan."

Erica nodded at him and sighed. "I had such a crush on you, Tristan."

"Me, too! But then you left so suddenly," Lisa scowled at Tristan, "I didn't have time to give you a proper goodbye."

"You had relationships with these women?" Skylar asked.

"Not exactly," Tristan muttered, not wanting Leilani to hear any more.

Lani felt sick Tristan would have ever been involved with these two women, but she wondered why Skylar was the one acting like a jealous girlfriend. *If anyone here is annoyed, it should be me,* she thought.

Jake, fortunately, wasn't aware of the hurt tone in Skylar's voice. He was more concerned with why Tristan was acting like he was cornered. *Why don't we just leave? There are four of us and only two of them. We outnumber them. What's the big deal?* he wondered.

"I remember when I first met Tristan. He was so gorgeous and charming, I would've run away with him on the spot. But he didn't have eyes for anyone but his precious Julianna," Lisa said. "I don't think he's given a flying fig about anyone since her. It's just love 'em and leave 'em, right, Tristan?"

"Who's Julianna?" Skylar whispered.

"Later, Skylar," Tristan hissed.

"Skylar, of course! You're as gorgeous as they say. How 'bout we grab a bite to eat," Lisa nodded her head toward Leilani, "and talk?"

"Jake, why don't you and Leilani head to shore now?" Tristan urged, feeling the situation was about to go very wrong very quickly. "Skylar and I will be along in a minute."

"No way, man. I'm not leaving Skylar behind. I'm staying."

"Jake, please," Tristan said gruffly.

"Fine," Jake relented, "but if you and Skylar aren't right behind us, I'm coming back."

Lani wanted to leave but Lisa still blocked her path.

"Lisa, you obviously want something from me. These two are going in and then we can get on with it," Tristan said.

"Whatever." Lisa moved out of Leilani's way and curled her lips into a contemptuous smile. "Have a nice night."

Erica watched Jake and Leilani paddle away and catch a wave to speed their journey to shore. "It's a pity you sent away the male. He's cute." She licked her lips. "I could eat him up."

"Yeah, Tristan, a little hors d'oeuvre might be nice before

we start," Lisa glanced again toward Leilani.

"Lisa, enough. Why are you here?" Tristan demanded.

"Same as you. Tasty waves," Lisa smirked, her eyes lingering on Leilani.

This is going nowhere, Tristan groaned. *Maybe some charm will help.*

"Listen ladies, sorry but there will be no meal tonight. Those are our friends, which means they're off limits. We abide by the Rules. That's how we get to live out in the open, free, with no trouble from the authorities or anyone else. Now come on, why are you really here? I know it's not to see me. Surely, two women as beautiful as you can get any man you want."

Tristan waited for them to respond. Seeing they weren't about to tell him anything yet, he decided to see if he could extract some information from them. "Hey, while we're talking, do you know anything about that teenage boy who got killed off of Imperial Beach a couple months ago? It was pretty reckless."

Lisa and Erica put their hands on their hips and stared Tristan down.

"Just curious," he assured them.

"Right. Don't be such a choirboy, Tristan," Lisa said. "I liked it much better when you were a bad boy."

Erica giggled. "You really were more fun back then."

Tristan tried to keep his annoyance at bay. "That boy wasn't even 18 yet, you know."

"We didn't kill him if that's what you're asking," Lisa insisted. "And whoever did is probably long gone if they know you and your little surf clique are here. You know, there's a rumor going around that you and your buds killed a couple fin-fangs up in Santa Cruz earlier this year. Know anything about that?"

"It's none of your concern, Lisa. Is that all? Nice seeing you both," Tristan said as he turned to leave.

51 – Fist Fight

Jake stopped paddling and looked over his shoulder. He left Cody in the ocean, alone, to die. He was not going to leave Skylar and Tristan behind. "Leilani, I've gotta go back. Those women seem kinda wacked. You go on. Watch from shore and call the police if you see anything weird."

"No. I'm not leaving you guys." Lani, who was still irritated that Tristan asked her to leave, was now also annoyed that Jake would think she couldn't handle herself with those two women. *Besides, who do those women think they are—blocking people's paths, being all obnoxious and flirty? Why doesn't Tristan tell them to get lost?*

Jake and Lani turned to head back toward Skylar and Tristan.

As Tristan turned to paddle to shore, he was alarmed to see Leilani and Jake moving toward them. He glanced to his right to tell Skylar to get Jake and Leilani home, but she wasn't there.

Turning back toward Lisa and Erica, Tristan felt his stomach flip. Lisa held one of Skylar's arms behind her back, restraining her. Erica held a wooden stake above Skylar's heart. Fortunately, Erica's back was to Jake and Leilani, so they wouldn't be able to see the stake. And from such a long distance, it simply looked as if Lisa had one hand on Skylar's shoulder; they couldn't see her other hand wrenching Skylar's arm behind her.

"Tristan," Skylar whispered.

"Erica! Lisa!" Tristan shouted. "What the hell …"

"Your reign is over, Tristan," Lisa interrupted. "You and your little crew have gotten carried away with your Rules. And especially with what happens to those who break them. The consequence for each Rule is … gosh, what is it again, Erica?"

"Gee, Lisa, I can't remember. Let's ask Skylar. Skylar, what's the penalty for breaking Rules 1 and 2?" Erica asked.

"Better answer her," Lisa said. "She's the one holding the stake."

"Death," Skylar replied.

"Death. That's right," Lisa said, acting as if she just remembered.

"What do you want?!" Tristan demanded.

"Dump your Rules. Break up your little gang. Quit killing your own kind," Lisa said.

"I can't do that, Lisa. Not when others out there get careless and threaten to expose us—all of us. Not when they mindlessly kill and leave carcasses all over the place." Tristan knew he had to do something to free Skylar and get rid of Lisa and Erica before Jake and Leilani reached them. "I'm trying to protect our way of life and protect some innocent humans along the way, like my friends here. That's all."

"They're just humans. And no one's innocent. Take your place at the top of the food chain with the rest of us," Lisa said. "You're an apex predator. Act like one."

"Fine then." Tristan plunged into the ocean. The instant he submerged, he morphed. Erica tried to dive off her board but was too late. Tristan sank his jagged teeth into her calf, before she could transform, and dragged her down into the water. He opened his jaws and pulled both legs deeper into his mouth. Driving his teeth into Erica's thighs, he whipped her body back and forth, ripping through her femoral artery. Once she stopped struggling, he clamped his jaws, crushing her.

Seeing Erica get pulled underwater, Skylar tried to twist free from Lisa's grip.

"Let her go!" Jake yelled.

"Stay out of this!" Lisa wrenched Skylar's arm behind her.

Beneath the water's surface, Tristan, still carrying Erica in his mouth, rammed the underside of Skylar's board with his snout, sending Skylar and Lisa flying.

"What was that?" Lani asked nervously. She then noticed Tristan was missing. "Where's Tristan? Tristan!"

Lisa regained control mid-air and angled her body so she pointed toward Leilani as she plummeted to the ocean. Just before striking the water, Lisa reared back her arm and punched the side of Leilani's head, behind her ear. The force knocked Leilani out cold and threw her several feet underwater.

Jake tried to swim for Leilani. But before he could reach her, Lisa appeared and punched him in the face.

Skylar, who had splashed down a few feet away from Leilani's lifeless body, poked her head out of the water in time to see Lisa hit Jake. *Oh no you don't, surf skank. He's mine and you're dead.*

She grabbed Lisa's board and threw it deeper into the ocean as far as she could, and then did the same with Erica's. *They won't be needing these anymore.*

Skylar then submerged and transformed. At 15 feet long, she was 2 feet longer than Tristan. She snapped her brown caudal fin and hurtled toward Lisa, hoping to reach her before she, too, transformed. Too late. Skylar faced off with Lisa, vampire shark to vampire shark. While both were about the same size, Skylar was fueled by jealous rage—by the image of Lisa punching Jake and by the thought of her being with Tristan.

Skylar struck first. She gnashed at Lisa's snout, sinking her teeth into Lisa's speckled light gray flesh. Lisa thrashed her body from head to tail, struggling to break free, but Skylar refused to let go. Skylar had killed more than a few Rogues since joining Tristan. She knew how to do battle and walk away unscathed.

While Skylar dug her teeth deeper and deeper into Lisa's snout, Jake tried to get his bearings on the ocean's surface. Slowly, the blackness that obscured his vision subsided into thousands of tiny white specks. *I really am seeing stars*, he thought, still dazed from Lisa's blow. As his vision cleared, he swam toward his board and tried to focus. *Where is everyone?* He couldn't hear anything moving and couldn't see anything other than surfboards scattered about the ocean's surface.

Several feet below, Tristan finished disposing of Erica's body with a few final bites. He turned toward the surface and saw Leilani floating, face down. *Leilani!* Forgetting to morph back into his human body, Tristan raced toward her but stopped before reaching her when her eyes opened.

Floating, head-down in the water, Lani found herself face to face with a great white shark. Her blue eyes widened as she gazed at the shark's sleek brown-gray body and large dark eyes. *Those eyes. They seem so familiar*, she thought. But as soon as the thought crossed her mind, she realized she desperately needed air.

Lani lifted her head, gasping and choking. When she caught her breath, she plunged her head underwater again to look for the shark but it was gone. *That shark. Those eyes.* Lani remembered exactly how she felt as a teenager at Sunset Beach, when she was thrown into the coral reef and awoke to find herself facing a great white. *There's no way it can be the same shark. No way. But I swear it looks identical …*

Tristan's voice interrupted her thoughts. "Leilani!"

She spun around in the water. "Tristan!"

He grasped her face in his hands. "Are you okay? Are you hurt?"

"My head." Lani raised her hand to the side of her head. "Lisa punched me."

"I'm taking you in," Tristan said.

"Wait! I saw a shark. It was right here."

"He swam away. Where are Jake and Skylar?"

"Here," Skylar said as they approached. "Everything okay?"

"Yeah. You?" Tristan asked.

"Yeah," Skylar nodded.

"Where are Lisa and Erica?" Lani asked.

"Gone," Tristan said. "Let's go in and make sure no one is hurt."

Tristan got to shore first. He held his surfboard over his groin and then quickly wrapped his towel around his waist. He accidentally destroyed his boardshorts when he transformed and didn't want to have to explain why he was naked. He dropped his surfboard and went to meet Leilani as she stepped onto the dry sand. He handed her a towel. "Hang on. I'll be right back."

Tristan quickly located Jake's and Skylar's towels and ran down to the ocean. He held up Skylar's towel, so Jake and Leilani wouldn't see she was naked, too. Skylar wrapped it around herself. He then handed Jake his towel, so it wouldn't look suspicious that he was playing towel boy for Skylar.

As soon as they were all on the sand, Tristan gently placed his hands on Leilani's shoulders, ran them down her arms, and clasped her hands in his. "Are you sure you're okay? Are you hurt anywhere else?"

"No. Just my head. What about you? I looked for you and couldn't find you."

"I'm fine." He pulled her close and turned to Skylar and Jake. "Are you guys okay?"

"Other than getting punched in the face by a girl, I'm fine," Jake muttered.

"I think my arm's lightly sprained but it'll heal quickly," Skylar said, feeling a pang of jealously over the concern Tristan showered on Leilani. With her good arm, she reached for Jake, hoping to make Tristan feel a bit of the jealously she did. "Jake, are you sure you're fine?"

"Yeah. Does anyone need to see a doctor?" Jake asked.

"No! No doctors," Skylar and Tristan said simultaneously.

"Torrey is a doctor," Tristan added. "She can help."

"A doctor? Isn't she kind of young?" Jake asked.

"Yeah, but she's a doctor nonetheless. Our very own Doogie Howser, you might say. Let's go to my place and call her," Tristan said.

"But shouldn't we call the police and report those women?" Lani asked.

"Not right now." Tristan lightly kissed the top of her head. "Let's get you home first and make sure you're not hurt."

52 – Treating Injuries

As soon as Tristan opened his front door, he was barraged by Logan, Cruz and Torrey, who were waiting inside.

"Tristan, Rogues …" Logan paused when he saw Leilani following behind. "Rogue waves, man. It's crazy out there."

"I know," Tristan said. "You guys okay?"

"Yeah, man," Cruz replied. "You?"

"No, not really," Tristan said. "I ran into a couple old acquaintances in the water. Skylar, Jake and Leilani were with me."

Logan, Cruz and Torrey glanced at each other, curious as to what exactly Jake and Leilani saw.

"What happened?" Logan asked.

"We can talk about it in a little bit. First we need to make sure these guys aren't hurt." Tristan turned to Torrey. "Torrey, can you take a look at Leilani and Jake? They both got punched in the head pretty hard."

"And Skylar's arm might be sprained," Jake added.

Torrey wrinkled her brow. She'd never seen Skylar hurt.

Skylar shrugged. "I'm fine now, Jake." She moved her arm around to show she was healed. "See? Good as new."

"Okay, Jake, Leilani, you guys get dressed and then let Torrey look at you. You can use the bathroom down here to change. Skylar, why don't you use the bathroom upstairs to change back into your clothes? I'm going to talk to Logan and Cruz for a minute," Tristan said.

"How about if I come with you? I want to know what happened out there. Who were those women and why did they freak out like that?" Lani asked.

"I want to make sure you're okay first. You're the smallest one here so that punch hit you the hardest. Torrey can tell us if we need to take you to the hospital or not. If anything bad happened to you, I could never forgive myself. So, please, let Torrey help you and I'll be right back," Tristan said.

As much as Lani wanted to go, her throbbing head demanded her attention. "Okay but come right back."

"I will." Tristan let go of her hand for the first time since they left the beach. He led Logan and Cruz upstairs to the master bedroom. "What happened? What did you guys see?"

"Rogues, man. We were surfing north of here and we saw three. Two men, one woman," Cruz whispered.

"Did they come after you?" Tristan asked.

Cruz and Logan shook their heads.

"But when we walked past, they kind of glared at us and laughed. I couldn't make out what they said … It was something about rain," Logan said. "Then we came straight here. What happened with you? Why are they hurt?"

"We ran into two Rogues, Lisa and Erica. I knew them from a while back, before I met any of you. They're from up north. They know about Santa Cruz and made a point of mentioning it. Then they flipped out. They held a stake to Sky and things devolved from there. Sky and I took care of them, so at least they won't be coming back," Tristan explained.

"How much did Jake and Leilani see?" Cruz asked.

"Not enough to know anything but it was close. Too close," Tristan answered.

"Do you think those two, Lisa and Erica, were with the three we saw?" Logan asked. As the most recent addition to the Nomads, he didn't have nearly as much experience fighting Rogues as the others.

"Probably," Tristan surmised, "and that means there's going to be more trouble. I should get back to Leilani before she gets suspicious. I think it's best if Sky and I keep Leilani and Jake close tonight. Why don't you all hang out here? I've gotta give them a story about what happened, and it'd be good if we're all on the same page. We need to keep them from going to the cops. Then tomorrow morning after they go home, we'll have a meeting—all five of us. We need a plan. Whatever's going on, I think this is just the beginning."

53 – Exes

Tristan, Cruz and Logan returned to the kitchen and watched as Torrey examined Leilani and then Jake.

"Okay, the good news is you're both going to be fine," Torrey declared, looking at Leilani and Jake, who were still seated at the kitchen table. "You each have a minor blunt head injury—nothing serious. I really don't think we're looking at severe blunt head trauma but let's be cautious tonight. You're probably going to have some bruising. Apply ice for 20 to 30 minutes at a time and repeat as needed every two to four hours. But don't apply it directly to your skin. Wrap it in a washcloth or hand towel, okay? Or, even better, use a bag of frozen vegetables wrapped in cloth. It'll conform better to the shape of your head."

Torrey paused to make sure they understood and then continued. "Now, if you start vomiting or experience confusion, drowsiness, weakness or an inability to walk, or a severe headache, let me know immediately. Tristan, Skylar, I want you to stay with them and monitor their conditions tonight. You don't need to keep them awake. In fact, some sleep would do them good. But check on them periodically. If they can't be awakened or if it's really difficult to awaken them, call me. Does everyone understand?"

Leilani, Jake, Skylar and Tristan nodded.

"Good. Tristan, do you want us to go now?" Torrey asked.

Cruz walked up behind Torrey and wrapped his arms around her. "You're so awesome, babe." He then whispered, "Now that you're done being a doctor, maybe we can go play doctor, if you know what I mean."

"I know exactly what you mean," Torrey laughed. "And I think everyone else does, too, judging by the embarrassed looks on their faces."

"Actually, I'd like you all to stay for a few minutes so we can talk about what happened tonight," Tristan said. "Unless Leilani or Jake want to rest and we can talk tomorrow."

"No, I'd like to talk," Lani said, "if Jake's feeling up to it."

"Fine with me," Jake said.

"Okay, let's all go to the living room." Tristan pulled a bag of corn and a bag of blueberries from the freezer, and two clean dish towels from a kitchen drawer. He handed them to Leilani and Jake. "Here, put this on your head where you got hit."

Tristan grasped Leilani's hand and led her to the couch, which rested against the wall separating the living room from the kitchen. Jake sat next to Leilani, with Skylar on his other side.

Cruz settled on one end of the loveseat, situated across from the couch and under the front window. Torrey sat on the other end and placed her legs across Cruz's lap. Cruz draped his arms over her legs.

Logan sprawled on the floor and waited for Tristan to begin.

Tristan stood at the head of the room, under the large Big Sur photograph, and clasped his hands together. "Well, I'm not sure where to start, since we were all surprised by Lisa and Erica showing up out of the blue. I really don't know what to say. Maybe you guys should start with questions? Leilani?"

"Uh, okay." Lani's head pounded but she had to know what was going on. *That whole encounter was way too strange.* "I guess first I'd like to know, who were those women? They didn't seem like normal, sane people."

"Lisa and Erica. I don't remember their last names. I met them individually several years ago," Tristan began. "I ran into Lisa later in Santa Barbara. I ran into Erica a couple years after that in Oregon."

"Tristan, it kinda sounded like you did more than 'run into them' or is that what you call it?" Skylar asked, still angry he had kept so much of his past a secret from her.

"Skylar," Tristan said calmly, "that's uncalled for."

"Uncalled for? I don't think it is, seeing how we almost got killed tonight by your psychotic ex-girlfriends," Skylar said.

Torrey, Logan and Cruz all glanced at each other, like schoolkids do when a student mouths off to the teacher. They knew only Skylar could talk to Tristan like that without being immediately shut down.

"So, exactly how many other crazy exes do you have that we don't know about?" Skylar asked. "You know, Tristan, I'm seriously beginning to question your taste in women."

Lani turned toward the other end of the couch, wondering if Skylar meant her. Skylar did.

"Do you really wanna go there, Skylar? Because we can go there if you want," Tristan threatened. "How about if we regale Jake with tales of a couple of your recent ex-boyfriends? Like Xan and … who was the guy before him?"

"Hey, man," Jake interrupted, hoping to reel Skylar and Tristan back from the edge, "I really don't need to hear about that right now. Let's all mellow out and get back to what happened tonight."

"Yeah," Lani agreed. "Like, what were those women doing here? And why did they turn so violent?"

"I wish I could say." *I'm not lying*, Tristan told himself. *I wish I could tell you both but it's too dangerous.*

"My guess is they got together on one of their little vacations and learned they had both been with me, though at different times," Tristan clarified for Leilani's benefit. "Honestly, both relationships were so brief I wouldn't even call them relationships," he added for Skylar's benefit, too. "I don't think either one was pleased I ended it quickly or that I left town afterward. I had no idea they'd still be upset so many years later. Like I said, my best guess is, my name came up in conversation so they started talking trash about me and hatched the idea to confront me. I doubt they planned to hurt anyone but clearly they're both a little unhinged. Leilani, Jake, Skylar, I'm sorry you got caught in the middle of this. I don't know what else to say."

54 – And Exes

Skylar decided she couldn't wait another minute. She had to know. "Tristan, I'd like to ask something else, if that's okay?"

"Only if it's quick. We're all exhausted."

"Okay then. Who's Julianna? Lisa and Erica made it sound like she was someone important to you, but I've never heard you mention that name before," Skylar said.

Oh my god, Skylar, now? Really? I need to play this right. Leilani knows about Julianna so I have to be truthful, but Sky is not going to take this well. Tristan thought back to the night he turned Skylar—the night she mistakenly thought he asked her to marry him. *She is not going to take this well at all. But I guess I have no choice.*

"Yes, she was someone very important to me, who I knew a long time ago, way before I met you," Tristan began.

"But who was she?" Skylar pressed. "A girlfriend? A lover? What?"

"Julianna was …" Tristan paused. Even though he could now say Julianna's name out loud without feeling a painful, gaping hole in his heart, it still hurt to say what she was. "Julianna was … my wife."

"Your wife? Your *wife*! You're kidding, right?" Skylar was unable to comprehend the words "Tristan" and "wife" together, since he had so quickly and cruelly dismissed the thought of marrying her.

Torrey and Cruz exchanged a quick glance and shook their heads. They knew Skylar was going to blow.

"Yes, Skylar. My wife. I'm sorry I never said anything to you. It was too painful. I was married to her for only a short time, when I was much younger. She was killed. It hurt too much to talk about so that's why I never told you—any of you. Except

Leilani," he added quietly.

Skylar jumped off the couch and exploded at Tristan. "You told her and not me?! How long have you known me? 10 years! How long have you known her? 10 minutes? I thought you weren't the marrying kind. I thought you didn't know the meaning of the word 'commitment.' I also thought you didn't keep secrets from me or any of us for that matter. I feel like I don't even know you anymore."

Tristan reached for her shoulder, "Sky …"

Skylar twisted away. "Don't touch me. Ever! Jake, we're leaving." She stomped out the front door and slammed it shut behind her. It crashed into the doorframe with a thud rivaling a sonic boom.

Jake, embarrassed by Skylar's outburst, helplessly looked at Tristan and Leilani. He opened his mouth to say something but came up empty.

"It's okay. Go," Tristan said to Jake. "Keep her safe tonight. I know she's mad at me but don't let her go out and do anything stupid. And she should keep an eye on you to make sure you're okay."

Jake sighed, "I'll try." He left quietly through the front door.

Tristan clasped his hands together, "I think that's enough drama for one night." He released his hands and pushed them toward the front door. "Everybody out. Good night."

He walked to the door and opened it. Torrey, Cruz, Logan and Leilani followed him.

"Hey, Tristan," Torrey said softly as she reached up to hug him, "I'm so sorry for your loss. I had no idea about Julianna. If you ever want to talk about it, my door is always open."

"Thanks, Torrey."

"Yeah, we're here for you anytime," Cruz added. "If I ever lost Torrey, I don't think I could live. Seriously. I'm really sorry about Julianna, even though I never got to meet her."

"Yeah, Tristan, I'm really sorry, man," Logan echoed.

"Thank you." Tristan closed the door.

"I should be going, too," Lani said.

"When I said 'everybody out,' I didn't mean you. I need to watch you tonight to make sure you sleep and also that you wake up. Remember what Torrey said? Go upstairs and lie down in my room. It's the first door on the left. I'll bring you some aspirin and water. I don't think I could take it if something bad happened to you. Let me keep you safe, at least for tonight."

"But I have some more questions for you."

"I'm sure you do. But we'll talk more tomorrow, okay? You need to rest. Your head is pounding," Tristan said.

"How do you know?" Lani asked.

"I just know. Bed. Now."

55 – Plotting

Up the coast, three surfers, ages 21, 22 and 25, milled about the beach, wondering what was taking Lisa and Erica so long.

"We should've never let them go alone," said the younger male, Ryan.

"I know, but they insisted. What could we do? I think Lisa still has a thing for Tristan. Probably Erica, too," theorized Alissa, the 22-year-old. "He is scorching hot."

"Quiet, Alissa. You better never let Dean hear you talking like that. He'll kill you," said the older male, Lance.

Alissa smirked.

"You think I'm kidding?" Lance asked, annoyed. "Let's go. I don't think Lisa and Erica are coming back. We need to tell Dean. He's not going to be happy about this."

"But it's not our fault they went off by themselves," Ryan said. "Plus, Dean is the one who started this whole thing— sending that graysuit to kill that kid in Imperial Beach. That was bound to attract Tristan's attention."

"Yes, idiot. That's what he wanted," Lance said.

Minutes later they stood at the door to Dean's rented house in Carlsbad.

"Enter!" Dean yelled from a chair in the corner of the dark living room. "Well?"

"Lisa and Erica went to talk to Tristan. They never came back," Lance explained.

"Why didn't you go with them?" Dean demanded, his face and shoulders enshrouded in shadows.

"They wanted to talk to Tristan alone," Lance answered.

"Fools," Dean said dismissively.

Lance, Alissa and Ryan wondered if Dean was talking about Lisa and Erica—or them.

"What's next?" Lance asked.

"We're going to stick with the plan. First, I'll try to reason with Tristan and show him that what he's doing—killing his own kind, those who he created—is wrong," Dean explained.

"But what if he doesn't listen? We can't continue to have Tristan and his crew killing us off because we don't adhere to his personal code of conduct," Lance said.

Ryan nodded, "Yeah, why don't we just take him out?"

"Do I really need to explain this?" Dean glared at Ryan. "Tristan is the only one who can create more of us. If we kill him, that's the end of the bloodline. Our species will eventually die out. We need to convince Tristan to change—to go from killing us to making more of us so we can rule the sea and eventually the land, too."

"And if he refuses?" Lance asked.

"Then we'll need to find another way." Dean leaned forward in his chair, so the light from the street lamp outside glinted off his white fangs. "If we can find out how he got the power to create us and replicate it, we won't need him anymore."

56 – Insecurity

Back at Skylar's place, Jake sat at the kitchen table, pondering how to ask what he was about to ask without sending her into another rage. "Um, Skylar? Can I ask you a question?"

Skylar set aside her dark thoughts, which focused solely on Tristan, and stared at Jake. With his blackening eye and downcast expression, he looked forlorn and miserable. She instantly felt bad. "I'm sorry. I was someplace else. How's your eye? Does it hurt?"

"Nah, it doesn't hurt that bad. I think my ego is bruised more than anything. I got my ass kicked by a girl, in front of the girl I'm …" Jake stopped.

"You're what?" Skylar asked.

"I don't know. You seemed pretty upset about Tristan tonight. It seems like you guys have a history and maybe it wasn't all that long ago and maybe you're not over him."

"I'm sorry. I got caught up in the moment. It wasn't so much that he was with Lisa or Erica or," Skylar gulped, "Julianna. It was that he didn't tell me. He left out these huge parts of his life. It felt like I didn't know him anymore and I thought he was my best friend."

"It seemed like he was more than your best friend," Jake countered.

"You're right. He was."

"So what happened?" Jake asked, though he wasn't sure he wanted to know. *Why wouldn't Skylar still be in love with Tristan? He's taller than me. He's better-looking. He's stronger. He's a better surfer. He seems to be able to get any woman he wants. He …*

"We were together for a while and it was pretty intense," Skylar began, interrupting Jake's inner litany of insecurities.

"But he couldn't give me what I needed. He didn't want to make a commitment. I did. So we broke up. It was the same cycle over and over. We'd go back to being friends, start hanging out, having fun. Things would be great, we'd get back together, he'd pull away, we'd break up. Finally, we ended things. I dated some other guys but they didn't work out. It turned out they weren't the guys I thought they were. But you're different. That's why I like you."

Jake tried to smile, despite his self-doubts. "Did you love Tristan?" *Please say no, please say no,* he thought.

"Yes," Skylar answered.

"Do you still love him?" *Please say no, please say no.*

"Forget about Tristan. He no longer matters to me. I'd like to see what happens with us." Skylar gazed so intently into Jake's eyes, he felt physically connected to her. The sensation was so strong, in fact, he didn't realize that she didn't answer his question.

Seeing Jake wasn't going to press the issue, Skylar relaxed. "I'm really sorry about tonight. I totally overreacted. I acted like a jealous girlfriend and I'm not. I want to be with you. And if I'm going to be with you, you should know my faults."

Skylar reached for Jake's hand and held it in both of her hands on the kitchen table. "Number 1, I can be self-centered. Not necessarily selfish but sometimes I have a hard time seeing beyond myself and my own needs. It's not intentional. Maybe it's because I was an only child and a pretty spoiled one at that. I don't know. I'm working on it. But sometimes you may need to direct my attention to things other than myself. Number 2, I can be impetuous. It's sort of the dark side of being spontaneous, which I am, too, but that's usually pretty fun. Sometimes I make decisions on a whim that don't turn out so great. Again, I'm trying to be better but it's part of my nature. Bottom line, I think I just have a hard time with empathy a lot of the time.

So, if I'm being a tool, tell me, okay?"

"Okay," Jake agreed. "But then you should know some of my faults, too. Like I have a hard time telling people if something's bothering me. I'll usually let things fester, hoping they go away rather than create a conflict. But then, since things don't change, I get more and more resentful and distant, which makes things worse. Things usually have to be pretty bad for me to say something. So I guess if I were to tell you that you were being a tool, you'd be, like, a major tool," he joked.

"Ha ha, very funny," she smiled. "What else?"

"I avoid difficult situations, even if it hurts other people." Jake turned away from Skylar and looked down at his hand in hers. "Like since Cody died, all these friends have been emailing me and texting me and leaving me voicemails, asking if I'm okay, if I need anything, if I want to grab a meal or some waves. And I've been ignoring them because if I see them, I'll think of Cody. And that hurts too much. So I blow them off when they're only trying to be nice. I know I'm driving them away but I can't bring myself to talk with them because it's too hard."

Seeing Jake's face cloud over, Skylar decided to put an end to the conversation. "Enough talk. It's time to get you to bed. Doctor's orders." She pulled him to his feet and guided him to her bedroom. "And I know just the thing to make you feel better."

57 – Model Couple

In the morning, Jake felt much more confident about his relationship with Skylar. Lying naked in bed next to her, he decided to ask about the other Nomads. He wanted to make sure there were no ex-boyfriends, other than Tristan, in the bunch.

"So how did you meet Cruz, Torrey and Logan?" he asked nonchalantly.

"Jake, are you trying to ask if I've been with anyone else in the group? If you are, the answer is no. Tristan was the only one."

"That's a relief. So how did you meet them? You all seem pretty tight."

"I met Cruz and Torrey together, of course, because they're always together." Skylar rolled her eyes, feigning disgust. "I hit it off with them right away. They were so friendly and fun. And Tristan loved them instantly. We started hanging out, surfing, and along the way became great friends. They love to travel as much as we do, so we started traveling to different surf spots together. They're just genuinely nice people."

What Skylar didn't tell Jake was that she had an ulterior motive in inviting Torrey and Cruz into the Nomads. When Skylar first met them, it was five years after Tristan turned her—and failed to ask for her hand in marriage. After spending a few evenings with the happily married couple, she thought they would be a good influence on Tristan. *Maybe they can show Tristan what I've been unable to. Maybe they can show him you can be married and insanely happy. Maybe they will plant the idea in his head that marriage is a cool thing. Maybe all he needs is a first-hand view into a successful marriage, with people who are a lot like us.*

After a week, Skylar told Tristan she met a really cool couple and he should come surfing with them. To Skylar's delight, Tristan immediately liked Torrey and Cruz.

Upon meeting the couple, Tristan enjoyed that Torrey only had eyes for Cruz. That meant there would be no conflicts with Skylar and no uncomfortable situations down the road. Tristan also liked that the couple was so easygoing. *It's so simple with them*, he thought. *There's no drama in their relationship, no possessiveness, no demands like there are with Sky. Maybe they'll be a good influence on her.*

The more Tristan hung out with Torrey and Cruz, the more he hoped the couple's passion-filled but drama-free lifestyle would rub off on Skylar. So, after a few months, when Skylar suggested turning them, Tristan said yes.

Skylar soon discovered, however, that having Torrey and Cruz around did nothing to encourage Tristan to get any closer to proposing, or even thinking about, marriage.

"Cruz and Torrey turned out to be great friends. Family, really," she told Jake.

58 – Boy Toy

"And what about Logan?" Jake asked.

"Logan's another story," she said. "Tristan met him surfing about six months ago. I remember Tristan telling me he met the funniest guy. He said Logan wasn't a particularly skilled surfer but his enthusiasm more than made up for his lack of natural-born talent. After a couple weeks, Tristan invited me to come out with them. I think Logan had a little crush on me at first."

Skylar didn't mention to Jake that she hoped Logan's crush would once again show Tristan how desirable she was and that he was crazy not to want to be with her. She wondered if it would make Tristan jealous if she asked him to invite this much younger and quite stunning male into the group. But after a few evenings hanging out with Tristan and Logan, Skylar changed her mind. She was so overtaken with Logan's boyish charm she decided she couldn't use him to get a rise, literally or figuratively, out of Tristan.

"But Logan got over me quickly when he saw I wasn't interested," she continued. "Now he's like a little brother. The great thing about Logan is nothing gets him down. Nothing! He has this incredible zest for life that's completely contagious. You know when you hang out with him you're going to have a good time and laugh a lot. He literally loves everything."

Jake leaned back and regarded Skylar as she smiled and spoke. *She is so hot. I am one lucky dude.*

59 – Lunch Plans

Shortly before 11 a.m., Tristan called Skylar's house. "Hey, how about if you and Jake swing by? Then we'll have our meeting after that."

"How do you know Jake is still here?" Skylar asked.

"Right," Tristan smirked. "So are you coming over?"

"We'll be there in a couple minutes." Skylar hung up and turned to Jake. "That was Tristan. He wants us to swing by his place."

"Okay," Jake said, feeling more confident about seeing Tristan now that he knew how Skylar felt about him.

Skylar and Jake walked down the shady, tree-lined street and entered Tristan's open front door. Skylar wasn't surprised to see Leilani there, but wasn't happy about it either.

"Jake! Nice black eye. How does it feel?" Tristan asked.

"Not too bad," Jake replied.

"Good. I was thinking, why don't you and Leilani hang out today? You can keep an eye on each other—make sure you don't start vomiting or walking funny or any of those other things Torrey mentioned," Tristan joked. Seeing Jake and Leilani's hesitation, he added, "It would make me feel a lot better. I'm sure Skylar would feel better, too."

"Uh, yeah. If it's okay with Leilani," Jake said.

"Sure," Lani agreed, though she didn't understand why Tristan was being so overprotective. "Why not?"

Skylar was about to say why the hell not, but stopped herself.

"So what are you guys doing today?" Lani asked.

"We're going to call a few old friends and see if they can shed any light on that whole Lisa and Erica thing, and why they turned up here out of the blue," Tristan explained.

"Oh." Lani wondered who exactly these "old friends" were

and how many were female.

"Leilani, how about if I get some take-out and meet you at your place?" Jake offered. "Or I can drive you home and we can pick something up on the way?"

"I'm fine to drive. Why don't you meet me at my house in an hour?" *This could be good,* Lani thought. *Maybe I can ask Jake if he's learned more about Rick or anything else. And I can get in a call to Garrison in the meantime.*

60 – Important Men

Back at home, Lani showered and dressed. She had at least 30 minutes before Jake was scheduled to arrive. *That should leave more than enough time for a call to Garrison,* she thought as she dialed his extension.

"Detective Garrison? Leilani … I mean, Lani Marley, FBI. We spoke at the beach the night of Cody Hansen's death. Do you remember?"

"Yeah," Garrison said. "You're the little pixie agent. What can I do for you?"

Patronizing as ever. Keep it together, Marley. The witness is hostile, not you. Question him nicely. He's a very important man, Lani chuckled to herself.

While training at the FBI Academy, Lani learned a trick from a senior female agent who told her, *"Men love to hear how busy and important they are. Whatever you can do to boost their egos and reaffirm their importance only helps you. Because then they feel the need to show you how important they are and divulge things they wouldn't ordinarily share. The bigger the ego, the bigger the mouth."*

"Thank you for taking my call, Detective," Lani began. "I'd like to ask you a couple questions. But I'm sure you're incredibly busy so I'll keep it brief. I know how important your time is."

"Yeah?" Garrison waited for her to continue.

"I'd like to mention up front that I'm not asking these questions on behalf of the Bureau. I'm actually on vacation. And I'm sure you have things extremely well covered and wouldn't need help from the Bureau anyway, right? So, the reason I'm calling is that the disappearance of that surfer, Rick Jennings, looks a lot like another case I'm working. I was wondering if you've learned anything new? I thought it might spark something with my case as well."

Of course, Garrison thought. *She can't solve her own case so now she's asking about mine. Typical.* "We have a few leads we're working. Nothing solid yet but we're getting close. I wouldn't want to jeopardize the investigation by divulging something too soon."

That means he has nothing, Lani knew. "That's understandable. What about anything else recently? Any violence or fights at local beaches, involving men or women?"

"Nothing out of the ordinary. Is there something I should know?"

"Nope. One more question, if that's okay. Have there been any other shark attacks or disappearances since the night Cody Hansen was attacked and Rick Jennings disappeared?"

"Hold on." Garrison flipped through a pile of folders on his desk. "Here it is. Yeah, two weeks ago five surfers went missing. They called themselves the Del Norte Reefers. One of their lowlife girlfriends called and said they never came home from surfing. I can't say I'm surprised. Those guys caused so much trouble it was only a matter of time before they crossed the wrong person and got what was coming to them."

"When's the last time they were seen?" Lani asked.

"Two weeks ago tonight. But I wouldn't worry about those scumbags. They've been in and out of jail since they were kids. Started with small stuff like stealing, drinking in public, drug possession. Then they got into more serious crimes—assault, battery, rape. But we've never been able to nail 'em for anything big. We've had more than a few reports of them getting violent with other surfers and people at the beach. But whenever someone files a report, they end up dropping the charges. Witnesses recant or refuse to testify. I'd say whoever took those guys out did the good people of North County a huge favor."

Lani sighed to herself. *Great. Police-sanctioned vigilantism. This guy is quite possibly the worst detective I've ever met.*

"Do these Del Norte Reefers have names?"

"Yeah, I can get 'em for you. Del Norte Reefers," he said derisively. "More like Teflon Reefers seeing as how we could never get any charges to stick to 'em. Looks like now they're the Dead-and-Gone Reefers."

"Thank you, Detective. I'd appreciate it. May I ask about one more thing, if it's not too much trouble?"

"Yeah, if it's quick," Garrison said. "I'm very busy."

And important, Lani joked to herself. "I'll make it fast. I heard you brought Tristan Pierce in for questioning last week in connection with the Jennings case. What made you bring him in?"

"We got a couple anonymous tips. A woman called in and said she saw Jennings' surfboard at Pierce's house. Around the same time, a man called in and said he saw Pierce with Jennings the day before he disappeared and that we could find Jennings' surfboard in a locked bedroom in his house."

"And what did you find?"

"Nothing that stuck. Apparently Pierce and Jennings were acquaintances. We did find a surfboard in Pierce's house that looked like Jennings' but we checked it out and found out it wasn't unique. There's a bunch of 'em that look exactly like that."

"And there's nothing else linking Pierce to Jennings?" Lani asked.

"No."

"Did anything unusual happen when Pierce was in custody? I heard he was detained for 48 hours and left the station a little worse for the wear."

"You hear a lot, don't 'cha? He was disrespectful so he was taught some manners," Garrison replied. "Are we done here?"

"Yes. Thank you for your time."

Lani groaned. *Tristan doesn't seem traumatized by whatever happened with Garrison. But he looks different, so I know it was something terrible. I guess I'll add that to the list of things that puzzle me about Tristan. Tall, dark, handsome, mysterious Tristan. You know, the mysterious part isn't all it's cracked up to be. I'd rather have him be like Jake in that respect. Jake is an open book. You can read Jake. With Tristan, several chapters are missing and I'm no closer to finding them.*

And who phoned in that other tip? It couldn't be Jake. So who?

61 – Lunch & Learn

When Jake arrived home from Skylar's, he checked his voicemail and email. The messages from friends were dropping off. He considered answering a few but couldn't bring himself to do it. Instead, he replied to a couple of work-related emails from a web designer friend. He'd asked the guy to handle his work for a few weeks so he could get his head together after Cody's death. The other designer, grateful for the work, said he'd be happy to oblige for as long as Jake needed him.

Jake switched off his computer and unplugged it from the wall. He didn't like to leave things sucking power from the grid when he wasn't using them. Energy vampires, he called them.

He grabbed his keys, wallet and sunglasses, and set out for Leilani's. On the way, he swung by a Roberto's taco shop to pick up lunch. He realized he hadn't eaten since the lasagna at Skylar's, which they barely touched before they went surfing. His stomach growled as he waited in line and placed his order.

Several minutes later, he rang Leilani's doorbell with two bags of Mexican food in hand.

"Jake, come in! And you have lunch. What do I owe you?" Lani asked.

"Nothing. It's my treat," he said.

"No. You treated me the last time we went out."

"Well, you can treat me next time, okay? Here, I got you a quesadilla with guacamole and a chile relleno. I hope that's cool. And for the carnivore in the room, I've got a carne asada burrito, three rolled tacos with guacamole, and a chicken burrito."

"I guess you're hungry," Lani laughed.

"You could say that." Jake was unable to suppress the grin forming at the corners of his mouth.

"I see." Lani smiled at how happy he seemed but still couldn't fathom what he saw in Skylar—other than her perfect face and body. "I'm not quite as hungry as you, but this looks awesome."

"Oh, I almost forgot the carrots." Jake reached into the bag and pulled out a small cardboard dish of pickled carrots, sprinkled with sliced jalapenos and onions.

"I love these!" Lani said. "I'll go get us a couple glasses of water. Go ahead and dive in."

After they finished eating, Lani decided to proceed, delicately, with a few questions. Jake was now a friend and she didn't want to betray their friendship while trying to get to the bottom of the growing number of files on dead and missing surfers.

"Hey Jake, I've been meaning to ask you about Cody ... and how you're doing with all that."

"I've been trying not to think about him too much. Every time I do, the pain comes flooding back. My mind flashes to him on the beach. I see the bites and all that blood. That's why it's been kind of nice hanging out with you and Skylar and Tristan and those guys. I didn't know you all when Cody was around, so I'm not constantly reminded of him like I am with my other friends—if I even have any friends left. I have pretty much blown everyone off. I was just telling Skylar last night that at first I had lots of messages but I haven't been able to bring myself to answer a single one. Now there are fewer and fewer. Pretty soon, there'll be none. But I kind of prefer it that way—to cut all my connections and start over." Jake raised his eyes to meet Leilani's. "Is that a terrible thing to say?"

"No, Jake, it's normal. I think anyone who's a real friend will understand you need some time. But I also think they'd love to hear from you when you're ready, to let them know you're okay."

"Yeah, I guess. I'm just not ready yet."

"I understand. You'll know when the time is right," Lani

assured him. "Hey, I've also been meaning to ask you something else but we haven't really had much time alone, without Skylar and Tristan around. I was wondering if you'd learned anything more about what happened to that surfer, Rick?"

"Not really. Tristan told me they knew Rick better than they let on at first. He said he felt weird talking about him when I first asked because I was so close to losing it, which I was. He said they didn't know Rick that well but that he was a beach leech and always going off half-cocked and getting himself in trouble."

"What do you think he meant by that?" Lani knew she had to tread lightly, to avoid arousing suspicion about why she was so interested in Rick and Cody.

"Who knows?" Jake wrestled with his thoughts. He stole a glance at Leilani's sympathetic blue eyes and decided to continue. "I don't know why, but I feel like I can't let it go yet. There was this vibe I got off Rick. I can't explain it. I've relived it in my head a million times since I passed him in the water and saw him talking to Cody. I got this feeling he had it in for Cody. But I, stupidly, dismissed it at the time. I know it sounds crazy but I can't shake the feeling he had something to do with Cody's death, even though I saw the shark bites myself. You probably think I'm crazy, right?"

"Not at all. Usually if you feel that strongly, in your gut, there's something to it. So no, you're not crazy. You just don't have all the answers yet. We'll find them. I promise."

Wanting to change the subject, Jake asked, "So what's with you and Tristan? Last night didn't look like your first date the way he was fawning over you."

"No, we had one other date before last night."

"And???" Jake raised his eyebrows.

Lani hesitated. "And I like him."

"But?" Jake pestered.

"But I get the feeling, after hearing from Lisa and Erica and Skylar last night, that he's great at getting women to fall for him, but not so great at sticking around afterward. Not that that's unusual male behavior."

"Hey, speaking as a male here, we're not all like that," Jake said.

"Maybe not all of you. But Tristan? I don't know. Evidence would prove otherwise. And that makes me a little wary," she confessed. "But don't say anything to Skylar or Tristan. I'm still trying to figure out exactly how I feel. When I'm with him, I feel great—better than great actually. But when I'm not, I start to have these doubts. Maybe I just don't know him well enough yet."

Eager to talk about something other than Tristan, Lani asked, "So did Skylar say anything about what happened last night? I mean, that was so bizarre."

"No, she didn't. Those women were so aggro. I have never in my life been punched in the face, let alone been punched in the face by a woman."

"Me neither. I didn't think grown women did that. I've gone over it in my head but cannot figure out what happened to set them off. Where do you think they went?" Lani asked. "I came to and they were gone."

"I don't know and I don't care. I really don't need another black eye. Though, this does make me look kind of bad-ass, right?" Jake tilted his head, giving Leilani a direct view of his bruised skin.

"Oh yeah. I'd definitely think twice before stealing your lunch money," Lani teased as she appraised Jake's face. "You know, it doesn't look that bad. You must heal fast. And I'm glad Lisa had the courtesy to punch behind my ear. I don't think a black eye would be a real turn-on."

"Don't underestimate yourself, Leilani. If anyone could rock a shiner, you could," Jake smiled.

62 – Family Meeting

Tristan assembled Skylar, Torrey, Cruz and Logan at his house. "We've got a serious problem," he began. "I've been thinking about it all night. What happened yesterday was definitely premeditated. Lisa and Erica were looking for me to give me a message. And I know those two didn't come up with this on their own. There's someone else pulling the strings."

"What exactly did they say?" Torrey asked.

"They told me to dump the Rules, dump you guys and quit killing Rogues. They said my reign was over," Tristan answered.

"Hey, that's what those three said last night! 'Reign's over.' It was 'reign,' not 'rain.' It's totally connected," Cruz said.

"So, Lisa and Erica denied killing that boy in Imperial Beach. But I think it's more than a coincidence some kid got killed, we showed up and now the county is crawling with graysuits—some of whom aren't exactly pleased with me. Lisa and Erica also said something else that might give us a clue," Tristan revealed. "They said there's a rumor going around we killed a couple graysuits in Santa Cruz earlier this year. I told them it was none of their business. But someone knows what we did and is obviously upset about it. Anyone have any idea who it could be?"

"No," the Nomads each answered.

"Tristan, you were the one who ordered the hit in Santa Cruz, right?" Logan confirmed. "So, it was a righteous kill."

"Yeah, but why else would they mention it?" Tristan wondered aloud.

"Do you think someone could've had ties to the Rogues we took out?" Torrey asked. "Like maybe one of them had a boyfriend or girlfriend or someone who now has a grudge?"

"I don't know but that's a good place to start," Tristan said. "Let's go over that night again."

63 – Meal Planning

Tristan recounted how earlier in the year, after watching the Mavericks Surf Contest in Half Moon Bay, he, Skylar, Torrey and Cruz headed down the coast to Santa Cruz. Since there hadn't been any suspicious shark attacks for a few months, Tristan decided to rent three places near the beach so they could relax and enjoy the local surf scene, from Steamer Lane to Pleasure Point.

A couple weeks into their stay, Tristan saw a story on the local news about a tragedy aboard a whale watching excursion. During an afternoon cruise, a family of four vanished. The disappearances weren't discovered until the ship docked. The father's body washed up on shore later the same day; it was riddled with shark bites. The mother and two kids were never found. There were no witnesses and the police found nothing to indicate any foul play.

The story reminded Tristan of his vampire days when he used to have the occasional "surf and turf" meal aboard sightseeing cruises in San Francisco Bay. He shuddered when he recalled how, when he was a mere bloodsucker, he used to mindlessly kill humans, good and bad, alike. He always killed for food and he never killed children, but he still wished he had been more discriminating. It took losing Julianna to show him how painful the consequences of indiscriminate killing could be.

After a day of hunting off the Santa Cruz coast, Tristan discovered two vampire sharks in the Monterey Bay, Andi and Andy. Tristan recalled they were high school friends who grew up in Santa Cruz. He remembered thinking it was funny they had the same name. Tristan turned them the night after they celebrated their 10-year high school reunion. *Was it 1973 or 1974?*

Andi had blue eyes and long brownish-blond hair that looked like copper in the sunlight, particularly at sunset. Her skin was evenly tanned a rich shade of golden brown. Andy's tan skin was two shades darker. He had wide brown eyes with long lashes and light brown hair. Each had a stocky build—the result of mixing the intense exercise of surfing with an intense love of eating.

Tristan trailed Andi and Andy, who were still best friends, for a few days to see if they had anything to do with the family's disappearance. He watched them swim back and forth near the Santa Cruz Yacht Harbor entrance, where whale watching cruises depart and dock, but saw nothing else out of the ordinary.

Tristan decided to call in Torrey and Cruz to do some reconnaissance for him. He thought since they had never met Andi or Andy, they might be able to squeeze some information from them.

The next evening, they all watched Andi and Andy head out to surf. Tristan then left to avoid being seen, and Torrey and Cruz waited on shore. Once they saw Andi and Andy coming in, they picked up their boards and strolled to the water.

Upon passing them, Andi and Andy knew Torrey and Cruz were vampire sharks like them.

"Graysuits! What's up?" Andy greeted them amiably.

"Hey! Not much, man," Cruz replied. "I'm Cruz and this is my wife, Torrey."

"Nice to meet you. I'm Andy and this is my friend, Andi."

"That's so cute!" Torrey exclaimed.

"Torrey, Cruz, nice to meet you," Andi smiled warmly.

"You, too," Torrey said. "Hey, Cruz and I were just thinking about some dinner. You know of any good dining around here? We're looking for something local and very, very fresh."

Andi and Andy exchanged a glance and smiled.

"There are a couple places we like to go. Are you concerned with the Rules?" Andi asked.

Torrey shot her a conspiratorial grin. "Not while we're on vacation."

"I thought you two seemed cool," Andi said. "I moved away years ago but Andy still lives here so he knows all the hot spots. A few days ago we had a fabulous meal on a whale watching cruise. But I'd probably avoid that for a little while. It attracted a bit too much attention. Once the media gets wind of a hot spot, you can't go back. It's a shame."

"Yeah, I think I saw something about that on TV. Bummer. But it sounds like it would be fun to look into, maybe further down the coast. So did you plan your meal in advance or did you choose something from the buffet?" Torrey asked.

"Even though we know we're supposed to plan our meals in advance and make sure the food is aged properly, sometimes it's fun to choose from the buffet. You get a wider variety that way," Andi shared a knowing smile with Torrey. "And sticking to a diet of only 'bad' food is so limiting. Sometimes you want something different, right? And the little ones are so tender and sweet."

Torrey and Cruz tried to hide their disgust with smiles.

"Well, listen, it was great running into you. And thanks for the dining tips," Torrey said.

"Sure. Enjoy the rest of your evening," Andi said.

Torrey and Cruz walked into the ocean and paddled toward the breaking waves. When Andy and Andi were out of earshot, Torrey turned to Cruz, "Eww. That woman is twisted. 'The little ones are so tender and sweet.' Sick!"

"They both are. Let's surf and get their stench off us. Then we'll go tell Tristan," Cruz said.

"That sounds good. I'm really glad you're here. I'd hate to do this alone." Torrey leaned over, "Promise you'll always be with me?"

"Always," Cruz answered with a kiss.

64 – Killing Time in Santa Cruz

Two hours later, Torrey and Cruz reported back to Tristan.

"They did it, man," Cruz said.

"Torrey?" Tristan asked for confirmation.

"Yeah, Tristan. They admitted it. It doesn't sound like it's the first time they've killed innocent people either, and it won't be the last. Even worse, they don't seem to have any issues with killing kids. I think Andi has acquired a taste for them." Torrey made a face to emphasize her disgust.

"That's what I was afraid of," Tristan said. "It's never easy making this decision but I've got no other choice. If this is the path they've chosen, we can't allow them to continue. There are Rules and there are consequences."

"Tristan, how about if you let Torrey and me do this one?" Cruz offered, eager to prove himself to Tristan, who had been so generous with them.

"If you think you're ready," Tristan answered. "I'll tell Skylar she can sit this one out. But how about if I go as backup? I'll be there if you need me. If not, you won't even know I'm there."

"Okay, that sounds good," Torrey agreed.

The next night Torrey and Cruz went to the same beach and paddled out after sunset. They waited, wooden stakes in hand, for Andi and Andy.

After an hour, they saw Andi and Andy enter the ocean. Torrey and Cruz smiled brightly as they approached.

"Hey, you two! Good to see you again," Torrey said.

"Yeah, you too. Did you find something for dinner?" Andi asked as she and Andy sat up on their boards.

"Yeah, we did," Torrey said as she positioned herself in front of Andi, and Cruz casually moved in front of Andy. "Something small and tender."

"Kids really are a treat, aren't they? I'd have one every day if I could," giggled Andi.

"Listen, there's something else we wanted to talk with you about," Torrey said.

"What's that?" Andi asked.

"Rule 1!" Torrey yelled as she thrust her stake through Andi's heart.

"And Rule 2!" Cruz added, jabbing his stake into Andy's heart.

Andi and Andy dissolved in blasts of ash, which crumbled into small gray mounds on their surfboards.

"Well, I guess that's that. How do you feel, babe?" Cruz asked.

"Surprisingly good," Torrey said. "I wasn't sure how I'd feel afterward, but I'm relieved that psychopath won't be killing any more kids. How about you?"

"Good. I think Tristan will be pleased."

Tristan popped his head out of the water. "I am. That was a perfect kill. Confirmed, quiet and quick. Nice job."

"So what do you want to do with the boards?" Torrey asked.

Tristan looked at the pyramids of ash, resting on the boards. "Let's leave 'em as a warning to any other graysuits who think about breaking the Rules."

65 – Clean Kill

When Tristan, Torrey and Cruz finished rehashing the sequence of events in Santa Cruz, they looked to Skylar and Logan.

"Guys? Anything about that sound out of the ordinary?" Tristan asked.

"No," Skylar answered. "I remember you guys telling me all this when we were there. I wasn't there for the killing but it doesn't get any cleaner than that. I don't see why there would be an issue with it."

"Logan, what do you think?" Tristan asked. "You weren't with us yet, so you can be the most objective."

"Tristan, man, it all sounds righteous," Logan said. "They broke the Rules. They got what was coming to them."

"Yeah, but why would Lisa and Erica mention it, if it didn't mean anything? We're missing something. Everyone stay alert," Tristan advised. "Let me know if you think of anything else that could help us figure out what's going on and who else may be involved. And let me know if you run into any new graysuits in town. I don't want any more surprises, particularly with Jake and Leilani around. All right, meeting adjourned. Who wants a drink?"

Torrey, Cruz and Logan decided to stay. Skylar, still angry at Tristan for keeping so many secrets from her, bolted and slammed the door behind her.

"Don't worry," Torrey patted Tristan's arm. "She'll come around. She always does."

"Thanks," Tristan smiled ruefully. "It's nice to have at least one woman in the family who doesn't hate my guts."

66 – Men in Gray Suits

Back at Lani's house, Jake's cell phone rang. Lani's chimed in a second later.

"Guess Skylar and Tristan are done," Jake announced with a smile as he pulled his phone from his pocket.

Lani answered her phone. "Tristan, how'd your afternoon go? Did you find out anything more?"

"Not really. Are you and Jake okay? No passing out or stumbling around?"

"No, we're fine," she laughed. "We're watching a movie."

"John Hughes, I presume? Hey, when you're done, how'd you like to come over for dinner? I can take over as nurse," Tristan offered.

"That's not necessary. I'm fine. But I would like to ask you more about last night," Lani said, hopeful he'd be open to more interrogation.

"I thought you might," he sighed. "Come over when you're done."

Thirty minutes later, Jake and Leilani climbed into his truck. He dropped her at Tristan's and headed to Skylar's.

"Leilani! Come in." Tristan embraced her and guided her to the kitchen. "I was just figuring out what to make for dinner. And these guys were just leaving."

"Right! Later, Tristan," Cruz grinned. "Nice to see you, Leilani."

"How are you feeling today?" Torrey asked.

"Good. And thank you again for last night," Lani said.

"No problem. You should be out of the woods but call if anything changes," Torrey said. "Anytime, okay?"

"Thanks, Torrey."

"Hey, Leilani, good to see you. Sorry to leave so fast,"

Logan said with a smile, "but I think Tristan wants to be alone with you."

As Torrey, Cruz and Logan ambled past the living room and toward the front door, the doorbell rang.

"Would you guys get that on your way out?" Tristan shouted from the kitchen.

"Sure thing," Logan said, reaching for the door.

Two men stood outside. The older one said, "I'm looking for Tristan Pierce. I'm an old friend, Dean Delsur. Is he here?"

"Hang on, dude." Logan closed the door part-way. He brushed past Cruz and Torrey, and scurried back to the kitchen. "Tristan, two men are at the front door asking for you."

"Who are they?" Tristan asked.

"Men in *gray suits*," Logan replied, emphasizing the last two words.

"Men in gray suits? That's funny. Isn't that slang for sharks?" Lani asked. "You know, like when you come home from surfing and say, 'I ran into some men in gray suits at the office today.'"

"Yeah," Tristan smiled distractedly. "I better go see who it is. Wait here, okay?"

Ignoring his request, Lani followed and watched from behind as Tristan opened the door.

"Tristan! I do have the right place. It's good to see you, man!" Dean exclaimed, throwing open his arms.

"Dean! This is a surprise." Tristan stepped onto the doorstep to wrap his arms around his old friend. "What are you doing here?"

Lani eyed the two men on Tristan's front porch. They were actually dressed in gray suits. Nice suits, too. The older of the two men, Dean, looked to be in his early 30s. At 6 feet tall, he stood eye to eye with Tristan but had a fairer complexion with aqua blue eyes and medium-brown hair. His hair was short on the sides and a bit longer on top, where it was brushed upward in a style that's meant to look spiky-casual but takes some time to achieve.

Lani scrutinized the younger man with Dean, who looked to be about 25 and stood 2 inches shorter than Tristan and Dean. He, too, had piercing light blue eyes and brown hair almost the same color as Dean's, but his hair was neatly combed back like he was headed to a business meeting. His skin looked incredibly smooth—more like a woman's skin than a man's.

Geez, are all Tristan's friends as good-looking as he is? And where do they all hang out? I could sell tickets and make a fortune, Lani thought.

"Tristan, I was hoping we could talk, but I see you have company." Dean glanced at the petite blond woman standing behind Tristan.

Tristan turned around and saw Leilani. She flashed him a smile.

"Maybe I could come in for a quick drink and we could arrange to get together another night?" Dean suggested.

"I'd love to, but now's not a good time," Tristan said apologetically. While he and Dean were very close at one time, Tristan felt uncomfortable about seeing another surprise visitor from his past and he didn't want to take any chances with Leilani there.

"I'm sorry. It's dinner time, right?" Dean looked from Tristan to Leilani, and raised his eyebrows as he looked back to Tristan.

"It's not like that," Tristan whispered, so Leilani couldn't hear.

"Hey, I have an idea. How about if you and your friends join me for dinner?" Dean offered. "I'd love to take you all out."

"These guys were just leaving. Logan, Torrey, Cruz, I'll see you later." Tristan ushered them out the door.

"Where's Skylar? I was hoping I'd see her tonight, too." Dean had always been attracted to Skylar but, in all the years he'd known her, she only had eyes for Tristan.

"Skylar's with her new boyfriend," Tristan replied.

"Tristan, are you going to stand and talk at the door all night or are you going to invite your friends inside?" Lani asked, wondering why Tristan was behaving so strangely.

"No, I mean …" Tristan fumbled, not wanting to explain why he didn't want to invite fellow vampire sharks into his home, which would then grant them access anytime they wanted it. "How about if we take Dean up on his offer and go out instead? When I asked you to dinner here, I hadn't checked my fridge. I have some leftovers from last night but that's about it. Are you up for going out? If you're not feeling up to it …"

"No. Going out is fine. I'll get my purse." Lani looked forward to finding out who this Dean person was and if he could provide any clues into the mysteries of Tristan.

"Great! There's this nice little Italian place a couple miles up the road. Do you want to follow me there?" Dean asked.

Tristan forced a smile. "Leilani, how does Italian sound?"

"Good," she said.

As they strolled into the front yard, Dean slapped Tristan's back. "It's really good to see you, man."

67 – Dean's Big News

Tristan and Leilani climbed into his black SUV and followed Dean's silver BMW to the restaurant.

"I'm sorry about this. I haven't seen Dean in a while. He's an old friend. If he's here unannounced, it must be something important. But I totally understand if you're not feeling well enough to go out tonight. If you want, I can take you home and you can rest, and then I'll come over as soon as I'm done with Dean." He hoped she would take the hint.

"Don't be silly. I wanna go out with you guys. So long as this 'old friend' doesn't go berserk and start swinging," she joked.

"Yeah, let's hope not." Tristan gave a feeble smile and stared ahead at Dean's car.

When they pulled into the parking lot, Lani noticed the younger man stayed in the car.

Dean walked up to Tristan and Leilani as they climbed out of the SUV. "Tristan, aren't you going to introduce me to this beautiful woman here?"

"I'm sorry. Leilani, I'd like you to meet my good friend, Dean. Dean, this is Leilani."

Lani noticed he didn't say, "This is my *girlfriend*, Leilani." She couldn't decide if she was bothered by it or not. *At least he didn't say "friend." That would've sucked.*

Lani reached out to shake Dean's hand. Instead, Dean grasped her hand and raised it to his mouth. He lightly kissed the back of her hand. "Leilani, a pleasure."

"Easy there, big guy," Tristan joked, cracking a genuine smile for the first time since Dean arrived.

He may not have said "girlfriend," but at least he's a little jealous, Lani smiled to herself.

"Isn't your friend coming in?" Lani asked Dean.

"No. That's Lance, my assistant. Sorry I didn't introduce you earlier. We're working this weekend and Lance is going to take care of some things while we're having dinner. He's hoping for a promotion, so I'm letting him try to impress me," Dean said.

The three of them walked into the dimly lit restaurant and settled in a corner booth, with Leilani in the middle. A tea light in a red glass bowl flickered in the center of the red-and-white checked tablecloth.

"So how did you and Tristan meet?" Lani asked, hoping to gain some insight into Tristan's past.

"We met in San Francisco when we were younger," Dean said. "It seems like a lifetime ago, doesn't it?"

"Yeah," Tristan mumbled.

Lani thought Tristan still seemed distracted but couldn't figure out why.

"So what are you doing in town?" Tristan asked.

"Business," Dean replied.

"Oh? What kind of business?" Lani asked.

"I'm a marketing consultant," Dean explained. "Businesses get themselves into trouble and call me in. I travel to their corporate office and move in for 30 to 90 days. I analyze their marketing program, figure out what they're doing right, what they're doing wrong, and what they should be doing to turn the company around. I then put together a reorg plan, with strategies and tactics for moving forward."

"Wow, that sounds impressive. Do you ever have to fire people?" Lani asked.

"No, I don't personally, but my recommendations sometimes involve cutting staff who are not being effective at their jobs."

"Hey, do you have a card? I have a friend who owns a business who might be in need of your services," Lani lied.

Dean removed a business card from his wallet and handed it to her. Lani made a mental note to do a background check on

Dean when she returned home.

"Could I get one of those, too?" Tristan studied Dean's card. "So you're consulting with a local company that's in trouble?" he probed, eager to find out why Dean showed up unannounced on his doorstep.

"Yeah. There's a biotech company in Sorrento Valley that needs help cleaning up its product marketing group—and its entire marketing department, really—before it launches a new product next year," Dean replied. "It's in beta testing now. The initial results look promising but the company is having trouble coming up with a cohesive strategy to bring the product to market."

"Nice. And you decided to stop by tonight because …?" Tristan asked.

The waitress arrived, interrupting them to take their orders. After she left, Dean resumed the conversation. "Now where were we? Oh yeah. Why am I here? Tristan, old man, I've got news. Big news," Dean grinned. "I'm getting married."

"Married? You? Get out!" Tristan's face broke into a huge smile.

"Yes, me, married," Dean beamed. "Can you believe it?"

"Congratulations, man. Who is she?" Tristan asked.

"Her name is Amanda and she is it. She's the one. I have waited my whole life for her."

"That's awesome." Tristan clasped Leilani's hand under the table. "So when do we get to meet her?"

"Soon. I can't wait for you to meet her. You will love her," Dean said.

The waitress arrived, set three wine glasses on the table, and filled each with Sangiovese. She placed the bottle on the table and left.

"I'm really happy for you." Tristan raised his glass, "To Dean and Amanda."

Dean and Tristan took a big swig of wine. Leilani took a small sip, not wanting to aggravate the dull throbbing in her head from her encounter with Lisa the night before.

Dean set his glass on the table. "Well what about you? I see you have an amazing woman as well." He turned his blue eyes to Leilani, who blushed.

At that moment, Tristan's cell rang. Seeing it was a call from Logan, he excused himself and walked outside to talk.

68 – Dinner, Interrupted

Tristan stepped into the parking lot. "Logan, is everything okay?"

"Yeah. I just wanted to make sure everything's cool with you guys. What's up?"

"Nothing so far. He says he's here on business and came by to tell me he's getting married," Tristan explained.

"Is that it?" Logan asked.

"Yeah. I think he's telling the truth. But stay on your toes. After last night, I'm still a little wary of surprise visitors."

"Okay. Later." Logan hung up.

Tristan glanced around the parking lot but didn't see Dean's assistant or his BMW. He dialed the biotech company Dean said he consulted for. He navigated through the unnecessarily complex voicemail system until he located Dean's extension. He entered the extension and then hung up upon hearing Dean's voice on the voicemail greeting.

I'm being way too paranoid, Tristan thought as he strolled back to the restaurant. *Dean's been nothing but a good friend to me since I've known him. And I probably would not have survived after Julianna died if it wasn't for Dean. I need to chill.*

69 – Getting Acquainted

While Tristan was outside, Dean took the opportunity to get to know Leilani better. "So, how long have you and Tristan been together?"

Lani wasn't sure how to answer. "Uh, not long. This is kind of our third date."

"Really?! That surprises me. I know Tristan and I can tell he's into you."

"Really?"

"Yes, really. He hasn't taken his eyes off you all night. I haven't seen Tristan act this way in a long time. Since Jul…" Dean stopped, waiting to see if Leilani knew about Julianna.

"Since Julianna?"

"Tristan told you about her? Then he really is into you. I don't think he's ever talked about her with anyone except me. And you know how she died?" Dean asked, curious about how much this human knew about Tristan's life.

"Yes, she was killed by a shark. I think Tristan still blames himself for leaving her alone in the ocean," Lani said.

Dean sighed. *She doesn't know what we are. I wonder how long Tristan will keep it from her.*

"Yeah, I don't think he ever got over the shock of losing her," Dean said. "But I have to say, there's a light in his eyes I haven't seen in decades."

"Decades? And how old are you exactly?" Lani laughed.

"I'm 32. So maybe 'decades' is exaggerating a little. But I can tell, you're good for him. You make him happy." He saw a look of skepticism cross her face. "What? What's that look?"

"Sorry. Was it that obvious? It's just … I don't think Tristan has ever had much trouble attracting women, so I'd think he's been pretty happy over the years," she smiled, only half-joking.

"No. I've known Tristan a long time and I can tell he's different with you. I'm happy for him. For you both," Dean raised his glass.

"What are we toasting?" Tristan asked as he slid into the booth beside Leilani.

"You and Leilani. I think you two are good together. I'm happy for you. And for me and my future bride."

Tristan examined Dean's eyes. *He looks like he's being genuine. I'm definitely getting paranoid in my old age,* he thought. *Dean has always stood by my side—through Julianna's death, through everything.*

Tristan clinked his glass with Dean's and Leilani's, and decided to relax. When he grasped Leilani's hand again, she noticed the tension she felt before in his body was gone.

As soon as they set their glasses down, Dean's cell rang. He looked at the caller ID and raised the phone to his ear. A few seconds later, he hung up. "I'm sorry. There's an emergency at the office. Some product testing went bad—really bad. We need to release a statement to the media tomorrow, so we need to get that drafted and then prep our spokesperson and CEO."

"I'm sorry to hear that," Tristan said.

"No, I'm sorry. I show up unexpectedly, drag you both to dinner, and then leave before we even get our food. So, dinner's on me tonight."

Tristan waved his hand across the tabletop, "That's not necessary."

"It's completely necessary. Tristan, I'll call you once I get this work thing under control. Maybe we can get together tomorrow? There's some wedding stuff I'd like to talk with you about."

"Sure. Thank you for dinner and congratulations again." Tristan stood to shake Dean's hand as he left.

"Leilani, lovely to meet you," Dean said.

"You're not going to kiss her hand again, are you?" Tristan teased.

"Have a good night," Dean smiled and waved his hand behind him as he left.

Lani turned to Tristan. "So I guess it's just us."

"That suits me just fine." He gazed into Leilani's deep blue eyes. "Hey, you didn't think Dean was charming, did you? And he's pretty ugly, too, right?"

"Uh huh. I'm so glad he's gone," she smiled.

As Tristan leaned in to kiss Leilani, she discreetly slipped Dean's business card into her purse.

70 – Hidden Agendas

Dean left the restaurant and climbed into the silver BMW, waiting outside the front door.

"How'd it go?" Lance asked.

"He was hesitant at first but we're good now. He doesn't suspect a thing," Dean said.

"And the woman? What about her?"

"Leilani. I think she could work to our advantage. I just need to figure out how," Dean said. "Why don't you drop me off at my place? Then return here and wait for them to leave. Follow them. Don't come back until you know where she lives."

71 – But Not Tonight

After dinner, Tristan drove Leilani back to his place.

"Would you like to come in?" he asked.

"Sure, for a little while. I'd like to talk some more about last night. I'm still confused about what happened," Lani said.

"Me, too. But I'll answer any questions you have as best as I can." Tristan dreaded the conversation that was about to occur, so he put on some music to fill the uncomfortable silences that were sure to follow. He sat beside Leilani on the couch in the living room. "What would you like to know?"

"Well, maybe we can start at the beginning and you can tell me how you met Lisa and Erica, and how things ended with each of them?" she suggested.

He raised his eyebrows. "How much do you want to know?"

"I don't need the gory details. Just tell me what happened."

Tristan recounted how he met each woman surfing and later spent time with each, without going into too much detail. "I was with Lisa for a month and Erica for only a weekend. I told them up front I wasn't looking for a relationship or anything serious. I was very clear about that. And they said they understood so …"

He paused as a thought struck him. He voiced the thought aloud to Leilani as he considered it himself. "I didn't think I was using them, but maybe I was … to numb myself, to forget about Julianna. It wasn't my intention to hurt anyone. I thought they understood it was casual. I swear I never said anything that would cause them to think otherwise. But maybe they felt something and I didn't want to see it because it would have complicated things for me."

Lani considered what Tristan said but still couldn't make sense of the previous night's events. "But why do you think they showed up after so long? Was it a coincidence they ran into you last night or do you think they've been looking for you?"

"I don't know. They seemed pretty mad, so maybe they were looking for me to get even in some way."

"And what happened while Jake and I were gone? We came back and saw Lisa holding Skylar and then she freaked out and went after me and Jake. It doesn't make any sense."

Tristan paused again. *I think I'm going to have to tell a little white lie here. Sorry, Leilani.*

"Lisa started picking a fight with Skylar," he fibbed. "I tried to talk her down. But then Erica got mad and pushed me off my board. You must've arrived right after that. I think they lost their minds. It was some kind of jealous rage that had been building and blew last night. I don't know what else to say. It's crazy."

Lani couldn't tell if Tristan knew more than he was saying or if he was as baffled by their behavior as she was. "But grown women don't go off like that. Is there anything you're not telling me? I can take it. And I promise I won't fly into a jealous rage."

"I've told you all I can."

"But it doesn't make any sense." Feeling frustrated, Lani decided to go in a different direction. "While we're having this uncomfortable discussion about your love life, can I ask you something elsc?"

"Go ahead."

"So, while you were outside, Dean asked me if I knew about Julianna. Did he know her?"

"Yeah. I met Dean shortly after I met Julianna. The three of us were great friends. He was the first one I told after Julianna was killed. He helped me get through it. Without him, I don't think I would have survived," Tristan recalled. "After that, I shut down. I couldn't talk about her anymore. Other than Dean, you were the only person who knew I was married—until last night."

"Speaking of last night, Skylar seemed … well, to put it

bluntly, she seemed like a jealous girlfriend."

"The situation with Skylar is complicated. We've, uh, dated off and on over the years. But I can assure you it's been over for a while and Skylar knows that."

"Still, she seemed awfully upset last night. Have you two 'dated' recently?" Lani asked as tactfully as she could. She tried to keep the mental image of Skylar and Tristan together from entering her brain.

"No. We haven't been together in almost a year."

"Were you guys ever serious?"

"Skylar was. I think she even wanted to get married at one point. But I could not conceive of ever marrying again after losing Julianna. Plus, I didn't feel for Skylar what she felt for me. My heart wasn't in it. To me, Skylar is a friend for life, but not a wife. I told her I didn't feel that way about her. Plus, that was years ago. I think she got it because she never brought up the topic of marriage again."

"So you and Skylar are completely over?"

"Yes," Tristan confirmed. "I swear."

"I believe you. But I think Skylar is still in love with you. Even if you've told her it's over, I can tell she's not over you."

"No. She knows it's over. Plus, she's into Jake now. You have nothing to worry about."

Tired of talking about Skylar, Lani decided to lighten the mood. "Well, she better be over you, because I don't want to get in another fight with one of your exes. Plus, I'm pretty sure she could kick my ass."

"I don't think you have to worry about that." Tristan smiled and leaned in to kiss Leilani. He then wrinkled his brow and pulled back.

"Leilani, there's something you should know. Even though I've known you only a short time, I want you to know that this, between us, is very real to me. This is not like with Skylar, or Lisa, or Erica, or anyone I've been with before. This is even different than I felt with Julianna. I can't explain it but I feel different with you. I feel like I want to be a better person … a different person than I've been. You make me want to be a better version of myself. There are things about my past I want to tell you, that I need to tell you, but I can't yet. I think I'm grappling with how I resolve my past with my present—and my future. Because I do see a future with you."

Lani peered into Tristan's warm brown eyes and felt her brain begin to cloud. Before it became too foggy, she asked, "What do you mean, 'your past'? You can tell me, Tristan. You can trust me." She wondered if she would finally get the answers to the questions that had been dogging her and her investigation.

"I will tell you everything. I promise. But not tonight. Please be patient with me a little while longer."

"Okay. But if we're going to be together, I need to know who you are. I need to know the real you."

"You do know the real me," he whispered. "It's my past that's not real anymore."

He kissed Leilani and offered to drive her home. The ride to her house was quiet.

He walked her to her door. "How's your head feeling? Do you want me to stay with you to make sure you're okay?"

"No, I'm fine," she replied. "I'll call you tomorrow."

They kissed goodnight and Tristan drove away.

As Lani walked inside, she considered doing a search on Dean Delsur but decided to put it off until the morning. She took two aspirin to dull the pounding in her head and crawled into bed, wondering what Tristan could possibly be agonizing about telling her.

72 – Open Invitation

Lani awoke the next morning grateful she felt no pain in her head. She went for a run, showered, brushed her wet hair, and threw on shorts and a tank top. She opened her laptop and typed "Dean Delsur" into a few search engines to see what came up on public sites. Seeing nothing out of the ordinary, she logged into the FBI database and typed in his name. As she hit "enter," the doorbell rang. She closed her laptop and got up to answer it.

She stood on her toes to peer through the peephole. "Who is it?"

"Leilani? It's Dean. Tristan's friend?"

What in the world is he doing here? Lani wondered as she opened the door. "This is a surprise. What are you doing here?"

"I felt bad about leaving so suddenly last night. I was hoping we'd get a chance to talk some more. I brought breakfast." He held up a small white bag and a cardboard container with two coffees. "I'm sorry. I'm intruding again, aren't I? I seem to be doing a lot of that lately. I can come back …"

"No, it's fine. Come in." She waved her arm inside.

Dean stepped through the door with a smile. "Listen, I want to apologize again for ruining your evening last night."

"You didn't. Did you get that work situation handled?"

"Yep. I put the right words in everyone's mouths—the spokesperson, the CEO and soon the media." He thrust a cup toward her. "Latte? I have bagels, too. Spinach or cinnamon?"

"Spinach. Thanks." As Lani reached for the bagel dotted with dark green specks, she glanced across the room to make sure her laptop was closed. "How did you know where to find me?"

"I have my ways," Dean grinned. "The reason I'm here is, I need to talk to you about Tristan. I'd like to ask him to be the best man at my wedding, but I'm not sure if I should."

"Why not?" Lani asked.

"As you know, when Julianna died, it messed him up. Bad. It really screwed with his head. He couldn't even say her name or say the word 'wife' without completely falling apart. But seeing him yesterday with you, it looks like he's finally gotten past it. The thing is, Tristan has not been to a wedding, even as a guest, since his own and that was years ago. I want him to be my best man, but I don't want to put him in a difficult position. So that's why I wanted to talk to you—to see if you think I should ask him, if you think he's ready." Dean raised his eyebrows, shooting her a hopeful look.

"Uh … I don't know. I haven't known Tristan all that long. I'm sure you know him a lot better than I do."

"You're right. I shouldn't have troubled you," he said. "I just didn't want to make Tristan uncomfortable."

"No, it's fine. You're a good friend for being so considerate."

"Hey, Leilani, could you not tell Tristan I was here today? I think it might embarrass him. And I'm not sure what I'm going to do yet, so it would be weird if you mentioned it and then I decided not to ask him."

"No problem," Lani said.

"I should probably go." Dean strode to the front door and stepped outside. "Thanks again for keeping this between us."

"Sure. Thanks for breakfast. And good luck with your decision." Lani closed the door, walked back to her computer and opened the screen. She resumed her search of Dean on the FBI database but turned up nothing unusual.

Is it a good thing Tristan and each of his friends don't have a criminal history or even a traffic ticket? Or is it weird? Can a person's history be too clean? Or do I think everyone's hiding something because as soon as I turned 18 I changed my name to hide my own family?

The thumping in Lani's head returned.

73 – Clingy

That evening Lani showed up at Tristan's door at 8 o'clock. He wasn't there so she walked toward the roar of the ocean. It sounded like white noise on a TV set, with the volume turned all the way up. She ran into the Nomads, returning from the surf.

"Leilani! Hey, what time is it? Am I late?" Tristan carried his board in one arm and wrapped his free arm around her.

"No. It's just now 8. I took a wild guess you'd be at the beach. So, what's with all the night surfing? Don't people do dawn patrol anymore?" she joked.

"Sure they do," Tristan answered, "but I don't like crowds."

"Yeah, and I don't care for the sun," Torrey said.

Cruz pointed his thumb toward Torrey, "I surf when she surfs. If she's on dusk patrol, I'm on dusk patrol."

"Anytime is a good time to surf," Logan said. "Night, day, whatever!"

"What about you, Skylar?" Lani asked.

"I just like it dark," Skylar sneered.

"Alrighty then," Lani said. "Hey, where's Jake?"

Skylar glared at Leilani. "We don't need to be together every second, you know? Clingy is so not attractive."

Lani's jaw dropped. She looked to see if Tristan heard, but he was talking with Torrey and Cruz. She sighed and walked over to him. He threw his arm over her shoulder again and they strolled toward his house, walking behind Torrey and Cruz.

Lani looked behind her. Seeing that Skylar was watching, she kissed Tristan's cheek. "I'm happy to see you."

"Me, too." Tristan pulled her close and planted a kiss on her lips.

I'll show you clingy, Lani thought, as the kiss lingered. Throwing one last glance over her shoulder, she was pleased to see Skylar was now the one with her mouth hanging open.

74 – Girl Talk

As they turned toward Tristan's doorstep, Lani said, "Hey, do you mind if I talk with Torrey for a minute? I want to thank her again for the other night."

"Not at all. I'll go change. Meet me inside when you're done." Tristan kissed Leilani again and headed inside his house.

Lani called out, "Hey, Torrey! Can I talk to you?"

Torrey, who was about 10 paces down the street, turned around. She gave Cruz a peck on the cheek. "I'll see you at home. Take my board?"

"Sure, babe." Cruz tucked her board under his arm and continued walking home.

"What's up? Are you feeling okay?" Torrey asked as she approached Leilani.

"Fine, thanks. I was hoping we could talk for a minute, since we never get a chance to talk alone without the boys around."

"You're right. They are always around, aren't they?" Torrey laughed. "At least they're nice to look at though, right?"

"Right." Lani sat on the curb and motioned for Torrey to sit beside her. "I wanted to thank you again for your help the other night. You took such good care of me and Jake."

"It was nothing. It was kind of nice. I haven't practiced medicine in a while, so it felt good. Though I'm sorry it had to be at your expense," Torrey added.

"So what made you give it up?" Lani asked, still wondering how someone who looked so young could be a doctor.

"It stopped being fun, which was a big surprise to me since I wanted to be a doctor since I was a kid. I studied hard in school. I took Advanced Placement classes in high school so I could motor through college. I received my MD from UCSD's School of Medicine. Then I completed my family medicine residency there, which was cool. I mean, how many residency programs have a link to the surf report on their website?" Torrey chuckled. "But when I was done with my training and considering going into private practice, I didn't feel the same passion for medicine I once did. So I stopped."

"That's it?! You stopped?"

"Yeah. I might go back to it someday," Torrey said. "Life is long. Who knows what I'll want to do 20 years from now?"

"But how did you just stop after all that work?" Lani asked, baffled by Torrey's decision.

"It wasn't that hard once I really thought about it. When I was in school and then training, I had three passions: medicine, Cruz and surfing. When I finished my residency, medicine was the one thing I didn't love anymore. That fire was gone."

Lani struggled to wrap her mind around what Torrey told her. *Who completes med school and all that training, and then quits?* "I'm sorry. That's just so hard for me to imagine after investing so much time and energy and money …"

"It is for a lot of people. But it was much harder for me to imagine staying trapped in something I no longer loved. I'd already done three years pre-med, four years in med school, and three years of residency. Then I took my certification exam and got my license to practice. But when I sat down to think about the next 10 years of my life, I couldn't see it spent as a doctor. People change, you know? People like to think once you start a career you're going to do it forever, particularly if you spend a ton of time and money on school and training. But it doesn't always work out that way. And if it's not what you want to do, then why do it? Why waste one more second of your life on something you don't love?"

"Oh, I dunno. Money? Stability? Security?" Lani said.

"But that's not a fair trade, Leilani. People think money makes everything worth it. But no amount of money is worth selling your life for. And that's what you're doing when you spend time working at something you don't enjoy. You're selling away little pieces of your life that you're never going to get back."

"Well, when you put it like that, it does sound like a bad trade," Lani said. "What did Cruz think? Were you and he on the same page?"

"Absolutely. Cruz is the best. He's my partner in every sense of the word. He was totally supportive while I was in school and training, and he supported my decision to leave."

"Wow, that's quite a guy you have there." Lani reflected on her ex-boyfriends and her family. "I can't think of a single person in my entire life who would have supported me like that."

"Tristan would," Torrey said.

Lani blushed and looked down at the cement curb. "I don't know about that. So how did you and Cruz meet?" she asked, eager to change the subject back to Torrey.

"When I was in med school, I used what little free time I had to surf. It kept me sane. I'd run into Cruz sometimes on the path to Black's Beach. He was an undergrad at UCSD. He'd be heading down as I'd be climbing back up the hill to go home. After saying hi to him every other day for a couple weeks, I asked him if he wanted to surf together the next time. He said yes. We've been together ever since."

"That's amazing. And how long have you been married?"

"We got married when I was in med school, a few months after Cruz graduated from college."

"What made you decide to get married so young?" Lani asked. "I'm sorry, I'm probably getting way too personal."

"No, it's fine. I like talking about Cruz. He is hands-down the most interesting person I've ever met. Before Cruz, I never had a relationship over three months. I would get bored with the guy, you know? But I've never gotten bored with Cruz. Every minute I get to spend with him, I consider myself to be the luckiest person in the world. That's not to say we don't spend time apart. We can and we do sometimes. When I was in school and in my residency, we had to spend a lot of time apart. But I love being with him. I feel more alive with him than I do without him. And when I'm with him, no matter where I am, I feel like I'm home."

Lani felt her cheeks flush again. She thought of how she felt around Tristan. It was kind of like how Torrey described. *I do feel more alive with him. And he's certainly the most interesting person I've ever met. But does that mean I'm in love with him?*

Torrey glanced at Leilani and smiled at the puzzled look on her face. *She realizes she's falling for Tristan. Poor thing. She's scared to death.*

Feeling Torrey's eyes on her, Lani lobbed another question, hoping to extract more details of Tristan's personal life. "And when did you meet Tristan? It was when he and Skylar were together, wasn't it?" Lani ventured.

Torrey paused, reluctant to talk about Tristan and Skylar. *But Leilani seems to already know they were together back then, so what's the harm?* "Yeah. Cruz and I met Skylar first. Then she introduced us to Tristan. We hit it off with Tristan right away. He was so cool and generous and fun. It was impossible not to like him. And he and Skylar together were a blast."

Lani clenched her jaw.

"Sorry," Torrey murmured.

"No, it's okay. I know they were together on and off for a long time, and that it was pretty intense."

"Yeah, but it's not like ..." Torrey stopped.

"It's not like what?" Lani asked.

Torrey lowered her voice. "I probably shouldn't say this. Skylar is a friend. She has always had my back. And I love

Tristan like a brother. But it was never going to happen for them. I've seen Tristan with women before, including Skylar. But I have never seen Tristan the way he is with you. He's different. There's something in his eyes I've never seen before."

Lani wanted to believe Torrey but questions and insecurities gnawed at her. "But, Torrey, Tristan says there are things in his past that may upset me or change my feelings for him. And that scares me. Do you know what it is he's not telling me? I don't want to fall for him only to have him turn around and leave, or stick around but turn out to be some terrible person."

"Tristan is not a terrible person. I can assure you of that. All I can say is Tristan is in a completely unique situation." Torrey paused to carefully choose her words. *How can I put this without betraying Tristan's trust or the oath we've all taken not to share our secret with humans?* "Tristan has a gift, a very unique gift. But it's a gift that can have a dark side. It's like when someone is psychic. It can be a blessing and a curse."

"You're not saying Tristan is psychic, are you?"

"No," Torrey laughed. "This gift he has … Okay, it's kind of like when two people decide to have a baby. They create this child out of love, with only the best intentions to raise a happy, healthy kid. The parents do all the right things and set the best example in every possible way. But the kid grows up and turns out to be a monster. When the parents conceived the child, they had no idea he'd grow up to be a bad person. It just happened—and there's no way the parents could have known and there's nothing they could have done to prevent it."

"Torrey, I have no idea what you're talking about. Are you saying Tristan has a kid?"

"No! I know I'm not making any sense. I'm saying maybe Tristan made some decisions and, at the time, he thought he was doing something good. But he didn't realize those decisions had consequences he could neither predict nor control. Despite that, he blames himself for those consequences and he's tried to fix the situation whenever he can."

"Torrey, I still don't understand. Does this have something to do with Julianna?"

"I didn't know about Julianna until the other night. But now that I do know about her, I'd say yeah, it probably does." Torrey realized she had dug a hole from which she could not extract herself. "Wait. Forget everything I said. I'm sure I've confused things even more. When Tristan is ready to tell you, he will. And when he does, please hear him out. Don't judge him until he has a chance to tell you everything. And, Leilani, know that Tristan does care for you. I can see it every time he's around you and even when you're not here. When someone says your name, he gets this look on his face ... it softens in a way. That's a really good thing. Tristan has been alone for so long."

"I wouldn't exactly say he's been alone." Lani felt petty, jealous thoughts of Skylar, Lisa, Erica and god-knows-who-else infiltrate her brain.

"Hey, you know you can be with other people and still feel alone, right?" Torrey asked.

Lani thought back to her childhood. That was exactly how she felt growing up. Her parents were there yet she always felt alone.

"Despite what you may think, Tristan has been alone all these years. Those other women filled his time but that was it," Torrey said.

"But he has you guys and Skylar ..."

"You know it's not the same," Torrey interrupted. "You can have the greatest friends in the world, but if you want one special person in your life and you don't have that—or if you had it and lost it—life can feel pretty lonely at times. I've never told Tristan this, but I would sometimes catch him watching Cruz and me, and he'd have this look. I could tell he wished he had someone, too. All I'm saying is give him a chance. I know if

Tristan could change some things about his past, he would. But that's a power even Tristan doesn't have."

Lani sat motionless, trying to absorb everything Torrey said.

Torrey gently nudged her. "You look a little dazed."

"Yeah, I think I am. But thank you, Torrey. I mean it. Tristan is lucky to have you for a friend."

"Thanks. But it's the other way around. Cruz and I are so lucky to have him in our lives. I like you, Leilani, and I think you and Tristan are good together. Give him a chance to tell you who he is."

"I'll try. I just hope it's soon."

"Me, too. See you later."

"Good night." Lani stood and gazed up at the stars. *Heaven help me. What am I getting myself into with this guy?* She took a deep breath and walked inside.

75 — Maybe

"Everything okay?" Tristan asked. "You were gone a long time. Are you feeling any pain? What did Torrey say?"

"I'm fine. We were just talking."

"Oh? What about?"

"I was getting to know her better. She told me about her and Cruz, and how they met and stuff," Lani said nonchalantly.

"Ah, girl talk."

"Uh huh. I like Torrey. She's really nice."

"She is." Tristan enveloped Leilani in his arms. "And do you think anyone else—oh, I don't know, in this room maybe—is really nice? That perhaps you might like to spend some time with?"

"In this room? Hmmm. Perhaps," Lani smiled.

"Perhaps, huh? Maybe?" he whispered, his mouth a quarter-inch from hers.

She touched her lips to his. *Maybe, Tristan. Maybe.*

76 – Finding Meaning

Jake sat at home, staring at his phone. *I can't believe I'm sitting by the phone, waiting for a woman to call. I'm a pathetic excuse for a man … but this man is dating the hottest woman in the county. So maybe I'm not that pathetic.*

A couple minutes later his phone rang. "Jake! Where are you? Come over!" Skylar said.

"Be there in five." Jake darted out the door. *Yes, I'm a pathetic excuse for a man. But at least I'm a happy man.*

Jake climbed in his truck but didn't turn the ignition. Instead, he gazed at his reflection in the visor mirror. *Happy? Yeah. I am actually happy, despite all that's happened. Maybe this is what was supposed to happen. Maybe I was supposed to find these people. Maybe I was supposed to find Skylar. I wish it could've happened a different way. I wish Cody could be here because he'd fit right in. Although, if he were here, he'd probably be the one with Skylar.* Jake smiled, thinking about how much the Nomads would've liked Cody.

But that's not the way it was supposed to be, I guess. Cody, if you're up there, man, I miss you. I will always miss you. But I now understand what Carlos was trying to tell me at your memorial. I'm supposed to miss you because you were so important to me. But I'm not supposed to stop living.

Jake rolled down his window and inhaled the warm, salty evening air on the drive to Skylar's. A few minutes later, he strode to her door. As soon as she opened it, he gave her a passionate kiss.

"Jake! What's gotten into you?" she asked breathlessly.

"It's what's gotten out of me. I'm done grieving. I feel like myself again, only better. Much better. And I think that's because of you."

Skylar saw a look in Jake's eyes she'd never seen before. She'd certainly never seen it with Tristan. She knew that, although Jake hadn't said it yet, he was in love with her.

77 – Three Little Words

Later that night, Jake lay next to Skylar, stroking her long, wavy chestnut-colored hair. He took a deep breath. Skylar felt his pulse quicken. She knew what he was going to say.

"Sky," he began, "there's something I want to tell you."

Skylar, who had waited so long to hear those three little words, now found herself hesitating. As much as she liked Jake, and as much as she wanted to be in love with him, she knew she wasn't. At least not yet. It was still Tristan she wanted to speak those words.

Not wanting to see Jake vulnerable or hurt, she decided to cut him off. She didn't want to put him through the agony of saying those words and waiting for a reply, if she couldn't say them in return. "Jake, I think we should wait. There's something you don't know about me."

"I know you, Skylar."

"No, you don't. There's something you don't know that you should know. But I can't tell you unless I talk to Tristan first."

"Tristan? What does he have to do with anything?"

"Because he made me this way," Skylar said.

"What do you mean? What way?" Jake asked.

"Please, Jake. You mean so much to me. I don't want to ruin this, but I will if I keep talking. Let's just talk in the morning, okay?"

"But all I want to say is …"

"No. Let's wait." Skylar kissed him and nestled on his shoulder.

Jake stared at the ceiling, wondering where the evening had taken a wrong turn. He left his house feeling great. He felt almost euphoric when he arrived at Skylar's. Now he felt confused. Darkness once again tinged the edges of his thoughts.

What if Skylar doesn't love me? Do I stick around, hoping she'll change her mind? Or do I leave? And if I leave, where do I go? I don't belong in my old life anymore. I thought I belonged here. But what if I'm wrong?

78 – Swear

Early the next morning, before Jake awoke, Skylar slipped out of bed. She threw on shorts and a hoodie, and scurried to Tristan's house. Seeing the sliding glass door to his bedroom partially open, she softly called out to him. "Tristan. Tristan, it's Sky. Tristan, I need to talk to you. It's important."

Tristan opened his eyes the third time his name was called. He looked at the clock and groaned. *5 a.m.* He climbed out of bed, doing his best not to disturb Leilani. He pulled on a navy blue t-shirt, which matched his boxer shorts, and tiptoed downstairs.

Lani pretended to sleep but watched him from beneath the covers. *He wouldn't put on a shirt to go to the bathroom or to get something from the kitchen, so where's he going?* She sat up in bed and listened. After hearing a door downstairs close, she walked across the bedroom to the sliding glass door. Standing behind the vertical blinds, she moved one blind to the side half an inch. She spotted Tristan and Skylar below.

Seeing Tristan raise his palms in the air, Lani guessed he was asking Skylar something like, "What could you possibly want at this ungodly hour of the morning?" Hidden behind the white plastic blinds, she strained to hear their conversation through the partially open door.

On the porch below, Skylar took a deep breath and began. "Tristan, I'm sorry to get you up so early but I need to talk to you. It's important."

"What?" Tristan grumbled.

"It's Jake. Things are getting serious and I don't know what to do. I think last night he wanted to tell me that he loves me." Skylar peered into Tristan's eyes, waiting for his reaction.

Lani silently gasped. *Jake, no! You're too good for her.*

Tristan smiled and pulled Skylar into his arms. "That's great. Unlike the last couple guys you brought home, Jake is a good guy. I'm happy for you."

Skylar twisted away. She didn't want Tristan to be happy for her. "I need to tell you something that's really hard for me. And I need you to answer me honestly."

"Okay."

"No, I mean it. Swear you'll tell me the truth," she said.

"Okay, I swear. What is it?" Tristan studied Skylar's face. He thought she looked almost like she did the night they killed the Reefers and she went home early. She looked like she was going to cry.

"Give me a minute. This is really hard." Skylar inhaled deeply, mustering her strength. "Let's sit down."

They sat on the porch swing, which hung below the master bedroom balcony. Lani kneeled on the bedroom floor and watched through the slits in the balcony floorboards.

"So the reason I'm telling you this is that I like Jake," Skylar explained. "But when I'm with him, it's not like when I'm with you."

"Skylar, don't …"

"No. Let me say this. I need you to listen and not say a thing until I tell you. Okay?"

He sighed. "Okay."

"Tristan, I have loved you from the first day I met you. You're all I've ever wanted. When I'm with you, I know you're the one. And if you would just open your eyes, you would see we are made for each other. But every time we get together, you eventually pull away. And I don't know why." Skylar wiped a tear from her cheek. "If you asked me to be with you forever, I would. I would have done it 10 years ago. I would do it right now. But I can't be your plaything anymore. When things end with Leilani—and they will end, Tristan, you know they will—you can't come back and pick up where things left off. I love you but I need to know if you can ever love me. If you need more time, because of Julianna or whatever, I can give you more time. But I need you to tell me if you think there's even the smallest chance you can love me."

Tristan froze. He knew that no matter what he said or how gently he said it, it would devastate Skylar and possibly destroy their friendship. Helpless, he looked at the sky, which began to lighten. "Skylar, please don't ask me to do this."

"I need to know, once and for all, if you think you can love me. If you need time, I've got time. But I can't take not knowing. It's killing me. Tell me."

"Sky, over the last 10 years, you have been the most important person in my life. You are my closest friend. You are the one person I've always known I could depend on, no matter what. I trust you with my life. You are so amazing in so many ways that any man would be lucky to have you. You know I would do anything for you. And you know I would do anything not to hurt you. But, Sky, I'm not in love with you."

"But could you ever be?" she pressed.

Tristan took a deep breath. "I've asked myself that question a thousand times. After I turned you, I beat myself up for months. I kept asking myself, *'What's wrong with me? I have this gorgeous, fun, smart, caring woman who wants to be with me, who loves all the same things I do, and I ... just ... can't.'* When we'd drift apart and then get back together, I would question myself all over again. *'What's my problem? Why can't I take the next step? Look at her! She's as amazing as she's always been.'* All this time, Skylar, all this time I thought I was broken. I thought something in me died that was never coming back. But then I met Leilani and I realized I wasn't broken. I could feel those things. I just didn't feel them when I was with you."

Skylar sucked in her breath like she'd been punched in the

stomach. "Wow, Tristan."

"I'm so sorry."

"No. I just can't believe what I'm hearing. So what are you saying? Are you saying you love her and you know for absolute certain you can never love me?"

"Skylar, don't," Tristan pleaded.

"No. I need to hear the truth. Forget about Leilani for a second. Do you think there's even the smallest possibility you could ever love me?"

"No."

Skylar shook her head as tears rolled down her cheeks. "Thank you for your honesty. I needed to hear that. There's one more thing I need to know. Did you ever love me?"

"No," he said softly.

"I am such a fool."

"No, you're not." He tried to wrap his arm around her but she batted it away.

"Yes, I am. But this is good. We can have a clean break." Skylar wiped the tears from her eyes with her sleeve.

"But I don't want a break. You're my best friend. I don't want to lose you. You mean everything to me."

"I don't want to lose you either. But when Leilani is gone, you can't come back to me like all those times before. I can't go through this again. This is the last time you will ever break my heart."

"Skylar, I don't want to hurt you. What can I do? I can't stand to see you in pain."

"Okay. Then give me someone who can give me what you can't. Turn Jake."

Lani leaned back and knocked the blinds. Startled, she dropped to the floor to avoid being seen.

As the plastic blinds swayed back and forth, Tristan looked up at the sliding glass door. Assuming a gust of wind knocked the blinds, he turned back to Skylar. Lani continued to listen, lying on the floor.

"Let's not rush this," Tristan said wearily.

"I'm not rushing. You said yourself Jake is a good guy. You like him, right?"

"Yes, I do. But don't you think you rushed things with Xan and Rick? I don't want us to make another mistake. And with all the chaos right now, and god-knows-who after me, don't you think we should wait?" Tristan asked. "Listen, I know you don't want Jake to get hurt. You saw what happened the other night with Lisa and Erica. Let's figure out what's going on before we make any big decisions."

"I'll wait a little while but I'm not waiting forever. Jake loves me. And now that I know how you feel, I think I could love him, too, in time."

"Shouldn't you be sure before you ask me to turn him?"

"When I ask you again, I will be. But will you do something for me in the meantime?" she asked.

"What?"

"Why don't you take him out surfing? Just the two of you. Feel him out. See if you think he'd want to join us. Our lifestyle isn't for everyone, you know." Skylar hoped he'd come to his senses and realize Leilani would never fit in with them.

"Yes, I'll take him out but that's all I'm doing for now."

"I better go before Jake realizes I'm gone."

"Skylar, I can't tell you how sorry I am. I wish things were different. I wish I could be different for you. I really do."

"It's too late, Tristan. The sun's almost up."

79 – Alone Again Or

Seeing Tristan rise from the porch swing and open the door to the house, Lani quietly crawled into bed and pretended to sleep. A minute later, Tristan entered the room, took off his t-shirt, folded it and placed it on a chair. He gingerly climbed into bed.

Lani lay on her side, turned away from him. She went over the conversation in her head. *What did Skylar mean when she said, 'Turn Jake'? And what did Tristan mean when he said she rushed things with Rick? Was Rick her boyfriend? If so, then she lied to Jake about barely knowing him, which would mean Tristan lied, too. But why?*

Lani had to admit she was happy to hear Tristan confess he never loved Skylar. But she worried about Jake. *Is Jake really in love with her? Can't he see through her? Yeah, she's gorgeous and all, but she's definitely not a nice person.*

And what did Tristan mean when he said people are after him? What people? After him how? And why?

What am I doing in the middle of all this? What am I doing here? How can I consider a future with this guy when I have so many questions?

Lani lay awake for an hour, asking question after question in her mind, before drifting into a restless sleep.

A couple hours later, over breakfast, Tristan noticed Leilani seemed somber. "Is everything okay?"

"Yeah. Why?"

"I dunno. You seem kind of quiet this morning."

"Sorry. I'm just tired. My head hurts." Lani's head did hurt, but not in the way Tristan thought. It hurt from wracking her brain trying to find answers to the questions that seemed to multiply each day she spent with him.

"Do you want me to call Torrey?" Tristan asked.

"No. I think I need to go home for a while and get some rest." Lani gathered her sunglasses and purse.

"Okay. Let me walk you out."

As Lani stepped outside onto the front porch, she saw Skylar and Jake approaching. They strolled hand-in-hand in the shade of the tree-lined sidewalk and up the walkway to Tristan's house. Lani rolled her eyes. Skylar was the last person she wanted to see. *And poor Jake*, she thought. *All this time Skylar has been with him, she's been in love with Tristan.*

"Good morning," Skylar said cheerily, flashing a bright smile from beneath a huge floppy hat. "Hey Tristan, didn't you say you wanted to talk to Jake?"

Tristan squinted at Skylar. She widened her eyes, silently telling him to get on with it.

"Uh, yeah. Leilani, will you give me a minute?" Tristan asked.

"Sure," Lani grudgingly agreed.

"Jake, why don't you come inside?" Tristan suggested.

As Jake stepped through the front door, Skylar bounced over to Leilani. "Leilani! Great to see you!"

Lani stiffened, surprised by Skylar's warm tone after what she overheard earlier that morning.

Once Skylar saw Jake and Tristan were wrapped up in their own conversation in the kitchen, she dropped the grin and her voice darkened to a condescending tone. "Leilani. You know you're not special, right? Tristan is a nomad at heart. He wanders, he hits some waves, then he wanders again. That's who he is. That's what he does."

Skylar glanced at Tristan again to make sure he and Jake were still talking, and then turned back to Leilani. "And he will leave you like he left Lisa and Erica and all the other blonds before you. He will leave you like he always leaves. He's pretending to get close to you now, right? Telling you how you're different from all those other women, how he feels different with you. Wait, you don't have to answer. I can see it all over your face. You're falling for it, too, aren't you? Falling for him? Yeah, that's about the time he gets the urge to move again. In a week, maybe two tops, he'll be gone, on to the next beach and the next blond. And you'll be here, alone again."

Lani glared at Skylar. Her eyes burned. She wasn't sure if she wanted to deck her or burst into tears. Her instincts told her Skylar was lying to hurt her, but she had to admit what Skylar said could just as easily be true.

"Wake up," Skylar said. "You're not really that naïve, are you?"

Lani concentrated on keeping her arms rigid by her side, so she didn't haul off and slap Skylar. *Like she deserves.*

Seeing Jake and Tristan walk back onto the porch, Skylar slipped her arm through Jake's. "Bye!" she yelled over her shoulder as they scampered down the sidewalk toward her house. "Great talking with you, Leilani!"

Lani stood on the porch, unable to move.

Tristan noticed an odd expression on her face. "What's up? You look like you're about to start spouting steam out of your ears. What were you and Skylar talking about?"

"Nothing," Lani mumbled. "What's up with you and Jake?"

"Nothing much. We're gonna go surfing tomorrow night. Just the two of us. I think Skylar wants us to bond or something."

"Huh, well, I better go."

"Are you sure you're okay? I can drive you home if you want," Tristan offered.

"No. I'm just tired."

"Okay." Tristan kissed her goodbye. "Call me later?"

"Yeah," Lani promised and sped away.

80 – Digging

When Lani got home, she threw herself onto the couch. *Get a grip! Skylar is playing you. Don't let her get to you. Forget what she said. She's just mad Tristan said he never loved her. And who can blame him? She's a terrible person.*

Feeling her world spiraling out of control, Lani did what she usually did to center herself. She went to her desk and grabbed a stack of case files. She took all the files related to West Coast shark attacks and surfer disappearances, and spread them in front of her on the floor.

Sitting cross-legged, she started with the most recent file, the Del Norte Reefers. She skimmed the criminal records of each of the five men. *Garrison wasn't kidding. These guys are despicable human beings. It probably is better they're gone. Sorry for doubting you on that one, Garrison.* Lani studied the photos in the file. One photo caught her eye. *Wait a minute. This one guy, the leader, looks a lot like Cody Hansen.*

She held up the photo in the light streaming through her window and stared at it. She then pulled Cody's photo from his file and held it next to the Reefer's.

So two surfers, who look almost identical, die in the ocean a few miles apart and within a few days of each other. Coincidence? And how does Rick Jennings fit into this? I wonder if there's a connection between him and the Reefers?

Lani opened the Imperial Beach file. *A teenage surfer dies from shark bites in south San Diego County. The Nomads, who were in Hawaii at the time of the attack, arrive in the county two days later.*

She leafed through the files on Cody and Rick. *Cody dies from shark bites, only minutes after Jake leaves him. Then Rick, who is the last one to see Cody alive, disappears without a trace. The*

Nomads are already in town, having arrived after the Imperial Beach incident. Rick's board, or a board like his, shows up in a locked bedroom in Tristan's house. The sheriff's department finds nothing to connect Tristan to the disappearance. Tristan tells Jake he knew Rick but denies knowing anything about Cody's death or Rick's disappearance. Skylar knew Rick, too.

So this morning when Tristan said Skylar rushed things with Rick, what did he mean? Were she and Rick romantically involved? Jake would know if that was the case, right? Unless she's keeping it from him—which, knowing Skylar, would make sense. She denied even knowing Rick at first, so would she really tell Jake that her ex was the last one to see his best friend alive? Or that her ex may even have had something to do with his death?

Next Lani opened the Santa Cruz file. *A family of four disappears on a whale watching excursion. The father's body washes up on shore with shark bites. The Nomads were in town at the time of the attack. Later that same week there were also unconfirmed reports of two missing surfers, a man and a woman in their early 30s, but no missing persons reports were ever filed.*

Lani reviewed the documents she'd compiled on the Nomads. *So the Nomads were in Santa Cruz when the family disappeared and the father turned up dead. They were in Encinitas when Cody was attacked, when Rick disappeared, and when the Del Norte Reefers went missing. But with the Imperial Beach case and all the other cases, the Nomads were hundreds or thousands of miles away when the disappearances or attacks occurred. They only showed up afterward.*

She closed the files and loudly exhaled. *I have no choice. I have to ask Tristan. But what will I tell him? I can't imagine he'll be thrilled to know I'm in the FBI and have been lying to him all this time. But, then again, he hasn't exactly told me everything about himself either. Man up, Lani. You got yourself into this. It's time to get yourself out.*

81 – Secret Call

As Lani scooped up the files and dropped them back in her desk drawer, her thoughts turned to Jake. *I need to warn him about Skylar before she breaks his heart. After all he's been through, I don't know if he can take it. Plus, I need to tell him what I overheard about Rick. I owe it to him.*

She dialed Jake's cell. It went to voicemail. "Hey, it's Leilani. I need to talk to you alone. It's about Rick. Call me."

A few hours later, Lani awoke to the sound of her ringing phone. "Hello?" she croaked.

"Hey, it's Jake. Did I wake you?"

"No. Well, yes."

"Ah, late night with Tristan?" he joked.

"Kind of. But not in the way you think," she replied.

"Whatever. Hey, you said you heard something about Rick?" Jake asked.

"Yeah, that's part of the reason I didn't get much sleep. Are you alone?"

"Yeah, for a few minutes. Skylar ran to the store. Why?"

"I overhead Skylar and Tristan talking this morning."

"This morning?"

"Yeah, it was early. Before the sun was up," Lani explained.

"That's weird. I didn't see her leave."

"Yeah, I think she wanted to talk to Tristan alone. Anyway, I promised I'd tell you if I heard anything and I heard something that sounded … suspicious. But you have to keep this between us. I don't want Tristan and Skylar to know I was eavesdropping."

"Okay," Jake agreed. "What'd you hear?"

"There's something Skylar isn't telling you about Rick. I don't know what it is exactly. But, like I said, I overheard them talking this morning and Tristan said something like, 'Don't you think you rushed things with Xan and Rick? I don't want us to make another mistake.' Do you know what he meant about Skylar 'rushing things' or them 'making another mistake'?"

"No. Tristan told me he knew Rick but he turned out to be an ass. Skylar hasn't said much about him other than she knew him, too, but not really well. What do you think they meant?"

"I don't know. But there's something else." Lani decided to spare Jake the pain of explicitly telling him Skylar was still in love with Tristan. "When they were talking, Skylar said something like, 'Give me someone who can give me what you can't. Turn Jake.' Do you have any idea what she meant?"

"'Turn Jake'? What the hell does that mean? Are you sure you heard her right?"

"I'm pretty sure," Lani said.

"I can ask Skylar about Rick again. But I don't know how I'd even begin to ask about 'Turn Jake.' Turn me how? That doesn't make any sense."

"Yeah, well, maybe just ask about Rick for now. But be careful and let me know what you ..."

"She's back." Jake hung up.

"... find out," Lani finished. She clicked her phone off.

Jake already lost his best friend. If it turns out Skylar is involved somehow, he will be devastated. If it turns out Tristan is involved, so will I.

82 – Button-Down

A few minutes after Leilani left his house, Tristan's phone rang.

"Hey, Tristan! It's Dean. My lunch meeting just got cancelled. Are you free in about an hour?"

"I could be. What do you want to do?" Tristan asked.

"How about if I swing by your place and we can figure it out? Another meeting's starting. Gotta make an appearance. See you soon."

Tristan smiled and hung up. He'd never understood Dean's penchant for the button-down, 8-to-5, work-a-day lifestyle.

Tristan met Dean while he was living in San Francisco with Julianna. The three of them used to go out at least once a week for dinner or drinks and have a great time. Dean would sometimes join them for weekend surf sessions. Other times, Tristan and Dean would hit the beach before or after Dean went to work.

Tristan remembered the night he turned Dean. Dean was the first human he turned into a vampire shark. Tristan wasn't even sure it would work. But Dean was willing to try and so was he.

83 – Spilling

It was early 1973. Julianna didn't feel like surfing so she stayed home to watch TV while Tristan and Dean went out.

Tristan had grown tired of keeping his secret. He was scared to tell Julianna he was a vampire, let alone a vampire with the ability to morph into a shark. As cool as she was, he couldn't predict how she'd react, so he put off telling her. Indefinitely.

At the same time, he was excited about his newfound power. It was exhilarating. He felt if he didn't tell someone he'd burst.

Tristan knew Dean was born in San Francisco so was probably familiar with the vampire rumors that had persisted in the city for decades. Tristan recalled hearing the same stories when he was a young man before a stranger in a street alley turned him. So, as he and Dean sat on their surfboards in the calm Pacific Ocean one evening, he decided to broach the subject.

"Dean, if you could do one thing for the rest of your life, what would it be?"

"What do you mean? Like, for work?" Dean asked.

"No. More like, what do you enjoy? What do you love?"

"This," Dean answered.

"You mean surfing," Tristan clarified.

"Yeah. This is it, man."

"You think you'll surf for the rest of your life?"

"Yeah, until I get too old and decrepit to carry a stick and paddle out," Dean smiled.

"So, if you lived to be 1,000 years old, you'd surf as much as you could for the rest of your life."

"Yeah!" Dean said. "Wouldn't you?"

"Of course. So, what if I said you could surf for, like, another 500 years? Would you want to?"

Dean considered the question. "Are you being serious?"

"Yeah, totally serious. Would you?"

He blinked at Tristan. "Then, yeah, I'd surf for 500 years if I could. What's this about?"

"I'm getting to that," Tristan replied, encouraged by Dean's response. "You've lived here your whole life, right?"

"Yep. Born and bred."

"Have you ever heard any stories about vampires in the city?"

"Vampires? Sure, since I was a kid," Dean said.

"Do you think there's any truth to those stories?"

"I dunno. I've never really thought about it. I mean, I've heard those stories as far back as I can remember. My dad told them to me and he heard them from his dad. So who knows? A lot of crazy stuff goes on in this city, right?"

"Right," Tristan affirmed. "What if I told you I think there's some truth to those stories? What would you say?"

"I dunno. Vampires in San Francisco? I guess if it was true, it'd be kind of awesome," Dean grinned.

Tristan couldn't tell if Dean was joking or not. "Do you really think so?"

"Are you serious, man?"

"Dead serious."

"Really? What do you know about it?" Dean goaded him to spill.

"A lot actually. But first I need your word you won't share any of this with anyone. Not even Julianna."

As Dean studied Tristan's expression, the smile faded from his face. *I don't think he's joking,* he realized. "Of course. You can tell me anything. You know that."

"I do. But what I'm about to tell you is going to turn your world upside down. I want to be sure you're ready. If you don't want to hear this, tell me now and we'll never speak of it again," Tristan said, hopeful Dean would ask him to continue.

"No, man, I'm ready," Dean said. "Lay it on me."

"Okay. But be prepared to have your mind blown."

Tristan then told Dean how he became a vampire on the streets of San Francisco in 1936. Dean listened intently, captivated by his story. Dean's brain told him such things were impossible but he knew, from Tristan's tone and the level of detail he provided, everything he said was true.

"So you're telling me you're a vampire? And you can turn me into a vampire if I want?" Dean asked.

"That's what I'm telling you. And there's more."

"How much more can there be? My mind is already blown."

"I'm not just a vampire. I'm a sea vampire. A vampire shark to be exact," Tristan said.

"A what?"

"You've heard of a vampire bat, right? Well, I'm a vampire shark. When I'm in the ocean, I can will myself to change into a shark and then back into my human body." Tristan's dark eyes glowed with excitement from telling someone about his special power. "I think I'm the only one, too."

"What do you mean? How did that happen?"

Tristan didn't know why, but his instincts told him to refrain from telling Dean about his experiences killing the three sharks in the Farallon Islands. It seemed too personal somehow. Plus, Tristan liked the idea of being the only one of his kind in existence. If someone else were to go to the Farallons and do the same thing with the same result, he thought it would make him less powerful.

"I don't know," Tristan lied. "I think it must have something to do with the fact that I spend so much time in the ocean, or maybe something unique with my body chemistry or DNA."

Dean splashed cold salt water on his face. "You're telling me the truth? You're not messing with me?"

"It's all true."

"And Julianna doesn't know? Why?"

"It sounds stupid but I'm afraid to tell her. She's cool with a lot of things, but this? It's so … out there. I know she loves me. But she loves me as a human. I'm not ready to risk losing her," Tristan admitted. "What if I tell her the truth and she leaves?"

"But you've got to tell her sometime. Maybe she'll want to be one, too," Dean suggested.

"Maybe. I think I need more time. I need to be sure. I feel like I've only got one shot to ask her. And if I screw it up, I could lose her forever."

"I understand. But I think you should try," Dean said. "So, why did you tell me?"

"Because you're my best friend and I trust you. And I know how much you love surfing. I thought you might like to join me," Tristan said.

"You mean become a vampire? Or vampire shark?"

"Yeah, if you want to. I haven't turned anyone yet, so I'm not sure if it will even work. If I bite you, I might turn you into a regular vampire. Or I might turn you into a vampire shark. Then if you become a vampire shark, I don't know what powers you'll have—if you'll be able to create a vampire shark, or a regular vampire, or nothing at all. So what do you think? Do you want to try?"

"Hmmm … It sounds pretty cool and all, surfing for 500 years. But I should probably give it some more thought. Tell me more about it and then I can decide."

Tristan explained to Dean all the major points of being a vampire: the myth of immortality, the heightened senses, the need to protect one's skin from the sun, the appeal of blood, and everything else he could think of.

"That all sounds like a fair trade for a very, very long life," Dean said. "I'll think about it, man. And thank you for trusting me with this. It must've been really hard to keep this to yourself for so long."

"You have no idea," Tristan laughed.

84 – Dean's Decision

Two days after Tristan told Dean he was a vampire shark, Dean called him. "Let's do it. I want to be a surf vampire."

"Are you sure?" Tristan asked. "Once I turn you, there's no going back."

"Yeah man, I'm sure," Dean said.

"What if I turn you and you're just a regular vampire, and not a vampire shark? Would you still wanna go through with it?"

"Yeah. I mean, it'd be cool to be able to turn into a shark. But even if I was just a regular vampire, I'd still be able to surf for 500 years, right?"

"Right," Tristan confirmed.

"Then, yeah, let's do it. Having the ability to live for hundreds of years? It's like you've found the fountain of youth!"

"Yeah, I guess so. When do you want to do it?"

"What are you doing tonight?" Dean asked.

"I guess I'm turning you," Tristan grinned into the phone. He was happy to finally have a friend be a part of his secret life. "Julianna will be home from work soon. I'll have dinner with her and then tell her I'm going to see you. I'll tell her it's a guys' night out or something. I'll come over to your place around 9."

85 – Experimenting

Tristan arrived at Dean's tingling with excitement. He rapped on the door three times. Dean, brimming with nervous energy, immediately opened the door.

"Last chance to change your mind," Tristan said as he entered Dean's apartment.

"Nope. My mind's made up. I want to be a surf vampire. I've been thinking about it since you told me and I think it sounds like the coolest thing ever."

"All right, here's what's going to happen," Tristan explained. "I'll step behind you and bite the side of your neck, a little below your ear. It'll be a really sharp pain. When I say sharp, I mean sharp. It's going to hurt like hell. I'll take some of your blood. At the same time, my fangs will release venom into your bloodstream. Then I'll step away and we wait. The actual transformation is a little different for everyone. It could take all night, maybe longer. Some people feel sick. I know I did. Other people don't feel much. They go to sleep like normal and wake up transformed. I'll stay with you to make sure it's an easy transition. I'll call Julianna later and tell her I've had too much to drink so I'm going to sleep it off here. Then when you're feeling strong enough, we'll go to the ocean and see if you can change into a shark. I hope you can. It is the most profoundly freeing feeling in the world." Tristan noticed Dean's heart beating rapidly. "Are you ready?"

"Yes," Dean answered.

"You're sure?"

"Yes. I'm ready," Dean said firmly.

Tristan stepped behind him. He bent Dean's head slightly to the right. "Here we go." He thrust his fangs into the left side of Dean's neck, piercing his flesh.

"Damn! That hurts!" Dean hissed through clenched teeth. "You weren't kidding."

After a couple minutes, Tristan released Dean and stepped around in front of him. "Come sit down." He guided Dean to the couch and handed him a clean towel to press on the two puncture wounds on his neck. "How do you feel?"

"My neck hurts but other than that I don't feel anything yet." Dean leaned back on the couch and clutched the towel to his neck to stop the flow of blood. He looked down at his blood-spotted shirt. "I guess this shirt's ruined."

"Sorry. I should have had you take it off."

"Don't worry about it. Near-eternal life or a shirt? I think I can sacrifice the shirt," Dean smiled.

"So what do you want to do now? Should we watch TV?" Tristan asked.

"Yeah, I guess. What does one normally do when changing into a vampire?"

"I dunno. I passed out in an alley," Tristan chuckled.

He got up to turn on the TV and sat next to Dean on the couch. They watched show after show, until they fell asleep listening to white noise.

In the morning, Tristan awoke first. He pulled the bloody towel away from Dean's neck and nudged him. "Dean. Hey man. How do you feel?"

Dean slowly opened his eyes. He reached up to the puncture wounds on his neck. They still felt sore. He walked to the window, opened it, and poked his head outside into the fog. "Oh god! What's that smell?"

"That, my friend, is the city," Tristan grinned. "You've turned. Your senses are now off the charts."

Dean shut the window. "How do you get used to that?"

"It takes a little time. Other than that, you feel good? You don't feel sick at all?" Tristan asked.

"No."

"Lucky bastard. I was nauseous for hours. Of course, I was terribly drunk when I was bitten. Maybe that's why," Tristan laughed.

"So what now?" Dean asked.

"Nothing. It's done. I should go home to Julianna. You can go about your day. Be sure to stay out of the sun though. Then call me when you're ready to go for a swim."

"Okay." Dean walked Tristan to the door. "I'm glad I did this. Thanks, man." He extended his hand.

Tristan gripped Dean's hand in his. "No. Thank you. I'm glad I finally have someone I can share this with. We're going to have a great time, you and me."

"We always do," Dean said as he closed the door.

86 – Swimming with Sharks

The next evening Tristan and Dean headed to the ocean. They left their surfboards strapped to the top of Dean's car.

"Let's wade out till we can't touch the sand and give it a try," Tristan suggested.

They strode into the frigid ocean water and walked until they could barely stand. They treaded water in the choppy waves.

"How is it?" Tristan asked.

"The ocean feels incredible! It feels like I'm melting into the water molecules around me." Dean swished his arms and legs to keep his head above water.

"That's good! That's a good sign. Now we'll go underwater and start swimming. As we do, I want you to picture being a shark. Imagine what it feels like to be in a shark's body. I'm not going to morph yet. I want to see what happens with you."

They dropped below the surface and swam side by side. Tristan watched, wondering if Dean would be able to do it. He saw Dean's expression change. *He's got it,* Tristan knew. *He's going to do it.*

A moment later, Dean transformed into a shark. The topside of his body was a mottled blue-gray color, the underside a grayish-white. He zoomed ahead, exhilarated by his strength.

Tristan morphed and caught up to Dean.

Dean looked next to him and saw a dark brown-gray shark with enormous teeth. His eyes widened with fear until he saw his own mottled blue-gray body and fins.

I did it, Dean rejoiced. *I'm a shark. This is, hands-down, the greatest day of my life!*

87 – Giving the Gift of Life

One month into his new life as a vampire shark, Dean told Tristan he wanted to try to turn someone to see if he, too, had the power to create a vampire shark. Tristan agreed but told Dean to choose his subject carefully.

"When I was turned, I didn't have a choice and that sucked," Tristan explained. "If you're going to do it, give that person the same choice I gave you. They should have the freedom to make an informed decision."

"Yeah, absolutely," Dean agreed.

"So who are you going to pick?"

"A guy from work. He's a cool guy. He's totally into the nightlife so I think he'll be perfect. He doesn't surf but he's an avid swimmer. So, whichever style vampire he turns out to be, I think he'll love it."

"That sounds good. There's one other thing though. Is he discreet? Being a vampire, shark or otherwise, requires the ability to keep our very existence a secret. There are a lot more humans than there are vampires. If word ever got out, humans would panic and grab their torches and pitchforks, if you know what I mean. When humans fear something, they don't try to understand it. They just kill it. That's their way. So discretion is paramount."

"Discretion. Got it."

"All right. Let me know how it goes."

A week later Dean reported back to Tristan. "No dice, man. I turned him into a vampire but he can't do the shark thing. I think he's kind of bummed. Do you think I did it wrong?"

"No. There's no right or wrong way. You bite someone on the neck and nature takes its course. I don't know why but I think I'm the only one who can create a vampire shark. Sorry, man," Tristan consoled Dean. Secretly though, Tristan relished the idea that he alone had this awesome power.

"Oh well. I tried," Dean said. "But Tristan, you can't keep this to yourself. This power you have is unbelievable. I love my new life. Love it! You have a gift, man. You've gotta share it."

Tristan considered what Dean said. He hesitated to create more vampires since it was sometimes hard to tell which could be trusted to be discreet and which couldn't. But he did love his life as a vampire shark. And Dean seemed to love his as well.

"I've never really thought about it before. Maybe."

"Think about it! We could create the most awesome tribe ever. Surf vampires everywhere!" Dean exclaimed.

In less than a month, Tristan, with Dean at his side, started turning willing young surfers into vampire sharks. Each time they went surfing without Julianna, they sought out the best, friendliest surfers and asked if they wanted to be turned. Tristan made sure he always gave them a choice and clearly informed them of what the transformation entailed. He told them to think about it for as long as they needed, and to find him or Dean when they had an answer.

Nine out of every 10 surfers they asked enthusiastically said yes. With the 1 out of 10 who said no, Tristan and Dean played the whole thing off like it was a big joke.

Tristan turned the willing surfers as they floated on their boards in the ocean. Dean talked each surfer through the process while Tristan released his fangs and bit. Once the bleeding stopped, they sent the surfer to shore and told him or her to get a good night's sleep.

One by one, month by month, the vampire shark population in Northern California grew. At first, they were a tight-knit bunch, surfing and swimming together as often as they could. But life gradually took them in different directions, and Tristan and Dean began to lose touch with the other "graysuits."

They started calling each other "men in gray suits" so they could talk openly in public. The phrase—which was soon shortened to "graysuits"—attracted a lot less attention than "vampire sharks," "surf vampires," "sea vampires," or any phrase with the word "vampire" in it.

Without Tristan's guidance, some graysuits got careless and sloppy. Instead of killing for food, some began to thrill kill—getting off on the hunt and the attack, and leaving bitten or half-eaten human carcasses strewn along the beach.

It was only when a vampire shark viciously killed Julianna that Tristan grasped the severity of the situation and realized his gift, for all the good it could do, could also have disastrous and tragic consequences.

88 – Taking the Gift of Life

After Julianna's death, Tristan was inconsolable. Dean tried everything he could think of to help get him through his darkest nights but nothing worked.

As grief and guilt consumed Tristan, he began talking about the need to create rules to govern how vampire sharks kill. He wanted to be sure no innocent humans suffered the painful death Julianna did, and that no graysuits suffered the heartache and anguish he did.

"I'm responsible. I didn't kill Julianna but I'm responsible. I created the monster that killed her. I need to fix this to make sure it doesn't happen again," Tristan told Dean.

"But it's not your fault. You can't let a few bad apples ruin the whole bunch," Dean reasoned.

"You're wrong. It is my fault. And the only way I know to fix it is to create laws or some kind of structure to govern our behavior. Humans have laws to make sure they don't run around maiming and killing each other. We need our own version of that, but something simpler. The human legal system is byzantine. It's way too complicated and ridiculous to be meaningful or practical."

"I dunno."

"Hear me out," Tristan interrupted. "I've come up with something I think can work."

"What?" Dean asked.

"Rules. I have two so far—the most important ones. Maybe I'll come up with more, maybe not. The most important thing is to keep it simple and I think I've done that."

Dean shook his head. "I dunno, man."

"Just listen. Rule number 1: Do not kill a child. That's simple enough, right? I mean, all vampires, regular and shark, know not to kill or turn a child. Everybody knows it's wrong so that one's pretty obvious. But Rule number 2—this one will make sure no one ever has to suffer and die needlessly like Julianna did."

"What's Rule number 2?" Dean braced for the answer. He knew trying to enforce rules in a group that was already drifting to the far corners of the globe would be difficult, if not impossible.

"Rule number 2: Do not kill, unless it's a righteous kill."

"What do you mean, 'righteous kill'?"

"It means you can't kill a human or vampire or vampire shark for no reason. If you're going to kill, it has to be because that person has proven beyond a shadow of a doubt they can't be trusted to interact with others. Like, a righteous kill would be if you're going to kill a murderer or a pedophile or a rapist— someone who gets off on killing people or committing an act so heinous that it injures their soul; someone who commits a crime against another living being that is so horrible, so vile that the victim will never fully recover from it. If you're going to kill someone, it has to be because the world will be a far better place without that person in it."

"But who decides if it's righteous?" Dean asked, though judging by the wild look in Tristan's eyes, he knew the answer.

"I do."

"And what's the punishment for breaking these Rules?"

"Death," Tristan answered. "If you break one of these Rules, you will be killed to make up for the life you took and prevent the taking of any others."

"Tristan …"

"Dean, there's no other way. We've got to make sure this never happens again. I can't bring Julianna back, but I can prevent this from happening to someone else. The only way to do that is to have the punishment fit the crime. You kill an innocent person, you forfeit your own right to live."

"But we're vampires. We *like* to feed on human blood," Dean tried to reason.

"No. We're better than vampires. We're more. We're vampire sharks. We can hold ourselves to a higher standard. We don't *need* to feed on blood to live. But, when we *want* to dine on fresh blood, we need to make sure we feed on someone who deserves to die. There's no shortage of evil people in the world. We're certainly not going to starve."

"But I don't think it's possible. We created all these graysuits over the past few years. I don't know how many we created. Do you? Is it 300, 400, more?"

Tristan flinched, thinking about the number of vampire sharks now roaming the world. "I don't know. But that doesn't matter."

"It does matter. Yes, many of the graysuits we created still live in the Bay Area but a lot have moved on and we have no idea where. It's like we walked out to the middle of the Golden Gate Bridge, ripped open a pillow and released the feathers onto the wind. Now, you think we can go find all those feathers, gather them up, and stuff them back in the pillow. We can't, Tristan. It's impossible."

"We've at least got to try. My mind is made up. We've got two Rules. Tomorrow we start spreading the word." Tristan's eyes darkened. "This is the way things are now. I created these lives. I can take them away."

89 – Destination Unknown

Thinking back on those early days made Tristan feel bad for questioning Dean's reasons for coming to see him. *Yes, Dean showed up unexpectedly, but he has been a loyal friend the entire time I've known him,* he told himself.

Tristan recalled how he and Dean spread the word about the Rules and asked vampire sharks to pass the word along to others they encountered. Those they told seemed to understand the need to live by a few carefully chosen rules to avoid attracting unnecessary attention from human law enforcement agencies.

After a few months, when they'd spread the word to every vampire shark within a 200-mile radius of the city, Tristan realized he couldn't bear to live in San Francisco anymore. The city held too many painful reminders of Julianna. He needed a clean break.

Tristan decided to travel, destination unknown. He asked Dean to join him but Dean didn't want to leave his home. Dean had lived in San Francisco all his life and he loved it. The abundance of foggy days created an ideal environment for a surf vampire who liked to spend his free time outdoors.

Dean also loved his work and didn't want to leave a job with a bright future. He worked in the marketing department of a small technology company. He enjoyed the creative challenges and opportunities in his job, and the company was really taking off.

He also liked the structure of his day—surfing before work, spending the day at the office, and surfing again in the evenings and on weekends. He even enjoyed wearing suits to work, particularly gray suits—his own private joke.

Dean hated to see Tristan leave but thought it would be good for him to get away for a while. Tristan left San Francisco in

1976. He visited every few years, never letting more than five years go by without seeing Dean. But it wasn't quite the same. Tristan missed his friend who had shared so much of his early life as a vampire shark and who had given him unconditional support in the dark months after Julianna's death.

Thinking about Dean, Tristan now felt guilty for not inviting him in when he arrived two days earlier. *Dean isn't like Lisa or Erica. Dean was the first Nomad, before I even had an inkling of forming the Nomads. He's never been anything but a good friend to me. Now he's getting married and I think he needs me. It's time for me to return the favor and give him the support he's come here for.*

Twenty minutes later, Dean arrived at Tristan's door with a bag of fish burritos.

"Dean, it's great to see you, man!" Spying the bag of food and smelling the aromas emanating from the bag, Tristan asked, "So we're staying in instead of going out?"

"I thought we'd have more time to talk if I picked something up on the way over, instead of having to drive somewhere, find parking, wait for a table … I hope that's okay," Dean said.

"Yeah. Come on in."

Dean brushed past Tristan with a sly smile. "Thanks."

Tristan showed Dean to the kitchen table. "So how long are you here? I have to say, I'm surprised to see you in sunny So Cal. I thought you'd never leave San Francisco."

"Me, too." Dean reached into the bag, handed a wrapped burrito to Tristan and grabbed one for himself. "It just felt like it was time for a change. So I started my own consulting firm. I mostly work up in the Bay Area but sometimes I'll take a job out of the area if the fee is sizable enough."

"That's cool. Do you ever get to take time off and travel?"

"Amanda and I are homebodies mostly. When we do travel, we usually don't venture more than an hour or two from home."

"So tell me about Amanda. I can't wait to meet her!"

"She's great. You actually met her once before. She's one of us." Dean smiled and took a big bite of his burrito.

"No way! Would I remember her?"

"I doubt it. I didn't even remember her. You'd think I'd remember us turning my future wife. But it was back in our days when we were turning a lot of people."

"So how'd you meet her again?" Tristan asked.

"At work. She was hired as an engineer at a software company. I ran the marketing department. I remember the first day I met her. As soon as I arrived at work, I could smell another graysuit and it turned out to be her. We went to dinner that night and things progressed pretty quickly from there."

"That's great, Dean. I'm happy for you."

"Thanks. So tell me about you. Who's this Leilani?"

"It's crazy. I met her two weeks ago. I can't explain it but she's different than anyone I've ever known. And I'm different with her. I feel things with her I haven't felt since Julianna. It's strange but I can actually see a future with this woman." Tristan shook his head in amazement, "This whole thing totally caught me by surprise."

"That is a surprise. Last time I saw you, I don't think you were able to look ahead a week, let alone imagine spending your life with someone. It's good to see you happy again," Dean said. "It feels like the old Tristan is back."

Tristan's face clouded. "No. The old Tristan, the one you met in San Francisco, is gone. He died a long time ago. But now I feel like I have a second chance—a chance to do it right this time. And I don't want to blow it."

"You won't. Don't worry so much. Everything will be great," Dean assured him. "You have Leilani. I have Amanda. Life is good, man."

"Life is good. I'm glad you're here."

"Me, too." Dean finished his burrito and checked his voicemail. "Hey, good news. My afternoon meetings have been cancelled. Product development needs another day to get their act together before they can meet with the marketing department. Are you free this afternoon?"

"Yeah. What do you want to do?" Tristan asked.

"I dunno. Just hang out. Is Skylar around? I'd love to see her."

"Maybe. She has a new boyfriend, so who knows if she's home or not," Tristan said.

"She has a boyfriend, huh? Is it serious?"

"It's hard to say with Skylar. I think it is for him. He's a stand-up guy though. I think he'd be good for her. He'd treat her right."

"Isn't that weird for you though? With you and Skylar and you know …?" Dean asked.

"No. Skylar and I talked everything out. She knows I've moved on. She's moving on, too. I think it's going to be good."

"I have to say, Leilani's cool and all, but I can't believe you and Skylar didn't end up together. That woman is smokin' hot. And she's had a thing for you for as long as I've known her," Dean said.

"Yeah, but it just wasn't there," Tristan said. "You can't make it happen if it's not there."

"With a woman like Skylar? Are you insane?" Dean asked, smiling.

"Hey, what about Amanda?" Tristan joked.

"I'm just sayin'. So should we go see if Skylar's home?"

"Sure. If you promise not to drool on her," Tristan laughed.

"I'll do my best. And hey, we don't need to mention any of this to Amanda."

"No problem. When do I finally get to meet her?"

"A couple days," Dean said. "I can't wait."

90 – Original of the Species

Tristan and Dean walked down the shady street to Skylar's house. She opened the door, surprised to see Tristan after their conversation earlier that morning.

"Skylar!" Dean stepped out from behind Tristan.

"Dean!" Skylar smiled and reached out to embrace him. "It's good to see you! It's been so long!"

Dean wrapped his arms around her. He put his head down to hers and inhaled. Her hair still smelled the same—like the ocean and tropical fruit.

Tristan walked behind Skylar and silently mouthed the words, "No drooling," to Dean.

Dean grinned and released her.

"Do you want to come in?" Skylar asked.

"Sure," Dean stepped inside. "Wow, it's great to see you! You look beautiful, as always."

Dean noticed Skylar's eyes looked red and puffy. "Are you okay? You look like you've been crying. If some guy is responsible for this, give me his name and address, and I'll go kick his ass right now." He clenched his hand into a fist, trying to make her laugh.

Skylar glanced at Tristan and quickly wiped her hand across her eyes. "I'm fine. I was just chopping onions."

"Ah, well, Tristan and I were wondering how to spend our afternoon. I was thinking we might go for a swim?" The thought of Skylar leaving behind her bikini and swimming naked excited Dean.

"Okay," Skylar said. "If we stay deep enough, the sun won't matter."

"Exactly! Tristan, you in?" Dean asked.

"Yeah." Tristan thought it would be good for he and Skylar

to hang out to quell any bad feelings that may have been stirred up that morning. He thought it would also be helpful to have Dean as a buffer between them.

"Just like that, Tristan?" Skylar said. "Don't you need to call Leilani and get her permission?"

"Ha ha, Skylar. She's probably working today anyway. So are we going or what?" Tristan asked.

"We're going!" Dean said.

The three of them spent the entire afternoon swimming up and down the coast, staying deep and far out of the way of surfers and swimmers. They arrived back at the shore at sunset.

Tristan swam to a rock where he'd tied their swimsuits and retrieved them. He handed Dean his trunks and Skylar her bikini.

He thought Dean's gaze lingered on Skylar a little longer than it should for a man about to be married. But Skylar was beautiful and Tristan suspected Dean had always had a little crush on her but never acted on it out of respect for him.

Dean turned to Tristan and smiled. "That was great! As much as I love my work, this was the perfect way to spend the afternoon. You guys wanna watch the sunset? Then I should probably go."

Tristan gazed at the sky. The peach-colored horizon deepened into shades of tangerine and mango, while the cerulean ceiling turned turquoise and then indigo.

Skylar snapped her towel and laid it on the sand. She sat down and stretched her tan legs in front of her. Dean sat beside her, and Tristan next to Dean.

Skylar noticed Dean hadn't been able to take his eyes off her all afternoon. She didn't think much of it since he was about to be married, but she had to admit she enjoyed the attention, particularly since Tristan took absolutely no notice of her anymore.

"So, Tristan, can I ask you a question?" Dean began. "I haven't met a lot of new graysuits. Are you still creating?"

"Not really. In the past few years, I've turned a couple people for Sky. I've also turned a few people who we really liked and thought would be a good fit with our group, like Torrey, Cruz and Logan. But I don't really do that anymore."

Dean looked down and absentmindedly doodled in the sand. "That's too bad. You have a gift, man. This here—what the three of us have—is it! This is the greatest life I can imagine. I can't believe you wouldn't want to share that with other people."

"Dean, we've had this conversation before. You, of all people, know why I don't. It's too unpredictable. It will never again be like the old days."

"I understand. It's just a shame more people can't live like we do. So how many new graysuits have you created?" Dean asked nonchalantly.

"Not many. Some years I may turn one or two; most years none. It depends on who I meet," Tristan answered.

"And how many do you kill for breaking the Rules?" Dean asked.

"Too many." Tristan stared at the horizon. "I wish I never had to kill another one ever again."

"You don't. I mean, you've always had a choice in this," Dean pointed out.

"No, I don't. There are Rules and there are consequences. That's the way it has to be," Tristan said.

"I understand why you feel that way. Believe me, I do. But it seems like we're losing more graysuits than we're creating. Pretty soon there won't be any of us left," Dean said softly.

"You're probably right," Tristan said. "But that might not be a bad thing."

"Tristan, how can you say that?" Dean countered. "Skylar, are you hearing this? What do you think?"

"I dunno. It's not really my call. Tristan knows what he's doing," Skylar said.

"Yeah, I know he does." Dean wanted to tread lightly to avoid arousing suspicion about his questions. "Speaking of creating, Tristan, did you ever figure out how you got your ability to turn people into vampire sharks? Why it's only you and none of the rest of us can do it?"

"I have no idea," Tristan lied. *Sorry, Dean*, he thought, *but the last thing I want is vampires flocking to the Farallons, eating radioactive sharks, and then going on a wild spree creating new vampire sharks all over the world.* "I think it's some genetic anomaly. I'm a freak of nature, I guess." He lifted the corners of his mouth into a slight smile.

"But don't you think about the future?" Dean asked. "We could be the first and last of our species."

"Some things weren't meant to last," Tristan said.

"No," Dean replied, "I guess not."

91 – Wedding Planning

Tristan, Dean and Skylar sauntered home, wrapped in their towels.

At Skylar's door, Tristan hugged her goodnight. "I'm really sorry about this morning," he whispered. "About everything."

"I know," she whispered back.

"It's all for the best. I promise," Tristan said.

Dean then hugged Skylar. "It was great to see you today."

"You, too," she said.

Tristan and Dean ambled back to his house.

"Hey, can I talk to you inside for a minute?" Dean asked. "It's important."

"Sure." Tristan unlocked his front door. "C'mon in. I'm gonna go get changed." He ran upstairs to his bedroom and returned a minute later wearing shorts and a t-shirt.

Dean changed back into his business clothes in the bathroom downstairs.

Tristan poured two glasses of water and called Dean into the kitchen. "What's up?"

"The reason I'm here is I'd like to ask you something about the wedding," Dean began.

"Sure, man. Shoot."

"I know we haven't seen each other in a while but … I was wondering if you would be my best man?"

"Really?! Yeah, man, I'd be honored," Tristan grinned. "And whatever you need for the wedding, you've got it. So when's the big day?"

"In two days."

"Nothing like waiting till the last minute!" Tristan laughed.

"I know. But it's going to be a really small wedding. And when I say small, I mean small. Only me, Amanda, the minister, you, and a few close friends. We got permission from a friend who works for the city to block off a cove in Solana Beach for the ceremony at sunset. And because we want our ceremony to be really intimate, would it be okay if you didn't bring Leilani? It's just that Amanda and I don't really know her and we're trying to keep things small and …"

"Dean, it's no problem. I totally understand and I'm sure Leilani will, too," Tristan assured him. "This is your day."

92 – Done Deal

Dean left Tristan and called his followers over to his house for a meeting.

"We're moving ahead with my plan," Dean began. "I talked to Tristan. He's barely turning anymore; one or two a year—and that's in a good year. He's killing far more graysuits than he's creating. There's no point keeping him around."

"But how do we get his power?" Lance asked. "We need his power so we can create more of us."

"Impossible. It's some genetic anomaly. It's nothing we can take from him and nothing we can create ourselves," Dean explained.

"But if we kill him, that's it. There are no more graysuits," Lance said.

"And if we leave him alive, that'll happen even faster," Dean retorted. "Our population declines faster and faster every year *because* he's alive. If we take him out, we can at least preserve the numbers we have. Plus, now that we know he's no good to us alive, we can finally make him pay for what he did."

Lance nodded.

"So is everyone clear on the plan?" Dean glanced around the room and saw heads bobbing up and down. "We need to be prepared. Tristan and his friends are strong and they know how to fight. They've killed lots of graysuits. They've been doing it for years. But we have two advantages: our numbers and, more importantly, the element of surprise."

Dean's thoughts turned to Skylar. "There's a member of Tristan's tribe who isn't happy with him right now. I think I might be able to convince this person to turn against Tristan and join us."

"But Dean, that's not in the plan," Lance said.

Dean flashed his fangs. "Lance, is this your plan or my plan?"

"Your plan."

"Exactly. And I know what I'm doing. We'll review the final game plan tomorrow night. After that, it's goodbye, Tristan. Goodbye, Nomads. Goodbye, Rules," Dean grinned.

Shouts of "Yeah!" and "Right on!" rang out in the group.

"And everyone? Don't eat too much in the next day or two," Dean added. "Once Tristan is gone, the human buffet is open."

93 – Single Life

While Tristan was out with Dean and Skylar, Lani put away her files and made a cup of tea. She sat in a plush chair, opened the window and felt the cool ocean breeze on her face.

I'm going to tell Tristan tonight. I've got to. I can't live like this. But what will I say?

She ran through different scenarios in her head. They all ended badly. *So I tell Tristan I'm in the FBI and ... He dumps me for lying to him and I never get the answers to my questions. He gets back together with Skylar, leaving Jake broken-hearted, too. Then he and the Nomads take me out in the ocean and I'm never heard from again.*

All right, those are potential downsides of telling the truth. What are the upsides? I tell Tristan, he says he understands and he finally tells me everything. It turns out he is in no way involved with people disappearing or dying. But then what? Do I run off with this guy, chasing waves? Does he settle down here? I can't see him putting down roots in one place.

Lani couldn't predict what the future held, but she knew things had to change. *Whatever happens, I'm ready. I can't lead a double life anymore and I would like to have a life that doesn't revolve around work 24/7. And, if I'm being perfectly honest, I would like Tristan to be a part of that life—whatever form it takes. But even if it doesn't work out that way, I can at least lead a single life again. Just one life. I swear, I don't know how undercover agents do it. They really should get paid more. Having one life is hard enough; having two is just plain crazy.*

She finished her tea and continued staring out the window. Her stomach twisted into knots as she mentally prepared for the conversation she knew she had to have with Tristan. She felt so tense she nearly jumped out of her chair when the phone rang.

"Tristan, hey, I was just thinking about you."

"Good things, I hope? Are you feeling better? You seemed a little off this morning," he said.

"Yeah, I needed some time alone to sort out a few things. Can we get together tonight? There's something I need to tell you."

"You wanna come over? Or should I come there?"

"No, I'll come over. I'll be there soon."

As Lani hung up, she thought of a line from a Bob Marley song: *One love. One heart.*

She sighed. *And one life. That will be such a relief.*

94 – Revelations

Lani knocked on Tristan's door. He opened it with a big smile and bent down to kiss her. "I'm so glad to see you."

"Yeah, I'm happy to see you, too," she mumbled, feeling anxious about what she had to say—and about how Tristan might react.

"Yeah, I can see that," he teased. "What's up?"

"We need to talk. Can we sit down?"

"Sure." Tristan led Leilani to the couch in the living room. He could sense her heart beating a mile a minute. "Is something wrong? Usually when someone says, 'We need to talk,' it's not good."

"No, everything's fine," she said. "It's just … you know how you said you'll tell me about your past when the time is right? Well I can't wait anymore—I have to tell you something about me. I don't know if it's the right time but I need to do it now. And I don't know where to start."

I'm already blowing this, she thought. *Pull yourself together.*

"Why don't you start at the beginning?" Tristan suggested.

"Because that's the hardest part," Lani smiled feebly. "I'm going to do this but before I begin, I need you to understand how much I care for you. I like you, Tristan, more than I've ever liked anyone. And I need you to know that."

"I do."

"Ugh. This is so hard. I'm just going to say it … When I first met you guys and told you I was an interior designer, that was a lie," she began.

"All right, so you're not an interior designer. I kind of guessed that when I first saw your house, remember?" Tristan smiled.

"Yes, I remember. And you were right. I have no decorating

sense whatsoever."

"So if you're not an interior designer, then what are you? What's the big secret?"

"I'm an FBI agent. I work out of the San Diego office. This time I've spent with you I've been on vacation. I haven't taken a vacation since I joined the Bureau so I've got a lot of time accrued," she explained.

"Okay, so you're an FBI agent on vacation and …?" he probed.

"And it's no accident I met you."

The smile faded from Tristan's face. "What do you mean?"

"Over the past few years, I've been looking into shark attacks and disappearances on the West Coast. Let me make it clear this is not a part of my official duties at the Bureau. It's something I've been doing on the side. I've lived by the ocean my entire life and I've never seen anything like I've seen in recent years. There has been a huge spike in attacks and disappearances, and it made me curious so I started digging. While I was digging I found that you and your friends kept popping up in all the places where these incidents occurred, like California and Hawaii. But with the exception of Santa Cruz earlier this year and the most recent incidents here in North County, you and your friends always turned up after the attacks, not before."

Tristan froze. *How did she find all that out?* Since he left San Francisco, he was extremely careful about what information was available on him and the other Nomads. In fact, the vampire shark community had a couple computer experts who regularly hacked into systems, such as the department of motor vehicles, college registrars, and government databases, to adjust birthdates and ages as needed. As an extra precaution, many graysuits also changed their identities and moved from time to time to avoid arousing suspicion about their incredibly slow aging.

"I don't understand. Why are you telling me this?" he asked, trying not to worry.

"Because I can't live like this," Lani said. "I feel like my life is spiraling out of control and it's all my own doing. When I went off on this wild shark chase, I was trying to find some explanation, some connection between these seemingly random attacks and disappearances. I didn't know what I was expecting to find … and then I found you."

"So you've been on the job all this time?" Tristan interrupted.

"No. It started that way. But it changed. The first time I saw you in that bar, the same night I met Jake, I felt something unlike anything I've ever felt before. I felt something … familiar. It was like we'd met before, even though I'd never seen you in person until that night. Believe me, I definitely would've remembered meeting you. You've turned my world upside down and now I feel like I've got to set things right again. I can't do that if I'm not honest with you. And the truth is, I have created a mess. I don't know what I was looking for. It was some gut instinct that ended up going nowhere and now I've probably ruined everything."

"Hang on. You haven't ruined anything yet. Why are you telling me this now?"

"Because I've been pestering you about telling me about your past and I've been hiding all this from you. I've been a total hypocrite. I feel like I don't even know who I am anymore."

Tristan thought back to their first date. "All that stuff you told me about your parents? Was that a lie, too?"

"No, Tristan. That was all true. I've never told that to anyone before you. Everything we've shared has been real. The only things I've lied about are my job and … my name."

"Your name? But you are Leilani Waters. I know you are."

"You're right. I am. I was. I changed my name when I turned 18 to Lani Marley. Marley was my middle name. My parents didn't exactly live their lives on the right side of the law. When I started college, I knew I was going to go into law enforcement, so I changed my name to distance myself from them."

Tristan shook his head. *How could I not have known all this? How could I not have sensed this?* "Sorry, this is a lot to process."

"I know it is and I'm sorry. I would take it all back if I could. But if I did, I never would have met you. And I would rather have had this time with you—even if I've destroyed everything—than to never have met you at all."

Tristan stared into Leilani's eyes. "I want to believe you. I want to believe you so much."

"You can, Tristan. I'm telling you the truth. I only hope it's not too late."

Tristan could tell from her eyes, voice, heartbeat, and body language that she was telling the truth. He ran through everything she said. As shocking and strange as it was, it all sounded plausible. Though he still couldn't figure out why she started looking into the shark attacks in the first place.

Humans usually write that stuff off to mother nature, he thought, *which is convenient for a predatory species that wants to swim below the radar. But maybe things are getting so out of hand that people are starting to notice. And, like Leilani, they're going to start asking questions about the killings and disappearances. And if they do, that'll definitely spell trouble for vampire sharks and all vampires, really.*

Lani began to worry about Tristan's silence. He looked like he was sizing her up and thinking about his next move. "What are you thinking? Do you hate me now? I would understand if you did." She cast her eyes to the floor.

"No, Leilani. I don't hate you," he said softly. *I guess when I think about it she hasn't done anything to me that I haven't done to her. I've lied, so I'm certainly no better than she is. In fact, I'm worse. She doesn't even know what species I am. At least I know she's a human.*

Tristan continued, "I would like to say I'm disappointed you felt you couldn't be honest with me from the start, and that all this time you felt like you couldn't trust me. But that would be hypocritical of me because I haven't been entirely honest with you," he confessed.

"What do you mean?" she asked. *Is he finally going to tell me?*

"These things that brought us together—they're all related. Your investigation, my past, the things you've been hiding from me, the things I've been hiding from you. You're not the only one who's been keeping secrets. I can understand how hard it's been for you and how much it's eating you up inside, because it's the same for me. I feel terrible for not telling you. But if I do tell you, it could drive you away and I don't know if I could stand that. And my secret isn't only about me. It involves the people I'm closest to as well."

Lani stared at Tristan. He looked like he was about to make a confession—a big one. She'd seen that look many times before, but usually in a cold, sterile interrogation room with a two-way mirror. "Tristan, you can trust me. And I will be completely honest with you from here on out. I hope you feel you can be the same with me."

"I want to, Leilani, I do. It's just that my secret is … different. If I tell you, I'm afraid you won't want to be with me. Like this morning, you seemed so distant. It felt like you were pulling away from me."

Lani considered confessing that she had been eavesdropping on him and Skylar. She decided to tell a half-truth instead. "You're right. I was distant. When I woke up this morning, I noticed you were gone. I heard voices so I looked outside and saw you talking with Skylar. I heard her say she's still in love with you. You have so much history with her, it made me feel insecure and then she said …"

"Leilani," Tristan interrupted, "if you had heard the entire conversation, you would have heard me tell her I never loved her and never will. It's you I want to be with."

"I want to be with you, too. But I feel like I'm in this void. You say you have these things in your past you want to tell me but can't yet. You say you feel these things for me …"

"I do."

"And I feel those things, too. That's what scares me. I feel like I'm falling for you but there are all these missing pieces. I don't want to be a Lisa who you spend a month with and then get tired of. Or worse, a Skylar who pines for you for years but can't break through this armor you surround yourself with. I feel like you can pick up and leave any day. You'll go on with your life and be fine, and I'll be left behind never knowing what was real and what was just … convenient."

"I would never do that to you."

"But you don't have any ties here," Lani argued. "No job, no obligations …"

"Those things don't keep people around who don't want to stick around," Tristan countered. "I want to be here with you. I am choosing to be here with you now."

"But what about Skylar, Torrey, Cruz and Logan? It seems like you guys travel around a lot. Aren't you going to want to leave soon? Find the next surf spot?"

"What? Where's all this coming from?"

Lani considered telling him about her exchange with Skylar earlier that morning but decided against it. "I don't know. I feel like things are so up in the air. A lot of that is my fault. I admit that. But where are you going to be six weeks from now? Or six months from now?"

"I don't know. And the reason is that I don't care. I could be anywhere. But wherever it is, I want it to be with you."

95 — Just Be

"But why would you want to be with me?" Lani asked. "I lied to you."

"Because I know you," Tristan said gently.

"Really? What do you know? That I'm a complete basket case?"

"No. I know you have a deep distrust of people so opening up isn't easy. I know you think you can rely only on yourself and no one else. My guess is all that comes from having lousy parents. If you didn't take care of yourself, feed yourself, get yourself to school, no one else was going to do it. Right?"

"Yes," Lani said quietly.

"And being completely self-reliant has served you really well in your life. You are a beautiful, brilliant, tough, talented woman who can do anything she sets her mind to—except maybe decorating," Tristan smiled. "Leilani, there are so many positives to being the strong, driven, determined person you are, we could be here all night and I wouldn't be able to list them all. But all that comes with a price. You live too much in here," he reached up and touched her forehead. "And not enough in here," he placed his fingertips over her heart.

He dropped his hand and took her hand in his. "Sometimes when I look at you, it's obvious you're a million miles away, running through a million questions or a million different scenarios in your head. Now that you've told me the truth about you and your work, I know part of the reason for that, but I don't think it's the whole reason. I think you've become accustomed to living in your head because it's a great way to avoid being hurt—analyzing everything but feeling very little. The problem is, when you live in your head like that, it starts to feel like the future is the only thing that's real. You forget to live in the present, breathe, and enjoy the moment."

Lani squirmed, feeling like she was under a microscope and Tristan was zooming in closer and closer.

"Let me ask you a question," he continued. "When you came to find me last night when I was coming back from surfing, did you even notice the color of the sky? Or the scent of the jasmine on the neighbor's fence? Or the tickle of the ocean breeze on your skin? Or were you thinking about finding me and then planning what would happen the rest of the night?"

She looked down. "No, I didn't notice any of those things you mentioned. I was thinking about the rest of the night."

"I thought so." He squeezed her hand. "Hey, I'm not saying planning is bad. It's a good thing a lot of the time. I've been very successful financially because I've been able to look ahead to the future and forecast what people are going to want and need, and plan accordingly. But when you spend your whole life looking to the future and wishing for tomorrow, you eventually realize you've wished your life away. And a human life is a very short life."

Lani thought about what Tristan said. *It's true. Each day I spend looking at what's around the corner, I'm ignoring what's here in front of me. And who's here in front of me.*

She looked into Tristan's soft brown eyes and felt her walls begin to shatter and fall away. A tear slipped from her eye. She struggled to hold back the others threatening to fall.

"Leilani, I hope you know I'm not saying these things to be critical. Not at all," Tristan said softly. "And I'm no better than you. I've simply been at another end of the spectrum. In my personal life, I've spent the last several years living only in the present, only in the moment. And, as a result, I think I probably hurt some people, like Skylar for one. I guess what I'm saying is there has to be a balance to everything."

Tristan glanced at Leilani's hand in his and gazed into her eyes again. "You know, the first time I saw you out on the water—that first wave you caught when Jake and I were watching and you glided into the tube … You were amazing. I saw you slip into another world. In those moments, all the thought and worry washed away from your face, all the tension melted away from your body. I could see the real you—and you are beautiful, Leilani. I see that every time you're in the ocean. I know that feeling because I feel it, too, when I'm out there. So what I'm saying is, I think I do know the real you. And I want to be with you—the real you."

Seeing Leilani perilously close to tears, Tristan caressed her hand with his thumb. "Listen, I know you've felt alone your whole life. I know how bad that feels because I've felt that way for longer than I can tell you. But you don't have to be alone anymore. You don't have to do everything or be everything. It's okay to rely on someone else if that person has your best interests at heart. I want to be that person for you. I want to make you happy. And I hope with all my heart you can be happy with me."

"I'm so sorry, Tristan, for everything." Tears streamed down Lani's face as she felt another rush of guilt about her deception. She remembered her call to Garrison, tipping him off about the surfboard in Tristan's house. She remembered hearing how Tristan had been beaten while in custody, and seeing how his face changed afterward. "I need to tell you …"

"No. Right now, you don't *need* to do anything. All you need to do is be. Just be."

Lani wrapped her arms around Tristan's neck and sobbed. He smoothed her hair, saying, "It's okay. I'm here for you," over and over.

As the tears rushed from her eyes, Lani felt all the years

of anger and sadness and hurt over her parents' neglect and ridicule spill from her body. She let go of all the failed relationships she cut off prematurely because it was easier to say goodbye than to face the possibility of getting hurt. She cried over the intense guilt she felt for keeping the reason she originally met Tristan and Jake a secret for so long. She cried for all the years she wasted building such high walls to protect herself from being hurt that she forgot to enjoy the simple act of living.

96 – Three Big Words

When there were no more tears left to cry, Lani pulled back from Tristan.

"Better?" he asked.

"Yeah. I'll be right back, okay?"

Lani stepped into the bathroom, splashed cold water on her face and dried her skin with a hand towel. She looked in the mirror. Her eyes were bloodshot and her face was splotchy from crying. But, despite her outward appearance, she felt better than she had in years. She felt lighter and ready to move forward with the rest of her life. She took three deep calming breaths and strode back to the couch.

"I need to tell you something," Tristan said as she settled in beside him. "But before I do, what should I call you?" He crinkled his eyes with a soft smile. "Leilani or Lani?"

"Leilani. I've tried to deny it, but that's who I am. Leilani Marley Waters."

"Okay then, Leilani it is. Leilani," Tristan took a deep breath, "I love you."

"I love you, too," she said.

He exhaled. "I can't tell you how happy I am to hear that. Listen, I know it took a lot of guts for you to come here tonight and tell me what you had to tell me. It also took a lot of faith I would listen to you and try to understand what you did and the reasons for it. Now, it's time for me to do the same. As much as it scares me, I need to tell you everything. I only hope afterward you'll still feel the same as you do now."

"I will. There's nothing you can tell me to change the way I feel."

"I hope that's true," he said. "But tomorrow, okay? I can tell you're exhausted and I am, too. It's been a really long day. We can talk after I get back from surfing with Jake."

"Tomorrow you'll tell me everything?"

"I promise. Tomorrow night." Tristan stood and pulled Leilani to her feet. "Would you like to go home or come upstairs?" he asked.

"Upstairs."

"I was hoping you'd say that."

97 – Best Man

The next morning, as he and Leilani lay in bed, Tristan remembered his conversation with Dean. "Oh, I almost forgot to tell you … Dean asked me to be his best man yesterday."

"He did?" Leilani pretended to be surprised, remembering that Dean had asked to keep his visit with her a secret. "That's great! When's the wedding?"

"Tomorrow."

"Tomorrow! That's quick!"

"That's what I said. I guess when you know, you know," Tristan smiled. "There's something else I need to tell you about the wedding. Dean made a point of telling me he wants to keep it really small. Just him and Amanda, me, and a few of their close friends. Are you okay sitting this one out?"

"Sure. I mean, I just met the guy so it's okay if he doesn't invite me to the most important day of his life," Leilani said.

"You're the best. Thanks for understanding."

Don't worry, Leilani, Tristan thought. *If all goes well tonight—and you don't run for the hills after I tell you what I am—there might be another wedding celebration soon. And Dean can be my best man.*

98 – Invitation Only

Later that morning, after Leilani had gone home, Tristan called another meeting.

"Thanks for coming, everyone. I need to tell you all something." Tristan paced in front of the photograph in the living room, while Torrey, Cruz, Logan and Skylar watched. "Give me a minute, okay?" He tried to gather his thoughts. He knew if he didn't choose his words carefully Skylar would explode again.

Torrey elbowed Cruz. "He's in love," she whispered in his ear.

Cruz raised his eyebrows at Torrey and looked over at Tristan. He chuckled silently to himself, *I know that look, man. I've had that look.* He turned to Torrey and mouthed, "Oh yeah."

"Actually there are two things," Tristan began. "First, Sky, would it be okay if I shared our conversation about Jake—about what you asked me? I think it might be good to discuss with the group before I go out with him tonight."

"Uh, okay. But I thought you said it was too early to consider," Skylar said.

"Yes, but this way when the time is right, everything will be thoroughly vetted and we can be sure we're choosing the right person this time."

"Fine," Skylar agreed.

"Sky is considering inviting Jake into our family," Tristan explained. "She hasn't made up her mind yet but she's thinking about it. I'm going to take Jake out later and feel him out a bit. You all know I like Jake. I think he's a stand-up guy. I think he'd be a good fit. If Sky wants to invite him to join us, I'm all for it."

Skylar looked up in surprise at Tristan. He smiled and nodded. She smiled back but was suspicious of his sudden change of heart.

"Everyone else on board if Sky chooses Jake?" Tristan asked.

"Yeah," everyone nodded.

"Any concerns? Any reasons why we shouldn't invite him to join us?" he asked.

"No."

Tristan clasped his hands together, "Good, we're all in agreement. Sky, there's something else we should discuss. When you're ready to make Jake the offer, I think you should tell him the truth about Rick and Cody. He deserves to know what happened."

"Are you crazy? No way. He doesn't need to know," Skylar countered.

"He does. If you're serious about having a future with him, you've got to be honest. If you don't tell him and he finds out, he'll never forgive you."

"He's not going to find out," Skylar insisted.

"Skylar, the truth always comes out and it's better if you're the one telling it. He's suffered enough, don't you think? If he finds out his girlfriend has been lying to him all this time about something so important, he's not gonna take it well. If you explain what happened and why we couldn't tell him, he'll understand," Tristan reasoned.

"It's nice you're so sure, but it's not your future we're talking about. It's mine. So I'll be the one to decide what Jake gets told. And I decide we tell him nothing. Let's leave it with what we already told him: We knew Rick, he turned out not to be a great guy, Rick's gone, case closed. Jake is finally feeling good. Telling him now is just going to open up that wound again. We all need to move on," Skylar argued.

"You're wrong. He needs to know," Tristan said.

"No, he doesn't. And while you're lecturing us on honesty, what about you and your little human? I'm guessing you haven't been entirely honest with her either," Skylar said.

"I'm glad you brought that up. Leilani and I had a long talk last night. She told me some things about herself, which I won't share now, but that took a lot of guts for her to tell me. I feel I owe it to her to do the same. I plan to tell her tonight about who I am and about what I am. It might take a while for her to absorb. So I'm not saying I'm going to turn her or even that she's going to want to be turned, but I thought you all should know since this involves all of us."

Tristan looked from face to face, hoping for support.

Skylar gaped at him. "You're not serious."

"Why wouldn't I be serious?" he asked.

"Because she's beneath you. Beneath us."

"Skylar …"

"No, this involves all of us and I say, no. Hell no! I don't like her. I won't have her in our family. You can have your little fling with her. But she's not one of us."

"Skylar, you don't get to decide that," Tristan said.

"I think we all do, like we just did with Jake. We all have a stake in this. And I know for a fact you're making a big mistake with Leilani. I don't know why you can't see that." Skylar stood up to leave.

"Sit down. We're not done."

"I'm done. I vote no on Leilani. You've ruined the last 10 years of my life. You don't get to ruin the next 10 by bringing that pathetic little human into our group. And if you say anything to Jake about Rick, I swear, Tristan, I'll kill you." Skylar stormed out the front door.

After the door slammed, Tristan turned to the rest of the group, "Well that went better than expected."

Torrey smiled and embraced him. "Don't listen to her. She's upset. She'll come around. And don't worry about Leilani either. She'd be lucky to have you. For what it's worth, I like Leilani and I think the two of you are good together. I hope it goes well tonight."

"Thanks, Torrey. That means a lot," Tristan said, grateful for the support.

"Yeah, Tristan," Cruz said, "if you're half as happy with Leilani as I am with Torrey, you're going to be a very happy man for a very long time. Good luck tonight."

"Thanks, Cruz," Tristan said. "Logan, that just leaves you."

Logan stood up and grinned. "Do what makes you happy. That's all that matters. If Leilani makes you happy, go for it, man!"

99 — Diversion

For 24 hours after Leilani's call, Jake wondered how to ask Skylar about Rick without having it seem like it was from out of left field. *Maybe I'll ask her before I go surfing with Tristan. But I need to think of a way to ease into it.*

Jake dialed Skylar's number and suggested meeting at her place before seeing Tristan. A few hours later, he stood on her doorstep, feeling anxious but determined.

Skylar opened the door, wearing a short, silky rose petal pink dress. Without a word, she pulled Jake inside and passionately kissed him.

"Wow! What was that for?" he gasped.

"I'm just happy to see you."

"Me, too. You look beautiful. Are we going out?"

"No. We're staying in. How about if you blow off surfing with Tristan and stay here with me?"

"If I knew you'd be wearing this tonight, I never would've agreed to go out with him in the first place," Jake grinned. "I probably shouldn't cancel at the last minute though. It seemed like he really wanted to surf tonight."

"He'll be fine. He can go by himself," Skylar said.

"No. I should go. But I promise I'll come straight back here when I'm done. And I'll make sure it's a short session," he assured her.

"All right," she pouted. "When are you supposed to meet him?"

"In 45 minutes."

"If I only have you for 45 minutes, why don't we make the most of it?"

Skylar undressed Jake and sat him down on the bed. As she stood in front of him, she lifted her dress over her head. Jake saw she wore nothing beneath it.

"Skylar," Jake whispered, "I …"

"Jake, shh. Later."

But Jake couldn't wait any longer. "I love you."

Skylar gazed into his eyes, kissed him and gently pushed him back on the bed.

100 – Last Chance

A few minutes before Jake was supposed to meet Tristan, he remembered why he'd come to Skylar's house.

"So, now that you know how I feel about you, I want us to be totally honest with each other about everything, okay?"

Skylar nuzzled her head on his shoulder. "Of course."

"You know how I asked you before if you'd ever had a relationship with any of the other Nomads, except for Tristan, and you said no?"

"Yeah, I remember."

"I know it's kind of weird to be asking this now but I just need to ask to get it off my mind, once and for all," Jake said.

"What?"

"Remember when I asked you and Tristan about Rick and you said you didn't really know him? And then after that, you guys said you knew him better than you originally said you did?"

"Yeah, I remember all that. Why are we talking about this now?" Skylar asked.

"Maybe I'm being paranoid but I was wondering if you and Rick were ever together?"

"Where's this coming from? Did Tristan say something to you?"

"Tristan? No. I just thought it was weird you guys were kind of evasive about him and I thought it would make sense if you were with him but you didn't want me to know," he explained.

"Jake, if I had something to tell you, I would. Forget about Rick. Forget about Tristan. Forget about everyone else. The only guy in my life—the only guy that matters—is you."

"All I'm saying is if there's something you need to tell me about Rick, now's the time to get it all out on the table."

"I swear I have nothing else to tell you," she assured him.

"So you're telling me absolutely nothing went on between you and Rick? He wasn't your boyfriend or anything? He was just a guy and nothing more?"

"Yes, that's what I'm telling you," she said. "You believe me, don't you?"

"Yes, I believe you." Jake glanced at the clock. "I'm so sorry to do this but I have to go meet Tristan. I'll see you back here afterward, okay?" He climbed out of bed and reached for his boardshorts on the floor.

"Okay, but make it quick. I'll be here waiting for you."

"Then this might be the quickest surf session ever. I'll be back as soon as I can." He bent down and gave her one more passionate kiss. "I love you."

101 — Rainbows

Jake met Tristan on the bluffs, at the pathway to the beach.

"I was beginning to think you'd forgotten," Tristan said.

"No, I remembered. I was with Skylar. I lost track of time."

"I see," Tristan smirked. "You ready?"

"Yeah, let's go."

They descended the path to the beach and strode to the water. Tristan glanced at Jake. "You look a little dazed, man. What's up?"

"Nothing," Jake replied.

"Riiiiight. What? Are you, like, in love with her or something?" Tristan teased.

"Maybe." Jake tried to hide his smile.

"Does she know?"

Jake's face broke into a grin. "Yes."

"And does she feel the same?"

"She hasn't said it yet. But maybe."

"That's great, man. I'm happy for you," Tristan said.

Jake and Tristan surveyed the waves under the light of the waning gibbous moon.

"Whoa! Did you see that?" Jake asked.

"What?"

"A rainbow in the spray of the wave. Look," Jake pointed, "there's another one."

"You can see that?" Tristan asked.

"Yeah. I've seen this during the day before, usually in the morning when the sun is shining. The wave crests, then the white spray blows back and turns into a rainbow. I've never seen it in the moonlight though. That's cool."

"Yeah, it is cool," Tristan agreed, still looking quizzically at Jake. "Let's head out."

As they paddled, Tristan pondered what Jake said. *He could see the rainbow. I've never known a human to see that at night. It's not even a full moon.* He glanced at Jake. *No way. He can't be. I would know. I would be able to sense if Jake was a vampire. So would Skylar. We'd be able to smell it. But, there's something going on with him. And that black eye he got from Lisa disappeared awfully quickly.*

102 – Interview

Tristan and Jake climbed on their boards and floated, waiting for waves. Tristan gazed at him again with a curious look.

"Jake, if you could do anything in the world for the rest of your life, what would it be?"

"Anything?" Jake pondered the question and said the first thing that popped into his head. "I'd surf."

"You'd surf?"

"Yeah. What would you do?"

"I'd surf." Tristan took a deep breath. "Do you mind if I ask you a few questions? They might seem kind of random, but bear with me, okay?"

"Oookaaay," Jake agreed, uncertain of where the conversation was heading.

"When is the last time you went for more than 72 hours without going in the ocean?"

"Three days without surfing?" Jake thought back. "Probably since before Cody died. I think I've gone surfing every night or at least every other night since then. It's kept me from going crazy."

"Have you been out surfing during the day, since Cody died?" Tristan asked.

"No."

"Why?"

"Because I surfed with Cody during the day," Jake said quietly. "Without him, it didn't feel right. That's when I started surfing at night and that's around the same time I met you guys."

"And what about your appetite? Any changes?"

"My appetite? What does that have to do with anything?"

"I just need to see something. Has your appetite changed recently? Maybe you don't eat much for a couple days and then all of a sudden you're ravenous? Or maybe you've developed a sudden taste for rare meat?"

"Yeah, actually, now that you mention it … I always used to get my meat cooked medium but I've been liking it more rare lately. And my appetite has been weird, like I won't be hungry at all for a day or two and then suddenly I'm starving. How did you know?"

This can't be possible, Tristan thought.

"Just a few more questions. Have you been particularly sensitive to the sun? Any unusual sunburns from being out during the day or under a full moon at night?"

"From the moon? You're kidding, right?"

"No, I'm not."

"No, no sunburns." Jake studied his skin. "But I have gotten pretty tan even though I haven't really been out during the day. Can the moon really do that?"

"Maybe. Now, this is going to sound weird, but does your head tingle when you get close to someone in the water?"

"Does my head tingle? I don't know what you mean," Jake said. "You're freaking me out, man. What's this about?"

Tristan ignored Jake's question. "Just one more thing. Will you do something for me? It's going to sound strange but give it a try—and trust me."

"Okay," Jake said. "I trust you."

"Let's get into the water."

Tristan and Jake rolled off their boards and treaded water.

"In a minute, I want you to submerge yourself and visualize what it would feel like to be a great white shark. Picture your body, your fins, your teeth. Think about what it would feel like to swish your tail fin and swim," Tristan said.

"What the hell are you talking about?"

"Please, Jake, this is important. Try it, okay? Go underwater and picture what it would be like to be a shark. But don't just think about it. Feel it—with every cell in your body. Okay? You ready?"

"Okay," Jake reluctantly agreed. *Why is Tristan is acting so weird? Pretend to be a shark? What's he up to?*

"Let's go underwater."

Jake dropped below the surface and closed his eyes. He pictured himself in the body of a great white shark. He imagined having a tail fin and what it would feel like to flick it. He snapped his fin. *Whoa, it feels like I really do have a tail fin*, he thought.

Jake opened his eyes and looked at his feet. But his feet weren't there. In their place was a caudal fin. But the rest of him was still human.

Jake and Tristan gaped at each other. Jake glanced down again and saw his feet. They raised their heads out of the water.

"What the hell was that?!" Jake demanded. "Did you see that?"

"Yes. I saw that."

"Was that a … fin?"

"Yeah, it was a caudal fin. But nothing else changed. I don't understand …" Tristan had never heard of someone morphing only part way. *When a vampire shark goes underwater and thinks of transforming into a shark, it's all or nothing. You appear either in human form or shark form; there's no in-between.*

"What do you mean, 'nothing else changed'?" Jake asked. "Did I just have a fin?!"

"I've never seen this before. How could this happen?" Tristan rattled his brain to think of what could cause only a partial transformation. "That day you were out with Cody, did you get bitten by a shark, too?"

"Bitten? No. I think I would know if a shark bit me."

"When you were in the ocean or right after you got back on shore, after you left Cody, were you bleeding anywhere on your body? Like maybe your foot or fingertips? Anything that might have been dangling in the water?"

Jake thought back to that day. His mind first flashed on Cody and all the blood that poured from his body after he pulled him from the ocean. He thought back further to when he first came out of the water. He walked to the parking lot. He saw the two women. *Wait a minute … they said I was bleeding.* "Yeah, my toe was bleeding. But I think I must have stepped on glass in the parking lot or something. It stopped bleeding right after I realized I was cut."

"Did you find any glass in the cut?" Tristan asked.

"No."

"Jake, I don't think you stepped on glass. That's not why you were bleeding."

103 – Becoming

Tristan climbed back on his board and ran his wet hands down his face. "Let's head in. We need to talk."

They surfed to shore, planted their boards in the sand and sat down.

"The last day you were with Cody, when you left him but were still in the ocean, what exactly happened? What do you remember?" Tristan asked, dreading the answer.

"I told Cody I was going in and he said he'd be right behind me. I started toward shore and I saw Rick paddling toward Cody. He had this look on his face when I passed him. I didn't like it so I climbed up on my board and watched. I couldn't see a lot because I was pretty far away by then. While I was on my board, I thought I felt something move beneath me, so I picked up my feet but didn't see anything. Then Cody waved me to shore and I went in," Jake explained.

"When you were sitting on your board, did you feel anything strange, like a pinprick?"

"No, I don't think so," Jake answered. "Tristan, what's going on?"

"Jake, I think you really are becoming one of us. But you're stuck in between … I don't know … I've never seen this before," Tristan stammered.

"What are you talking about?" Jake demanded. "You are really starting to freak me out, man."

"I need to tell you something about us … about you. This is way sooner than I was planning to do this. And Skylar's not here. Wait! Let's go to Skylar's. I need to talk to her and then we can talk to you together."

"What? No. Tell me now. What the hell is going on?"

"I really want Skylar here for this," Tristan insisted.

"No. Tell me what's going on now!"

"All right, but tell Skylar I didn't want to do it this way. Tell her I wanted her to be here with you." Tristan did not want to face Skylar's wrath twice in one day.

"Whatever. I'll tell Skylar whatever you want," Jake agreed.

"First, I need your word you will not tell anyone what I'm about to tell you. Once I tell you, you'll know why secrecy is vital to our survival."

Survival? That's kinda dramatic, Jake thought to himself. "Okay, I swear, I won't tell anyone."

Tristan took a deep breath. "Here's the truth, Jake, as unbelievable as it is … Skylar, Torrey, Cruz, Logan and I are not what you think we are. We're not … human."

"Not human?" Jake squinted his eyes and glared at Tristan, trying to make sense of what he was hearing.

"We're vampires but with one key distinction. We're vampire sharks."

"Vampire sharks? What the hell is a vampire shark?" Jake asked.

"A vampire shark is a vampire with the ability to transform into a great white shark in the ocean. I was the first of our kind. While any kind of vampire can create another vampire, only I can create a vampire shark."

Tristan watched the disbelief creep across Jake's face. He'd seen the look on humans hundreds of times before. Tristan told Jake how he became a vampire, and created other vampire sharks, and how Julianna's death opened his eyes to the consequences of his actions. He told Jake about the Rules, why he created them, and why he and the Nomads traveled the world to enforce them.

104 – The Whole Truth

Tristan saw the wheels turn in Jake's mind and a spark flicker in his eyes.

"Was Rick a vampire shark?" Jake asked.

"Yes," Tristan admitted. "Rick was a newborn. He was recently turned. He was supposed to take out the head of the Del Norte Reefers."

"The Reefers were vampires?"

"No, they were human but the very worst kind of human. I could tell you about all the horrific crimes they committed against other humans—worse than vampire sharks, I assure you. Rick was going to do his first kill and take out the leader. He was supposed to wait for me so I could make sure there were no mistakes. But Rick left early—going off half-cocked as usual. When I realized he'd gone ahead, I raced to the beach. As soon as I saw Rick headed toward Cody, I knew he was going to kill him. I knew he had the wrong guy. Jake, I swear, I swam out as fast as I could to try to get to Rick in time. But I must not have been paying attention—I was so focused on getting to Rick and stopping him. I remember grazing something on the way out. I thought it was a fish but … I think it was you. I think I accidentally nicked your toe with my fang as I swam by. I think the reason you haven't gone out surfing during the day isn't because of Cody. It's because every cell in your body has been telling you not to. I swear, I didn't mean for this to happen. Everyone I've turned has made a conscious decision to be turned. Only one other time have I made a mistake and that was with Skylar. Everyone else I've turned has been a very deliberate bite to the neck and only when the person has chosen to have it done."

Jake scowled at Tristan, shaking his head in disbelief.

"I think when I nicked you, I must have released a tiny amount of venom into your blood. That's why you haven't completely turned. You're stuck in between. You're still mostly human, which is why you smell human. But you're part vampire shark, which is why you could change your feet into a fin," Tristan speculated.

"You're crazy, man. Vampires? Vampire sharks?" Jake scoffed. "You're insane."

"I wish I was. But think about it. Think about how you feel in the ocean. It's different than it was before. It's more … vivid, right? More visceral? It feels like you're not only in the ocean, but a part of the ocean?"

Despite the fact that Jake's brain struggled with the things Tristan told him, his body told him it was true. And he had seen his own tail fin, after all. He tried to corral his scattered thoughts. "Let's put aside for now that I'm supposedly part vampire, part human. Let's just set that aside. You're telling me Rick killed Cody and you've all known about it all this time and you never said anything to me?"

"I wanted to tell you. You have to know that. But I couldn't tell you without telling you what we are. And that would have put all of us at risk. If I told you Rick killed Cody, you would've gone to the sheriff and they would've brought us all in for questioning, not just me."

"The cops brought you in for questioning?" Jake asked.

Tristan recounted his experience with Garrison. He told Jake about how, if vampire sharks do not submerge themselves in salt water at least once every 72 hours, they age five years an hour until they find salt water again or until they die. He then revealed that he aged 90 years after Garrison beat him and locked him up. "If we were locked up, waiting for trial, we'd all be dead within a week. Me, Skylar, Torrey, Cruz, Logan—all of us."

Jake considered what Tristan said but was not satisfied. "You still should have told me. All this time I've been driving myself crazy, reliving that day in my head over and over, trying to figure out what happened and if I could have prevented Cody's death in any way. I've been beating myself up all this time for leaving him alone in the ocean. And all this time you knew."

"I wanted to tell you the truth. But don't you understand why I couldn't? I would have put a lot of lives at risk other than my own. I couldn't do that. I took care of Rick to ensure he'd never make another mistake like that again. I know what it feels like to lose someone to a vampire shark."

Jake admitted to himself he didn't know how Tristan could have told him about Rick without giving away their secret. But that didn't make it any easier to accept.

"But you said you didn't even like Rick. So why did you turn him? Especially since you said you were so careful after what happened to Julianna."

"I can't," Tristan shook his head.

"You have to. If I'm stuck here—between the human world and whatever world you live in—because of Rick and because of you, you owe it to me. You have to tell me the truth. The whole truth."

"I was asked to turn him." Tristan hoped that would satisfy Jake but he knew it wouldn't.

"Who asked you?"

"Jake, please."

"Who asked you to turn him?!" Jake demanded. "It was Skylar, wasn't it? Rick was her boyfriend, right? She asked you to turn him and you did, even though you didn't trust him."

"Jake, I can't. I promised."

"You don't have to. That's it. My girlfriend's ex-boyfriend killed my best friend. And all this time she never thought to tell me." Jake's eyes burned. "Tristan, you said you wanted to tell me what happened but couldn't because you were afraid of what would happen to everyone. And I believe you, okay? I believe you. But what I want to know is, did Skylar want to tell me?"

Tristan didn't answer. He couldn't without betraying Skylar.

"She didn't, did she?" Jake shook his head.

"Why don't you come back to the house with me? Let's talk this out. Things are really complicated right now. We can work through this though. You, me and Skylar can work through this," Tristan pleaded.

"No. We can't. All this time she said nothing. I told her I loved her and she said nothing!"

"Please come home with me. Leilani's coming over. We can talk this out," Tristan said.

"Leilani? Does she know? Is she one, too?" Jake asked.

"No. She's human and she doesn't know anything. I was actually going to tell her tonight. She's probably on her way over right now."

"And after you tell her what you are, are you going to tell her about Rick? About what really happened?"

"Yes, I said I'd tell her everything tonight. I told her if we're going to have a future together, she needs to know about my past."

"So then everyone would know who killed Cody except me, the only person who ever knew him," Jake anguished. "I've gotta go talk to Skylar. Now."

"I'll go with you. We can talk to her together. She can explain why …"

"I'm not going there for an explanation. I'm going there to tell her it's over." Jake grabbed his board and set off toward Skylar's.

"Jake, wait!"

"Leave me alone, Tristan! You've screwed up my life enough!" Jake shouted. "I wish I never met you! Any of you!"

On the way to Skylar's, Jake saw Leilani approaching.

"Jake, hi! Are you and Tristan …"

"Not now!" Jake yelled as he ran by. He then stopped and turned around. "Hey, Leilani! You want some advice? Run. Go home as fast as you can and forget you ever met Tristan or any of them. Seriously. Go now. You'll thank me for it later."

Tristan ran up as Jake jogged away.

"What happened? Why is Jake so upset?" Leilani asked.

Tristan wiped his hands across his face. "I don't even know where to start."

"Why don't you start at the beginning?" she suggested with a smile.

Tristan put his arm around her and kissed her forehead. "Because, as a very wise woman once said, that is the hardest part."

105 – Lies

Jake stormed into Skylar's house. "Skylar!"

"Up here!"

He bolted upstairs and into the bedroom.

She sat up in bed. "I'm glad you're back. Now where were we?"

"Don't, Skylar, just don't." Jake snatched her dress off the floor and flung it at her. "Get dressed. Meet me downstairs." He turned and left.

"Jake!" She slipped her dress over her head and ran downstairs. "What's wrong?"

"What's wrong? Where do I begin? How about with Rick? I know he was your boyfriend," Jake said. "I know he killed Cody. I even know why he killed Cody. Of course, he didn't mean to kill my best friend. It was just mistaken identity. No big deal. Just the wrong guy wearing the wrong trunks, right?"

"What are you talking about?"

"This whole time you've been with me, you knew who killed Cody. It was your boyfriend. Was that funny to you? Have you been laughing at me this whole time? Am I a joke to you?"

"What did Tristan say to you?" Skylar asked. "He's lying. He just wants to hurt me …"

"Nothing! Tristan didn't tell me a damn thing. I put the pieces together. Don't you see? All this time you've known me, you knew I was suffering and you said nothing. You knew my best friend was killed. You knew who did it. You said nothing!"

"No, you don't understand. Please let me tell you my side of things," Skylar begged.

"You lied to me. Everything we've had has been a lie." Jake's face twisted in grief and disgust. "I never want to see you again. I never want to hear your voice. I never want to see your face. We're done. And if you ever come near me, I'll tell the world what you are. You're a monster."

"Jake, please, let me …"

"Never again!" Jake slammed the door and sped home in his truck.

106 – Three Questions

While Jake and Skylar's relationship was imploding, Tristan and Leilani walked to his place.

"I'm sorry I'm running late," Tristan said as they entered his front door. "Things with Jake took an unexpected turn. Give me five minutes. I'll be right back and then we can start."

Tristan was determined not to veer from his plan for the night. He quickly showered, brushed his teeth and his hair, and dressed in black pants and an espresso-brown button-down shirt that make his eyes sparkle. He rushed back downstairs.

"Ooh, you look nice! Are we going out?" Leilani asked. "I thought we were staying in and you were going to tell me …"

"We are," Tristan interrupted, "but I have something special prepared for you."

"You do? Hey, is Jake okay? He seemed pretty upset. Maybe I should call him."

"I'd wait. Give him a chance to cool down," Tristan suggested.

"What's wrong?"

"He learned some things tonight that were pretty upsetting. He and Skylar are probably having a huge fight right now."

"What's going on?"

"I'll tell you later. I promise. And then we can call Jake together. I'd like to check on him, too. But first, I want to talk about you," Tristan said. "Take a seat in the living room and I'll be right back."

Leilani sat on the couch and straightened her skirt. She wore a periwinkle sleeveless dress with a v-cut neckline and long, flowing skirt. She wasn't sure how late they were going to talk and she wanted to be sexy but comfortable.

Tristan reached into the refrigerator and removed a tray of

organic strawberries and a bottle of champagne. He set two champagne flutes on the tray and carried everything to the coffee table. He lit two white taper candles and poured the champagne.

"First, I'd like to make a toast to you." He raised his glass. "Thank you for telling me everything you told me last night. I know it was tough. You were able to do something I haven't been able to do yet and I admire your courage."

Leilani raised her glass to Tristan's. "Thanks, but it feels weird to be toasted for lying and then admitting it."

"Nevertheless, it took guts. And that's not all we're toasting. I also want to toast you for being you. Until you came into my life, I thought I was incapable of ever falling in love again. I thought it was impossible for me to feel those feelings. You showed me what I was missing in my life. And now that I've found it, I don't think I can live without it ever again. I love you, Leilani, more than I've ever loved anyone."

"But Julianna ..." Leilani interrupted.

"I loved her but it was different. I didn't love her enough to tell her who I really was. If I had, she would have had the opportunity to make a choice and she might still be alive today." Tristan set down his glass to give Leilani his full attention. "I love you enough to give you a choice even if it means you might not choose me. Even if it means I risk losing you."

"You're not going to lose me," she assured him as she set her glass down. "I love you."

"I know. And that makes me happier than I've been in a hundred years," Tristan said.

"A hundred years? That's probably a bit of an exaggeration, don't you think?" Leilani joked.

"Not really," he answered with a cryptic smile. "Before I start, I want to ask you three things. Number 1: Will you please listen to everything I say tonight and try not to judge? Please let me explain and you can ask me as many questions as you want. I will be 100 percent truthful with you. Agreed?"

"Yes," she replied.

"Number 2: Will you please promise me you won't storm out? I need for you to not just listen, but to try to *understand* everything I tell you. It may take all night but I'd like you to stay until you understand everything. Agreed?"

"Yes."

"Before I get to question number 3, I want to tell you that I don't want an answer to this question until you have a chance to think about everything I'm going to tell you tonight. I don't want an answer until you're sure. If it takes an hour or a day or 10 years, take as long as you need. Agreed?"

"Yes," Leilani promised.

"Thank you. Here goes … Leilani, I want you to know I am completely, totally, 100 percent in love with you. You are the one. I want to spend the rest of my life with you." Tristan knelt on one knee in front of her. "So my third and final question of the evening is, Leilani, will you marry me?"

Leilani started to speak but Tristan stopped her. "No, please don't answer yet. I have here in this box a ring. I would like nothing more than to slip this ring on your finger tonight. But first, I need to tell you who I am. After you know everything, you can give me your answer whenever you're ready. I just want you to know this is how I feel about you. Nothing you say or nothing you ask tonight will change my feelings for you, so be as brutal as you need to be to get the information to make your choice."

Leilani looked at the box in his hand. "Tristan, I …"

"No, please don't answer yet."

"It's okay. I'm not going to give you an answer. I promise I will listen to everything you say and I promise I will try to understand. But I want you to know how much this means to me. Thank you."

107 — HIStory

"All right, let's begin." Tristan took a deep breath. "Leilani, when I say I want to spend the rest of my life with you, I'm not talking about the next 50 years. I'm talking about the next 500 years."

Leilani cocked her head and reached for a strawberry. *500 years? He likes to exaggerate, doesn't he? It's sweet though,* she thought as she bit into the juicy red berry.

"I can see you thinking, 'Oh yeah, 500 years. He sure likes to exaggerate,'" Tristan smiled.

Leilani raised her eyebrows. "Are you a mind reader? Is that what you're trying to tell me? Because you're pretty much right on. But you forgot the part where I said, 'That's sweet.'"

"No, I'm not a mind reader. And I'm not exaggerating."

"What do you mean?"

"I said 500 years because I'm not exactly … human. I was once. I was turned into a vampire in 1936. That means I can live to be 800 or 900 or even 1,000 years old."

"I'm sorry," Leilani interrupted. "I thought you just said you were a vampire."

"Yeah, I did. And that's not all I am. I'm something more."

Tristan explained to Leilani how he was turned into a vampire, against his will, in San Francisco. He shared how 36 years later he developed the ability to transform into a great white shark. He told her about how he and Dean turned hundreds of young surfers into vampire sharks and how that led to Julianna's death. He told her how he created the Rules to prevent that from happening to anyone ever again. Finally, he explained how he and the Nomads travel around the world to locations where shark attacks have occurred to determine if a vampire shark is responsible and, if so, to eliminate the offender.

Leilani sat motionless, quietly absorbing everything he said.

When Tristan finished, he noticed her arms and legs were crossed—defensive body language. He decided to take a break. He leaned back on the couch and took a drink of champagne.

"Is that everything?" she asked.

"Those are the high points. There's some stuff I need to tell you about Jake and Skylar, but let's start with what I just told you."

"Tristan, you have to understand that all this is completely unbelievable, right?"

"I understand. If you want I can prove it to you," he offered.

"How? Are you going to show me your fangs?" she asked sarcastically. She took a swig of champagne.

"I can, if you'd like."

"Sure. Why not?"

Tristan opened his mouth and released his fangs. Leilani jumped and nearly dropped the champagne flute in her lap.

"Okay, that was good," she admitted as she struggled to make sense of Tristan's stories. They were so wild she was completely thrown for a loop. *Why on earth would he tell me he's a surf vampire or vampire shark or whatever he calls it? What could possibly be his motive? I would say it's to push me away, but then why would he ask me to marry him?*

Leilani checked to make sure she hadn't spilled champagne in her lap and decided to push ahead. "And maybe next you can turn into a shark for me."

"I would but I can't unless I'm in the ocean. We can go if you want but you've already seen me in shark form. Twice." Tristan hoped to jar Leilani's memory and chip away at the wall of doubt she was busily constructing.

Leilani blinked. *Twice? What does he* ... Immediately, her mind flashed to the night they ran into Lisa and Erica. She saw a brownish-gray shark underwater headed toward her. She looked into the shark's eyes and felt recognition. *And that looked like the same shark I came face to face with in Hawaii, during my final surf competition, when I woke up underwater.*

"No," she shook her head.

"Yes," Tristan said gently. "That was me. You saw me the night we encountered Lisa and Erica. I saw you floating face down and I panicked. I was so concerned with reaching you I forgot to change back into my human form. You looked into my eyes. I saw you. You recognized me even though you didn't know it at the time."

Leilani sat back. *Oh my god.* "And the other time?" she asked, though she knew the answer.

"It was when you were 16, during a surf competition. You said it was your last one. I was swimming around, watching the competition from below. I saw you get thrown into the coral and get knocked out. I swam over and saw your head bleeding. There was something about you, something I couldn't explain. I floated there staring at you, trying to figure out what I was feeling and you woke up. You looked at me for quite a while. That impressed me. Humans usually see a face like mine and swim for their lives. But you stared at me, until you had to surface for air. I was afraid you were going to tell people you saw a shark, so I left. I didn't want to be hunted and killed for inadvertently scaring a teenage girl."

Leilani tried to deny what she knew in her gut was true. "But I told you that story about how I saw a shark during that competition. How do I know you're not telling me this because you already know that stuff?"

"Because you were wearing a bright yellow bikini. There was a black band, about a half-inch wide, across the top of your bikini top and bottoms. You were wearing a gold chain with a small dolphin charm around your neck. And you had a cut on your right shoulder and bicep. When you hit the coral with your head, it also sliced into your shoulder and arm."

Leilani stared at him. She hadn't told him what she was wearing or about the cuts on her shoulder and arm. *It's all true. Everything he's saying is true.*

"Are you still with me?" he asked. "You look a little sick."

"No, I'm here. I think I need a minute. I've entered this whole alternate reality I never knew existed and it's been right here in front of my eyes. Give me a minute to get my bearings."

She thought back on her relationship with Tristan and the nights they spent together. *Nights. Nights only for the most part. I've seen him at his house during the day but we've never been out together, other than when he walks me to my car. Not breakfast, not lunch, not surfing. Only surfing at night.*

109 – Grilling

After a few moments, questions began racing through Leilani's mind. "You said I could ask as many questions as I want?"

"Absolutely."

"You do realize I'm an FBI agent, right?" she smiled. "I'm pretty good at this."

"Yes, for the last 24 hours at least," Tristan smiled back. "Fire away."

"Well the obvious question is, if you're a vampire, what do you eat?"

"I eat whatever I want. I eat regular food mostly, though I do like my meat raw or rare, which I know grosses you out since you're a vegetarian. And that means you're going to like this next part even less. When vampire sharks break the Rules, sometimes we kill them with wooden stakes but sometimes we turn into great whites and go after them in the ocean. When we catch them, we eat them. It's one fish eating another fish, or sometimes a fish eating a vampire."

Leilani's eyes widened. "That's gross."

"To you it is. It's not gross to a shark. Great white sharks generally don't like humans. They're too bony. There's not enough meat and fat like there is on seals and other animals. But to a shark, a human is simply a piece of meat—nothing more, nothing less."

"And what about humans?" Leilani asked. "In the movies, vampires are always desperate for human blood."

"Vampires do love human blood but they don't need it to live," Tristan explained. "They have it as a delicacy, so to speak. I don't like vampires much. Most of them have learned to blend into human society and have found ways to dine on blood without killing people. But some of them kill indiscriminately and it makes me sick. I used to be like that. Believe me, I'm not proud of it. I hate to even tell you about it but I promised I'd tell you everything. And now when I think back on the people I killed for food, I'm filled with regret. I think about their families who were waiting for them to come home. I think about the lives I destroyed. Losing Julianna gave me a perspective I had lost. She taught me how to feel like a human again. But that doesn't erase the things I did that I am deeply, deeply ashamed of."

"You killed people for food?"

"Yes," Tristan confessed. "I didn't think twice about it when I was a vampire. But when you know better, you do better—and I know better."

"What about since then? Have you killed humans since you became a vampire shark?"

"I told you about the Rules. Rule number 2 is: Do not kill, unless you're certain it's a righteous kill. That applies to vampire sharks as well as humans."

"So you do kill humans?" she asked.

He nodded yes.

"But who do you kill? And what gives you the right to decide to kill anyone?"

"It's complicated. First, let's look at it from a biological point of view. Let's look at the food chain. When you're a shark eating a human, it's no different than a human eating the flesh of a cow or pig or fish. It's just flesh. The thing with most humans is they think they're above it all. They like to say they're at the 'top of the food chain' so they can eat whatever animal they choose. They may be at the top, but they're still *part* of the food chain. A human is an apex predator but there are lots of other apex predators, too. When a shark or grizzly bear or lion eats a human or another animal in their natural habitat, they're not doing anything immoral. They're simply eating a meal. It's for survival. To a shark, eating a human is no different than eating a seal. One piece of meat is not more or less valuable than another. It's all food."

Tristan saw the doubtful look on Leilani's face and pressed forward. "Now *that* is quite unlike humans. Humans think their lives are more valuable than any other creatures. They pollute the ocean with trash and sewage and chemicals and noise and a million other things, and think it's their right and their privilege because they're 'at the top.' They kill for sport and leave the earth strewn with animal carcasses to rot and waste. They shoot animals from boats and jeeps and helicopters, leaving the poor creatures to die alone, writhing in pain. They kill for money, too. Like those poachers who slaughter elephants—who are highly intelligent creatures, by the way—for their tusks. And did you know millions of sharks are killed each year for shark fin soup? People slice off the shark's fin and toss the bleeding animal back into the ocean to die. I mean, imagine taking a human, hacking off his arms and throwing him in the ocean to flail and drown. Humans also kill each other for ridiculous reasons like greed and religion and jealousy. Humans are not superior to any other creature on this planet, believe me."

"So you just kill anyone? The human race is like one big buffet to you?" Leilani asked.

"No. You're missing the point. Let me explain," Tristan said calmly. "While I don't believe humans are better than any other creature, I do know what it feels like to lose a human. Julianna died because a rogue vampire shark, who I created, took a bite out of her for sport and left her to die. He wasn't feeding. He was hunting for fun, for the thrill of the kill. That is wrong. It's wrong for a vampire and it's wrong for a human. When vampire sharks—who follow the Rules—kill to feed, we don't target some random person. We never kill children. Ever.

I told you that's Rule number 1. Even most regular vampires have the sense not to kill kids. We only feed on the worst kind of humans—those who kill other humans or mortally wound their souls. We kill humans the world is better off without."

"But how do you decide who's a bad person? What gives you the right?" Leilani demanded.

"We only target humans who have broken human laws but who managed to slip through the system and offend again. We're simply doing what your byzantine legal system can't do."

"So you're telling me you kill and eat humans when you're a shark, but it's okay because they're bad humans," Leilani said sarcastically.

"Yes. Humans are part of the food chain, like I told you. By only targeting those who deserve to die, we are a lot more fair-minded than many humans. I told you we don't kill for sport. When we kill, we kill for food and nothing goes to waste. Unlike humans, we don't do things like torture our food for profit or to save a few bucks. Humans are not a good model for the humane treatment of their food. Vampire sharks don't imprison chickens in tiny cages that are too small for them to spread their wings or even turn around because more chickens can be raised more cheaply. We don't isolate baby cows in tiny pens and restrict their movement so their muscles can't develop and then call it veal. We don't force-feed corn down birds' throats to fatten their livers and then call it foie gras because 'fattened liver' supposedly sounds more palatable than what it really is—tortured goose. Most humans simply don't care if their food comes from humanely treated animals. They don't care about the pain they inflict on other species."

"Tristan, I get your point. And I already know all that stuff. A lot of that is why I chose to become a vegetarian in the first place."

"And I respect your choice," he said. "I'm simply asking

you to consider that humans are not a great example of the right way to kill and eat food."

"You're right. I'm not arguing that with you. But what gives you the right to choose to kill a human?" Leilani asked. "How do you know they won't change?"

"I don't. But what gives them the right to hurt or kill more people because one day, maybe, possibly, far off in the future they might see the light and change their ways? When we decide to kill humans, it's because they've already proven— repeatedly—they can't be trusted to interact with other humans."

"Did you kill that boy in Imperial Beach?" Leilani demanded.

"No. That was a rogue vampire shark and he was dealt with. I told you, we don't kill children."

"What about the Del Norte Reefers? They disappeared recently and no one seems to know a thing."

"Yes, the other Nomads and I killed them."

Leilani's eyes widened. "Why? Why them?"

"Do you have any idea how despicable those guys were? Do you know the horrific things they did?" Tristan asked.

"I saw their case files. They had some terrible things in there like assault and rape and ..."

"Those are just words on a page. Every one of those words has real, human consequences. The reason we went after those guys was for a friend. He didn't ask us to, but it was the right thing to do. This friend told me some things in confidence but I'll tell you because I trust you and because I think it might help you understand. Okay?"

"Okay," she replied. "But I don't think I'll ever be able to understand killing someone."

"Do you know Mark, the owner of the surf shop a couple doors down from the Italian restaurant we went to with Dean?" he asked.

"I know of him. I don't know him personally."

"Well I do. He's a good friend and a good guy. Earlier this year, his little sister was going through a rough time. She flunked out of college in her freshman year and was feeling lost. She went to the beach one night. The Reefers were there, having a bonfire. They asked her to join them for a drink. She went over and they fed her beer after beer until she passed out. She woke up the next morning in the sand, bloody, naked and alone."

Leilani winced.

Tristan continued, hoping to show her why he was right to remove the Reefers from the human race. "They took turns with her all night as she lay there unconscious. When she awoke in the morning, she couldn't remember much. She remembered drinking with them but not much after that. She didn't know if it was just the alcohol or if she'd been drugged, too. She found her clothes on the beach and drove herself home. She cleaned herself up, took some aspirin, and went to bed because she was in a lot of pain. She was too embarrassed to call anyone because she blamed herself for drinking with those guys. After a couple days, though, she finally called her brother because she couldn't stop hemorrhaging. He took her to the hospital. The doctor told her that her injuries were so severe she can never have kids. When she sleeps, what happened to her comes back in flashes in nightmares. She has post-traumatic stress disorder and a huge pile of medical bills. And those guys were never prosecuted. By the time she made it to the doctor, the DNA evidence was gone. Because her memory was trashed, there wasn't much to build a case on. She was too terrified to file a report but, even if she did, it probably would've gone to Garrison and he's bungled cases like this before."

Leilani sat quietly, empathizing with the woman's pain as Tristan went on.

"The thing is, that's not the first time those guys have done something like that. And if they continued to exist, it wouldn't be the last. That woman will carry the physical, mental and emotional scars from that night with her the rest of her life. They didn't kill her but they destroyed the life she dreamed of having. If the legal system worked, they'd be put away for life. But it didn't, so we chose to enforce our Rules upon them."

"But Tristan …"

"Listen, I know it's not a perfect system. Nothing is perfect. Your system isn't perfect. My system isn't perfect. But it's better than nothing. And I feel much better about you or anyone else going to the beach alone knowing those guys are gone."

As much as Leilani liked the idea of Tristan getting the Del Norte Reefers off the street, it still felt wrong to do it by killing. "I understand what you're saying. But I don't think I can go along with killing someone, no matter how terrible they are."

"I understand," he said. "But think about it. It might not seem like it, but we're doing humans a favor."

110 – Mistakes

"What about Cody?" Leilani asked. "What happened to him?"

"That's why Jake was so upset tonight." Tristan told her how Rick mistook Cody for the head Reefer and that he tried to stop him but failed to make it in time.

"And all this time you knew what happened to Cody and didn't tell Jake? How could you not tell him, knowing how much he was hurting and feeling guilty about leaving Cody behind?"

"I wanted to, but I couldn't without giving away our secret about what we are. And it wasn't my call. It was Skylar's. I begged her to tell Jake but she refused."

"Skylar? Why was it her call?" Leilani asked.

"Rick was her boyfriend. Skylar asked me to turn him. I didn't think she knew him well enough but I couldn't tell her no."

Leilani's thoughts raced back to the conversation she overheard between Tristan and Skylar the morning before. *That's what Tristan meant when he said she "rushed things with Rick" and that he didn't want them "to make another mistake."*

"And Jake found out tonight Rick was Skylar's boyfriend?" she asked. "And that he killed Cody?"

"And that she said nothing."

Leilani leaned back on the couch. "Poor Jake."

"There's something else he's upset about. But he should tell you himself. It's not my place to tell you," Tristan said.

"Can we call to see if he's okay? He's probably freaking out."

Tristan dialed Jake's number. It went straight to voicemail. "Jake, it's Tristan. I'm calling to see how you're doing, so call me back. I'm going to put Leilani on." He handed her the phone.

"Jake, Tristan told me what happened with Rick and Cody, and with Skylar. I'm so sorry. Please call my cell, even if it's the middle of the night. I'm worried about you. Call me when you get this. Bye."

111 – Midnight Confessions

"Leilani, there's something else you should know about vampire sharks. We can't go for more than 72 hours without being in the ocean." Tristan explained the aging process and dire consequences for every hour spent out of the ocean after three days. "That's why it's so dangerous to get mixed up with the police. If you get thrown in jail—even if it's a mistake—you can very quickly die there."

"Have you ever gone more than 72 hours without being in the ocean?" she asked.

"A few times, mostly when I was younger. Once I traveled inland and nearly died. That's when I realized we need salt water to live. Another time I just didn't make it into the ocean for a few days. I did the math and figured out we lose about five years for every hour spent out of the ocean, after three days."

"What about recently?" She braced herself for the answer.

"Yeah, I was brought in for questioning regarding Rick's disappearance. Garrison slammed my face into the table, repeatedly. Then he blamed me for it and locked me up for the weekend."

Leilani gasped. *I know why Tristan's face changed. He aged while he was in jail. How much? 50 vampire years? 100?*

"Does it hurt? To age that quickly?" she asked.

"Like you wouldn't believe." As Tristan answered, he saw the color drain from Leilani's face.

"I need to tell you something," she said. "I started to tell you last night but I need to tell you now."

Leilani explained how, during the barbecue, she found Rick's board in the guest bedroom and phoned in an anonymous tip. "I'm sorry. I only wanted to see if the sheriff found anything. Garrison later said there was a second call, pointing him to you.

But I'm part of the reason you were locked up. I'm so sorry. I didn't know the consequences, that it would cause you pain, that it could kill you …"

"You phoned in a tip?" Tristan asked, surprised by her confession.

"Yes, but it was before I really knew you. Before our first date. That's the last terrible thing I have to tell you about myself. You know everything now. I swear."

"I believe you," he said. "I wish you hadn't done that, of course, but there's no way you could have known what would happen. I know you didn't mean for me to get hurt. But you said there was a second call?"

"That's what Garrison said."

"Do you have any idea who it was?" Tristan struggled to figure out who else would have phoned in a tip about him and Rick's board. "Do you think it could have been Jake?"

"No. I think Jake would've told me if he found something in your house or if he called the sheriff."

"Then who would've done it?"

"I don't know." Leilani stared at the floor, deeply regretting causing Tristan pain and the loss of several years of his life.

"Leilani?" Tristan gently waved his hand in front of her face. "You look like you're far away again. It's okay about the phone call. I forgive you. Really. You didn't know. You couldn't have."

"Thanks. I don't know what to say. I think my mind is on overload."

"I understand. That's why I want you to take as long as you need." He wrapped his arm around her. "I would like nothing more than for you to say you'll marry me and be my wife. Now that you know who I am, you can decide if you want to be with me."

"Do you mean I'd be with you as a human … or that you'd want to turn me?" she asked hesitantly.

"I don't care. I just want you. That's all that matters. You can be whatever you want to be. I just hope you want to be with me. Would you like to stay here tonight? Or would you like to go home?"

"Neither," she answered. "I think I need to go to Jake's."

"I'll go with you."

"No, it's better if I go alone. Something tells me Jake isn't going to want to see you or Skylar tonight." Leilani gave Tristan a tired smile.

"You're right. But call me afterward. Let me know you're both okay."

"I will."

"I love you, Leilani."

Leilani wanted to say it back, but was too tired to know how she felt. Instead, she smiled and kissed Tristan's cheek. "Thank you. I appreciate you trusting me enough to tell me all this tonight—and for forgiving me for what I did. I'll think about everything you said. I promise."

"That's all I ask," he said. "Call me later."

112 – Cold Comfort

On the drive to Jake's, Leilani cranked up the stereo and blasted the air conditioning to keep herself awake. She parked near his apartment and trudged to his front door in the damp, chilly night air.

She rang the doorbell but there was no response. She knocked. "Jake! It's Leilani." She knocked again. "Jake, please. I need to know you're okay."

"Go away!" he shouted from behind the door. "I don't want to talk to anyone right now."

"Please let me in, just for a minute. I need to see you. I'm worried about you."

Jake unlocked the deadbolt and opened the door a crack. "There. Now you've seen me. I don't want to talk."

"You don't have to talk. Can I come in for a few minutes? I can make us some tea or something to eat."

Jake opened the door a little wider. Considering that an invitation, Leilani barged in. To prevent Jake from stopping her, she marched straight to the kitchen and rummaged around. She found a box of tea bags in the cupboard and set some water to boil in a pan on the stove. She opened the refrigerator. *Not much to choose from here.* She removed a small loaf of bread and half-stick of butter.

"Tea and toast?" she offered.

"Whatever. I'm not hungry," he muttered.

"That's okay. I am. I'll make enough for both of us in case you change your mind."

Leilani pulled two mugs from the cupboard and set a chamomile tea bag in each. She dropped two slices of bread into the toaster. She worked quietly, waiting for Jake to begin talking first.

She removed the boiling water from the stove, poured it into the mugs and carried them to the kitchen table. She buttered the toast, placed it on two small plates and carried those to the table as well.

Leilani nodded to Jake to come sit with her. She took a bite of toast. "I never imagined toast could taste so good. I'm exhausted."

Jake took a seat. "So did Tristan tell you what they are?"

"Yes, he did," she said softly.

"Did he tell you Rick was one of them and that he killed Cody?"

"Yes, he told me that, too. I'm so sorry." She removed the tea bags from the mugs. She pushed a mug toward him. "Here, take a drink."

Jake raised the mug to his lips. He felt the warm liquid slide across his tongue and down his throat. It felt soothing.

"All this time, Leilani. All this time they've all known and no one said a damn thing." He quickly wiped away a tear forming at the corner of his eye. "I was finally starting to feel normal again—to feel good even. And now this."

"I know. I'm so sorry. I can't imagine how you must feel."

"You know, after you called me and told me what you overheard, I went to Skylar. I asked her point blank about Rick and she didn't say anything. I even told her I loved her. I'm so stupid. I betrayed Cody. I was with the woman who was with the man who killed him."

"Jake …"

"No," he interrupted. "I should have known. How could I not have known? I started out looking for those guys so I could find out what happened to Cody. Then I got sucked in. They all seemed so great. Surfing every night, having fun, no responsibilities. I fell right into it. I blew off my friends. I blew off my work. For what? For a woman? She's not even human."

Leilani didn't know how to respond. She knew nothing she said could alleviate his pain.

"What's wrong with me?" he lamented. "How could I not have known?"

"It's not your fault," she tried to comfort him. "There's no way you could have known."

He ignored her. "I didn't even tell you the best part. It turns out, I'm one of them."

Leilani set down her mug. "What do you mean?"

"Tristan didn't tell you?"

"He told me what happened with Rick and how he didn't get there in time. He said there's something else you're upset about, but he wanted you to tell me."

"How big of him," Jake said bitterly. "It turns out while Tristan was trying to save Cody, he accidentally nicked me with one of his fangs. Apparently some of his venom mixed with my blood. It wasn't enough to turn me completely, just partway. So I'm not quite human anymore but I'm not one of them. I'm stuck somewhere in between."

Leilani's eyes widened in surprise. "But how is that even possible?"

"You tell me. You're dating the king of the vampire sharks."

"Jake ... I found out about all this tonight, just like you. I don't know how this stuff works. I don't even know what to think about any of this or Tristan or ..."

Leilani's trembling voice pulled Jake from the pool of self-pity he'd been wallowing in all night. "I'm sorry, Leilani. I shouldn't be taking this out on you."

"It's okay. I can't imagine what you must be going through. I want to help but I don't know how," she said.

"You are just by being here. I think you're the only friend I have left," he said.

"Tristan wanted to come. But I told him to stay home. I said you probably wouldn't want to see him."

"You got that right."

"I know it doesn't help, but I do think Tristan was trying to save Cody. He feels terrible about what happened. He knows how painful it is to lose someone so violently like that," Leilani explained.

"Maybe, but he's also the cause of all this. He turned Rick. He's got to take some responsibility."

"I think he does."

"What about you? Do you love him—knowing what he is, what he does?" Jake asked.

"I don't know. I thought I did. But I was in no way prepared for this. I don't know what to think or how to feel about anything."

"Welcome to my world." Jake took another drink of tea. "So do you have any deep dark secrets you'd like to share with me? Might as well get everything out in the open, right?"

Leilani looked down at the crumbs on her plate. "Actually, yes."

Jake glared at her, knowing there was no way he could stand another betrayal.

"I don't know if this is the right time but I'd rather tell you now than later. When the paramedics were trying to revive Cody, I was there in the parking lot talking to the detective in charge. I heard about a shark attack over the sheriff's radio and rushed down," she said.

Jake remembered seeing a woman with blond hair talking to the detective, but he only saw her from the back.

Leilani went on to tell Jake about her job, her investigation, and how it led to Tristan and the Nomads. "I'm sorry I lied to you. I just wanted to find out what happened to Cody and to Rick," she explained. "That's all."

"I should probably be mad at you," Jake said, "but I'm not.

Out of everyone, you were the only one who was trying to help me."

"I still am." Leilani reached across the table to touch the back of Jake's hand. "I care about you."

"That wasn't just part of your job?"

"No. Our friendship was never part of the job. Throughout all of this, I've wanted to find out what happened to Cody as much as you. I knew how much pain you were in. I only wanted to help."

"I know," he sighed.

"We'll get through this. I'm here for whatever you need, okay?"

"Okay. I think, right now, I need some sleep." He pushed his mug to the center of the table.

"That's a good idea. How about if I stay here on the couch? I'm too tired to drive home and I can be here if you need me. Then in the morning, we can have a big breakfast, talk this out and figure out what to do next," she suggested.

"Okay." Jake got up from the table. "Let me get you a pillow and blanket."

"Thanks. Do you mind if I call Tristan? He was worried and I promised to call to let him know you're okay."

"Do what you gotta do. But I don't want to talk to him."

"I understand," Leilani said. "Try to get some sleep. I promise things will look a little better in the morning."

"I doubt that. But thanks for saying it anyway."

113 – Just

After Leilani left, Tristan called Dean. He needed a sympathetic ear and knew Skylar would be in no mood to talk with him. "Dean, it's Tristan."

"Tristan? What time is it?"

"It's late." Tristan glanced at his clock and realized what day it was. "Oh my god. I shouldn't be calling. You're getting married tonight. Forget it. We'll talk another time."

"No, if you're calling at this hour, it must be important," Dean said.

"Are you sure? I don't want to trouble you, today of all days."

"It's no trouble," Dean insisted. "What's wrong?"

"What's not? Skylar's boyfriend dumped her and I'm pretty sure she blames me. I told Leilani what I am and she left. I have no idea what's going through her head or if she's even coming back," Tristan said. "It's just … I feel like my world is crumbling around me and I don't know how to stop it from happening."

"Dude, I'm coming over. Give me 15 minutes." Dean smiled. His fangs glinted in the faint light streaming from the illuminated screen on his phone.

This is even better than I imagined. I won't have to destroy Tristan. He's already got a head start doing it to himself. Dean thought of a line from a Radiohead song, *You do it to yourself, you do and that's what really hurts is you do it to yourself.*

Fourteen minutes later Dean arrived at Tristan's house. Upon entering, he spied the champagne bottle and half-full glasses in the living room.

They sat down at the kitchen table and Tristan recounted how he proposed to Leilani and told her about his life as a vampire and vampire shark. He then revealed what happened with Rick,

Cody and Jake. He didn't mention Jake was now part vampire shark. He thought Jake should be the one to tell people. But he did share how Jake freaked out about Skylar's relationship with Rick and went to her house to break up with her.

"So that's it," Tristan concluded. "I told Jake the truth and now Skylar probably never wants to see me again. I told Leilani the truth and she bolted. I don't know if she's ever coming back."

"Man, you've had quite a night," Dean said.

"What should I do? I feel like everyone is turning against me."

"Tristan, you worry too much. You told Leilani to take her time thinking things over. That's what she's doing. You probably blew her mind. Give her some time to piece it back together. She'll come around. Skylar's another story. She doesn't react well when things don't go her way. We should go talk to her."

"I really don't think she wants to see me right now," Tristan said.

"We should go anyway. If she won't see you, I'll talk with her and try to calm her down."

"All right. But then you should get home. I've already taken up too much of your time. You need your rest before the ceremony later."

"Don't worry about me," Dean assured him. "I've got everything covered."

114 – Sever

Tristan and Dean walked to Skylar's house and knocked on her door.

"Thanks, man. I don't know what I'd do without you tonight," Tristan said.

"No problem," Dean replied. "That's what friends are for, right?"

A couple seconds later, Skylar flung open the door, expecting to see Jake. "I'm so sorry," she blurted out before realizing it was Tristan and Dean. "Tristan, I told you if you told Jake anything about Rick, I'd kill you. Get out of here! I never want to see you again!"

"I didn't tell him. He figured it out. Let me explain," Tristan pleaded.

"No!" Skylar yelled. "You just don't want me to be happy. You can't stand for me to be with someone else. I'm sick of it. I'm sick of you and your twisted mind games. I wish I'd never met you."

"I didn't tell him. I swear …"

"You ruined my life. You destroy everything you touch. You killed my relationship with Jake on purpose. I knew I couldn't trust you!"

Emotionally exhausted from the long evening, Tristan snapped. "Oh, like I can trust you?! You've had it in for Leilani since the beginning. You know that first night we all went surfing with her and Jake? Remember when she wiped out? You had nothing to do with that, right?"

"I told you I didn't," Skylar hissed. "I was waxing my board. I hadn't even made it into the water yet. It's not my fault your girlfriend can't surf."

"Really? Then maybe you can explain something to me.

When I carried Leilani to shore to make sure she was okay and you ran over from waxing your board, why was your hair all wet?"

Skylar lunged at Tristan, screaming, "I hate you!"

Dean caught her flailing arms and held her back. "Tristan, go. I'll take care of this," he said calmly.

"Dean, no, this is my mess," Tristan said.

"Go, Tristan!" Skylar shouted. "Nobody wants you here!"

"Shut up down there!" a voice yelled from a neighboring house.

"The neighbors are going to call the police. Tristan, go home. It'll be okay," Dean said. "I'll call you later."

Tristan turned and left. Still holding Skylar, Dean walked her inside her house. He breathed in the scent of her hair. A twisted smile escaped his lips as the door closed behind them.

115 – Twisting

"Skylar, he's gone. Calm down," Dean soothed as he led her to the couch.

"I hate him," she seethed.

"I know. And you have every reason to. What he did was unforgivable."

"So he did do it? He told Jake about me and Rick?" Even though Skylar had accused Tristan of doing exactly that, she wasn't sure if it was actually true.

"Tristan is my oldest friend … but I can't stand by and watch this go on any longer. You need to know the truth." Dean grimaced like it pained him to betray Tristan.

"What do you mean?"

Dean began to spin his lies, hoping to trap Skylar in his web. "Tristan told me tonight that he told Jake about you and Rick on purpose. He said you were getting too close to Jake and he wanted to put an end to it."

"But why? I thought he liked Jake. And he's got that pathetic blond so why would he care what I do?"

"Because he's Tristan. He wants it all. He wants to have Leilani but keep you on the side for when he gets bored. He said all he has to do is snap his fingers and you'll come running back to his bed. He said he can have you whenever he wants because that's what he's been doing the past 10 years," Dean lied.

Skylar gasped. She felt sick to her stomach.

Dean draped his arm across her shoulders, pretending to comfort her. "I'm so sorry to have to be the one to tell you this. But I can't stand to see him treat you like this anymore."

"But Tristan wouldn't …"

"Wouldn't he? He killed Rick, right? Rick was yours. Tristan had no right to do that. What about your other boyfriends?"

"You mean like Xan?" Skylar asked.

Dean had no idea who Xan was. "Like Xan. And what happened with him?"

"Tristan took him out surfing and left him to turn to a pile of ash in the sun," Skylar recalled.

"Are you starting to see a pattern here? He doesn't want you to be with anyone else. He sees you as his property. And there's something else. But I don't know if I should tell you. I don't want to see you hurt."

"What? Please, Dean. I need to know."

"Did you know Tristan proposed to Leilani tonight?"

Skylar felt tears sting the corners of her eyes.

"He did. Sky, you've been with this guy 10 years and has he ever said he loves you?"

Tears began to roll down her cheeks. "No. He said he would never love me."

Dean reached up and wiped her tears with his fingertips. "You're too good for him. You can't let him treat you like this. He's never been serious about you. You should hear the things he says about you when you're not around." Dean wrinkled his face, pretending to be disgusted.

"What did he say?" Skylar asked, alarmed to hear Dean say such things about Tristan.

"No, I'm not going to repeat the vile things he said. You need to leave him, once and for all. You need a clean break, a fresh start."

"But where would I go?" Skylar felt utterly and completely lost.

"You could come away with me," Dean offered.

"But you're getting married today."

"Skylar, don't you see? It's you. It's always been you. I could never tell you because you were with Tristan and I couldn't betray him. But I don't care anymore. He doesn't deserve you. He never did. You are the most beautiful, most amazing woman in the entire world. Any man in his right mind would be lucky to have you."

"But what about Amanda?" Skylar asked.

"I'll tell Amanda it's over. The wedding's off."

"But don't you love her?"

Dean cupped his hands on the sides of Skylar's face and stared into her eyes. "I fell for you the first time I saw you. But with Tristan around, I never thought I had a chance. You deserve someone who'll give anything to be with you. If you said you wanted to run away tonight and get married, I'd do it in a heartbeat. That's how special you are." *The web is spun,* he thought. *Here comes the prey.*

"You'd really do that?"

"In a human heartbeat. Just say the word." He could tell from her rapidly dilating pupils he was saying all the right things.

"I ... I don't know what to say."

Dean's blue eyes blazed with excitement. "Say yes! We don't have to get married tonight but let's start a new life together, away from everyone and everything."

Skylar looked at his beaming face. *He's offering me everything I ever wanted from Tristan. But Tristan betrayed me. He ruined my life. He's not the person I thought he was. Maybe I do need a fresh start—away from Tristan, away from everyone. But this is all so sudden.*

"Sky, you deserve to be happy. Forget about everyone else and worry about yourself for once."

Stung by Dean's account of Tristan's numerous betrayals, Skylar agreed. "Okay. Let's do it."

"Are you sure?"

She nodded, "Yes. Let's go away together. Just you and me."

"We are going to have such an amazing time! You will not regret this," Dean promised.

116 – Dreaming

As soon as Leilani climbed under the blanket on Jake's couch, she fell fast asleep. Her mind struggled to process all the information from her marathon conversation with Tristan.

While she slept, she dreamed of a wedding. She stood on the beach, staring at the bride and groom. After a moment, she realized she was the bride and Tristan was the groom. She felt her white gown blowing in the sea breeze as he placed the ring on her finger. Before she could place the ring on his finger, she heard screaming. She turned and saw Jake carrying Cody's bloody body. Jake set Cody down in the sand and tried to revive him. She and Tristan ran down the aisle to help. There was blood everywhere. Leilani looked at her white gown, which was now turning crimson with blood. She looked down at the sand again and saw it wasn't Cody lying on the ground bleeding to death; it was herself. There was a large bite taken out of her side. As she lay in her wedding gown, bleeding, Tristan leaned over her saying, "Leilani, I ..."

Leilani bolted upright, sweating and panting. She glanced down at her body to make sure she was still in one piece. *Relax. It was only a nightmare.* She struggled to calm her breathing. *If it was just a dream, then why am I still so anxious?*

117 – Breakfast

Later that morning, Jake walked out to the couch and found Leilani dressed in shorts and a t-shirt. "Hey, did you go home and change?"

"I woke up early so thought I'd go home and freshen up," she explained. "And I promised you a big breakfast so I went to the store and picked up all the fixings. I hope you're hungry."

"Thanks. But you didn't have to do that."

"I know I didn't have to, but you've treated me to two meals and now I'm treating you. I'll get started on breakfast. Why don't you go shower and then join me in the kitchen?" Leilani wanted to get Jake moving so he wouldn't wallow and fall into a depression.

"Okay," he agreed, too groggy to protest.

Leilani prepared a fruit salad and then chopped vegetables and shredded cheese for an omelet for Jake. She whipped up pancake batter and started pouring the first pancake when he returned to the kitchen.

She handed him a glass of mango juice. "Your juice, sir."

"Thanks." Jake eyed all the food on the countertop and stove. "I don't think this kitchen has ever seen this much activity at one time."

"Well, I did say a big breakfast. If you're hungry now, there's fruit salad on the table. Your omelet and pancakes are coming right up." She turned back to the stove to continue pouring the pancake batter. She then dumped two beaten eggs into a hot skillet.

"Thanks, Leilani," Jake said.

"No problem."

"No, I mean, not only for breakfast—for coming here last night, for being here this morning. Thank you."

"Really, it's no problem. You're actually doing me a favor. I'm not ready to face Tristan yet and this gives me an excuse," she smiled. "How are you feeling today?"

"A little better. I still feel like my heart got ripped out, trampled, and handed back to me, but better," he said. "You know, last night before you got here, I felt like I was at the bottom of a deep, dark hole. Now I feel like I'm climbing out but I don't know where to go. I think I mostly feel lost, like I have no idea what to do with the rest of my life."

"I know exactly what you mean. And I wish I could say something to help but I've got nothing." She removed the omelet from the pan and stacked three pancakes on Jake's plate. She served herself three pancakes and walked the plates to the table.

As she took her seat and poured maple syrup on her pancakes, Jake studied her face. "You look tired. Did you sleep okay? I'm sorry. I should've offered you my room and I could've slept on the couch."

"The couch was fine. It was the nightmares that kept me up," she confessed.

"You wanna talk about it?"

"Not really. Last night was just … intense. I feel like I woke up in one world yesterday and a completely different world today."

"Tell me about it. My ex is a vampire shark. Oh yeah, I'm one, too," Jake laughed.

"Yeah, so's the guy who asked me to marry him," Leilani added.

"What?! You didn't tell me Tristan proposed."

"Yeah, last night. I haven't given him an answer. He told me to think about it for as long as I need to."

"What are you going to say?" Jake pointed to his plate, "This omelet is amazing by the way. Forget interior design or the FBI. You should be a chef."

"Thanks. Cooking helps me relieve stress. I think it's the chopping and smashing and grating and throwing things into sizzling pans," she smiled. "Honestly, Jake, I have no idea what I'm going to say. I'm still having a hard time getting my head around this whole vampire shark thing and the Rules and the killing. It's so outside my sense of reality and morality. I don't know what I feel. Wait. Yes, I do. I feel confused. That's what I feel."

"I hear that. Who would've thought that night we met at that bar we'd be here today discussing vampires over breakfast? Life is a trip, Leilani. Life is definitely a trip."

"Well, at least we're on this trip together," she said. *You're not alone in this, Jake. And fortunately, neither am I.*

118 – Fresh Start

An hour before sunrise, Dean rose from Skylar's bed. He touched the side of her face. "Sky," he whispered, "I should go. It's better if Tristan doesn't see me here."

Skylar groaned. "Who cares about Tristan?"

"No one. But we need a clean break. I don't want him or the other Nomads coming after us. Tristan thinks he owns you. He'd rather see you dead than with someone else. It's better if we just disappear and start fresh," Dean said.

"But I have to say goodbye to Torrey, Cruz and Logan."

"No. If you do, they'll tell Tristan. It's safer for us if you don't."

"Don't you think you're being a little paranoid?" Skylar asked.

"No. If you knew the things Tristan said, you'd say I'm not being paranoid enough. You have to trust me," Dean said.

"I do but …"

"I know it's hard. But your safety is my top concern right now. Pack your bags and your board. Don't talk to anyone. I'll meet you back here at 8:30 p.m. sharp. We'll leave from here for the airport."

"Where are we going?" Skylar asked.

"Leave that to me."

"But what are you doing today? Why can't I come with you?"

"Because I have to cancel the wedding. I need to see Amanda and tell her in person. It's not the kind of thing I should do over the phone. Then I need to go to the wedding site and send home anyone I can't reach today. I'm the one calling this off so it's only fair I deal with the consequences," Dean explained.

"You're right. I'm sorry."

"No, I'm sorry I have to leave you alone today. I'll take care of everything and I'll see you here, 8:30 sharp. Don't forget."

"I won't forget," Skylar promised.

"After tonight, it's just us. You and me."

119 — Clearing

When Jake and Leilani finished breakfast, he cleared the dishes.

"Really, I'm fine," he assured her. "You should go."

"Okay. I guess I should talk to Tristan. I left kind of suddenly last night. I should try to see him before he has to leave for the wedding."

"What wedding?"

"His friend, Dean. He's here in town on business. He asked Tristan to be his best man. The wedding is this evening. I'm not invited. It's a small ceremony—friends and family only."

"Tristan's going without you?" Jake asked.

"Yeah. Dean is one of his oldest friends. I've only met the guy once or twice. I told him it was fine," Leilani shrugged.

"Where's the wedding gonna be?"

"The beach, of course. It is Tristan's friend, after all. I'm sure you know the spot. It's that secluded cove in Solana Beach, with the stairs you can access from the street." She explained where the ceremony was going to be held—and confessed how relieved she was that she didn't have to go. "A wedding is the last place I need to be with Tristan today."

"Yeah, you're probably right," Jake agreed. "Try to get some rest later, okay? You look pretty tired."

"I will. I'll take a nap while Tristan's gone. Maybe it'll help me clear my head. I'll call you later."

"I'm fine," he said. "There's no need to check up on me."

"Good. Then it will be a short conversation."

120 – Processing

Tristan's phone rang shortly before dawn. "Leilani?"

Dean spoke into his headset in his car, "No, man. Sorry to wake you. I wanted to tell you Skylar's fine. She just needs a couple days to cool down. I explained it wasn't your fault about Jake and I think she gets it. But you know Skylar. She's hotheaded. She'll come around. But don't try to call her for at least the next 24 hours. Give her some time. It'll be better that way."

"Okay, thanks. Are you just getting home?" Tristan asked, worried he'd kept his friend up all night.

"No, I got home hours ago," Dean lied. "I woke up and realized I forgot to call to let you know how things went. Go back to bed. Everything will be fine in a few days. I'll see you tonight."

"Thanks. I owe you." Tristan hung up. He thought about calling Leilani but decided to give her space as well. *Why is it that the one thing the most important women in my life need right now is to NOT hear from me?*

He turned over and tried to fall asleep again. A few hours later his phone rang.

"Tristan, it's Leilani. Did I wake you?"

"I was hoping you'd call. It's good to hear your voice."

"Can I come over? I need to talk to you."

"Yeah, I'll see you soon." Tristan quickly dressed and went downstairs to prepare some food for her arrival. He tried not to worry about why she wanted to talk with him. *It could be a good thing as easily as it could be a bad thing, so stop stressing about it,* he told himself.

Hearing Leilani knock at the door, he yelled, "Come in! I'm in the kitchen."

She walked in and saw him preparing sandwiches.

"I hope you're hungry," Tristan said, smiling.

"I'm sorry. I had breakfast with Jake."

"Of course. I should've asked."

"No, it was sweet of you to make lunch. Maybe we can have it later?"

"Sure. So you were at Jake's all night?" Tristan trusted Leilani but wished she would have wanted to be at his place instead of Jake's.

"Yeah, he was feeling pretty bad. I forgot to call you, didn't I? I'm sorry. I meant to, but I must've fallen asleep as soon as my head hit the pillow. I was too tired to drive home so Jake let me sleep on his couch. I also wanted to make sure he was okay this morning. So to get him up and moving, I made a big breakfast. I would've invited you but he still isn't ready to see you," Leilani explained.

"It was nice of you to do that for him. Jake is lucky to have you as a friend. So what about you? How are you doing with everything I told you yesterday?"

"I'm still processing but better. It's a lot to take in."

"I know. And thank you for keeping your promise to listen to everything. I appreciate it. It must've been difficult," Tristan said. "So you said you wanted to talk?"

"Yes. There are some things I don't understand. I haven't made up my mind yet because I'm still conflicted about some things. But if I'm going to consider a life with you, there are some things I need to know."

Tristan smiled broadly. *Consider a life with me ... She's still considering it. That's good. Don't blow this, man.*

121 – The Future

Tristan offered Leilani a seat at the kitchen table while he put the sandwiches in a covered dish and placed it in the refrigerator.

"So where do you see yourself in the future?" Leilani began. "Are you traveling? Are you here? And what happens when you hear of someone breaking the Rules? Do you pick up and leave to go take care of that? I'm not sure where I'd fit into your life."

"Leilani, I told you. I don't care where I am as long as I'm with you." He took a seat next to her at the table.

"But if you could choose, would you stay in one place or would you travel?"

"If you wanted to, I'd choose to travel. Maybe it's the shark blood running through my veins, but staying in one place is the less appealing option of the two," he said.

"So settling down, buying a home—that's not your ideal?"

"No, but I would understand if that's what you want. Personally, I've never understood the concept of buying land. The earth and the ocean belong to everyone. The idea that someone can say, 'This piece of land or this stretch of beach here is mine and you have no right to it,' is bizarre to me. Early native cultures had it right. They roamed, they hunted, they gathered, they roamed again."

"So given the choice, you would travel?" she interrupted.

"Yes. Given the choice, I would travel *with you*," he clarified.

"And what if a rogue vampire shark breaks the Rules? Would you go there?"

"Yes, because it's my responsibility. I created every vampire shark in existence. If one breaks the Rules and starts killing, it's my responsibility to stop it. I can usually take care of these things pretty quickly though. So you could come with me or you could choose to stay home. Whatever you want."

"But isn't it dangerous?" she asked.

"I've been doing this a long time. There's no need to worry. And Torrey, Cruz, Logan and Skylar are a big help."

Leilani pondered what he said. "Here's the thing … I still don't know how I feel about the Rules. I don't know enough about vampire sharks to condone killing them. Maybe it's the right thing to do, maybe it's not. But I do know enough about humans to know killing is wrong. If I'm going to be with you, you can't kill humans. Ever. Even if they're the worst kind of humans. That's not your choice."

"But Leilani, even after everything I told you …"

"I heard you. And you make a very good argument. With guys like the Del Norte Reefers, it's hard to argue against it. But I still think killing is wrong. And I can't be with you if you're some kind of vigilante, killing humans you deem unfit to live. You can feed on something else, not humans."

"I would like to respectfully disagree with you. I don't think killing is wrong if you're killing the right people. Humans remove predators from their environment all the time. A grizzly bear who wanders into a campsite and attacks someone is promptly shot, and sometimes many other innocent bears are, too. When we go in and remove a human, we do it with precision. It's not haphazard."

"But what about Cody?"

"That was a mistake made by an idiot who didn't follow the Rules. Leilani, if you had experienced what I've experienced or had seen the things that I've seen, I'm pretty confident you would see things my way," Tristan said.

"I don't think I would—and I've seen some pretty gruesome things in my job, by the way. Even with everything you've told me, I can't consider being with you if you kill people. I need you to promise me you will never kill another human," Leilani insisted.

"If you feel that strongly about it, it's done."

"Really? Just like that?" she asked.

"Just like that. You know I would do anything for you. Humans are off the table. But I can't stop enforcing the Rules with my own kind. I have to. It's the only way I can take responsibility for my actions. When vampire sharks fail to take responsibility for their actions and kill indiscriminately, I have to intervene. I *have* to, to save human life," he said.

"I understand you feel responsible. But it's hard for me to wrap my mind around the fact that killing is a good thing, even with vampire sharks. But since I don't fully understand the whole vampire shark thing, I won't ask you to change that— at least not yet." Leilani paused as a thought occurred to her. "Hey, do you remember that barbecue at your house and how Cruz freaked out that Jake was going to barbecue shark fillets? Why was that if, as you say, flesh is flesh and all? I mean, I'm assuming Cruz has killed some humans and vampire sharks. So why was he so upset?"

"Because the shark Jake brought is endangered. Humans aren't," Tristan replied. "In fact, humans are the reason why so many animals, like sharks, are endangered, sick and dying. A key difference between vampire sharks who abide by the Rules and humans is that we only take what we need to survive. Look around the planet—in the water, in the air, on the earth. Things in nature don't take more than they need to survive. Humans do and that's where they create problems for themselves and every other species."

Leilani tried to think of an argument to defend humans in this instance but couldn't come up with one so decided to change the subject. "And what about the whole daylight thing? How does that work if you're a vampire?"

"If you're a newborn vampire and are exposed to direct sunlight, you turn to a pile of ash. The same thing happens if you get a stake to the heart. Those are, without a doubt, two of the quickest ways to kill a vampire. A wooden bullet through the heart works, too, but a gun is so noisy. It usually gets snatched away before the human has a chance to use it. And, truth be told, vampires enjoy the hand-to-hand combat of fighting with stakes. They think guns are for weaker species like humans," Tristan explained.

"To answer your question, vampires can build up a tolerance to sunlight and even tan. But when you're going to have your skin for centuries, you're mindful of how much sun exposure you get. Over the last few decades, sunscreen has made life much easier for vampires." He grinned, "It also works great for surfing under the light of a full moon."

"You're kidding!"

"I'm not."

"So that's why you smelled like sunscreen that night we went surfing after we had dinner here! It wasn't your trunks. It was you," she realized.

"Yep. Sunscreen at night is a dead giveaway of a vampire shark. I buy only the unscented stuff but it still reeks like sunscreen. What else? I can see you still have concerns."

"What about Skylar, Torrey, Cruz and Logan? If I'm with you, what happens with them? Are we all traveling together like one big happy family? Though I can't imagine Skylar would be happy about anything involving me," Leilani grimaced.

"Skylar aside, I think you'd fit right in with everyone so we wouldn't have to change anything. We might travel with them and surf the same places and hang out sometimes, but we'd have separate homes and separate lives," Tristan explained. "If traveling with them makes you uncomfortable and you want it to be only the two of us, we could discuss that, too."

"And I never see anyone going to work or hear anyone talking about work, except Dean," Leilani said. "Do you support them financially?"

"Skylar has her own money. I pay the way for anyone who needs it. Like right now, I'm supporting Torrey, Cruz and Logan. They didn't ask me to. I offered. I think it's the least I can do for them joining me and helping me enforce the Rules. I have the means—much more than I could ever need for myself—and I enjoy sharing it with people who make me happy. That's something you should know about me. Things don't make me happy. People make me happy. I would share my money with you, too. If you wanted to quit your job today and never work another day in your life, you could. But it would be your choice."

"I don't even know what to say to that," Leilani said.

"Think about it. Think about what you really want out of life. If you could do anything, what would you do?" Tristan asked. "I have my answers. I'd surf and I'd be with you. You need to find your answers."

122 – Confirmation

Several hours after Dean arrived home, he called Lance. "Everything set for tonight? We can't afford to make any mistakes. Everything must be perfect."

"Everything's set. What did you decide about Skylar?" Lance asked.

"She won't be at the wedding today. I decided not to tell her about our plan. But she is leaving Tristan's crew. She'll join me tonight after the festivities and we'll be leaving town together. No one is to speak a word to her about what happens tonight. After Tristan and the other Nomads are gone, no one is to speak of them ever again."

"Okay. But I have to ask, do you trust her? She's been with Tristan 10 years. She's gotta have some loyalty to him if she's been with him all this time," Lance said.

"I've taken care of that. She's done with Tristan. She's with me now. And Lance," Dean added, "never question my decisions again. I've told you twice. There won't be a third time."

123 – Home

Tristan touched Leilani's face. "I understand how hard this is for you to take in. But, despite everything I've told you and how complicated life must seem now, it's not. It's actually very simple. I love you. That's all that matters. Do you still love me?"

Leilani took a deep breath. She shut out the chorus of concerns chiming in her head and listened to her heart. "Yes, Tristan, I love you."

Tristan breathed a sigh of relief.

"But I need more time to think about your proposal," she added.

"That's fine. I'm just thankful you're still here."

"And you swear you won't kill any more humans from here on out?"

"I swear. You have my word," he promised.

Leilani dropped her head back on the chair and yawned.

"Tired?" Tristan asked.

"Exhausted. After I left here last night, I stayed up with Jake. I didn't sleep well because I had bad dreams. Then I got up early to make breakfast."

"Why don't you go upstairs and take a nap?" he suggested. "Like you said, it's better not to drive if you're this tired."

"But you have to get ready for the wedding later. I'll be in your way."

"You are never in my way. Go get settled in my room. I'll move my stuff down to the guest room. It's no problem. A nap will do you a world of good. You'll see."

"Okay. Thanks."

Leilani trudged upstairs and climbed into bed, while Tristan moved his tux and assorted toiletries to the guest room. By the time he got back to the bedroom, she was asleep. He kissed her cheek and shut the bedroom door.

If she's still here, she's not leaving. I can feel it, Tristan thought. *She may not know it yet but I do. She's going to say yes. Leilani, you don't need to drive home. You are home.*

Tristan walked down the hall smiling to himself. His vibrating phone broke his reverie. "Dean! What's up? Are you ready to walk down the aisle?"

"Yeah. But what's up with you? You sound a lot better than you did last night," Dean said.

"I am. Leilani came back."

"That's great. I'm sorry again she won't be able to join us at the wedding. I'd love to have her but Amanda wants to keep it small."

"Dude, it's no problem. Leilani totally understands."

"Okay. And you'll be at the beach at 6:30?"

"Yes. But are you sure you don't need anything before then?" Tristan asked. "As best man, I really haven't done anything. No bachelor party, no rehearsal."

"Because I don't want any of those things. I need you there at the ceremony. That's it," Dean insisted.

"You got it."

"What about Leilani? What's she doing today?"

"Resting." Tristan looked down the hallway and smiled. "At home. Hey Dean, thanks again for talking me off the wall last night. Things really are better today."

"No problem, man. See you at the wedding."

124 – Decision

Leilani awoke around 6 p.m. She felt like she'd been asleep for days—and felt more refreshed than she'd ever felt in her life. She sat up in bed and stretched her arms over her head. Her mind was crystal clear. She had only one thought: *I know what I'm going to tell Tristan.*

A few minutes later, Tristan slipped into the bedroom, dressed in a tailored black tuxedo. "You're awake!"

"Wow! You look nice!" Leilani exclaimed. *Just when I think this guy can't get any better-looking, he gets better-looking.*

"Thank you." He sat beside her on the bed. "Are you feeling better?"

"Much. Thanks for letting me crash. I needed it."

He leaned over and softly kissed her lips. "Anytime. Mi casa es su casa." He kissed her again. "I'm really glad you're here."

"Me, too," she said. "Do you mind if I stay here while you're gone? I thought maybe we could continue our conversation when you get home. I have an answer for you, but I don't want to rush it in the few minutes before you have to leave for the wedding."

"You can stay as long as you like." He got up and retrieved a key from his dresser. "Take this. This is your home, too."

"Thanks." Leilani wrapped her fingers around the key. "You should get going. The best man cannot be late to the wedding."

"All right. But at least give me a hint. Will I be happy with your answer? Because, if not, maybe you should think about it some more," he suggested.

"I wouldn't want to spoil the surprise," she smiled coyly. "I'll see you tonight."

"I can't wait." Tristan leaned down and kissed her again. "I love you. More than you can possibly know."

"I love you, too."

125 – The Big Day

Fifteen minutes later Tristan arrived at the cove, still smiling from hearing Leilani say she loved him and excited about seeing her again later. As he parked on the street, he saw police tape blocking the stairs that led down to the cove. *Dean's friend in the city must've done that. I guess that's one way to ensure you have a private ceremony.*

Tristan bounded down the concrete stairs, gazing at the ocean. Upon reaching the 42nd step, he spotted the cove on his right. He noticed four red and white poles, tiki torches, and an archway in the distance. He jogged down the remaining 100 stairs as the sun disappeared below the horizon.

When Tristan got closer, he saw the tall wooden poles marked off a walkway in the sand. Two poles stood at the back and two at the front; they were shrouded in red and white ribbons that fluttered in the ocean breeze. Between the poles was a red satin walkway, lined with tiki torches. The torch flames illuminated the path down the walkway to the white arch adorned with red and white roses. There were more tiki torches on both sides of the archway, which was centered in front of the cliff wall that encircled the cove.

Dean, dressed in a gray tuxedo, stood in front of the arch. Tristan sauntered down the red satin aisle and took his place next to him. He patted Dean on the back, "This looks great, man. It's perfect. You ready?"

"Yep. I've been waiting for this moment for a very long time," Dean smiled.

126 – Primping

After Tristan left, Leilani quickly drove to her house. She wouldn't be back again until tomorrow so wanted to make sure she had everything she needed for the night.

She took a bag from her closet, rummaged through her drawers, and threw in some clothes and an ivory silk nightgown. She reached for her toothbrush and assorted personal items and tossed them in the bag's outer pocket.

She rushed from room to room, grabbing every candle she could find and flung those into the bag, too. She raced back to Tristan's.

Leilani used her key to enter Tristan's house and locked the door behind her. She strode to the kitchen and looked at the clock. *The ceremony's probably getting started,* she thought.

She had no idea how long or how short the wedding ceremony would be, or if there would be a reception. She wanted everything to be perfect when Tristan arrived home.

She placed the candles all over the living room and ran up to Tristan's bedroom. She undressed and jumped in the shower. Feeling the hot water stream over her head, she wondered how she came to this point in her life, which was so far from anything she ever imagined for herself. As the bathroom filled with steam, her brain and heart engaged in battle.

Am I really going to do this? Am I really going to marry a ... vampire shark? I never even heard of such a thing 24 hours ago. That's crazy, right? But when she thought of Tristan, she knew he was the one she'd been waiting for her whole life. He was the one she wanted to be with. She felt a spark when she first gazed into his eyes at the age of 16, though she thought it was fear since he was in the body of a shark. When she saw him two-and-a-half weeks ago that first night at the bar, she felt the same spark again when her eyes connected with his across the room.

My entire life has made sense. I don't know if this makes any sense whatsoever. In fact, it probably doesn't. But it feels right. For once, I'm going to rely on my feelings. My whole life I've relied on my thoughts and I've felt alone. For the first time, I feel like I'm not alone. I feel like I belong ... with Tristan.

But, even so, I can't completely discount what my head is telling me. So for my heart, I will say yes to Tristan's proposal. But for my head, I will insist on a very long engagement. That way I can make sure this is going to work.

Leilani turned off the shower. She towel dried her skin and her hair, swiped on some deodorant, and slipped into her ivory nightgown. She blow-dried her hair and put on a little makeup.

She stared at her reflection in the mirror. *Okay, Leilani, this is it. Heart, you win this battle. Head, stay alert.*

127 – Here Comes the Bride

After standing next to Dean for a while, Tristan grew restless.

The minister arrived and took his place under the flower-adorned arch behind a wooden podium.

Four men and three women arrived and stood in the sand. They stared expectantly at Dean. Tristan assumed they were impatiently waiting for the ceremony to begin, like he was.

Tristan recognized one of the men from the night Dean showed up at his door. *He invited his assistant? It didn't seem like they were that close.*

"Is this everyone?" Tristan asked.

"Almost," Dean answered. "The maid of honor should be here any minute. Then Amanda will make her big entrance."

As if on cue, a woman appeared carrying a surfboard above her head. She wore a red chiffon strapless dress, with a fitted bodice and a short cascading ruffled skirt.

Tristan saw something shiny on top of the board. The hairs on the back of his neck rose. *Something's not right.* He looked at Dean, who smiled, and then back at the woman carrying the surfboard.

Tristan casually reached inside his jacket. He touched his phone and speed dialed Torrey and Cruz. Tristan pressed the speaker button so they could hear him, and then he turned down the volume so no one would be able to hear Torrey or Cruz.

Dean turned to Tristan, curious about what he was fumbling with in his jacket. Tristan removed a mint and smiled at Dean as he popped it in his mouth.

The maid of honor set down the surfboard, picked up the shiny silver container and presented it to Dean. She took her place with the other women and men.

Tristan scanned the beach but didn't see anyone else

approaching. "Dean, where's Amanda?"

"She's right here. Let me formally introduce you." Dean removed the lid from the silver urn and poured the ashes into his hand. "Amanda, meet Tristan. Tristan, meet Amanda."

128 – Wrong Number

Jake was home watching TV when his phone rang. He picked it up but didn't hear anyone. He was about to hang up when he heard Tristan ask, "Dean, where's Amanda?"

"Tristan, it's Jake. Not Dean. You've got the wrong number," he said into his phone. He was still in no mood to talk to Tristan.

Then Jake heard another voice he didn't recognize. The voice said, "She's right here. Let me formally introduce you. Amanda, meet Tristan. Tristan, meet Amanda."

Did Tristan accidentally dial his phone from the wedding? Jake wondered. He was about to hang up again until he heard Tristan say, "Dean, what the hell's going on?"

Something's wrong. Jake couldn't explain it but he knew he had to get to Tristan. He threw on a t-shirt over his boardshorts, grabbed his keys and ran to his truck. He sped to the beach, listening to Tristan and Dean.

129 – Guest of Honor

"Tristan, surely you remember Amanda. Or have there been so many executions they're just nameless, faceless piles of ash to you?" Dean demanded.

"What are you talking about?" Tristan asked.

Dean's voice grew harsh. "Not what! Who! This precious pile of ash in my hands is what's left of Amanda. We called her Andi. You, Torrey and Cruz met Andi earlier this year in Santa Cruz."

Andi and Andy, Tristan remembered. *But that was a clean kill.*

"Ah, I see from your face you do remember. Andi was my fiancée. But you wouldn't know that because you've been so busy roaming the globe killing us off, you've neglected to keep in touch with your friends. And, when you did meet Andi, what did you do? Instead of getting to know her and finding out she's engaged to your old buddy Dean, you and your little disciples murdered her. For what?! Killing a few worthless humans? They're food, Tristan! They're inferior to us! Andi was mine and you killed her. That means you broke my Rule—never kill your best friend's girlfriend! You know what the punishment is for breaking my Rule, right?"

"Dean, come on, man. You know the Rules and why we have them. It's to prevent situations like this. Andi knew what she was doing when she killed those people. There were kids, man. Kids! She knew the consequences," Tristan explained.

"Your Rules are ridiculous!" shouted Dean. "We're done living by your Rules. If you remember, I never even wanted them in the first place. I tried to talk you out of them. Now your Rules have cost me someone I cared about. Your reign is over, Tristan."

"You don't want to do this," Tristan said.

"Yeah, I do. I've been planning this moment since the night I discovered Andi in a pile of ash on her surfboard." Dean turned to face the wedding guests and slapped his hand on Tristan's back. "You're our special guest of honor, Tristan. We're going to begin the reception now. Guess who we're serving for dinner?"

Tristan shook his head in disbelief, turning from Dean to the guests. "Dean, don't."

"First, we're going to make you suffer," Dean hissed. "Remember how bad a bite from one vampire feels? Try nine. My friends here are going to drain you of nearly every ounce of your blood. Then, when you're a drop away from death, they'll stake you and leave your ashes to scatter in the wind. It'll be like you were never here. And we can finally get back to feeding on whatever humans we want, like we're meant to. It'll be good for the planet. Humans are a plague. They're breeding unchecked, consuming and polluting everything around them. We're their natural predator. Circle of life, right, Tristan?"

"Dean, no." Tristan wondered how his friend could have turned into such a bitter, cruel, evil person.

"Dinner!" Dean yelled.

In a flash, the minister—who had been standing behind Tristan—seized the wooden podium, spun it 90 degrees, lifted it over Tristan's head and shoulders, and slammed it down on him. The wooden rod, which connected the reading surface to the four-footed base, pressed against Tristan's chest, pinning his arms to his sides.

"Don't do this!" Tristan struggled beneath the rod.

Dean strode down the aisle and headed toward the stairs. "Too late, Tristan, it's done. While my friends here are feeding on you, I'm going to grab some dinner of my own. I think I feel like something … blond."

"Don't you touch her!" Tristan shouted. "I'll kill you! I'll kill you, Dean!"

"Promises, promises," Dean said as he strolled away. "Lance, let the feeding frenzy begin!"

130 – Racing

When the minister crushed the wooden rod against Tristan's chest, his phone switched off. As soon as Jake realized the connection dropped, he dialed Leilani, who was in the shower at Tristan's house.

Jake hurriedly left a message. "Leilani, it's Jake. Something's wrong. The wedding's a set-up. They're going to kill Tristan. Call Cruz, Torrey and Logan and tell them to meet me at the cove. I don't have their numbers. I'll call Sky. I'm on my way to Tristan now. Stay home and don't let anyone in your house. I'll call as soon as I can."

He dialed Skylar's number. It went to voicemail. "Sky, it's Jake. The wedding's a set-up. Dean's gonna kill Tristan. I'm on my way to him now. Get the others. Meet me at the cove where the wedding is. Call me or Leilani if you need directions. Hurry!"

As Jake approached the stairs to the beach, he saw a silver BMW speed away from the curb. Jake zoomed into the parking spot, cutting off another car. He turned off his ignition, reached under the passenger seat and grabbed his titanium dive knife.

The driver in the other car was about to yell at Jake for stealing the parking spot, until he saw Jake exit his truck carrying a knife.

Jake ducked under the police tape and darted down the stairs toward the beach. Nearly a third of the way down, he saw the cove. He crouched down and continued descending the stairs, knife in hand.

131 – Reception

As Tristan stood with his arms pinned under the wooden rod of the minister's podium, he assessed the situation. *One man behind me, four men and four women in front of me. Nine on one. It's not ideal but I can do this. Focus and take them down one at a time. The quicker I take them out, the quicker I can get to Leilani.*

With that thought, Tristan abruptly thrust his upper body forward, flipping the minister over his shoulders and head. As the minister flew through the air above him, Tristan freed his arms and grabbed the wooden tiki torch closest to him. He plunged the base of the torch into the minister's heart as his body hit the sand. The minister dissolved into ash. *That's one.*

Seeing Tristan spring into battle mode, Lance rattled one of the four wooden poles shrouded in red and white ribbons. The 12-foot pole broke apart into eight stakes, each 18 inches long. Lance kept one stake for himself and, with rapid-fire motion, tossed the others to the wedding guests.

"Tristan, there's no point in fighting," Lance said. "There are eight of us and only one of you. Go quietly into the night, dude."

"Eight on one? I won't even break a sweat," Tristan boasted. *Now it's time to play with them, undermine their confidence.* "You do know who I am right? I created Dean. I created you. I created every vampire shark in existence. I'm a god. I'm immortal. I'm not some pathetic vampire who's going to die in a few centuries."

The men and women nervously looked at Lance.

"Don't listen to him!" Lance instructed. "He's messing with you."

"Dean didn't tell you about my power, did he?" Tristan asked. "Why do you think he left so suddenly?"

132 – Nobody's Home

Dean drove straight from the beach to Leilani's house. He rang the doorbell but heard no movement inside.

That's odd, he thought. *Tristan said she was home resting.*

Dean knocked and called out Leilani's name. He picked the lock on the front door and walked inside. "Leilani? It's Dean. Tristan's hurt. He needs you."

He marched into the kitchen and then the bedroom. "Leilani?" He entered the bathroom and poked around. *No toothbrush. She's not here. She must be at Tristan's. Hmmm, that could work out well. Now I can participate in the killing of Torrey and Cruz, too.*

Dean ran back to his car and dialed his phone. "Yeah, it's me. Do you have Torrey and Cruz yet? ... No? Good. Change of plans. Leilani's at Tristan's. Go there first. Subdue her. Then call Torrey and Cruz and have them meet you there. We can do it all at Tristan's and pin Leilani's murder on him. It'll be the icing on the cake. I'll be there in a few minutes."

133 — Wedding Crasher

Tristan glanced up at the stairs and saw Jake approaching. The others had their backs to Jake. They should have been able to detect his scent but were too distracted by Tristan's theatrics.

Good, Tristan thought. *Now the element of surprise is on my side.*

"Enough with the lies, Tristan," Lance said. "You're no longer our meal. You're dust."

Lance and the seven other wedding guests lunged at Tristan. *One at a time,* he reminded himself.

As stakes struck at him from all directions, Tristan grabbed the two arms closest to him. They belonged to a man on his right, Ian, and woman on his left, Diane. Tristan gripped Ian's wrist in his right hand and Diane's wrist in his left. Making an "X," Tristan swiftly crossed his arms in front of his chest, plunging Ian's stake into Diane's chest and Diane's stake into Ian's chest. They disappeared in a poof of ash on either side of him.

Spying this from the steps, Jake stopped in his tracks. *They're all vampires,* he realized. *What do I do? Do I really want to get involved in this? I don't owe Tristan anything. He turned the guy that killed Cody. And he turned me into some kind of freak human-vampire-shark hybrid. I should turn around and forget I ever saw this.* But Jake knew he couldn't let Tristan die alone. He looked at Tristan, facing off against six vampires. *I can't let them kill him. And what would I tell Leilani? I've at least gotta try to help him.* Jake silenced the debate in his head and sprinted toward Tristan, clutching his dive knife in his right hand.

Upon seeing Ian and Diane disappear, Lance reached for the other pole at the top of the walkway. It was a solid 12-foot piece of wood.

While Tristan focused on the five vampires in front of him,

Lance ran behind Tristan and swung the pole like a baseball bat. The wood cracked against Tristan's shoulder blades, knocking him to the ground. While Tristan was splayed out on his stomach, one of the five vampires, Melanie, stepped over him, raising her stake for the kill.

Tristan flipped onto his back in time to see Melanie's glowering face and a stake rapidly approaching his chest. Tristan grabbed the stake with his right hand just before it struck his skin. With his fingers wrapped around the pointed end of the stake, he violently flung his arm to the right, causing Melanie to lose her balance. While she toppled and fell to Tristan's right, he ripped the stake from her hand. He sprang to his feet, crouched above Melanie who was now lying in the sand, and jammed the pointed end into her chest. She burst into a heap of ash.

Tristan rose to his feet. He hurled the stake toward Lance's chest but Lance snatched it from the air before it connected with his skin.

"Ben, Alissa! Now!" Lance yelled.

Ben and Alissa rushed at Tristan with their stakes raised. Ben charged at Tristan from the front and Alissa from the back.

Jake, who had finally reached the red satin walkway, froze in horror as Tristan stood immobile. At the last instant, as Ben and Alissa swung their stakes downward to strike, Tristan jumped to the side. Unable to halt their momentum, Ben and Alissa smacked into each other. As their skulls and bodies thudded together, the force of the collision knocked their stakes from their hands and each fell backward into the sand.

Tristan seized the stakes off the ground and gripped one in each hand. While Ben lay dazed on the ground, Tristan stooped down and rammed the stake in his left hand into Ben's chest. Tristan rose and turned back to Alissa. As Alissa leapt to her feet, Tristan whisked his right arm above his head and threw his stake toward the center of her chest. A gust of wind scattered

Ben's and Alissa's ashes in all directions.

Lance stood at the front of the satin walkway, facing Tristan. Behind his back, he gripped the stake Tristan had thrown at him. His knuckles turned white. "Dammit! Work together!" he shouted to the remaining man, Ryan, and woman, Dana.

Seeing Lance was about to turn toward the ocean and discover Jake, who now crept toward them, Tristan taunted him. "Lance, how many more of you need to die? Dean doesn't care about you. That's why he left you here. He knew you wouldn't survive."

"No, he knew you wouldn't survive." Unexpectedly, Lance hurled his stake at Tristan's chest.

Tristan, distracted by Jake's approach, tried to sidestep the stake but was too late. The stake struck him, slightly to the left of his heart. The blow wasn't precise enough to turn him to dust but it was strong enough to pierce his body several inches, slicing through him almost all the way to his back. Blood began to spill from the wound.

From behind, Jake raised his dive knife and rammed it between Lance's shoulder blades. His skin made a disgusting slurping sound as the blade sliced into his body. Blood dribbled from Lance's mouth, down the front of his shirt, as he struggled to reach the knife handle protruding from his back.

Looking past Lance, Jake saw Tristan sink to his knees. As Tristan reached up to remove the stake from his chest, Jake yelled, "No! You'll make it worse!"

Seeing Tristan injured, Ryan and Dana leapt toward him.

Jake left Lance, still flailing to reach the knife buried in his back, and raced to Tristan. Jake tackled Ryan, who was about to strike Tristan from the front. As Jake and Ryan wrestled in the sand, Dana moved in for the kill.

Dramatically playing up his injury, Tristan hung his head and swayed on his knees as if he might topple over, hoping to draw Dana closer.

Dana grabbed Tristan's hair and wrenched his head back, exposing his throat. "You don't remember me, do you?" she asked. "I know it was just a weekend but I thought you really … Well, it doesn't matter what I thought. Now I get to take this stake and break your heart."

As Dana positioned her stake to the right of the stake already protruding from Tristan's chest, he seized her wrist. She was surprised by the strength of his grip. He tried to force her arm back but she was strong.

Jake broke free from wrestling with Ryan. Dana thought if she released Tristan's hair or the stake, he could overpower her. She hoped Ryan would tackle Jake before he reached her but Jake was too quick. Jake tackled Dana from the side, doing his best not to hit Tristan.

As Jake landed on top of Dana, the stake rolled from her hand. Jake grabbed it. Sitting on her pelvis, he stabbed her but missed her heart. Dana pushed Jake off but he held onto the stake, pulling it from her wound. Blood streamed from her chest.

While Dana and Jake faced off, Ryan looked from Jake to Tristan, not sure who to attack first. Seeing his indecision, Tristan took the opportunity to swipe a stake off the sand. The sudden movement caused a fresh wave of blood to gush from his chest.

Jake turned away from Dana. He swung his arm back like he was going to throw his stake at Ryan. He hoped to fool Dana into lunging at him.

Fangs bared, Dana swooped toward Jake's neck. Keeping his body turned to Ryan, Jake whipped his arm behind him and jammed the stake into Dana's chest as she approached. Jake looked over his shoulder to make sure he connected with her heart this time, and watched her dissolve into a lump of ash.

"Jake!" Tristan yelled.

Jake turned his head in time to see Ryan barreling toward him with a stake. He used his forearm to block Ryan's arm. Ryan swung the stake at him again. Jake deflected it with his other arm. They tussled. Swipe, deflection, swipe, deflection.

"Stake!" Jake shouted to Tristan.

Tristan tossed his stake to Jake. More blood flowed from his chest.

With one hand, Jake ripped the stake from the air and faced off with Ryan.

"What are you? Human?" Ryan asked. "You're in way over your head, dude. Drop the stake and I'll make it a quick kill. Resist and I'll make it slow and painful."

"Whatever, man," Jake said. "Do you have any idea what the past 24 hours have been like? I have nothing left to lose. Bring it."

Ryan took another swipe at Jake but missed.

Jake goaded him. "Is that all you got?"

Ryan leapt toward Jake, swinging his stake but missing again.

"Tristan, I thought these guys were supposed to be able to fight," Jake jeered, knowing each verbal jab caused Ryan to become more infuriated and less precise.

Ryan darted toward Jake again but caught his foot under the satin walkway. Seeing Ryan start to fall forward, Jake swung his arm up as hard as he could, hoping his stake connected with Ryan's heart. Jake felt the force of Ryan's body fall down onto the point. Just as he thought he'd missed the heart and would have to run for another stake, Ryan evaporated in a cloud of dust.

Jake turned and saw Lance standing in front of Tristan, near the archway. Lance had successfully removed the knife. Blood flowed freely down his back. He wrapped his hands around the stake in Tristan's chest.

Jake spotted his knife in the sand and ran to retrieve it.

Tristan grabbed Lance's hands but couldn't pry them loose without pulling the stake from his chest. He knew if he did that, he'd lose a lot more blood—probably too much to make it to Leilani in time.

Lance gripped the stake and tried to wriggle it free from Tristan's chest. "Does that hurt?" he taunted Tristan. He wiggled the stake again. "How about now?"

Tristan squelched the scream that wanted to escape his lips as Lance twisted and turned the stake in his chest. "Not really," Tristan grunted. "I'm immortal. Tonight I'll be good as new. And you'll be dead. Your body's not going to have time to heal itself before you bleed out—or till I turn you to dust."

Tristan glanced over Lance's shoulder and saw Jake sneaking up behind him.

Again, Lance tried to free the stake from Tristan's grasp. "You're a liar."

"And you're dead," Tristan said.

Jake reached over Lance's right shoulder and slit his throat with the dive knife.

Instinctively, Lance raised both hands to the gash in his neck, releasing his grip on the stake still protruding from Tristan's chest.

"Does *that* hurt?" Tristan sneered.

Jake ran to retrieve a stake lying on the sand near a pile of ash and threw it to Tristan.

Tristan caught the stake and speared Lance's chest. "How about now?" he asked right before Lance exploded in a spray of ash.

Tristan dropped the stake in the sand. "We need to get to Leilani! Dean's after her."

"No, we need to get you an ambulance. I'll get Leilani."

"No! No ambulances. No hospitals. No police. We need to get to Leilani. Let's go."

134 — No Answer

Jake helped Tristan walk across the beach and back up the 142 stairs to the street. Blood oozed from Tristan's chest.

Jake opened the passenger door and helped him climb into the seat. He eyed the stake jutting from Tristan's body. "I think you'll wanna skip the seatbelt today."

Jake ran around the hood, opened the driver's side door and reached behind his seat. He handed a clean beach towel to Tristan. "Here, use this to sop up the blood." He climbed in and turned the ignition. "Where are we going? Leilani's house or yours?"

"Mine," Tristan said.

"I tried calling Leilani's cell on the way here. There was no answer," Jake said.

"Let me try. You drive. Dammit! I should've never let Dean in my house."

Tristan dialed Leilani's cell. Her phone, which sat in her bag in Tristan's bedroom, went straight to voicemail again. "It's Tristan. Dean tried to kill me and he's coming to kill you. Jake and I are on our way. If you get this, go to Torrey and Cruz's. Dean can't enter since he's never been invited in there. Call my cell and let me know you're safe. I love you."

Tristan turned to Jake. "Can't you drive any faster?"

"I'm going as fast as I can. There are too many cars on the road," Jake replied. Traffic slowed to a crawl. "It's gridlock. There must be an accident or something."

Tristan scowled at the cars in front of them. He saw they were stuck. There was nothing Jake could do. "I'm sorry. We just have to get to Leilani." He leaned his head back on the headrest and turned to Jake. "Hey, how did you know where to find me?"

"What do you mean? You called me. I heard you and Dean

talking and figured something was wrong so I raced down here."

"What? I thought I was dialing Torrey and Cruz. I must've dialed you by mistake. God, Jake, after everything that happened yesterday, I can't believe you came," Tristan said.

"I had to. You were in trouble."

As they inched ahead on the highway, Jake glanced at Tristan's chest. "Dude, we need to get you to a hospital. You're dying. I know you're not immortal. C'mon, let me take you in."

"No. I told you, I'll be fine. If they get me in the hospital, I'll become a lab rat because my body is different from a human's. My heartbeat is different. I heal differently. They'll keep me and I'll die from lack of exposure to salt water. They'll also file a police report, which is the last thing we need," Tristan said.

"But your chest!"

"My body wants to heal but it can't with the stake still there. You were right to tell me not to remove it though. If I do and I can't get to Torrey in time to stitch me up, I could bleed out before my body has time to heal on its own. Torrey is smart. She'll know what to do. Torrey! I need to call her. Dean's probably going after her and Cruz, too. They were in Santa Cruz with me. They're the ones who killed Andi, Dean's girlfriend."

Tristan dialed Torrey and Cruz. There was no answer so he left a message. "Dean is the one behind everything. He tried to kill me. He's after Leilani and he'll probably come after you, too. If Leilani hasn't gotten my message, she's still at my house. Get her and bring her to your place. You haven't invited Dean in so he can't enter. Jake and I are on our way. Be careful."

Tristan dialed Logan next. No answer. "Where is everyone?!" He left a message instructing Logan to get Leilani to Torrey and Cruz's condo.

Jake glanced at Tristan's chest again. "Does it hurt? The stake?"

"Yeah. It feels exactly like you'd imagine it would feel. But what's even more painful is picturing Dean reaching Leilani before we do. It's killing me not knowing if she's safe or if Dean's with her. I'm gonna try Skylar."

Tristan dialed and left a message. "Skylar, it's Tristan. Don't hang up! I know you don't like Leilani but she's in trouble. Dean's gone crazy. He tried to kill me. He's going after her next and he might be after you guys. Get Leilani and bring her to Torrey and Cruz's. Do not let Dean in! I'm on my way."

Tristan hung up. "I'm going to try Leilani again."

135 — Tied Up

Logan bolted to Tristan's house and banged on the front door. "Leilani, it's Logan! Something's wrong! Leilani! Let me in!"

Leilani had just finished lighting all the candles in the living room when she heard the pounding at the front door. She peered through the peephole. "Logan?"

"Leilani! Let me in! It's an emergency. Tristan sent me."

Leilani opened the door slightly and peeked outside. She was in her nightgown and self-conscious about having Logan see her half-dressed. "What's wrong?"

Logan burst inside. "Have you talked to Tristan since he left?"

"No. Why? What's going on?" she asked.

Logan shut the door. "Something went wrong at the wedding."

"What? Tell me what's going on. Why are you so upset?"

He led Leilani to a chair in the living room. "Here, sit down. I'll call Tristan and let him know you're safe."

Logan placed his hand on Leilani's shoulder to gently guide her into the chair and dialed. "It's Logan. Leilani's here. Where are you? … All right. See you soon."

Leilani reached for Logan's phone. "Let me talk to him."

"He hung up. He'll be here in a minute. Everything will be fine."

A moment later, Tristan's front door opened.

"In here!" Logan yelled.

Dean turned to the left and entered the living room. He was still dressed in his gray tuxedo. He carried a dark gray briefcase. "Leilani! I'm so glad you're here! You won't believe what happened today."

Leilani started to rise from the chair but Logan gripped her shoulders and pushed her back down.

"Logan, let me up. Where's Tristan?"

Dean set his briefcase on the floor next to Leilani's chair. "I'm sorry to be the one to have to tell you this but Tristan's dead."

"Dead?! What do you mean, he's dead?" Leilani demanded.

"Dead as in deceased, as in gone, as in not coming back." Dean leered at Leilani in her ivory nightgown and glanced around the room at all the candles. "And what a shame, Leilani, because you look stunning tonight. And candles? How romantic. You must've had a special evening planned. It's a shame he'll have to miss it."

"Dean, what's going on? Where's Tristan?!" Leilani asked.

"Enough with the questions! I told you Tristan's dead. Now be quiet like a good little human or I'll silence you permanently." Dean turned to Logan, "Let's tie her up and gag her. Then go get Torrey and Cruz."

Dean removed his tuxedo jacket and opened his briefcase. He reached for a roll of duct tape while Logan held Leilani to the chair. She screamed but Dean forced her jaw shut and taped her mouth closed.

"I said quiet," Dean hissed.

Logan held Leilani's arms down while Dean tore off a long piece of tape. She tried kicking but Dean pressed her legs against the chair and stepped on her feet. He knelt down and wrapped the tape around one ankle, binding it to the chair leg. He did the same with the other ankle.

Logan continued to grip Leilani's arms as she thrashed against him. Dean strung more tape around her, slightly below her collarbone, and secured her upper body and arms to the back of the chair. He taped her wrists, palms up, to the arms of the chair.

She continued to struggle but the tape didn't budge.

The front door opened. Torrey called out, "Leilani?"

Logan yelled, "In here! Hurry!"

Torrey and Cruz ran into the living room. They saw Leilani tied to the chair.

Leilani screamed beneath the tape and violently shook her head "no" to try to warn them.

"Logan, why are you just standing there?" Torrey demanded.

Cruz and Torrey didn't know Dean had disappeared into the kitchen and returned carrying a large cast iron skillet.

Leilani saw Dean sneak up behind Cruz. She screamed with her eyes and motioned her head in Dean's direction, but couldn't warn Cruz fast enough with the tape on her mouth.

Dean bashed Cruz in the back of the skull, knocking him to the floor. Torrey curled her hand into a fist and swung at Dean but Logan grabbed it before she could make contact.

Dean slammed the skillet into Torrey's forehead. She collapsed next to Cruz.

"Let's tie them up," Dean said. "I've got cuffs, too. Tape alone isn't enough to hold them."

Leilani looked helplessly at Torrey and Cruz crumpled next to each other on the floor. *What the hell is going on? Where's Tristan? He can't be dead. What are Dean and Logan doing? What do they want?*

Leilani whipped her head around to see if there was anything she could use to free herself or use as a weapon against Logan and Dean. There was nothing.

Dean ran to the kitchen, grabbed two chairs from the table and brought them back to the living room.

Logan and Dean lifted Torrey onto a chair. They cuffed her hands behind her, cuffed her ankles, and taped her to the chair. When they were done, they did the same to Cruz. They positioned the chairs so Cruz and Torrey faced Leilani.

"Don't worry, Leilani. They're quick healers," Dean said. "They'll wake up in a minute. Then the real fun begins."

136 – Jam

Traffic slowed to a crawl. Jake strained to see the highway ahead.

"What's the holdup?" Tristan asked.

"I dunno. I can't see a thing. Hang on, we can get off here. I know some back streets." Jake veered off the highway into a neighborhood.

"This is taking too long," Tristan worried.

"We'll get there, Tristan. We'll get there," Jake reassured him as he zoomed through the residential streets.

137 – Bloodlust

"Logan, until they wake up, what do you say we start with a snack?" Dean suggested.

Dean and Logan gazed hungrily at Leilani and bared their fangs. Leilani struggled against the tape and shook her head. *No,* she thought, *this is not happening. If I only had a knife or something sharp, I could cut through this tape and ...*

"It's okay," Dean soothed. He ran his fingers along the side of Leilani's face and down her neck. "We're not going to turn you into a vampire. That requires a bite to the neck. But we are going to feed on you for a while and that means we can bite you anywhere else."

Dean kneeled beside Leilani. He placed his hand on the tape on her wrist and inspected her inner arm. "This looks tasty. Ooh, nice blue veins. Logan, what do you say we start with the wings?" Dean plunged his fangs into Leilani's forearm, slightly past the edge of the tape.

Leilani gasped from the razor-sharp pain. She willed herself not to cry. *I will not give you the satisfaction, you sick, twisted freak.* She steeled herself against the pain and the disgusting thought of Dean's mouth pressed against her flesh.

Dean sucked for a few seconds. "Sweet. Did you have maple syrup today? It's nice. Logan, you gotta try this."

Logan knelt in front of Leilani on the other side. "Don't mind if I do." He squeezed her bicep. "There's a little more meat up here. I think this is where I'll start."

Logan gored Leilani's upper arm. "You are sweet," he agreed. "No wonder Tristan liked you so much."

Dean gradually moved up Leilani's inner arm, making fresh bites every 2 inches or so. Logan did the same, moving in the opposite direction on her other arm.

"You know what, Logan? Wings are fine but I'm really more of a thigh man." Dean pulled away from Leilani's arm. Blood dripped from his fangs and spilled from each of the wounds on her arms.

Leilani looked around the room again for something, anything, she could use to defend herself. There was nothing.

138 – Retaliation

Torrey moaned and lifted her head. She tried to focus. She saw a blurry white figure streaked with red. As her vision cleared, she realized it was Leilani. Blood ran down Leilani's arms and pooled on the floor. *Oh my god. They're feeding on her!*

"Torrey, you're up!" Dean said. "Leilani, will you excuse me for a minute? Logan, feel free to continue your meal."

Dean stood. "Torrey, so good to see you. You think your husband might join us anytime soon? I can't start unless you're both here. Cruuuz, Cruuuz, wake up! We're waiting."

Cruz stirred upon hearing his name. He tried to move but couldn't. He opened his eyes and saw he was restrained. He looked to the side and saw Torrey tied up as well.

Dean walked to Torrey and stroked her hair. "You're a very lucky man, Cruz, to have such a beautiful wife."

"I'll kill you if you touch her!" Cruz roared, straining against the cuffs and tape.

"No, you won't. Now shut the hell up or I'll kill her now!" Dean threatened.

Cruz glowered at Dean and then noticed Leilani, still tied to the chair and bleeding. Logan continued to feed on her. "Logan? What the hell are you doing? Get off her!"

Dean slapped Cruz's cheekbone. "I thought I told you to shut the hell up!" He straightened his tie and glared at Cruz and Torrey. "Before we begin, I'd like to tell you both Tristan is dead. So he won't be coming through the door to save you."

Torrey and Cruz exchanged a worried glance. They wondered if it could be true.

"Now I'm sure you're all wondering, am I going to kill you?" Dean looked from Leilani to Torrey to Cruz. "The answer is …

yes. Of course, it's yes! Why else would I be here, right?" he laughed. "What I haven't decided is the order in which you'll die. Leilani's kinda petite. Will Logan drain her of her blood before I finish with the happy couple here? I don't know. But it'll be fun to find out."

Dean paced between Leilani, Torrey and Cruz. "And I'm no mind reader, but I bet you're all wondering *why* I want to kill you. I can see it in your eyes. 'Dean, why are you doing this? You seemed like such a nice guy, so handsome, so charming.' I bet that's what you're thinking, right?"

Dean turned his gaze to Leilani. "Let's start with you. I know you're the most important person in Tristan's life right now. I even know he proposed to you last night, which, as luck would have it, makes this so much more meaningful for me. You see, earlier this year, Tristan took someone very special from me—someone who I proposed to. So, Leilani, that means you have to die. Fair is fair."

He turned to Torrey and Cruz. "Now, when I say Tristan took someone from me, I mean Tristan ordered the kill. Tristan and his stupid Rules. So, as of today, there are no more Rules."

Dean looked from Torrey to Cruz and back to Torrey. He knew from Logan that Torrey killed Andi, but wanted to see if she'd admit it. "I know one of you killed my fiancée. The question is, which one?"

"Dean, let Leilani go, man," Cruz pleaded. "She has nothing to do with the Rules. She …"

Dean punched Cruz in the face, breaking his nose. Blood spilled from his nose, down his chest and onto his lap.

"Cruz, I've already told you twice to shut up. There won't be a third time. The next time you speak out of turn, I'll stake your wife through the heart," Dean threatened. "Where was I? Oh yeah. In Santa Cruz earlier this year, one of you killed a woman named Andi. I loved Andi. I thought we were going to spend the rest of our lives together. Life is funny though. Now that I'm finally getting my revenge for Andi's untimely death, I'm not as upset about it as I once was because I have someone new. But my buddy, Logan, was upset by the killings, too. You see, Andi and Andy were like parents to him. They practically raised him when his own parents ran out on him. I promised Logan we'd get even with Tristan and whoever did the killing. So, what I want to know is, which one of you killed my fiancée?"

Cruz glanced at his wife and turned back to Dean. "It was me. I killed her."

"Cruz, no! It was me, Dean. I did it," Torrey confessed.

"Torrey, please, babe," Cruz begged. "Be quiet. Dean, it was me."

Leilani couldn't hold back the sobs anymore. She could choke back the tears from her own pain, but couldn't bear to watch what was going to happen to Torrey and Cruz. Logan groaned, disgusted by Leilani's tears. He buried his fangs in the side of her calf.

Cruz wanted to demand again that they release Leilani, but was afraid Dean would kill Torrey if he opened his mouth.

Dean sized up Cruz and Torrey. "You both say you did it. Interesting. Which one of you is lying to protect the other? Which one of you loves the other more?"

Dean removed a wooden stake from his briefcase. He held it between Torrey and Cruz, turning the pointed end from one to the other. "Eenie, meenie, miney, mo." He slammed the stake into Cruz's chest, purposely missing his heart by an inch.

Cruz screamed in agony as Dean wrenched the stake back out of his flesh.

"Did I choose right?" Dean asked.

"Yes," Cruz grunted, "it was me. I killed Andi."

Torrey screamed, "Dean, stop it! I killed her. Please don't hurt him. Andi killed kids. I told Tristan. I did it! I staked her!"

"Logan, would you like to do the honors?" Dean asked.

Logan looked up. Leilani's blood dripped from his fangs. "I'd love to. I've been waiting months for this!" He rose to his feet and reached for Dean's stake. He raised his arm and thumped the stake into Torrey's chest, a half-inch from her heart.

"I'll kill you, you filthy bloodsuckers," Cruz spat.

"One time too many, Cruz." Dean pulled the stake from Torrey's chest, raised it over his head and smashed it into Cruz's heart. Cruz collapsed into a pile of ash on the chair.

"No!!! Cruz!!!" Blood gurgled from Torrey's chest as she screamed.

Leilani struggled in her chair. She wanted to reach out to Torrey but the tape kept her immobile.

Dean stared at the pyramid of ash that used to be Cruz and smiled smugly. He turned to Torrey, "You took my future wife. I took your husband. Now we're even."

He glanced at his watch. "I hate to cut this short but I lost some time when I went looking for Leilani at her house earlier. Logan, be sure you drain Leilani of every last drop of blood. When she's dead, finish off Torrey. I'll leave the stake here for you. I've got a plane to catch."

"You got it," Logan said. "It'll be my pleasure."

Dean grabbed his jacket and briefcase, and left through the front door.

Hearing the door close, Logan turned back to Leilani. "You know, it didn't have to be this way," he said. "If the cops had just done their job and arrested Tristan for Rick's death, you wouldn't be here now. I don't know how much easier I could've made it for them. I called and told them Tristan killed Rick, and where to find Rick's board. All they had to do was detain Tristan for a week. He would've been dead."

The second call, Leilani thought. *It was Logan. Logan called Garrison about Tristan.*

"But they released him," Logan continued. "And now, because of their incompetence, Dean's here barking orders at me and you're here bleeding to death. Stupid humans. If you weren't so tasty, there'd be no point to keeping any of you around. And you, Leilani, are pretty damn tasty."

139 – Departing

Dean headed toward Skylar's house, where he'd parked his car. He set his briefcase inside the trunk and pulled out some fresh clothes. He changed and threw his blood-spattered tux in a garbage bag. He tossed the bag in a neighbor's trashcan sitting on the curb.

He wondered why he hadn't heard from Lance yet. He called Lance's cell but there was no answer. "Hey, you were supposed to call me when you were done with Tristan. I'm leaving for the airport in a minute. Call when you get this."

Inside the house, Skylar had her bags packed and ready to go. She sat on the couch and checked her purse to make sure her driver's license and passport were there. She saw her cell phone blinking and called to retrieve her messages. "Message 1: Sky, it's Jake." She clicked the delete button. *Sorry, Jake, I'm over you. I've got Dean now. Too bad if you realized you made a mistake. Your loss.*

"Message 2: Skylar, it's Tristan. Don't hang up! I know you don't like Leilani but she's …" Skylar clicked delete again. *Seriously? He's calling me about Leilani? Dean's right. It's better if I leave. There's nothing for me here.*

She turned off her phone, removed the battery, and threw the phone in the trash. *I'm done with you all. I never want to hear from any of you again.*

Skylar heard a knock at the door. She opened it to see Dean standing there smiling. "Right on time!" She noticed red specks on his face. "Is that blood?"

"What?"

She pointed, "On your face."

"I must've cut myself shaving. Lemme go wipe it off." Dean ran to the bathroom and washed his face. As he dried himself with a towel, he glanced in the mirror to make sure there were no other telltale signs of human or graysuit carnage on his body.

"You ready? We've got a plane to catch," he said as he returned from the bathroom.

"Maybe I should say goodbye to Torrey, Cruz and Logan. It's not their fault Tristan's such a jerk."

"Sky, we don't have time. Plus, I told you it's better if we leave and don't tell anyone. We don't want them coming after us. You know how Tristan is. It's nice of you to worry about everyone but don't you think it's time you focus on yourself for once? C'mon, our future awaits!"

Dean lifted the handles of Skylar's suitcase and board bag, and carried them to his car. Skylar clutched her purse and carry-on tote. She turned out the lights.

"To new beginnings," she told herself.

140 – Ash and Blood

Jake skidded to a stop in an empty spot on the curb, one house away from Tristan's. He sprinted up the sidewalk, through the yard and burst through the front door. Tristan followed, leaving a trail of blood behind. As they turned toward the living room, they saw Torrey cuffed to a chair and bleeding. Then they spied Logan feeding on Leilani's leg, slightly above her knee.

"You're dead!" Tristan charged at Logan, who jumped up and made a break for the back door. Tristan tried to run after him but couldn't with the stake protruding from his chest. "Jake, I can't run. You've gotta go after him for me."

But Jake stood frozen, staring blankly at Leilani. Her ivory nightgown was now crimson with blood. His mind flashed to Cody. *Blood. Too much blood.* His heart pounded in his ears. The periphery of his vision clouded and darkened.

"Jake," Tristan repeated. But Jake didn't move.

Tristan grabbed Jake's arms and shook him. "Jake!"

Jake could see Tristan's mouth moving but couldn't hear the words over the thumping of his heartbeat in his ears.

"Jake!"

Finally, Jake heard his name. The blackness receded.

"Logan! Go after Logan!" Tristan yelled.

Jake nodded and dashed out the back door.

Tristan removed the tape from Leilani's mouth. "Are you okay?"

"Oh my god!" Leilani gasped. "Your chest!"

"Don't worry about me. Are you okay?"

"Yes. Help Torrey!"

Tristan turned to Torrey and saw the pile of ash in the chair next to her. He looked into her bloodshot eyes and back at the empty chair. "No." He tore through the tape and ripped apart the handcuffs on Torrey's arms and legs. He placed his hands on her shoulders and stared at her tear-streaked face. "Torrey, no."

"Dean killed Cruz. Cruz tried to protect me. Dean killed him right in front of me. I'll die without him, Tristan. I'll die," Torrey sobbed.

"Torrey, hang on. I'm going to free Leilani. I'm here. Just hang on." Tristan turned back to Leilani. He crouched in front of her and removed the rest of the tape.

Leilani wanted to throw her arms around him but couldn't with the bloody stake sticking from his chest. "Tristan, we need to get you some help!"

"I'm fine. We need to fix you up first. You've lost a lot of blood." Tristan rose to his feet but stumbled.

"You're turning pale." Leilani guided him to the couch. "Lie down. Torrey, can you help him?"

Torrey, who was still bleeding from her own chest wound, knelt beside Tristan's head and shoulders. His eyes rolled up into his head. "Tristan, can you hear me?" she asked. "Tristan?"

Jake ran back into the living room, breathless. "I couldn't find Logan. I don't know where he went."

"Jake, run to my place and get my black bag," Torrey said. "It's in the closet by the front door. Hurry!"

Jake darted outside again.

Torrey crouched over Tristan, opened his eyelids and examined his eyes. "Tristan, can you hear me?" She felt for a pulse.

"Yes," Tristan wheezed. More blood escaped from his chest. "Torrey, I'm sorry about Cruz. It's all my fault. I'm so sorry."

"Tristan, no. It was Dean. And Logan. They're to blame, not you," Torrey said.

"Leilani?" Tristan whispered.

Kneeling next to Torrey, Leilani reached for Tristan's hand. Her voice shook as she fought back sobs. "I'm here. You're going to be fine. Torrey's going to fix you right up."

While Leilani held Tristan's hand, Torrey walked to the kitchen sink and scrubbed her hands clean. Jake returned with her medical bag. Torrey pulled out a syringe and some gauze. She quickly irrigated her own stake wound, which fortunately wasn't nearly as deep or as wide as Tristan's, and shoved a ball of gauze inside to slow the flow of blood. She washed her hands again and returned to Tristan.

"I'm going to give you some anesthesia," Torrey explained. "I need to remove the stake and stitch you up, and it's going to hurt like nothing you've ever experienced before."

"No, no anesthesia. I need to talk to Leilani," Tristan insisted.

"Tristan, please listen to Torrey," Leilani said.

"No. I need to talk to you," he said.

Leilani looked to Torrey but Torrey saw there was no use arguing with him.

"Tristan, you can talk to Leilani in a minute. Jake, get some kitchen towels from the drawer and tie them on Leilani's wounds. She's losing too much blood. I can only work on one patient at a time and Tristan is more critical right now," Torrey said.

Jake grabbed a pile of clean dish towels, tore them into strips, and tied them around the multiple wounds on Leilani's arms and legs.

"Tristan, you have two minutes. Then we'll get started," Torrey said. "Jake, come outside with me. I'll see if I can pick up Logan's scent."

141 – Forever

"Tristan, I'm so sorry," Leilani cried.

"Why are you sorry? I'm the one who should be apologizing for getting you mixed up in all this," he said.

"No! You were right! They're monsters. And now Cruz is dead. Cruz and Torrey were trying to save me. Dean and Logan have to be destroyed. They …"

"Listen to me. None of that matters now. All that matters is you're safe. We need to get you to a hospital. You've lost too much blood." Tristan turned her wrist over. "You're still bleeding."

"No, not until I know you're okay. Why don't we go to the hospital together? I can make sure …"

"No. If I go to the hospital, I'll die there or in a jail cell. At least here, I have a fighting chance. If Torrey can't fix me, I'll have Jake take me to the ocean. If I have the energy and can morph into a shark, the salt water should accelerate the healing," he explained. "We don't have much time before Torrey comes back. I need to know. What were you going to tell me tonight? What's your answer?"

"Yes, Tristan. I was going to tell you yes, I'll marry you."

"I have something for you." Tristan reached into his pants pocket and removed a small velvet box. "I should be kneeling for this but maybe we can make an exception this time." He smiled and pulled a sapphire ring from the box. The blue round cut stone glittered, as did the small white diamonds encircling the stone and the band.

He held the ring in his fingers. "I chose this ring so, whenever you look at it, you'll know exactly how I feel about you. I chose the sapphire because my love for you is as deep as the ocean; the diamonds because it's as vast as the stars;

and the circular band, of course, because it's never-ending. Leilani, will you marry me?"

"Yes, Tristan. I love you," she smiled through her tears.

Tristan slipped the ring on her finger. She bent down and softly kissed his lips.

"I will love you forever," Tristan whispered.

"Forever," Leilani whispered back.

142 – Surgery

Torrey and Jake returned to the living room. Leilani moved around to the end of the sofa. She stood above Tristan's head and gently stroked his hair.

Torrey knelt beside Tristan. "Before I start, I have to tell you I don't know if I can do this. I'm not a surgeon. And this stake is deeper than any I've ever seen. I'm not sure how you've survived this long. The stake is keeping your body from healing itself. But once I remove it, there's going to be major bleeding. I don't know how much internal damage there is—my guess is it's pretty severe—and I don't know if I'll be able to stitch everything up in time. There's a good chance you could bleed out. The flow of blood might be faster than your body's ability to heal itself. Plus, an operation like this can take hours under the best of circumstances. And this," Torrey waved her arm around the living room, "is not the best of circumstances. Are you sure you want me to do this?"

"Is there any other way?" Leilani asked.

"No," Torrey replied.

"Yes, I'm sure," Tristan answered. "And no anesthesia. I need to be able to morph later. I think if I can get to the ocean I can heal more quickly."

"I'll do a local anesthetic. That shouldn't interfere with your ability to focus and morph. But it's going to be no match for the pain." Torrey positioned Jake next to her. "On the count of 3, Jake, I want you to pull the stake as hard as you can. Pull it straight out, in one smooth movement."

Leilani bent down to kiss Tristan's forehead. Her tears dropped onto his face. "I love you, Tristan."

"I love you, too," he said.

Torrey counted, "1, 2, 3."

Jake yanked the stake as hard as he could. It released from Tristan's chest with a moist sucking sound and flew from Jake's hands across the room. It landed in a magazine rack.

A geyser of blood gushed from Tristan's chest as soon as the stake wrenched free. He screamed in agony. His fangs descended as he labored to breathe through the searing pain. Beads of sweat broke out across his forehead and then his entire body.

Torrey quickly cleaned the wound and began stitching the damaged tissues back together.

Leilani had never seen anyone work so quickly or so nimbly. She knew Torrey was doing everything she could to save Tristan, despite being severely injured herself and losing the love of her life only minutes ago.

While Torrey worked, Jake gathered up the ribbons of duct tape and cuffs, and threw them in the trash. He took the trash bag outside and placed it in a neighbor's trashcan.

Finally, Torrey finished and taped bandages over Tristan's wound. His breathing slowed.

"Did it work? Is he going to be okay?" Leilani asked.

Torrey took Tristan's pulse again. "There was too much damage. I did what I could but it's not nearly enough. His body was ripped apart inside. He lost a lot of blood. And he's not healing quickly enough. We need to get him to the ocean. It's his only hope. Jake, help me. We need to carry him."

Tristan looked up and saw Leilani hovering over him. He clasped her hand and touched the engagement ring on her finger. "Forever," he whispered. Tristan's hand went limp and his eyes closed.

"Jake, we need to go now!" Torrey said.

Jake grabbed Tristan's feet. Torrey gripped his torso. They headed for the back door.

Leilani followed but after a few steps, the room spun. She

looked down and saw fresh blood spouting from one of her wrists and from her thigh. The dish towel ribbons on her arms and legs were soaked. "Jake," she mumbled.

Jake and Torrey turned and saw Leilani fall to the floor.

"Jake, call 911. Get an ambulance here. As soon as you hear the sirens, run. Leave through the back door and come help me with Tristan," Torrey said.

"But what about you? You can't carry him," Jake said.

"Yes, I can. Call now, then come as quick as you can." Torrey lifted Tristan over her shoulder and carried him out the back door.

143 – Payment

At home, Logan threw his clothes and passport in a black duffle bag, and secured his surfboard in its travel bag. He looked at his watch. He still had several hours until his flight departed for Australia but he didn't want to stick around in case Tristan or Torrey came looking for him.

The first-class flight and $100,000 in his checking account were payment from Dean for his services infiltrating the Nomads over the past several months and assisting with the killing of Torrey and Cruz.

Logan debated whether or not to call Dean to tell him he didn't actually finish the job. *Should I tell Dean that Tristan showed up and I had to book on out of there before killing Leilani and Torrey? On one hand, I should because if Tristan survives, he'll be looking to kick Dean's ass—and mine, too. On the other hand, if I tell Dean, he could take his money back for not finishing the job. And I did my part. I gave up months of my life, playing the enthusiastic little soldier to Tristan. Man, that sucked.*

Logan loaded his bag and board into his car. *No way. If I call Dean, he'll get mad and want me to clean up the mess. Forget that. We got our revenge. And what Dean doesn't know won't kill him. Probably.*

Logan turned his key in the ignition. *I just need to disappear. So where should I go until my flight leaves?*

144 – Sliver

Jake dialed 911. He gave Tristan's address and said, "A woman is passed out. She's bleeding to death. She needs medical attention. Send an ambulance right away."

Jake hung up. He tried to wake Leilani but couldn't get her to respond. He held her in his arms until he heard sirens in the distance. "Leilani, if you can hear me, I've got to go help Tristan. I'll come to the hospital later to check on you. Stay strong."

Jake dashed out the back door and down the path to the beach. He caught up with Torrey about 3 yards from the ocean. She stood, with Tristan draped over her shoulder, staring at the horizon.

"Torrey?" As Jake approached, he noticed she was bleeding again from her chest wound. The gauze was gone and blood flowed down the front of her body.

"Jake, take Tristan off my shoulder. Gently," she instructed. "I can't move."

Jake pulled Tristan into his arms. "Do you want me to help you to the ocean, too?"

"No. I think when I got staked earlier a sliver broke off in my chest. Carrying Tristan must've jostled it loose. I can feel it pressing against my heart," Torrey said. "If I take another step, it's going to puncture my heart."

"What should I do?" Jake asked.

"Take Tristan to the ocean. My board and Cruz's board are out there. We left them when we heard Leilani scream. Find one and use it to get Tristan to deep water. Keep Tristan in the salt water as much as you can. See if it revives him. If he regains consciousness, tell him to morph. That's all we can do."

"But what about you?"

"Just go!" Torrey urged. "I know what I'm doing."

Jake rushed toward the water with Tristan.

As soon as Jake turned away, Torrey whispered, "I'm coming, Cruz." She gingerly lifted her foot and took a step forward. The sharp wooden sliver that remained in her body rotated slightly and stabbed her heart.

Hearing a soft, whooshing sound behind him, Jake turned in time to see Torrey's ashes scatter in the wind.

145 – Deeper

Jake splashed into the ocean. After wading out several feet, he lowered Tristan's body into the salt water. He draped one arm over Tristan's shoulders and chest, and tucked his hand under Tristan's armpit, making sure he had a firm hold. With his other arm, he swam deeper into the ocean, searching for the surfboards.

Jake spotted a board and swam to it, clutching Tristan under his arm. He threw one arm over the board and kept one on Tristan. "Can you hear me? Tristan?"

As they floated in the current, every minute or so, Jake spoke to see if Tristan would respond. After about 10 minutes, he thought he felt Tristan flinch at hearing his name.

"Tristan? It's Jake. Can you hear me? We're in the ocean."

"Leilani," Tristan whispered. "Where is she?"

"The hospital. She's going to be fine," Jake assured him, hoping it was true. "We can check on her later."

"Torrey?" Tristan asked.

"She didn't make it," Jake said softly. "I'm sorry."

Tristan sighed heavily.

"Relax, man. Just feel the ocean, okay?" Jake looked back at the beach. The tide had dragged them quite a bit south. *That's probably good. There was a lot of blood on the trail to the beach. The sheriff is probably all over it by now.* "I'm going to swim us deeper. I don't want us to be visible from the beach."

"Mmhmmm," Tristan mumbled.

After swimming and floating for an hour, Jake felt Tristan stir. "Tristan? Are you feeling any better?"

"A little. I think the salt water is helping. I want to see if I can morph. Let me go for a couple seconds."

Jake released Tristan. He sank underwater. Jake took a deep

breath and dropped his head below the surface to keep an eye on him. Tristan closed his eyes and concentrated. Jake saw his body flicker—shark, human, shark, human. Then it stopped. Jake pulled him back up.

Tristan placed his hands on the surfboard and rested his head on his hands. "It takes energy to morph. I'm not strong enough yet."

"Then we'll float for a while more till you are." Jake swam to the opposite side of the board. He draped his arms across the top and placed his hands next to Tristan's, in case Tristan started to slip.

After a few minutes, Tristan spoke. "Jake, thank you. I've done nothing but bring pain and chaos to your life. And despite everything, you risked your own life to save my life and Leilani's. I can never thank you enough for what you did today. I'm really sorry for everything."

"No, man. I'm sorry. I overreacted yesterday. I know why you couldn't tell me about Rick without giving away your secret. I also know Skylar told you not to tell me anything and that you didn't want to betray her." Jake paused, thinking back to the bloodbath at the cove and at Tristan's house. "Seeing Dean and Logan and those other vampires tonight, and how sadistic and vicious they were, I now understand why you do what you do. I know why you had to kill Rick and that it wasn't your fault he killed Cody. I know you did everything you could to get to Cody in time to save him."

"I appreciate that, but it is my fault. I turned Rick. It doesn't matter if Skylar told me to. I made the decision to do it. And I accidentally turned you, at least part of the way. I'm so sorry. I wish I could give you your life back." Tristan sighed, exhausted from a lifetime of regret. He took a deep breath of salty air. The comforting sound of the water lapping around his shoulders and head helped to clear some of the fogginess in his brain.

"No, man, don't apologize. You were trying to save Cody. I get that." Jake scooped some salt water across the top of the board to wet Tristan's head and hands. "While we've been floating out here, I've been thinking ... I want you to finish the job, if you're up to it."

Tristan raised his head slightly and eyed Jake. "You mean turn you?"

"Yeah. I mean, I'm already halfway there, right? I can't let Logan and Dean get away with what they did to you and Leilani, and to Cruz and Torrey. They're murderers and they'll kill again if we don't do something. I want to do this."

"Vengeance is not a reason to turn."

"That's not why I'm doing it," Jake said.

"Why are you doing it then?"

"Because the ocean is where I belong. It's where I've always belonged. Before Cody died, it was where I went to have fun. After he died, it was where I went for solace. The ocean has always been the only place I feel comfortable. It's where I feel like myself. It's where I feel at home."

"But what about yesterday? You were pretty freaked out," Tristan countered.

"Yeah and I was also pretty mad at you. But when you asked me to imagine myself as a great white and my feet morphed into a fin, it felt pretty incredible. I can't explain it but it felt ... right."

"If you do this, there's no turning back," Tristan said. "You have to be 100 percent sure."

"I am. I'm 100 percent sure this is what I want."

"Then I have one last question for you." Tristan gave him a small smile. "Jake, do you want to surf forever?"

"Yeah," Jake grinned. "Or at least several hundred years, right?"

"Right. But forever sounds cooler."

146 – Turning

"So how do we do this?" Jake asked.

"Usually, I'd come up behind you and bite your neck. But I don't think I have the strength to hold on to you. How about if you come over here next to me and rest your head on the board? Then I'll lift my head and use gravity to help me puncture your skin with my fangs. But I have to warn you, it's a pretty sharp pain."

"Worse than a stake to the chest?"

"No," Tristan grimaced, "but it still hurts like hell."

Jake swam to Tristan's side of the board and faced him.

"Are you sure you wanna do this? That this is who you are?" Tristan asked.

"Yes," Jake reaffirmed. He rested his head on the board next to Tristan's.

"Okay then." Tristan lowered his fangs and lifted his head. He let his head drop forward and plunged his fangs into Jake's neck. After a minute, he pulled his head back and rested it on the board. Blood dripped from his fangs into the ocean. "That should do it."

Jake gripped his neck and swam back to the other side of the board.

After Tristan caught his breath, he explained that it could take up to 24 hours for the transformation to be complete. "You're my brother now, Jake. You really are one of us."

"Thanks. I could use a brother," Jake said. "Right now, you're the only family I've got."

147 – Floating

After an hour, Tristan told Jake he felt strong enough to float on his own.

"I can't leave you here alone," Jake argued.

"You can and you will. There's nothing more you can do."

"But you're still bleeding. I can see it leaking from your chest."

"Yes, but you being here isn't going to stop it. I need you to check on Leilani. I'm not strong enough to go myself or I would. I need to know she's okay," Tristan said.

"I'm not leaving you here," Jake reiterated.

"Jake, this is where I belong. If I'm going to heal, it'll be here in the ocean. There's nothing you can do for me. I'm going to try to morph again in a little bit. Maybe your blood will help give me the strength to do it this time. I want you to go to the hospital and make sure Leilani's okay. Then you can meet me later and tell me how she is. We're pretty far south. I think we're close to Fletcher Cove. How about if you go to the hospital and come back here later? You can meet me, just offshore, around 2 a.m."

Jake wrestled with the idea of leaving Tristan alone. "And what if you're not there?"

"If I'm not there, I didn't make it."

"No way. I'm not leaving you here to die alone."

"Listen," Tristan snapped, "if that's what's going to happen, it's going to happen with or without you here. In the end, we all die alone."

Jake stared out at the dark horizon.

Tristan softened his tone and continued, "There's one other thing I need. After you see Leilani, I need you to go to my house. Be sure to wait until after the sheriff is gone and be careful no one sees you. You're a vampire shark now, or at least you will be soon. You need to be in salt water at least once every 72 hours. You don't want someone seeing you breaking in and calling 911. When you're in my house, go to the kitchen and open the broiler door. Taped to the bottom of the black cookie sheet is a CD. Take it with you and open it when you're home. It has the information to all my bank accounts and my sources for getting new identities. If I make it, we'll need that to relocate. We can't stay here with all the carnage Dean and Logan left behind. But if I don't make it, then you and Leilani take it all. With Torrey and Cruz gone and Skylar god-knows-where, you and Leilani are the only family I have left. Use it to build new lives."

"I'm not leaving you."

"Jake, I'm begging you. Please, go to Leilani. Please, do this for me."

Hearing the desperation in Tristan's voice, Jake relented. "Fine. I'll go. But I better see you later. Fletcher Cove. 2 a.m."

"Thank you."

Jake let out a long sigh of despair. He wanted to grant Tristan his wish but felt terrible about leaving him. He lifted his elbow onto the surfboard and offered his hand to Tristan. "I'll see you later?"

Tristan clasped Jake's hand. "I hope so. Tell Leilani I love her and that I'll do everything in my power to make it back to her. If I don't make it, take care of her for me."

"You'll make it back," Jake promised.

148 – Ride

Jake released his grip on Tristan and the surfboard. He swam toward the gold lights dotting the shore. He couldn't tell if his eyes burned from the salt in the ocean or the tears spilling from his eyes.

Get a grip, man, he told himself. *Tristan needs you to do this. He'll be fine. Do what he wants and then get back here as quick as you can. Tristan will be here. He has to be.*

When Jake climbed onto the shore, he remembered his wallet in the back pocket of his boardshorts. He undid the Velcro on his pocket and removed it. Everything was soaking wet. He touched two soggy $20 bills. *It's still cash money, right?*

Jake walked up the hill and turned north on Highway 101. He saw three surfers he knew having pizza and beer on the front patio of Pizza Port. He nodded, "Hey, man."

"Jake! We haven't seen you around. How are you?" one of the surfers asked.

"Hey, Daniel. I've been better. Anyone have a phone I can borrow? I need to call a cab. My truck is up in Encinitas and I need to get it," Jake explained. "It's kind of an emergency."

"A cab? Nah. I'll give you a ride," Daniel offered.

"No, you guys are eating," Jake said.

"I'm done." Daniel shoved his last three bites of pizza into his mouth. "Let's go," he mumbled.

"Okay, thanks, man. I'll see you guys later," Jake said to the other two surfers, knowing he wouldn't.

"Later, man!" they shouted.

As Jake walked away with Daniel, he heard the two surfers speaking in hushed tones. "That's the dude whose friend got killed by that shark." "No way!" "Yeah, no one's seen him since the paddle out. I think he quit surfing." "Hell, I might too if I saw my friend get eaten by a shark."

Jake ignored them and followed Daniel to his car, a rusted green 1977 hatchback.

"It's a beater but it still runs," Daniel smiled. "So what happened to you? You're all wet."

"Uh, impromptu surf session," Jake said.

"Righteous."

They drove in silence to Jake's truck, parked one house down from Tristan's. There was still one sheriff's car in front of Tristan's house and some activity in the doorway. Jake recognized Detective Garrison from the night Cody died.

Daniel surveyed the scene. "Dude, what happened here?"

"I dunno. Guess I missed all the excitement," Jake lied.

"Is that Garrison over there?" Daniel asked. "That dude's a total dick. I hate that guy."

"Yeah. Hey, thanks for the ride, Daniel. I really appreciate it."

"No problem. I haven't seen you out surfing in a while. Give me a call if you want to go sometime, okay?"

"Okay. Thanks again." Jake slipped into his truck and drove away.

149 — After Hours

Jake went home to change out of his wet shorts. He checked his messages. Leilani had left a message with her room number at the hospital. *She's okay,* he sighed with relief. *Tristan will be happy to hear that.*

There were no other messages. Jake was surprised he hadn't heard back from Skylar. He called and left another message, unaware her phone was in the trash.

A few minutes later, Jake hopped back in his truck and drove to the hospital in Encinitas to see Leilani and keep his promise to Tristan. When he arrived, it was after visiting hours. He waited until the nurse left her desk to get a cup of coffee and then snuck down the hall to Leilani's room. He tiptoed inside, not wanting to wake her if she was sleeping.

As soon as he crossed the threshold, Leilani bolted upright. "Jake, I was so worried about you guys! I passed out and didn't wake up until the paramedics were loading me into the ambulance."

"We were worried about you, too. One minute you were up and the next you were crumpled in a ball on the floor. I waited with you until just before the ambulance arrived but you were out cold," he recounted.

"You did? Thank you. Where's Tristan? And Torrey? I've been going crazy here by myself."

Jake decided not to answer her until he was sure she was strong enough to hear the news. "First, tell me what the doctor said. Are you gonna be okay?"

"They want to keep me here a day or two for observation. They've got me on fluids and antibiotics. They said I lost a lot of blood and almost didn't make it but I'm going to be fine."

"What did you tell them?" Jake asked, curious about how

she managed to explain all the bites on her arms and legs.

"I told the doctors and the sheriff that I got attacked by two big dogs. I said I was house-sitting for a friend and I stepped outside to get the mail, and these dogs came out of nowhere and chased me. I told them I ran to the first house I could find and that fortunately the door was unlocked, but no one was home. I said I tried to close the door but the dogs burst through and attacked me. I told them the dogs bit my arms and legs, before I could beat them back with a chair. Then the dogs ran away, leaving trails of blood behind."

"Wow, that's quite a story," Jake said.

"Yeah. I was pretty delirious when I came up with it. I don't know if they bought it but what other explanation is there? I'm covered with fang marks. They're obviously not human bites. Fortunately, Garrison's not the sharpest tool in the shed. He'll probably pester me for a day or two and then give up."

"So you're going to be okay?"

"Yes. They want to start me on rabies shots so I need to figure out a way to get out of that. I'll probably have some scarring but I'll live," Leilani said. "Jake, please. Tell me about Tristan and Torrey. Are they okay? Where are they?"

Jake hesitated. Leilani knew the news wasn't good. "Please tell me," she begged.

Jake explained what happened to Torrey and that she died saving Tristan's life.

Leilani took a deep breath. *She and Cruz are together now. I don't think she would have wanted it any other way,* she reassured herself. "And what about Tristan?"

"I don't know," Jake answered honestly. He relayed what happened at the wedding and how they rushed to find her afterward. He shared how, after the ambulance came, he and Tristan made it to the ocean and floated south. He explained that Tristan tried to morph but couldn't get it to stick. "Tristan said the best thing for him was to stay in the salt water. He insisted I come to check on you. I tried to stay but he wouldn't let me. I swear, if it was up to me, I wouldn't have left him but it was what he wanted. He asked me to come back tonight and find him … if he makes it."

Leilani sniffed loudly, trying to keep the tears at bay. She didn't want Jake to feel bad for leaving. She knew Tristan wouldn't let him stay, no matter how strongly he insisted. "Thank you for everything you did today. You saved Tristan's life and mine."

"I didn't do enough," Jake countered.

"Jake, you did. If it weren't for you, both Tristan and I would be dead. We owe you our lives."

"No, you don't. You and Tristan gave me my life. After Cody died, I was a shell. I was empty. Meeting you guys brought me back to life." Jake's voice quivered. "Especially you. You're the one person who's always had my back."

Leilani grasped his hand.

Jake cleared his throat. "Before I left, Tristan wanted me to tell you something. He wanted me to tell you he loves you and he'll do everything in his power to make it back to you."

Leilani nodded and smiled, but the tears started falling. "I'm sorry. I really don't cry very often. But this just sucks. Not knowing if he's alive or …"

Jake squeezed her hand, "I know." He decided not to share that Tristan wanted to leave them all his money if he didn't return. *If Tristan comes back, it won't matter,* he reasoned. *If he doesn't come back, then I'll tell her. There's no use upsetting her more. Especially since he's probably coming back.*

A nurse appeared in the doorway and glared at Leilani. "Visiting hours are over. Your friend has to leave."

Leilani nodded and turned to Jake. "Call me as soon as you know anything."

150 – Vampire Shark Adrift

After Jake left to swim to shore, Tristan floated. Blood seeped from his body into the ocean.

He tried to morph but failed. He waited a half-hour and tried again. As he shifted from human to shark to human, a dolphin appeared.

"Is that really you?" Tristan asked.

The dolphin bobbed his nose up and down.

As Tristan shifted from human to shark again, he felt the dolphin's movement with his lateral line. The nerve impulses traveled to his brain, helping him to hold his shark form.

The dolphin wriggled his body and swam closer. Tristan felt a tingling sensation across his head as his vast network of electroreceptors detected the dolphin's electrical field. Tristan concentrated with all his might to hold his shark form but after a few seconds he felt himself fade. He returned to his human form.

Tristan stared at the dolphin and tried to morph again but couldn't.

"Thanks for trying, Cody," Tristan smiled. "I guess it wasn't meant to be."

Tristan floated on the surfboard another half-hour before he felt himself begin to lose consciousness. Slowly, his hands slipped off the board and his face dropped into the water. Everything turned black.

151 – Mementos

Jake drove to Tristan's house after leaving the hospital. The sheriff's car was gone. Yellow crime scene tape blocked the front door.

After making sure no neighbors were watching, Jake crept to the back door. With his elbow, he broke a pane of glass on the French door. Careful to avoid the shards in the frame, he unlocked the door and let himself inside.

He turned right into the kitchen. He squatted and opened the broiler door, removing the black cookie sheet. He rose to his feet, turned it over and set it on the tile countertop. The CD was there. He removed the tape and stuffed the plastic case in his pocket.

He entered the living room. The couch, chairs and patches of the floor were drenched in blood. A lot of it was Leilani's but some of it also belonged to Tristan, Cruz and Torrey. *I wonder what the forensic investigation will turn up. Do they even know what vampire shark blood is?*

Jake walked upstairs. He peered inside the door of a bedroom and saw rows of surfboards. He flinched when he saw Rick's board.

Rick. This is all his fault. If he wouldn't have killed Cody, none of this would've happened … But I guess that wouldn't have stopped Dean and Logan. They still would've gone after Tristan, Torrey and Cruz. And if I hadn't been here, Tristan might have died, probably with his engagement ring in his pocket. Or maybe he never would've met Leilani, which would have been even worse.

Jake glanced around Tristan's bedroom. He opened the walk-in closet and saw a bag with clothes sticking out. Judging by the petite size, he guessed they were Leilani's. He reached inside the bag and found her wallet, phone and keys as well. He set the bag by the door to take with him when he left.

On the shelf next to the door, he spotted a book with an old leather cover. He opened it and discovered it was a photo album of Tristan. There were pictures of him as a child and as an adult when he was human. There were then pictures, about one a decade, after he turned.

He shoved the album in Leilani's bag and carried it downstairs. Spying a rack in the corner of the living room, he walked over to it in case there were any other photo albums Leilani might want. He flipped through the contents. It appeared to be all magazines. When he reached the last one, his fingers felt something hard. He peered inside and saw a bloody wooden stake. He lifted it from the rack.

This is the stake I pulled out of Tristan. Garrison must have missed it.

Jake wrapped his hand around the stake. It was so wide he couldn't touch his fingers to his thumb. He couldn't imagine how Tristan made it from Dean's fake wedding to his house to the ocean after being impaled with it.

Jake put the stake in his other pocket and slipped out the back door.

152 – Searching

Jake showed up at Fletcher Cove at 1:30 a.m. He paddled out and waited for Tristan. At 2:15, he removed his knife strap from his ankle, slipped out of his boardshorts, and tied them to his leash. He dove underwater and pictured himself as a great white shark. After a few seconds, he morphed. He was amazed by how powerful he felt in his new body. He searched and searched for Tristan but found nothing.

He surfaced in his human form. He scanned 360 degrees around him. He sniffed the air. He listened. *Nothing.*

Jake alternated between shark and human form, searching a larger and larger area. After three hours, there was still no sign of Tristan.

He slipped back into his shorts, refastened the strap to his ankle, climbed onto his board and headed toward shore. He felt a light breeze on his face. *Wait.* He lifted his nose and sniffed the air. *It can't be.* Facing the shore, he surveyed the water. *Logan.*

Jake reached down to the knife strap. The strap no longer held his dive knife. That had been left at the beach after he slit Lance's throat. Now, the strap held the stake that killed Tristan.

Silently, Jake paddled toward Logan. When he was a few feet away, he stopped. His heart pounded and his knuckles turned white gripping the stake behind his back. "Logan?"

Logan turned, startled by Jake's voice. "Jake? I'm surprised to see you here."

"You broke the Rules, man."

"There are no Rules anymore. I'm sure Tristan's dead by now."

"No, man. Tristan sent me to bring you your last meal."

"What? You?" Logan's fangs descended.

"No. A nice, big, bloody stake."

Jake whipped his arm forward. The stake struck the center of Logan's heart, turning him to a cloud of dust. The dust and the stake dropped onto his board.

Drained of energy and emotion, Jake surfed to shore. He knew he had to get home before sunrise. He also knew he had to be the one to tell Leilani that Tristan wasn't coming back.

153 – Breaking the News

Jake drove home in silence. Numb, he parked his truck in its usual spot. He didn't remember the ride home.

He walked inside and collapsed on his couch in the dark. He closed his eyes and fell into a shallow sleep.

After a while, he got up, showered and threw on a pair of boxers. He served some leftover fruit salad from his breakfast with Leilani, settled at his desk and flipped on his computer.

One ruthless killer down, one to go. Jake did an Internet search for Dean Delsur. Seeing no recent postings, he tried a different tactic. He input the terms "great white shark" plus "attack" and the current date.

Bingo. Jake located a new story posted on a surf blog in the Hawaiian Islands. It described how two surfers had disappeared just before dawn. Witnesses reported seeing two sharks in the area. *If one of them is Dean, I wonder who the other one is.*

Jake noted the location of the disappearances. *I doubt Dean had enough time to rent a house or a condo, so he and his accomplice are probably staying in a nearby hotel*, he theorized.

Jake loaded Tristan's CD into his computer and made a copy of all the files. He found a file marked "IDs" and opened the folder. He scrolled through a list of telephone numbers until he found a local area code. He dialed the number. "Yeah, Tristan Pierce gave me your name. I'm sorry to call so early but it's an emergency. I need two California driver licenses, two Social Security cards and two passports. ... Yeah, I'll email you the info and photos. ... Yeah, I can send you the money electronically. ... Can I pick them up at noon today? ... Yes, rush charges are fine. ... See you then and thank you."

Jake hung up. Even though it was going to be a warm day, he put on a long sleeve cotton shirt, pants and a cap to protect his newborn vampire skin. He rubbed sunscreen onto his face, neck and hands.

He put Tristan's CD in its case, tucked his wallet into his back pocket, grabbed his car keys and his darkest sunglasses, and headed to the hospital. He carefully avoided exposing himself to direct sunlight. Luckily, the sky was mostly overcast.

At the reception desk, he saw the nurse who kicked him out of Leilani's room the night before. "I'm here to see Leilani."

"I'm sorry. Only family is allowed."

"I am family," Jake lied.

"Oh, you must be the fiancé," the nurse said. "She was calling out for you last night. Bad dreams. This way, Mr. Pierce."

The nurse led Jake to Leilani's room. She was sleeping.

"Poor thing," the nurse whispered to Jake. "I've never seen such a vicious attack. If you can wait, it would be best to let her rest and talk with her when she wakes up on her own."

Relieved Leilani was sleeping, Jake quietly closed the curtains on the room's only window and sat in a chair next to her bed. Within five minutes, he fell fast asleep. He dreamed of being a shark, swimming faster and faster, searching for something and finding nothing but darkness.

Jake awoke to a soft voice. Someone touched his hand. It was Leilani.

"How long have you been here?" she asked.

"I dunno. What time is it?"

"Almost 10 a.m." Leilani grew worried. *If Tristan was okay, Jake would have said something by now.* "Did Tristan …"

Jake shook his head. "I'm sorry. I was there all night. I looked everywhere. He wasn't there."

Leilani reached for the box of tissue by her bed. Jake shut the door. He didn't want the nurse to come in and kick him out again. He sat beside Leilani and held her as she cried. He didn't know how long they held each other before she pulled away.

"I'm sorry. It's going to take me some time. I thought I was going to spend my life with him. Now I have to get used to the idea of spending my life without him," she said.

"Don't apologize," he said softly. "I'm going to miss him, too."

The door opened and the nurse entered. "Everything okay in here?"

Leilani smiled weakly. "Yeah. Just got some bad news."

"Maybe you should leave now, Mr. Pierce," the nurse said.

Leilani raised her eyebrows at Jake. She turned back to the nurse. "No. I need him here. Please."

"Okay, but you need your rest." The nurse took Leilani's vital signs and left the room.

When she was gone, Jake apologized. "Sorry. They wouldn't let me in unless I was family. She assumed I was Tristan so I went with it."

"No, it's fine. I'm glad you're here."

154 — Parting Gifts I

"I need to tell you something else," Jake said. "I don't know if it will make you feel better or worse, but you need to know."

Leilani braced herself for more bad news. *Tristan is gone. What else could he tell me that would make me feel worse?*

"Logan is dead," Jake said flatly. "He'll never hurt you again."

"What?! How?" Leilani asked.

"When I realized Tristan wasn't coming, I started toward shore. I ran into Logan. I killed him with the stake that killed Tristan. So he won't be coming back. Ever."

Leilani lay back in her bed. She couldn't decide how she felt about Logan's death. "I guess I feel … relieved?" She glanced at Jake. "He didn't hurt you, did he?"

"No, I'm fine." Jake reached down to the floor. "After I left Tristan last night, he asked me to go by his house and get something. While I was there, I found your bag in his room. I thought you might want it."

He retrieved Tristan's photo album from the bag and handed it to her. "I also found this in his bedroom. I'm pretty sure he'd want you to have it."

Leilani flipped through the first few pages. "Is this Tristan as a kid?! And here he is as an adult …" She paused on a page. "This must be after he got turned. He looks different—like something's changed in his eyes." She continued leafing through the album. "Judging by the fashion, it looks like there's a picture only every 10 years or so. And here, this must be Julianna. They look so happy."

"Turn to the last page," Jake urged.

She skipped to the final page and spotted a photo of her and Tristan, together, in his backyard. "Where did this come from?"

"It's from the barbecue at Tristan's. You know, the night Cruz tackled me for bringing shark? I forgot Tristan asked me to take this. Look, you can see Cruz and Torrey in the background by the barbecue. Tristan asked me to be sure to get a picture of the two of you. I think he knew even then that you were destined to be together."

Leilani stared at the photo. Tristan's expression looked so happy. "Thank you. I can't tell you how much this means to me."

Jake's face reddened. "Yeah, well, the real reason he sent me to his house was to get this." He handed her the CD case. "Tristan said if he didn't make it back, he wanted to leave everything to us. He said we were the only family he had left. I looked at it this morning. It's got all his bank accounts, access codes, everything. He said he wanted us to use it to start new lives."

Leilani stared at the shiny silver CD in the clear plastic case. "I don't know what to say."

"Me neither."

Leilani handed the CD and photo album to Jake and asked him to put them in her bag. *Something is different about him,* she noticed. *And he reeks like sunscreen.*

Jake saw Leilani appraising his appearance. *She knows,* he thought. "Uh, yeah, there's something else I need to tell you. About me. Though I think you've probably already guessed it. While I was with Tristan yesterday in the ocean, I asked him to finish the job and turn me." He waited for her reaction.

Leilani swallowed hard. "Jake, why?"

"A lot of reasons. The main reason is that I discovered it's who I am."

"And this is what you want?"

"This is what I am."

She stared into his eyes, trying to wrap her head around his decision to become a full-fledged vampire shark. "Okay. Just as long as you're still Jake."

"I'm still Jake—just new, improved and waterproof Jake," he smiled. "Listen, you should get some rest. I'll come back tonight around dinnertime. There are a few things I need to take care of this afternoon. When do you think they're going to release you?"

"They're waiting for some test results. Hopefully tonight, maybe tomorrow morning. Detective Garrison is supposed to come back today. I hope they release me before I have to deal with him."

"Just go in the bathroom and pretend you're throwing up or something. Tell him to come back tomorrow," Jake said. "By then, you'll be outta here."

"That's not a bad idea." Leilani clasped Jake's hand as he rose to his feet. "Thank you for everything. I don't know how I'd get through this without you."

"I'll see you later. Get some rest."

The nurse entered as Jake was leaving. "Goodbye, Mr. Pierce."

"Later."

As soon as Jake left, Leilani's thoughts turned back to Tristan. She buried her head in her pillow and cried until she fell asleep.

155 – Identity

Jake left the hospital and headed to see the man he'd contacted earlier. He arrived in Fairbanks Ranch about 10 minutes to noon. He pulled up to the security gate, and gave his name and the name of the man he was meeting. The guard called the man to confirm, wrote down Jake's license plate and opened the gate.

Jake wound through the streets lined with immaculate houses and landscaping. He located the address, pulled into the circular driveway and walked up to the huge arched wooden door.

Before he could knock, the door swung open.

"Jake?" the man asked.

"Yes. I called earlier. Tristan Pierce sent me."

"Come in."

Jake stepped into the entryway. The floor and walls were covered in luxurious dark green marble. He caught a whiff of the man's slightly salty scent. *Vampire shark,* he knew.

The man closed the door and walked to a small marble-topped table in the foyer. He grabbed a plain manila envelope and returned to Jake. "Here you are. I trust everything is to your liking?"

Jake opened the envelope and inspected the contents. "Yes, thank you. You do excellent work. May I contact you again in the future if I need new documents?"

"Of course. Please tell Tristan I said hello." The man showed Jake to the door.

Jake returned home. He booked two plane tickets online. He packed a carry-on bag, and slid his computer and travel documents into a soft-sided briefcase. He sealed his surfboard in its travel bag. He took a nap for a few hours and then carried his bags to his truck.

156 — Leaving

Jake arrived at the hospital shortly before 6 p.m. He passed Detective Garrison in the hall. Garrison did a double-take. He could tell Garrison thought he looked familiar but couldn't quite place him. Jake gave him a slight nod and continued on his way.

Jake entered Leilani's room but it was empty. Startled, he looked around, fearing she'd been released and hadn't contacted him or that Dean had come back for her. Then he spotted her bag in the corner of the room.

A moment later, Leilani emerged from the bathroom. "Jake, I'm glad it's you. I thought it was Garrison coming back. I did what you said. It worked like a charm. He totally bought it. Once I started dry heaving he couldn't leave here fast enough."

"Good. Do you think he'll pester you for more information?"

"No. I told him the story about the dogs again. He thought it was a weird coincidence I ended up in Tristan's house while fleeing the dogs, but he has no other explanation. And, other than my blood, they couldn't identify any of the other samples they took at the scene. They blamed it on some glitch in their equipment. I guess it's not designed for vampire shark blood. The good thing, at least in this instance, is that Garrison's lazy. He'll probably keep the file on his desk for a week, so it looks like he's doing something. Then it'll get buried as new cases come in."

"So, are they ready to release you?"

"Yep. I just finished the paperwork. Thanks for bringing my bag with my clothes. I came in wearing my nightgown and it was covered in blood …"

Jake hugged her. "It's okay," he whispered.

"Does the pain ever go away? I can't stop thinking about him."

"I wish I could tell you that you'll feel better in time and that it won't hurt so much. But the truth is, you'll probably always feel that hole in your heart. When Cody died, my friend Carlos told me something. He said the reason the loss felt so great was because Cody was so great. It's the same for you and Tristan. The pain you're feeling right now is directly proportional to how important Tristan was to you. When he died, he took a part of your soul with him and that leaves a hole behind. Carlos told me I was lucky I had that hole, because it showed what a big impact Cody had on my life. I didn't understand it at the time, but he was right. If I wasn't so fortunate, it wouldn't hurt so much. You had that with Tristan. It was short—way shorter than it should've been. But you had it, Leilani. That's what matters."

Leilani smiled through her tears and took a deep breath. "Okay, I'm ready to go."

Jake carried her bag and steered her to the parking lot in a wheelchair.

"I hate that they make you use these," she said. Once they hit the pavement outside the hospital doors, Leilani stood. She was still sore from the multiple puncture wounds on her arms and legs but determined to walk on her own.

As she climbed into Jake's truck, she saw his bags in the cab behind his seat and his surfboard in the truck bed. "Are you going somewhere?"

"Yeah," he answered, "and if you're feeling up to it, I hope you'll come with me. With my new capabilities as a vampire shark and your investigative skills, I think we'd be a great team."

Jake revealed his plan to Leilani as they drove. "I'm going to Hawaii. I was on the Internet. There was a shark attack this morning, before dawn. Two surfers disappeared. I think it's Dean. He probably flew there last night, checked into a hotel, and went straight to the beach. And he has someone with him.

Two sharks were spotted."

"Who? If Logan's dead, who would be with him?"

"I don't know. But if Dean's out there killing innocent people, I have to stop him."

Leilani pondered who could be with Dean. The answer struck her like a bolt of lightning. *Skylar. She's the only one who was unaccounted for yesterday. In all the chaos, no one thought to look for her.*

"Hey, Jake," she said gently, "do you think it could be Skylar?"

"Skylar?! No. No way," Jake answered without thinking. "She might be a liar and the worst girlfriend ever, but she's not a cold-blooded killer."

"I know you might not want to hear this but Skylar was … Well let's just say she wasn't a very nice person, particularly with me. I think she was upset I was with Tristan. And none of us have seen her since yesterday. Have you heard from her at all?"

Jake's heart dropped to his stomach. Skylar hadn't returned any of his calls. "We need to make a stop."

As Jake raced to Skylar's house, he wasn't sure what would be worse. Either he'd arrive at Skylar's and find she'd left town, which would mean she's with Dean. Or he'd arrive and find a pile of ash in her house.

"Stay here." Jake parked at the curb and marched to Skylar's door. He was about to knock when someone exited the front door. "Who the hell are you?" he demanded, thinking it could be one of Dean's vampire soldiers. *No, this woman smells human.*

"I'm the landlady. Who are you?" she demanded right back.

"Sorry. You startled me. I'm looking for Skylar Sirena."

"Skylar? She's gone. She left me a message saying she had to leave town suddenly. She told me I could keep her security deposit and she left me a check for next month's rent, in case I had trouble finding another tenant. Nice girl," the landlady grinned.

"Did she say where she was going?" Jake asked.

"No. No forwarding address either. But a beautiful girl like that? I bet she has a new boyfriend," the landlady said with a knowing smile.

Jake trudged back to Leilani, who sat in his truck with the window rolled down.

"Did you hear all that?" he asked.

"Yes. I'm sorry, Jake."

"Whatever. So are you coming to Hawaii with me?"

As Jake pulled away from the curb, Leilani inhaled the night air through the open window. She smelled fresh cut grass mixed with the pungent scent of the ocean.

Should I stay or should I go? she wondered. *With Tristan gone, there's nothing left for me here. There's my job but I don't think I can go back there, at least not for a while. But if I go with Jake, what am I going to do? Hunt down Dean and Skylar? Then what? Surf?*

"Leilani? You look a million miles away," Jake said.

Leilani stared straight ahead out the windshield. "More like 2,500 miles," she said slowly. "I'm going with you."

Driving in the darkness, Jake felt a smile creep across his lips.

157 — Parting Gifts II

Jake parked at the curb in front of Leilani's house and walked inside with her.

As Leilani closed the front door, she said, "I need to make a call and get my things together. Why don't you have a seat and give me about a half-hour? Help yourself to the fridge."

"Okay." Jake sat on the couch and closed his eyes.

Leilani retreated to her bedroom and shut the door. She dialed the special agent in charge of the San Diego Division and requested a 30-day leave of absence from the FBI. She explained that she had sustained severe injuries from an attack by two vicious, possibly rabid, dogs and that she needed time to recuperate and deal with some personal matters as well.

The special agent in charge, who had always appreciated Leilani's work ethic and her years of tireless service, granted her request. He knew she wouldn't ask for the time if it wasn't absolutely necessary. He told her to complete the required forms and return the paperwork to him within 24 hours. She made a mental note to complete the forms on the trip to Hawaii and email them from the plane.

Leilani hung up and quickly packed. She put on a long sleeve shirt and a long skirt to cover all her bandages and bite marks. She threw her meds in her carry-on bag, along with her laptop.

They were about to hop back in the truck when a light bulb went off in Jake's head. "Hey, is it okay if we make one more stop? Then we can take a cab from there to the airport?"

"Yeah, sure. What do you need to do?" Leilani asked.

"Return a favor."

Jake drove to Daniel's house and parked in the driveway next to the rusty green hatchback. While Leilani called for a taxi, he wrote a note to Daniel. "Daniel, you gave me a ride when I really needed it. Now I'd like to give you my ride. I'm leaving town and don't know if I'm coming back. Please tell everyone goodbye. The pink slip and keys are in the glove box. Enjoy your new wheels. Peace, Jake."

Jake pinned the note under the windshield wiper and patted the hood. "Now I'm ready."

158 — Red Eye

Forty minutes later, Jake and Leilani were at the airport. They flashed their new identities and checked their surfboards on the red eye flight to Honolulu. They strode through security with their carry-on bags. They took a seat at their gate and waited for the flight to board.

Jake leaned in close to Leilani and whispered, "Hey, I've been thinking about something. I don't think we should tell anyone Tristan is gone. We should let everyone think he and Torrey are still alive and that the Rules are still in force. If word gets out Tristan is dead, it'll be chaos. He was the only one keeping a lid on things."

"I hadn't really thought about that, but you're right. It'll be better if everyone thinks Tristan and the Nomads are traveling around the globe as usual," she agreed. "But what about Dean? He's probably spreading the word he killed Tristan."

"Maybe. But as soon as Dean sees me and I tell him we killed all his wedding guests and Logan, he'll realize he made a fatal mistake by not killing Tristan himself. And by then, it'll be too late."

Jake glanced up at the TV screen tuned to CNN. He nudged Leilani as the newscaster read from the teleprompter, "Two experienced surfers were reported missing in Hawaii early this morning. They were last seen just before 5 a.m. in the ocean near their Waikiki hotel. Another surfer reported seeing two great white sharks in the vicinity of the surfers shortly before they disappeared. Search and rescue crews are scouring the waters off the coast of . . ."

Jake and Leilani turned away from the TV and grimaced. They didn't have to listen to the rest of the story. They knew more than anyone on the news desk or at the scene. The killing had begun. Again.

159 — Family

"We're now ready to begin general boarding," the flight attendant announced.

Jake turned to Leilani. "Are you ready?"

"As ready as I'll ever be," she answered. "They haven't left us much of a choice, have they? We have to go."

They stood and ambled toward the flight attendant collecting boarding passes.

"Jake, I want to thank you for taking care of all this." Leilani looked at her ID and boarding pass. "So, what made you choose these names?"

"I think Tristan would've wanted it that way."

The flight attendant smiled broadly as she reached for their boarding passes.

"Leilani Pierce. Welcome aboard."

"Jake Pierce. Welcome."

THE END

Thank you for reading DARK SURF!

If you enjoyed it, would you please take a moment to leave a review at your favorite online retailer? Thanks!

The next book in the
DARK SURF series
is coming soon!

Can't wait to see what happens?
Visit DarkSurf.com and sign up for *DARK SURF Nightly*.

Be the first to hear about the next book
and all DARK SURF news!

Acknowledgments

Thank you to:

Steve Zmak (stevezmak.com) for providing such a stellar example of what it means to be an artist. Your artistic vision, talent and integrity are a model for any working artist to aspire to—no matter what the medium. Your encouragement and faith in me were invaluable as I embarked on this adventure to write my first novel, an exhilarating and sometimes terrifying task. Your keen insights, suggestions and contributions to my first draft definitely made this a better story. You are the world's best "logic editor" and your creativity is transcendent.

Norma, Veronica, Charlene, Manuel and Noah Correia for a lifetime of love and support. You have always believed in me and encouraged me, while giving me the space to live my life. You have each taught me the value of hard work and, more importantly, the value of family. I am so fortunate to call you mine.

Tom and Claire Zmak for your love and encouragement. You are the epitome of what parents-in-law should be and I am so very lucky to call you family, too.

Robert Alexander, Christine Arenson and Susan Boettner for generously giving your time to read an early draft of DARK SURF. Your comments, edits and encouragement were incredibly valuable and I am grateful to have you as friends.

Paula Criswell for your editing expertise, your guidance and support over the years, and your generous spirit. I am eternally grateful to you.

Christina Grant for your thoughtful suggestions and edits, which were so helpful in writing DARK SURF. And a special thank you for arranging our daylong and weeklong writers' retreats, which are super-productive and (just as important) super-fun. As a fellow writer and author, you are an inspiration.

Jill Kramer of Waterside Productions for taking a chance on an author writing about vampire sharks of all things. I deeply appreciate your hard work, expertise and enthusiasm, and everything you've done for me and DARK SURF. And your suggestion for the tagline, "Surfing's in their blood," is brilliant.

Bill Gladstone of Waterside Productions for generously giving your time to talk with an aspiring novelist, for immediately getting the surfer/vampire/shark concept, and for offering to introduce me to Jill Kramer.

Rick Frishman for hosting Author 101 University and providing a place for writers to network with each other and experts in the publishing industry. And a big thank you for suggesting I meet with Bill Gladstone at a meet-the-agents session.

Barry Krost for your stellar efforts to get DARK SURF to the right people so we can turn this story into a major motion picture.

Norman Stephens for your hard work, professionalism and integrity. I am very fortunate to have the opportunity to work with you to try to bring DARK SURF to the big screen.

Christopher Shy and ShadowCatcher Entertainment for allowing me to use such incredible artwork for the cover of DARK SURF. Christopher's images are truly amazing. Even in my wildest dreams, I never imagined having artwork as cool as this on the book cover—so thank you, thank you, thank you for sharing it with me.

David Branfman for your expertise, your guidance and your kind words. It gives me such peace of mind to know you're only an email or phone call away.

Jane Deuber for your insightful coaching that helped me carve more time for fiction writing into a 24-hour day. You are a shining example of how to play in the big leagues with enthusiasm, clarity, integrity and balance.

Leslie Eicher for too many reasons to mention. Since day one of my career, you have been a role model to me. More important, you are a true friend. I am so grateful to have you in my life.

Mary Jeanne Vincent for your friendship, support and encouragement throughout this journey. And thank you for asking how it's going each time we meet for lunch. It means a lot.

Roger Smith of RAS Design Media for building such a kick-ass website for me at DarkSurf.com.

Steve Zmak (once again) for designing such a kick-ass website for me at DarkSurf.com, and for designing this book.

Robert Krantz for your advice and guidance, and inspiration through your own writing and movie projects.

Kate Dzierzek, Tricia Krantz and Lisa Mumford for years of friendship and support, and for making my life so much more fun.

My friends from UCSD, who—even though we don't get to see each other very much—inspire me from afar. From my B-House buddies to the Hotelers to my fraternity friends to everyone in between: "You can check out anytime you like, but you can never leave." And that's a good thing because you guys rock.

My extended family and friends in California, Nevada, Montana, Texas and everywhere else. Some of you are mentioned here and some are not, but you have all been a great support to me.

Bands such as the Kaiser Chiefs and Wavves for writing music that's so awesome to play as I write. Songs from *Employment* and *Off With Their Heads* (Kaiser Chiefs), and *King of the Beach* and *Afraid of Heights* (Wavves) immediately put me in the zone for writing about these characters and locales. Many of these tunes are woven into the fabric of DARK SURF and have a permanent place in my iPod. I will always associate these songs with the amazing time I had putting this book together.

U2 (who I must mention if I'm mentioning bands) for decades of creativity and inspiration. Your relentless commitment to your work, your fans and the causes you believe in is a model for artists in any field.

Surfrider Foundation (surfrider.org) for everything you do to protect our oceans, waves and beaches. Your work is so incredibly important and I'm proud to call myself a member of your organization.

Surfers everywhere for your love of and respect for the ocean, and your everyday acts of bravery and heroism.

YOU for taking time out of your life to read this book—and as Tristan Pierce once said, "A human life is a very short life." Thank you for taking this journey with me. It's just the beginning!

**For information about T.C. Zmak
and the DARK SURF series:**
TCZmak.com
DarkSurf.com

Follow T.C. Zmak:
Facebook.com/TCZmak
@TCZmak

About the Author

T.C. ZMAK was born and raised in San Diego, and graduated from the University of California, San Diego (UCSD) with a bachelor of arts degree in communication. T.C. now lives in Marina, California on the picturesque Monterey Bay. Read more about T.C. Zmak at TCZmak.com.

www.ingramcontent.com/pod-product-compliance
Lightning Source LLC
Chambersburg PA
CBHW021423240626
47153CB00001B/8